PERFECT ORDER

A BILLIONAIRE STEALTH ROMANCE

TRACEY JERALD

8 Perfect Pursuit 8/20/24

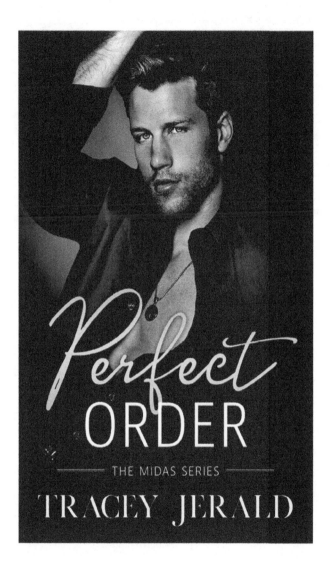

Perfect
ORDER

— THE MIDAS SERIES —

TRACEY JERALD

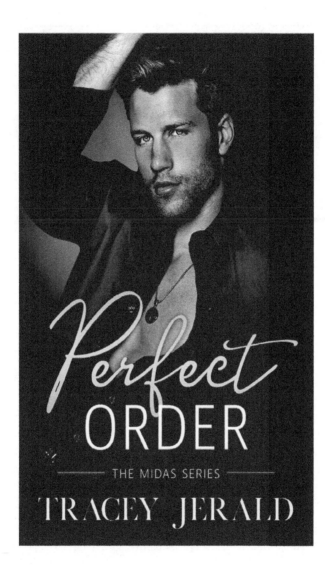

Perfect
ORDER

—— THE MIDAS SERIES ——

TRACEY JERALD

Perfect
ORDER

TRACEY JERALD

A Midas Series Standalone Novel

Tracey Jerald

101 Marketside Avenue, Suite 404-205

Ponte Vedra, FL, 3208

https://www.traceyjerald.com

Book Layout © 2017 BookDesignTemplates.com

Perfect Order/ Tracey Jerald

ISBN: 978-1-7358129-3-9 (eBook)

ISBN: 978-1-7358129-4-6 (Paperback)

Library of Congress Control Number:TBD

Lyrics for "Gettin' Stiggy Wit It" written by Daniel Fitzpatrick. Used with permission.

Editor: One Love Editing (http://oneloveediting.com/)

Proof Edits: Comma Sutra Editorial (https://www.facebook.com/CommaSutraEditorial)

Cover Design by Tugboat Design (https://www.tugboatdesign.net/)

Photo Credit: Wander Aguiar

Model: Philippe Bélanger

PR & Marketing: Linda Russell - Foreword PR (https://www.).

To Amy Rhodes—beloved friend, incredible human, and claimer of book boyfriends. Kane is waiting for you with open arms. Thank you for everything you do for me.

And to Dan Fitzpatrick. Leanne wouldn't be quite the same without you. Neither would any of us.

ALSO BY TRACEY JERALD

Midas Series

Perfect Proposal

Perfect Assumption

Perfect Composition

Perfect Order

Perfect Satisfaction (Coming in 2022)

Amaryllis Series

Free - An amaryllis Prequel

(Newsletter Subscribers only)

Free to Dream

Free to Run

Free to Rejoice

Free to Breathe

Free to Believe

Free to Live

Free to Dance

Free to Wish

Free to Protect (Winter 2022)

Glacier Adventure Series

Return by Air

Return by Land

Return by Sea

Standalones

Close Match

Ripple Effect

Unconditionally With Me – A With Me in Seattle Novella

Go to https://www.traceyjerald.com/ for all buy links!

PLAYLIST

Carrie Underwood, Ludacris: "The Champion"
Norah Jones: "Come Away With Me"
Goo Goo Dolls: "Better Days"
Stevie Nicks, Lindsey Buckingham: "Landslide"
Stevie Nicks: "If You Ever Did Believe"
Jessica Riddle: "Even Angels Fall"
Edie Brickell & New Bohemians: "A Hard Rain's A Gonna Fall"
Lady Gaga, Bradley Cooper: "Shallow"

Madonna: "Live to Tell"
Sarah McLachlan: "World's On Fire"
Madonna: "I'll Remember"
Heart: "These Dreams"
David Gray: "Babylon"

THE MIDAS TOUCH

In Greek mythology Midas, wandering one day in his garden, came across the wise satyr Silenus who was rather the worse for wear. Midas treated him kindly and returned him to his great companion, the god Dionysos.

In return for this, Dionysos granted Midas a wish. The king, not realizing the repercussions of his decision, chose to be given the magical ability to turn any object he touched into solid gold. Simple things, everyday things, Midas took for granted were instantly transformed by his touch into solid gold.

The full consequences of this gift soon became evident. At the barest touch, flowers, fruit, and water turned to gold. Midas became sick of this world he world surrounded himself with and sought to relieve himself of it.

Those finding themselves burdened with an abundance of perfection gifted to them by the gods often seek relief to reverse their fortune.

Except when that gift is love.

\

PROLOGUE
EIGHTEEN YEARS AGO FROM PRESENT DAY

"Come on, Lee!" my younger sister by four minutes shouts as she races across our backyard in New Hampshire.

I race after her, calling, "Go on ahead, Lee! I'll wait here."

She flaps her hand behind her and begins running as fast as she can after the bunny we both saw. We're both positive we can convince our parents to let us keep him—her?—if we can just catch it.

Lee seems to think she can run it down. Maybe she's right; she's superfast. But I think if I wait it out, I can catch it right here by waiting.

So, I sit, content to let the warm summer sunshine wash over me. Pulling out one of the carrots we pulled from our mom's garden out of my pocket, I brush it off and take a bite. The sweet tang rushes into my mouth as I chew.

Every day should be like this, I think as I fall backward and stare up at the puffy clouds dotting the blue sky. Just me and my Lee. Home together, forever and ever. No school to keep us apart during the day.

"And we get to sleep in the same room at night," she pants as she collapses next to me. Yanking her own carrot out of her pocket, she chomps down.

I smile without looking over at her, knowing she's done it again—read my thoughts without my having to say a word. "It drives Mom nuts when we do this."

"Talk without words? I know."

I roll to my stomach and stare into my own face, down to identical freckles that have sprouted this summer. "She was talking to Daddy. She said the teachers are concerned we cheat at school."

Lee's face becomes indignant. "We do not. They put us in separate classes just for that reason."

I sigh. The one thing different between Lee and me is our tempers. I'm much slower to anger, whereas my identical twin flares at the slightest poke. "Lee, she said the teachers are concerned, not that *they* are."

And as quickly as it bursts, her fire burns out. "Oh." Lee chomps down on her carrot again, reminding me I want some more. At the exact same moment, we both moan, "So good," before we collapse into a heap of giggles—something we get yelled at a lot for doing late at night because we won't go to sleep.

I think about the rabbit hopping along in the woods and declare, "Lee, we can't take it away from its family."

"Why not?" She pouts.

"Because it would be lonely. Imagine if someone ever tried to take you away from me." Just the thought of ever being without my twin causes my heart to pound in a painful way. The pressure hurts.

Lee rubs her hand over her stomach. "Stop thinking like that. It hurts too badly."

"Promise me. Nothing is going to ever happen to take you away from me." Tears leak from the corner of my eyes onto the soft green grass under my head.

"I promise, Lee. I'll never allow anything to ever take me away from you." She throws herself into my arms and hugs me so hard I feel it lodge behind my ribs against my heart, which is where all of my memories of Lee and me live.

Suddenly, she stills before whispering, "Look, Lee. Look!"

I twist my head around, and it's not just one rabbit in front of us but an entire family. "It's a mommy, a daddy, and babies." I reach out for Lee's hand to find it already there. "It's so beautiful."

"Let's give them the rest of our carrots," she suggests.

Without another word, I begin breaking my carrot into smaller pieces before softly tossing it into the grass. The bunny Lee was chasing before hops forward bravely and snatches a piece in its mouth. I point and whisper, "That one's you."

"Why?"

"It's fearless. Just like you."

Lee studies the other rabbits and points out another. "That one is you. It's watchful of the others."

I giggle. "That's so not me."

"Um, yeah it is. Who shoved Baxter Masters because he was bullying Marcie on the playground?"

"Well, he shouldn't say such mean things," I say indignantly.

"And who can beat anyone at a staring contest?"

"Let's practice now. I'll show you," I cry eagerly.

We face each other with legs crossed and grab hold of each other's hands. Both of our eyes close. Simultaneously, our eyes open. Neither of us blinks until we hear the back door open and our mother shout, "Kylie, Leanne! Which one of you has been rooting around in my garden?"

Together, as we've done everything since before we were born, we answer, "It was me."

Our mother just sighs before she turns and walks back inside.

And we both fall backward against the warm grass, still holding hands when I declare, "I love you, Kylie. Always."

"And I love you, Leanne. Forever. No matter whatever happens."

KANE

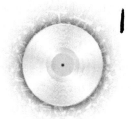

1

TWO YEARS FROM PRESENT DAY

Beckett Miller's new single 'Live the Dream' just hit number one on the Billboard charts. While Wildcard has issued his standard statement, he's storming around New York like someone just lit his favorite silk shirt on fire. What's wrong, Beckett? Trouble in paradise?

— **StellaNova**

"Hey, Ma," I answer the phone call from my mother just before striding across the Avenue of the Americas to enter Rockefeller Plaza, where I'm supposed to meet my boss for an 8:00 a.m. meeting. "You're up awfully early."

"When have I ever not been up with the roosters, Kane?"

"Never." I duck around a few people scurrying down the street directly in my path. "The problem was you also never went to bed late enough for me to have any fun either."

Her raspy voice laughs in my ear. "Too true, sweetie. I do believe it was that very thing that got you in trouble when you took out...what was her name?"

"Megan Jo." My mother has the mind of an elephant. After I returned home broken from my last mission, it was her unshakeable faith in me that got me through the horrid days. And the worst of the nights. "I was what? Seventeen? Are you ever going to let that go?"

She grunts out her assent, and all it makes me want to do is laugh, but my mother didn't raise a stupid man when she wielded a wooden spoon like a music conductor. Nor did Uncle Sam reinforce what I learned with years of counterterrorism training to have me step into such an obvious trap. My shoulders stiffen when I realize what else I learned at the hands of varied members of the US federal government, but I know down to my bones that I will always be faithful to the memories of the men and women I served with.

Until the last breath leaves my body.

"Kane, are you listening to me?" she grunts.

I have to grin. No one I've ever met has caused me to be myself quite like my mother. It's why I don't feel a single ounce of guilt admitting, "Not a single word, Ma. Were you complaining about the hens again?"

"No, but I should be! Dratted things aren't laying eggs."

I glance down at my watch, thankful I have a few moments before I need to head upstairs. "Ma, we've talked about this. It's likely your damn rooster is too old to..."

"The absolute last thing we should be discussing are cocks, Kane. I believe the last time we *did* discuss them, you were around sixteen, and your father mumbled something about condoms before leaving it up to me. Can you explain to me why the hell does that man think I'd know more about some slimy latex than the man who wears it?"

At this point, I'm doubled over laughing. "Ma, stop. I beg you. Please. I can hardly get my breath."

"And now you want to lecture me about my beautiful Rufus not being manly enough to do his duty to his lady birds?" The umbrage in her voice is completely legitimate, and any other time but now, I'd be all about continuing this conversation.

"Ma, you know there's no way I'd ever cut you off—"

"Darn tootin', Kane. You know better than to interrupt your mother..."

"—but not today. Not when I'm about to have a discussion with one of my bosses about my potential readiness to go out in the field again," I conclude.

There's silence on the other end of the line. And in the blink of an eye, Fern McCullough drops the humorous monologue my sister and I swear should have secured her own television show years ago. An eerie silence extends between us before she probes gently, "Are you ready, sweetheart?"

I tip my head back and stare up at the powerful spire that seems to reach up into the sky with no end. "I'm stronger, and if I don't give this a chance, I'll never know, will I?"

"There's so much I want to say to you."

"You have about seven minutes to..."

"We love you, Kane." My throat closes up as she sums it up in four simple words that mean everything. I can't manage any words, but I don't need to. "Wherever you are, no matter what you do, your family always loves you. You know that deep down, son, right?"

I clear my throat before I manage, "Yeah, Ma."

"Good. Now, go show them the man you were born to be. And if they don't recognize you for the warrior you are, well, they can just go straight to hell."

"I'm pretty certain they've already been there," I start, but I'm talking to thin air. My mother's hung up on me, likely unwilling to show me her emotions. I slip my phone back inside my suit jacket and pull out my badge so I can easily slip through Security. But instead of pressing my usual floor when I hit the elevator, I lean over and press the button for the executive floor.

As the elevator rises, I mentally go through the responses I'll provide when I'm asked if I'm ready because I know I am. I was made to serve and protect. I was made for this.

And I'm ready to get back to doing what I was born to do.

Hudson Investigations was built on the principles of two men—Caleb Lockwood and Keene Marshall. Beyond the lucrative work they're awarded from our government, they have a well-earned reputation of integrity for helping reunite families in their Missing Persons and Protective Services division.

I've been working with this illustrious team since I first came on board a few months ago. And much like the men who started the firm, I quickly learned there are few things in life more rewarding than being able to provide answers to people who don't have any.

It makes me curious if Caleb has a new assignment, which causes conflicting emotions inside of me. While I'm anxious to prove I'm capable enough to be back in the field, I abhor the idea there's a person out there who is lost, perhaps permanently. Even though our job is to provide closure, there are days when I'm more than ready to toss back a few drinks with my colleagues to numb the pain over what we've discovered once we've secured our target.

I remain ramrod straight in my chair in the lobby, even through the call Tony, Caleb and Keene's administrative assistant, receives. "Yes? I'll let him know you're ready for him." After he hangs up, he stands. "Kane, if you'll follow me."

Pushing to my feet, I stride forward, a frown of concern touching my lips. "Do you have any intel on the target you can share?"

Tony shakes his head. "The key players are waiting for you inside. You'll get all the information you need."

"Thanks for nothing," I mutter as we reach the door.

"I get that a lot." He reaches past me and knocks.

"Enter," I hear Caleb call out.

I reach for the handle and push the door open. After taking two steps into the room, I come up short because sitting in front of Caleb's desk is none other than the world-famous rock star Beckett Miller. And despite the usually gregarious demeanor he has on his face when I've seen him in the press, the man appears completely shut down. In fact, he's downright rude when he ignores my presence and returns his attention to Caleb. "This is truly ridiculous, Caleb."

"It isn't, Beckett. We're having this conversation because of the fact one of your fans managed to get her ass past your doorman. What do you want next? To find one sprawled in your place? I mean, our systems are good, but they're not impenetrable."

"Well, isn't that fucking reassuring," the tattooed rock god drawls. "And what is Captain America over here supposed to do? Make sure my dick is covered so no one gets a picture of it as I'm jerking off in bed?"

A very clear understanding of what my assignment will be forms. Suddenly, I'm almost wishing Caleb had waited a few more weeks before he decided I was ready, but I'm not about to screw up this chance. While Beckett continues to spew out all the reasons why he doesn't need protection as he cavalierly gallivants around the city, I wander over to the windows.

"You're being an obtuse ass, Beckett," Caleb shouts.

"And you, Carys, and everyone else knows I need to be free to live my life," he counters. He slumps forward in his chair, his back angled slightly away from where I'm standing.

I know when I've been dismissed, but it's high time someone reminded Mr. Miller of the reason he's sitting in my boss's office. I guess the person to do that is going to be me.

Like a snake striking, I lunge for him. Within seconds, I have his head encased in my arms. All it would take is a little pressure one way or the other to either ruin his singing career or simply end the conversation in a very permanent way. I lean down and hiss, "Now, try to get away, rock star."

Beckett makes a high-pitched squeal that reminds me of the pigs on my parents' farm. He kicks his long legs out frantically. His arms flail, and his panicked "Caleb" comes out off-key. Probably the first time that's ever occurred, I think with a touch of amusement.

Caleb quirks a brow at Beckett before calmly asking, "Kane? If you don't mind letting Beckett go. I think he's paid for his crack."

I quickly remove my arms and step back as Beckett leaps to his feet, a muscular man who's both humiliated and terrified. "My goal wasn't retribution, Caleb. It was to demonstrate to Mr. Miller how ridiculously vulnerable he is. I presume he had some spatial awareness as to where I was in the room."

Beckett's chest heaves up and down. He twists his head from side to side before he frowns. "It doesn't hurt."

"Of course not. I merely incapacitated you. I wasn't trying to harm you in any way."

The tattooed man in front of me visibly swallows. "You said I'm vulnerable. What do you mean, anywhere?"

I tick off some examples. "From a side street, in your favorite coffee shop, on the elevator coming here. Anywhere you go, you have to presume there's a bogey lurking. You're a very high-value target, Mr. Miller."

"You have no idea how high," Caleb murmurs laconically, but I don't glance in his direction. I know what my purpose is here today, and it's to convince this too-stubborn man to accept he needs protection.

"What does this entail?" Beckett asks.

Before Caleb can answer, I jump in. "At least three individuals in a diamond formation for day to day every time you leave your residence. That means three teams for round-the-clock coverage. Hudson would be able to supplement with additional personnel for premieres or other large events so long as we know about them in advance."

He nods before taking my place at the window. "All I wanted was the music. I never expected any of this."

"Those who are blessed with success never do," I inform him firmly but succinctly.

"Blessed. That's one word for it." Beckett turns away from the Manhattan skyline and directs his words to Caleb. "Done."

"Excellent. Kane, if you don't mind giving us a few minutes to work out some final matters?"

"Not at all." I hold out my hand. "Sir. I'll apologize for the tactics but not the outcome."

"Maybe you're more like the Winter Soldier than Cap," Beckett muses.

Ignoring his dig, I finish my apology. After all, it won't help the company if I managed to piss off who I presume will be a lucrative client. "I assessed the situation, and Caleb's words didn't appear to be penetrating. I thought a demonstration would..."

"Wake me up? It sure as hell did." Beckett takes my outstretched hand. "Thank you."

"It's been a pleasure." I turn to leave when I hear him call out, "Your name is Kane?"

I whirl back to face him. "Yes, sir. Kane McCullough." I barely refrain from giving him my last rank and serial number. That's when I begin to feel the room spin because Beckett Miller says to Caleb, "Either he heads my team, or I'm not signing anything."

Caleb arches his brows so high they disappear beneath his hairline. "Kane? Are you certain about that?"

Beckett gives me a full inspection that would have done my drill sergeant proud. I remain unmoving when he declares, "Yeah. I'm sure. If I have to have a bodyguard, I want the guy who will be the last one standing. Is that you, Kane?"

His words leave a burning streak across my heart, but he can't know that. Instead, I reply, "Yes, sir."

Caleb slaps his hands on the desk. "Then there's nothing left but the paperwork. Kane, you're officially on duty."

Despite the unknown knocks I've taken since I was discharged from the Marines, those words spark a glow inside me that never should have been extinguished. I face Beckett head-on. "I won't let you down, Mr. Miller."

That's when Beckett grumbles, "I sure as fuck hope not. Hey, do you think you can teach me that crazy head-hold thing?"

A booming laugh erupts from Caleb as I easily deny my new protectee. "No."

"It could come in handy," Beckett says petulantly.

"And terrify those of us who are going to be guarding you. It takes years of practice to be able to attack with that kind of control," I counter.

Then my balls draw up slightly when Beckett reminds me in a *sotto* voice, "We're going to have years together, Kane."

God help me, what did I just agree to? Beckett Miller's sadistic grin swims before me as I make my way to sit back in front of Caleb's desk.

That's right—a second chance at life after the other one was shot to hell by my own gun.

Leanne

 *2*

TWENTY-TWO MONTHS FROM PRESENT DAY

Saratoga Springs, N.Y. After twelve years on the market, local residents will be pleased to know the old Spa City Saddlery has been sold. There's no new information on what the new owners plan on doing with the property, however, there has been no request to transition it to a commercial property.

"Leanne, why don't you get space in the city? Then we could live together again."

When I whirl around to face my twin, it's like staring into a mirror image. Christ, more so than ever since today we're dressed more alike than we have been since we were kids. A pure coincidence. To protect ourselves against the elements of the warehouse I'm inspecting for purchase, we both donned black leather jackets and jeans. And while my jeans are a deep dark blue and hers are torn in enough places to make me question how they're remaining on her legs, a stranger coming through the door would still believe they were seeing double. If it were to occur, my sister would merely smirk while I rolled my eyes—at least on the outside. After all, we've had twenty-three years of people guessing our identities incorrectly.

Then again, I'd just pray I'd be quick enough to slip out one of the concealed weapons I've taken to carrying so I'd be able to save Kylie. She's the most important thing in my world.

"There are too many reasons to name," I tell her.

"Try," she urges.

We're standing in a run-down office space that easily requires a quarter of a million to be dropped for the heavy cable I need to be laid, and that's before the cosmetic repairs, let alone the secure spaces. In some ways, Kylie's right. It would be so easy to saunter into some Manhattan high-rise with everything nice and perfect, sexy and sleek. All I'd have to do would be to drop a large chunk of my savings and rely on someone else to do the work.

And therein lies the problem. I live in a world where trust isn't granted easily, if ever.

I step around the large hole the previous owners left in the floor and pick my way carefully to the window. Twisting to the side, I imagine where my desk would be placed and lean back just a bit. There in the distance is the view of Hadley Mountain the Realtor told me about. "Although this location has organic protection built into three sides, it's a benefit overall. Some external offices, conference rooms, maybe a break room could have a view." If I decide to purchase the space, by the time I'm done, over seventy-five percent of the space's improvements will be unrecognizable to someone like Kylie. With the security integrity improvements I plan on installing, false ceilings and floors will be commonplace.

Then again, my sister won't have the clearance to enter those areas. Only a select cadre of my employees ever will.

"Rocks, trees, and weeds, Leanne. What the hell is so appealing about that? And for Christ's sake, did they just make saddles here, or were there actual horses stabled here?" She sniffs the air even as she scuffs her high-heeled boot on the office subfloor I can visualize being ripped out and replaced so easily with cabled wire bundled tightly beneath it.

I open my mouth and quickly snap it shut. Much like my twin was made for the new stardom she's beginning to enjoy since she was first spotted singing at a nightclub in Manhattan, I was made for the shadows—those housed by the bits and bytes of the far reaches of the internet, to be exact.

My mother jokingly called the differences in our careers the first branches off the trunk of the Lee Tree. "It doesn't mean you aren't as close as ever, but you're developing your own personalities," she explained when my sister got in my face about why I wouldn't waste a credit hour at MIT to take "A music theory course. Just one. I take computer science, Lee. Why can't you do this for me?" she shouted.

Back then, I fought a war with myself to share with her what I was really doing, but I'd taken a vow. I couldn't; I still can't. Now without endangering us all.

She wanders up next to me. "The only thing I can say about it that's a benefit is you'd be the same distance from me as the parents."

"And I'd have better shopping," I joke.

"That's the truth." Saratoga Springs is an adorable college town that sports some of the finest horse racing in the country, attracting a high-end clientele and some exclusive boutiques. "I personally don't understand why people flock here..."

I interrupt her. "You might one day. There's an incredible concert pavilion here."

She stills. Uncertainty leaks into her voice, "Do you really think so?"

"Of course I do! Why this sudden doubt?" Kylie's talent is being bandied about by some of the bigger names in music.

"Here you are buying a building—Christ, Leanne, a building— and I'm still hoping I can sell out theaters in New York."

I grab her hand and squeeze hard. "I believe in you."

"You have to; you're a part of me. I bet it's taking me longer because you used to suck down my oxygen in the womb," she grumbles. But she still bumps my shoulder, showing her gratitude for my never-ending support.

"No, I believe in you because you're doing this because you love it. Not for money, not for entitlement, but because you have to sing in a way most people need to do things like breathe. And get over yourself. I didn't take your oxygen; you likely took mine for those pipes." A grin lifts her lips, so I continue. "We might be two people—very different ones—but you'll always complete me, Lee. You always have, always will. I'm not whole without you." I remind her of the very simple reason we called each other by the same name for years—when and where it matters the most, we've been the same since person since we both cried to be free from our mother's womb.

A second later, Kylie's arms are wrapped around me. "You're right."

"I always am," I remind her drolly.

She pinches me before admitting, "I got scared for a moment. It's real. You're not going to be nearby."

I reassure her, "I'm just a phone call away."

"I know. And no matter what, you're right here." She wedges her hand between us to press her fingers against her heart. Blowing out a gusty sigh, she declares, "I just have to persevere. I can do this."

"You can. In fact, I'm so certain of it, I'll make you this bet."

"What's that?"

"When you become some big-name star, I'll do my best to keep the tabloids off your back."

She shakes with laughter. "Now that, my darling sister, is a dare."

I groan. "What did I just do?"

"For once, you were impulsive. Now, let me be practical in return. Make an offer on the building. It's exactly what you've been looking for." Kylie pulls back, and we communicate without words.

It's the beginning of the rest of our lives. And as always, she's there for me.

Just like I'll always be there for her.

A few weeks later, I'm down in Manhattan to spend a long weekend with my twin. We're wandering around the city to walk off her nerves due to the show she's performing that night. Impulsively, she's decided she has to have the outfit on display in the window of the largest Free People I've ever seen. Just as she dodges in between the people meandering at Rockefeller Center to make a dash for the door, my phone rings. Glancing at it, I see it's my Realtor.

Indicating I'll follow her in just a moment, I answer it and ask Shari, "Give me some good news."

"If you truly believe acquiring that run-down building is good news, I guess that's what I have. I even got it for lower than asking."

The emotions coursing through me must be better than having won the lottery. My pulse is leaping, and my heart is pounding. I know I just won the first battle in the many wars I'm about to fight on behalf of what I know is fair and righteous—a mission that's been instilled in me for years. And when my plans are complete, the people I plan on recruiting to join me will be ready to charge a ridiculous amount for the things we've already been doing. "It's perfect for what it will be."

"And that is?" Shari probes.

I ignore her question and instead ask, "When do we close?"

"Well, if you're financing, that could take some time."

"I'm paying for the building outright." I learned years ago to leave as little of a footprint on the internet as possible. I plan on paying for as much as I can in cash. Fortunately, between an inheritance left to me and Kylie by our grandparents, plus the money I've stashed away, I should be able to afford everything I need.

Just barely.

"Oh, well, if that's the case, then terrific. I'll call you back with a date."

Before I can respond, I accidentally hang up on her when I'm bumped into by someone on the sidewalk. "Umph!" I let out an inadvertent sound as I stumble to the left.

A barrage of footsteps passes by me even as strong arms clasp mine. "Are you all right?" The intensity of this man's ocean-blue eyes causes my heart to bounce my ribs around, making me forget what the hell I even cared about.

Almost instinctively, I reach up and cup his shoulder. "I'm...fine." God, what a lame word for the man who transformed my insides into a melty pool of liquid wax.

His lips compress, doing nothing more than drawing my attention to them. My own part of their own accord in a primal reaction. *God. What the hell is this feeling?*

But before I can wrap my mind around it, he's stabilizing me, declaring, "Good." Then without another word, he strides away with a fluidity that pulls his dress slacks lovingly against long legs that lead to the most remarkable ass I've ever seen.

I don't know what causes me to do it—he's a damn stranger—but I shout after him, "Too bad I didn't catch your name, buddy. Maybe you're a 'get them off and go' kind of guy, but I'm not that kind of girl."

He freezes midstride before whirling around. The only people looking at us are the tourists, which means pretty much everyone. His lips curve into a facsimile of a smile. "I actually do know who you are, Ms. Miles." And it's with that, he slips into a black SUV in the passenger seat.

"How on earth does he know...holy crap!" Overwhelming excitement for my sister overrides the flutters in my stomach over an encounter with an incredibly hot guy that still has my stomach doing somersaults. I dash toward the door of Free People, shouting, "Kylie! I think you were just recognized!"

Our twin senses in complete sync for the moment, she happens to be coming out the door. When she hears me, she screams, "What do you mean?"

After I recount what just happened, we jump up and down, hugging in the middle of the sidewalk. And I spend the better part of the afternoon while she gets ready for the performance stripping the internet of our impromptu dance. Just like I promised.

Of course, I look for Ocean Eyes in the audience that night. And the next when Kylie, as Erzulie, blows the roof off the same club before I drive back to Saratoga to fork over a hunk of my savings to begin a new road in my life.

Ah, well. I can't cry over what wasn't meant to be. And what's meant to be right now is lurking in the shadows to allow people to sleep easier in their beds at night.

Even if they don't know it.

KANE ³

FEBRUARY- TWO YEARS LATER

@BeckettMiller... you're unbelievably awesome. And gorgeous. Ditch the blonde and marry me. I'd look good on the red carpet too! #beckettmiller #biggestfan #premiere
   — @LMozzo, Celebrity Fan

My hand reaches out and slaps on the sensor before I punch in a series of numbers. The elevator in front of me slides open. I step in, shifting my impeccably tailored suit jacket imperceptibly so the butt of the weapon won't catch on the material when I move.

Day after day, the constant routine has healed my wounded soul to merely a scar. While I know the memories of what happened overseas in the mountains of Azerbaijan will haunt me and possibly make me unfit for some of the more complex assignments I know I have the skills to contribute to at Hudson Investigations, I've made it to the other side of the hellhole I was living in when I first came back stateside. But I know there will be some things I can never put it on the line for ever again.

So, instead of being sent in on high-value kidnap-and-rescue missions with regularity, thereby utilizing my background as part of a Force RECON company and interrogator, two years ago I demonstrated just enough of my skills to snag Beckett Miller's attention.

Instead of putting everything on the line, feeling the adrenaline spike with every mission I take, I spend a good deal of time repeatedly lecturing one of the world's most famous rock stars about safety protocols.

It wouldn't be so bad if Beckett wasn't so hell-bent on ignoring the basic rules of protection that were established for his own good. When a man has as many potential targets on his back as Beckett does—between crazed fans, potential kidnappers, and jealous whack jobs who would simply prefer he doesn't exist—it infuriates me he doesn't take his protection more seriously. Especially when I know my sins come back to haunt me in the depths of night when I wake up sweating because my hands feel like they're mired in the warmth of blood of the people I loved—people I swore I'd protect, even as it gushed past my fingers too fast for me to stop it.

In the world I live in, death doesn't always give closure. More often than not, it leaves the survivors with unanswered questions—the most important being *why?*

Distracted, I step off the elevator that leads directly to Beckett's penthouse and almost crash into a luminous blonde. Famed singer Erzulie jumps back a foot, stammering, "Excuse me. I wasn't expecting anyone to come out of Becks's elevator."

I give the woman in front of me a head-to-toe perusal. She's dressed in shredded jeans with a sheer blouse and a pair of cowboy boots with a coat thrown over her arms. She's attractive, but there's no spark. Nothing electrifying about her. I'd swear she's an entirely different person than the woman I crashed into a few years ago outside of Rockefeller Center. Maybe inside she is. After all, I've changed from the man I was back then. Somehow, I've regained parts of my soul I never expected to.

Now, something about her sends up a warning flare inside me every time we come into close contact—which really isn't that often. Maybe it's the way her eyes are guarded instead of the way I felt that day, as if I could drown in the dark, fathomless blue. But instead of being left with a feeling of yearning as I was that afternoon, I find myself wary as she gives me a similar visual inspection before skirting past me to step onto the elevator I've just exited. "We had an early morning meeting with Kris," she explains needlessly as she mentions the head of their record label—Kristoffer Wilde.

"That's not my concern, Ms. Miles," I return softly.

An annoyed expression flashes across her face before her trademark smile replaces it, and she declares loftily, "Well, I was grilled by your goons about why I needed to come up and wake Becks from his beauty sleep."

I can't prevent my lips from twitching because if nothing else, Kylie Miles is amusing. "That's because of the fact he'll take that out on the rest of the team all day."

She fakes a stagger, clasping her hands against her chest in shock. "No! Not our Becks."

My eyes flit to the closed doors of the penthouse. "If you're feeling generous, you could share if it went well."

"That depends on whether you enjoy wearing a tuxedo?"

I visibly shudder. Kylie drawls, "That was about Becks's reaction when Kris explained his latest brainchild. You two can commiserate together the rest of the day." She pushes the button to take her down in the elevator.

Just as the doors close, I call out, "When is all of this happening?"

"Tomorrow!" is shouted back at me just as the doors close in my face.

When I'm certain I'm alone again, I let loose the groan I was suppressing in her presence. I've suffered more than my fair share of military dress uniforms to last a lifetime. The idea of donning one for any reason is tantamount to having bamboo shoots shoved under my fingernails. "And I still remember what that felt like," I mutter, clenching my fingers tightly.

As much as it would be so easy to discredit every word out of Erzulie's mouth, everything she said is too easy to substantiate, so there's no reason for her to make up some ridiculous story about my needing to find a tux just to be annoying. First, her mere presence is proof enough. After all, her words ring true about Beckett's security being too tight. I should know—I designed it that way. So, while the suspicious side of me wonders if she's pushing some sort of agenda, there's not a chance she's lying.

Unfortunately, that means we're all going to suffer some formal shit tomorrow night I should have known the schematics for weeks ago to have planned a team of twenty to guard Beckett against. Not plan something half-assed with less than a day's notice.

Moving to the penthouse doors, I put my hand on the knob just as it flings open. "Hey, Ky? You left your phone. And it says..." Beckett Miller is standing there in his trademark shirt unbuttoned to almost his waist and jeans. In his hand is a cell phone that's ringing. I note there's not a name, but instead, it says *L2 — Emergency Contact.* "Hey, Kane. Ky was just here."

Lifting my cell, I press a button and speak calmly into it. "Please have Ms. Miles detained. She forgot her cell phone." I hold out my hand, and Beckett sheepishly places it into it. "Don't—"

"Go anywhere without calling someone. I get it. Not like I don't hear it on repeat every day."

Briskly, I whirl around and head back down the elevator to meet Erzulie downstairs. But the suspicious side of me can't help wonder who L2 is and if I need to be concerned they're going to have any impact on Beckett.

In the back of the car with Beckett and Erzulie the next night, my jaw is locked. It has nothing to do with the two people bickering across from me about everything from who should get out of the car first to whether or not Erzulie should ditch her stylist's choice of sequined boots for more traditional heels. Or whether Beckett should undo just one more button on his already open shirt to "Allow your tattoos more visibility. I mean, that ink is shit hot, my friend," Erzulie eggs him on.

"Do you think? I mean, I can barely tuck in the shirt as it is. My tailor didn't send over a long," Beckett moans.

"Ugh. Yeah. No, that won't work. I mean, there's decadent, and then there's sloppy." Erzulie shudders.

I'm giving serious consideration to shooting them both instead of defending them against a threat. The possibilities of putting myself out of my misery are endless. But I'm certain my bosses wouldn't appreciate me shooting one of their largest clients outside of the US government. And besides, my awful mood has nothing to do with their antics and everything to do with the complete lack of cooperation I received from the theater for this premiere. The blasé "We don't expect any trouble" set my temper aflame.

"No one expects any problems, Ms. Wexford." I tried patience.

"Then none should happen." I swear, if I didn't know better, I'd think Wexford was a founding member of the Field of Dreams religious sect. Only in this case, praying for the lunatics not to come wasn't quite going to cut it.

"Let me explain how this is going to work. I'm going to have four people exiting the limo surrounding Beckett and Erzulie..."

"Four? I didn't plan for an extra four people," she twittered. The sound was like nails running down a chalkboard.

If she thinks four is bad, wait until I'm done. "And another ten behind the cameras along the red carpet. This way, they are protected the entire way up to the doors. Once inside the theater..."

"You expect me to have an additional fourteen people at my premiere?" She descended from her transcendent plane to screech.

"Either you accommodate the fourteen, or you'll be missing two key individuals—Beckett Miller and Erzulie," I threatened.

Her silence was a clear acceptance of my plan.

Now the sheer banality of the conversation makes me want to whip out my Sig Sauer to shoot the tires out of the limo we're riding in to stop us from arriving. Any of us. Just so I don't have to sit through any more torture in this lifetime. After all, haven't I been through enough?

And to think I have hours more to endure. I can't prevent the small groan that escapes my lips.

It's Erzulie who chuckles. "And to think I believed nothing disturbed your resting work face." She assumes a stoic mien that causes Beckett to howl with laughter.

Before I can respond, Beckett jumps in. "Nah, Kane looks more like this." He assumes a stern teacher expression.

"Only when I'm talking to you," I inform him drolly.

Both of them burst into laughter. "All kidding aside, thank you for doing this tonight...Kane?" Erzulie holds out her hand.

I take it and shake it firmly. "Just my job, ma'am."

"Ugh. I just got my first 'ma'am,' Beckett," she jokes. A friendly smile is tossed at Beckett. And I immediately notice there's no heat between the duo. They're exactly what they claim to be—friends.

Huh. Interesting. And yet, when she touched me, there was no flash of the fire from that first meeting. Maybe I just imagined what happened between us all those years ago? *And maybe you should cut her some slack because you ran into her on the street and she doesn't remember you.* I chastise myself for being a moron over an incident that pulled me from a temporary abyss she had no idea she helped me through. I take her outstretched hand and shake it firmly. I'm rewarded with a bright smile that does nothing for me. Not a damn thing. The tension headache that's been brewing eases some. That is, until Beckett speaks again.

"She's Kylie, Kane. You're likely to see her a lot. The label is tossing around the idea of having her go on tour with us."

"We'd be a disaster together. You're like a toddler on steroids," she informs him primly.

Before I can assimilate the entirety of the conversation—and oh, someone save me. The souring of my stomach from the security nightmare due to the Wonder Twins on tour together—we pull up to the theater, and the noise level rises to unbearable levels. I immediately slip in my earbud and lecture the two childlike adults who want to fight each other for the car handle. "No one leaves the car before me."

Beckett rolls his eyes at Erzulie. "Here goes 'Professor McCullough.' I told you he'd have made a great lecturer."

Instead of rising to Beckett's bait, I say mildly, "That's right. Remember what we discussed at the penthouse."

Much to my surprise, it's Erzulie who ticks off, "Stay within the formation. The team will move with us as we talk to reporters and fans. We don't have freedom until we're safely inside the pavilion. If you tell us to drop, no questions."

Incredulous, I ask Beckett, "Why can't you listen like as well as her?"

Before he can respond, Erzulie answers, "I have a twin who... specializes in security."

What? A twin? My mind reels at the concept. "It would be interesting to meet her," I say honestly as I open the door handle and slip out.

Just as I step from the car, I'm positive I hear her laugh behind me. "I bet it would be." But I don't have much time to process her words. It's time for my job to begin.

I never know if something is coming.

But I have to be prepared in the event it does.

Leanne

NOVEMBER - PRESENT DAY

Some of your favorite celebs turn fashion into an art. Leading the fall list of best-dressed is genre-defiant singer, Erzulie. Her style is much like her vocal capability. Not everyone can mix fitted sequins, exaggerated over-sized wool cardigans, and thigh-high leather boots tighter to make it trendy.

— **Eva Henn, Fashion Blogger**

November - Present Day

"What's this I'm reading about you and Beckett Miller? I thought you just went on tour together for a few months after the premiere. You swore to me there was nothing between you," I demand.

My twin just chortles. "Trust me. We're just friends."

"Then what is this innuendo from StellaNova? According to them, you're practically living with the man." Hurt runs through my voice. It's not that I'd be upset by my sister getting involved with someone—anyone. It's that she hadn't told me first, and I'd be reading about it in a tabloid.

"They're a bunch of blowhards," my twin tries to soothe me. "Trust me, I am nowhere close to living with Beckett or any man. I am having way too much fun to settle down."

I begrudgingly cede that point. But still— "You'd tell me first?"

"I promise, Leanne. If I eventually fall for some megahot star, you will be the first to meet him," she vows. "Now, if you really want to know who I was sleeping with while I was on that tour, we'll be here all night."

"Oh, God. Just assure me you didn't break anyone's heart."

"Not at all." Her face takes on a seductive cast. "And if I can get my ass into the studio, you might hear all about it on my next album."

One beat, two, and the two of us burst into laughter. "You're completely incorrigible."

"Of course I am. We're each other's mirror, Leanne," she reminds me.

"That's what Mom always claimed, but I swear to you, expect to get the third degree from her about Beckett Miller. I swear, her crush on him is ridiculous. Even Dad's annoyed by it." Kylie groans so loudly, I'm certain the people outside my office can hear it. "Listen, the man's hot as hell. It's not my fault she has her fantasy of you settling down and producing musically inclined babies with their daddy's eyes." I taunt my sister even as my fingers fly across the keyboard. I scan an email sent from my handler, which includes the press release we were authorized to announce earlier today. His message sends a surge of pride through me. *And to think I wasn't sure if this was going to work in our favor. Excellent work, Qaza!* I quickly type back, *It was a group effort. Let's bring the team together for a call to see how to mine the data for the intel we're looking for.* Then I refocus on Lee's indulgent face.

"If you talk to Mom before me, disabuse her of that."

"Good luck with that."

"Listen, Beckett is gorgeous, and honestly, I do want you to meet him. But there's someone much more important for you to meet."

"Good, because I was starting to get a complex. Wait, what? Who do you want me to meet? He's not some troglodyte, is he?" I ask suspiciously.

Kylie sticks her tongue out at me as I grin back at the face that's identical to my own. Even our hair is cut similarly, hanging in long, angled layers. It's crazy how despite the hundreds of miles between us, we've never drastically altered our appearance. We've always had this odd twin connection that our mother calls our twin ESP. If one of us did something, a few days later the other would do the same thing. Pulling her legs up to her chest, she reminisces, "No, the guy I want you to meet is one of Beckett's bodyguards."

"What makes you think we'd get along?" I twist my head away and scan something that flashes across my screen.

"Because he's just your type. Hot, smart, and a smart-ass. Plus, he's a little bitch about Beckett's security."

I whip my head around stick my tongue out at Kylie, who laughs uproariously before reminiscing, "Remember the way we used to go on and on about Beckett and Brendan? And now they're people I interact with. What dimension did I step in?"

"Do you remember the way we used to drool over the life-sized posters we had hanging of them in our room as kids." We both giggle helplessly.

That's when she confesses, "I was astounded when Kris set up that date for Beckett and me for the premiere back in February."

"Wait. You're you, and he's him. You're telling me it was all a setup?"

Nodding, her blonde hair floating in the wind off the balcony of her New York City condo, she gives up gossip rags like StellaNova would kill for. "Complete setup. The record label wanted to see if they could spark some promo. With the way the fans reacted, they decided to send me on tour with Beckett, Mick, and Carly."

"And there wasn't a spark between the two of you? Even from the beginning?"

Kylie had just brought her mug of tea to her lips. She quickly sets it down. "Between me? And Becks? You have got to be kidding."

"Because of his age?" Just as my sister's about to respond, I hurriedly respond, "Because I don't care about the fact he could almost have fathered us, the man's shit hot."

"There's no denying that." She frowns thoughtfully. "But take it from me, there's just something...sad about him. Like he's been damaged somehow."

My antennae shoot straight up. "Damaged how?"

"I'm not certain. But when it's about the music, he's great. He's been an incredible mentor about how to improve my sound. But when the conversation turns to anything personal, he clams up. Completely annoying."

"Not everyone wants the world to know every detail about their life personal life, my darling. Maybe he keeps his shit locked up tight, despite the trash the tabloids report about him," I remind her, but mentally, I'm wondering if I need to run a more thorough check on Beckett Miller.

Uproarious laughter ensues. "You'd know that better than anyone, my little secret keeper." Before I can retort, she continues. "My record label thinks I can do no wrong."

I scoff. "If they only knew. By the way, where's the gift of my new Dolce & Gabbana handbag for intercepting the photo of you table dancing at Redemption that your former douchebag bedwarmer released to Sexy&Social?"

"You're going to hold me to that?" Kylie tries to inject a wounded tone into her voice, but I know her better. I hear the underlying laughter.

"Damn straight."

"Okay, fine. I assume you want black to match your soul? Black leather? Like those sadist hacking skills you keep under wraps?"

"Technically, I'm a white hat."

She snorts. "Yeah. Okay. Sell it to someone who doesn't know you the way I do."

"Now, now. Play nice with the person who holds your reputation intact." I give it a moment's thought. "But black works. I'm not certain I own much white. Frankly, do I own anything that doesn't match black?"

"Yeah, the answer's no. I've seen your wardrobe. I tend to be the one a bit more colorful when it comes to clothes."

"When you wear them at all, darling," I inform her sweetly.

A wicked smile crosses her face. "There is that. But there's something about being so good at being bad that's completely freeing. You should give it a try sometime."

I make a mental note to dig deeper in the dark corners of the web to make certain I'm not missing anything to protect my sister's image. "You worry me. You know that, right?"

"Everything worries you."

"There might be some small grain of truth to that," I admit, relaxing in my chair, and change the subject. "How does it feel to be represented by Wildcard?"

"Oh, a million times better than that douchebag at the Neo Agency. Have I mentioned how grateful I am you managed to find that information on Hutnik for me to back away from my contract with him with barely a word?"

"I still don't understand why you didn't just ask your lawyer..." I stumble over her name.

"Carys. Carys Burke. And that's because I was embarrassed as hell."

"Over what?" I demand.

"She encouraged me to hold out before I signed with anyone. But I was impatient. I wanted to *be* someone, Leanne. I had stars in my eyes, I guess. I saw the glamor of what was being offered without understanding what was being asked of me." Her eyes take on a faraway look. "I'll never do that again."

"And you didn't." My sister's recently departed agent tried one too many times to imply she owed him sexual favors for the success of her career. Using sleuthing search skills I'm certain I taught myself in the eighth grade, I collected enough information about him to find out she wasn't the only one he'd tried that crap on. I was infuriated to find some of his attempts were successful, and Kylie used it to get him to cancel their contract, leaving her open to be signed by Wildcard right before handing the evidence over to the heads of the Neo Agency.

When I last checked, Mr. Hutnik was seeking out other employment. Too bad, so sad.

As satisfied as I was at the easy resolution, I worried the ass was going to seek out retribution. After all, Kylie's now a *someone*, and I'm not certain how quiet I could have kept this if the shit went to the press since technically what I did wasn't exactly legal, nor was it sanctioned. But she's my Lee, and I'll do anything, take on anyone, to protect her.

My voice softens. "Have I mentioned how proud I am of you lately?"

"And even though I understand about every fourth sentence you utter when you start talking about a new system you've overtaken, you must know I feel the same about you. I mean, look at what you've built."

I twirl away from the quad monitor setup that has a constant flow of data streaming to wonder, "We both have what we've always wanted." I hold my fingers crossed in my lap. There's actually a great deal I want I still haven't achieved, but those discussions can't be had here.

They never can.

"Looks like."

If it had been anyone but the other half of myself saying that to me, I might have believed her cheerful rejoinder. But something in her voice sends chills up my spine. I tread carefully. "Something up?"

"No...maybe? Just something happened. It's left me feeling a bit odd."

Every hair on my body raises. But just as I'm about to probe for more information, my computer sounds with an alert of an attack on the company network. I whirl back to see a stream of encoded data bouncing off the external firewall protecting my DMZ. *Damn, this is the last thing I need right now.* Even as my fingers are flying to drag anyone with the skills to combat this out of their beds, regardless of their nocturnal activities, I order my twin, "Spill it."

She opens and closes her mouth. "Not right now. You're working on something important..."

"Nothing is more important than you, my Lee," I reassure her, even as my fingers clatter at an alarming pace against my main keyboard.

She opens her mouth just as a second alarm sounds. I yell at the offending device. "Christ! It's Friday at eleven. Don't people have a life?"

"Obviously not, or you wouldn't have a company that just beat out half the known universe for an enormous government contract," she says drolly. "This can wait. The fate of the world as we know it can't."

I roll my eyes. "It's not that bad."

"Would you tell me if it was?"

I hedge just a little too long, and my sister laughs. "Ah, so are we talking about the compromise of all my electronic devices or potentially a missile heading to blow up StellaNova's headquarters? If it's the second, do you think—just this once—you could let it go? For me? Please?"

I can't help it. I burst out laughing, but that sound withers away when my sister plainly states, "I miss you. I know I just said I have everything I ever wanted, but somehow I always imagined you by my side when it happened."

"I know. Me too." The secrets I hide are different now. Even as exciting as they are, they're nothing like the ones you giggle over in the middle of the night with the person your heart beats for and with.

"It's been too long since we've seen each other."

I chew on my lip, mentally solving the attack as well as rearranging my schedule for the next two weeks. "Listen, I'm heads down planning for the face-to-face meeting with the representatives from government. They have to come in and inspect the facility within fourteen days of the award. Do you have plans next weekend?"

Kylie shakes her head. "Nothing concrete. Why?"

"Let's do a sisters' weekend together starting next Friday. You, me, and the Plaza. I'll drive down to the city. We can have a massive sleepover."

"And catch up in person," she muses. "I approve of this mightily."

My smile is crooked. "Good, because I wasn't going to let you back out."

"You know, for someone who is four minutes older, you're awfully autocratic."

"It comes from running my own business. And I'm only older because they grabbed me out first," I remind her.

"True. Besides, being younger does have its perks. I got more time to cook. It made me better-looking."

I scoff. We're completely identical unless she gets a bone up her ass and decides to do something funky with her hair.

"...and more talented. Guess that's why I may have a shot at singing a duet with Brendan Blake on his next album."

My jaw drops. My fingers stop moving. My office could be infiltrated by the enemy and I'd never know it. I shriek, "And you waited this long to share this with me?"

Suddenly, my office door flies open. I knew I should have engaged the security locks. Someone blearily manages, "You got 'em already?"

I yell, "Get out! Out, out, out!" The door quickly snaps shut.

Kylie sighs. "Honestly, babe. This isn't a good time."

I mutter, "It's our time. It's always supposed to be."

"I know. But life happens. Things...happen." An odd note in her voice has me yanking the handline out of the cradle.

"What is it?"

She shakes her head. "Nothing too serious, I hope."

"Are you sure?" I demand. The way her attitude keeps flipping and flopping is seriously beginning to worry me, but she hasn't said the one thing guaranteed to make me stalk out the door of my office and to say the hell with everyone and everything. I know everything about Kylie because she can't hide a damn thing from me. Our ridiculously traditional parents would wither away if they knew about the way her life has deviated from the girl who left New Hampshire to sing: the booze, the men, the photos of the drugs—which she swears was just a onetime thing.

Then again, it's not like my life has followed a path of roses either. My eyes glance to the side, where I keep my system that can only be accessed with my retina scan and a fingerprint sequence. My own version of the old-fashioned children's toy Simon. It's just the kind of games I play on it are ridiculously dangerous.

"Listen, it's not a big deal. Really, you won't see this on any scandal sheet."

I flat out ask, "Are you in trouble?" I wince as my watch vibrates with a text from the one man who can send a frisson of fear down my own spine. *Are you on this, or do I need to send in a different team.* Fuck, Kylie might not be, but I'll have someone's boot up my ass if I don't get this numnutz out of my network.

She stands and reaches over to pick up her mug. "It's nothing that won't hold. Go deal with your bleeps and blips. And I promise not to fall asleep next week when you tell me about it."

"You'd better not."

"I love you, forever, Leanne," she says.

"And I love you, Kylie. Always," I vow. Pressing End on the call, I turn my full attention to the upper monitors and the jackass who thinks there's a chance in hell of breaching my network.

Wrong. And unfortunately for them, by the end of the night, I'll be turning all his information over to my new best buddies at the DoD—which will ultimately filter up to the man who controls many of my own movements. After all, I'm perfectly fine with being bad when there's something good waiting for me at the end of it. Thus far, no feeling has given me the same excitement as beating another hacker at their own game. Well, I amend internally as I turn up my sister's latest album, except for watching my sister onstage, accepting her first Grammy Award.

That's the only thing that's come close.

Leanne

Saratoga Springs, N.Y. Castor has been awarded a $172 million prime task order by the Department of Defense to protect against cyberattacks.

— **Castor Newsroom**

My cell ringing is what wakes me the next morning. Without looking at the caller ID, I mumble, "Unless the server room is on fire, you know you can kiss my ass."

My mother laughs. "I certainly will not."

I roll over and manage to pry my eyes open. I didn't stumble into my bed until close to dawn. "Hey, Mom. Did you just get off shift?"

"Hello, Leanne. No, honey. I wasn't working last night. Your father and I were having breakfast before he went off to put in his orders for the stocks he wants to trade. That's when he showed me an interesting tidbit in the local paper. I was calling to congratulate you on your new contract, but now I feel like I first need to lecture you about overworking."

I yawn in her ear, even as I scooch into a sitting position. Dragging my tablet off my end table into my lap, I scroll through my company email to see if there's anything urgent. "Just had a thing at work that ran late. I didn't get home until dawn."

"I don't suppose I'm interrupting anyone who would actually be worshiping at the altar of your rear?" There's a note of hopefulness that has me bursting into laughter.

"Gee, Mom. Way to be a bit obvious there. Why not ask me if I got sweaty in between the sheets with someone last night."

"Because that's so crass, darling."

"Do you ever grill Kylie like this?" I grumble.

"No." Just as I'm about to unload my feelings about that on our mother, she explains, "With her I have to come right out and ask because I never know if the press is making something out of nothing. Like this thing with her and Beckett Miller? I mean, honestly? While I have a ridiculous crush on him your father just can't understand, the man could almost *be* her father. And despite your best efforts to make her look like an angel, Leanne, I know my girls better than you think."

"I don't know what you're talking about, Mom," I reply airily.

"Uh-huh. You're not doing her any favors."

"More favors than you know," I mutter under my breath.

"What was that? I didn't quite hear you."

"Just that she favors you." I think quickly on my feet, mentally congratulating myself for getting that one past my mother, but she goes on to say, "But she inherited my temperament at that age, which is why I know she's likely causing a ruckus and you're doing exactly what your father did."

"Which is?"

"Doing everything possible to keep her hot mess express from hitting the newspapers."

I can't rein my laughter in. "What a way to speak about your youngest child."

"When you next chat with your sister—and I don't mean in that crazy telepathic way you two seemed to perfect in utero—tell her the local paper quoted a very nice mention of her performance at a place called Brooklyn Steel?"

Enthusiastically, I inform her, "Kylie mentioned it. Said there were amazing acoustics and her show sounded so terrific, the label is debating releasing the live recording."

"Really? Well, isn't that wonderful."

"I'm so proud of her, Mom."

"I'm proud of *both* of you, despite the fact your work rarely appears in the paper, darling. Don't think your father didn't come rushing down to the breakfast table this morning when he saw Castor's press release. Why didn't we hear about that from you?"

"We were under a gag order." I was under much more than that as I force myself to dredge up the memory of a deep voice screaming at me on the secure line issuing threats I ended up reporting to the DoD. Freaking Messenia.

"You couldn't have told us?"

For just a moment, a twang of guilt hits. Then, memories of the way the sleepy little town where I grew up could miraculously manage to spread gossip without a single person saying a single word makes me shudder. Calling upon all the diplomatic negotiation skills I used to secure the deal in the first place, I soothe her ruffled feathers. "Mom, I could have put the entire contract at risk. Who knows who might have been listening?" *And I don't just mean our government*, I think ruefully, recalling the attack on the company's network last night. Despite the fact I've taken a large step back from what I used to do, I'm ridiculously cautious for entirely different reasons.

I can't deny there are times I yearn for anonymity—when I was only an obscure college kid who was simply someone's unknown best friend or their worst shadow. Then after an infamous Defcon where I was noticed, and subsequently approached on campus, my whole life changed. Mind whirling, I recount my first interaction with my boss.

"Why are you here?"

"I'm here for you." He crossed his still-impressive arms over his chest.

I remember shrieking at him. "Privacy is the very core of Defcon. Who the hell are you to shatter it?"

"The man who's going to save the life of you, your parents, and your twin. You have no idea of the people who are taking notice of you, little girl. Now, do you want to give up the theatrics and have an adult conversation, or would you like to draw a little more attention to us?"

I crashed into him as I stormed past, calling him an asshole. But I agreed to the conversation.

In all the years I've worked for him, I've begrudgingly retracted calling him an ass. He's laid it all on the line, multiple ways. And he's never asked for more than any of us give, than he himself has given. So what if I've been forced to give up free time because certain authorities need me to assist under dire circumstances when computer experts, governments, and corporations needed my skills to accomplish certain missions? Instead of using my skills for my own amusement, now they're used to keep people safe.

Only once have I felt the games went too far and debated quitting, putting it all behind me and focusing solely on the jobs my cover affords me. Early in my career, intel I passed along to a Marine led to a bloodbath in Azerbaijan. My handler verbally castigated me when I approached him with my weakness. He took a much-needed hard line, reminding me of the oath I swore. I'll never forget him telling me to come back when I had my head on straight. "These are people's lives you're saving. You can't quit on them."

I went back to New Hampshire to get perspective, blaming the loss of a bug bounty for my behavior. While there, my father reasoned, "You need more than this in your life, Leanne. Structure. Balance. You can be the best at what you do without being notorious."

"You mean like Kylie," I teased. My twin's antics were going to turn my platinum-blonde hair gray well before its time.

"You need to be the best in a very different way. You're identical, but you don't need the fame the way she does. Find your balance; it's out there."

As if his words woke me, I began investigating what it would take to disengage myself from the ties that bound me so tightly to a future that was destroying me one click on the keyboard at a time. I established Castor and what jobs I would continue to accept under the aegis of my new corporation. Shaking my head to clear it from the foggy memories of the past, my smile is in my voice when I tease my mother. "Besides, I would have called later."

"When you woke up."

"Mom, when have I kept normal hours?" Not since I learned the truth lives buried in layers of night. And people with something to hide fear the dark.

"Sadly, not since you were in high school, darling. I still remember the first semester you came home from MIT and were up three days straight in some...what's it called again?"

"A hackathon. And I damn well won it." It was much more than a hackathon, but there are things I can never share with my mother. Things I'll take to the grave.

Horror fills her voice. "Leanne Miles, tell me you weren't up all night participating in something of that sort. You're a legitimate businesswoman now."

I cross my fingers before responding. After all, if I tried to explain what my company really does to my mother, she'd likely have a heart attack on the spot. And that wouldn't be good for Mom to be wheeled into the hospital where she's a trauma nurse due to her daughter's carelessness. "Of course not, Mom. I hire people for that sort of work." Which is completely true. I now manage my own team of twelve that get off on the hunt as much as I do. And while we still have other work, it's the things we tackle for Uncle Sam I suspect she'd never understand, perhaps even severely disapprove of.

She lets out a sigh of relief. I almost feel guilty about the small fib until I think about all the crap about my sister I destroy regularly. Thoughts of Kylie appearing on the front page of a tabloid table dancing with her legs wrapped around the hips of a popular movie star flit through my mind. "Yeah, that would go over well," I mutter.

"What would, darling?"

"Nothing, Mom. I was thinking about work." Because some days, the alerts about my sister rival the volume of work my boss punts my way.

"Do you have to go in today?"

"Yes. It's going to be crazy for the next few weeks." I explain the bare bones of the contract to her and make plans to visit after I visit my twin in the city.

"Then, I'll let you go, darling. I love you."

"Love you too, Mom." I hang up.

Jumping out of bed and making my way into my bathroom with my tablet in my hand, I think about the attack on Castor last night. I almost pity the poor bastard whose system we used my newest program against. Dioscuri—named after the Gemini twins, Castor and Pollux—identifies and copies all computer data and location information before incapacitating the target in a way that allows the target to continue to operate. It starts an automatic recording of all activities and moves the data to a backup drive the owner can't access without a secret key that only Dioscuri has access to. It's proven handy in numerous court cases as evidence. And it's the same tool the government just acquired the exclusive use of and support for the next three years.

It was a brainchild I began developing in secret after I overheard one of my team bitching about their system getting wiped during the war games they participated in during Defcon and how they missed a court date as a result of it. It reminded me of my high school days when too often, I cavalierly would be the shadow probing my way into companies like my own to see how many layers I could strip away, how many files I could seize, how much data I could accumulate.

Only I never got caught.

There's no stopping the enemy. If someone's determined, they'll use any manner necessary to win. Even as I fend off the smaller attacks with ease, I'm always carefully stepping, trying not to wake the sleeping beasts who are simply waiting for an opportunity to unleash their cyberattacks on my network as a pathway into data much more valuable.

A familiar ping jerks my attention away from the simple pleasure of blow-drying my hair and refocuses it. Immediately, I'm cautious as I lean over. I let out half of my breath in relief as I glimpse a picture of Kylie at Redemption—the hot nightclub in Manhattan. But only half. Picking up the tablet to study the photo, everything inside me clenches up. I have a window of ten minutes to stop the script that will automatically erase Erzulie's antics, leaving her angelic indie goddess reputation intact. But after a quick perusal, the knot inside me relaxes. "Thank God. It's just a different one from the night she was table dancing." Unconcerned about this one being online, since she's simply holding a drink and laughing, I zoom in to get a good look at who she's talking with. Because his face is splashed all over social media, and then there's the fact he's a damn hottie, I easily recognize Redemption club owner, Marco Houde. I drag my finger around the screen to see if there is anyone else of notice before letting out a long whistle. "Who in the hell is *he*?"

In a black suit with a blue shirt that emphasizes his dark blond hair and chiseled jaw, my heart skips a beat at the pure perfection of his face, which is turned away from where Leanne is standing. I love the feeling of pleasure that floods through me as I zoom in on his magnificent profile.

It's *him*. Ocean Eyes. The man who I'd begun to think was merely a mirage, though he invades my dreams at regular intervals that I've woken reaching for my vibrator.

Finally, I have a photograph to run through my sources when I have a free moment, which means—I think wryly—I'll get to it in about three or four years. "Or maybe I can convince her to make a return trip to Redemption next weekend. Even if he's not someone she knows, one can only hope this guy is part of Redemption's regular clientele." Mentally, I plan on tossing a little black dress and heels into my bag.

But for now, I have to focus on the here and now. And for me, that means a world most people don't acknowledge in their minds because if they did, they'd be afraid of their shadow. Then again, that means they'd have to admit they have a shadow. A constant one.

And it's being monitored.

KANE

We can't choose our family, but we can choose our friends. Trust me, that's so much better.

— @PRyanPOfficial

My hands shake as I scroll through the contacts. Pressing Send, I hold the phone to my ear and wait as the first, then second, ring happen.

I'm almost grateful when I'm sent to voicemail. "Hey, Brit. It's Kane. I just wanted to call and check in on how you and Maddie are doing. I'm thinking of you both." I disconnect the call.

I'd be a liar if I expressed disappointment she didn't pick up. I'm always terrified one day she's going to answer and tell me the truth about what she thinks of me for sending her loved one to his certain death. And someday, I know I'll need to be strong enough to endure her censure. Just the way I did from the government that ordered us to conduct the op in the first place. But again, I've received a reprieve.

I'm still sitting there clutching my phone with my elbows braced on my knees when I hear a knock on the doorframe. My colleague Mitch is leaning against the jamb. "Anything you need?" His face holds the understanding only another person who's witnessed death recognizes. It's why I don't immediately tell him to go shove his support up his ass and stalk away, as I've done with so many others.

"I imagine twenty years from now, I'll still be trying to absolve myself for his death," I declare bluntly.

He nods, his face reflecting the same weighty guilt mine does. Though we served in different capacities, Mitch—a former cop—still carries his own wounds. And like mine, they're normally not visible. So we don't get bogged down in the mistakes of the past, I drag us both into the present. "What's up?"

"Beckett's schedule for the next week." He holds out the typed papers to me.

I scan the pages, noticing how light the schedule is, and groan. "We're screwed. He doesn't have enough to keep him busy. This means we're going to be flying somewhere on a whim, or we're going to be traipsing around New York. Either way, it's a security nightmare."

"Thank you."

I frown. "For what?"

Mitch's mouth curves. "I bet the guys you'd say something almost exactly like that. I just won twenty in the pool we have going."

Despite the lingering nausea threatening to claw its way up my guts from my earlier call, my lips twitch. "I'm not sure I like becoming predictable."

Mitch is quick to dissent. "Oh, it's not you who's predictable, Kane. Beckett, yes. You, no."

"Still." I frown down at the paper. "Maybe it's a good time to go over the security protocols to Beckett's place."

Mitch groans. "And there goes that twenty."

I bark out a laugh. "Get out of here." Mitch turns to leave, but before he does, I call out, "Hey, Mitch? Thanks."

He shrugs. "You've done it for us."

"Yeah." I wait for him to leave and then push to my feet. Striding over to the window, I give myself a moment to recall the mission.

It was a night mission, and there wasn't much more than the HUMANIT to go by. Three helos were in the staging area, but by the time we entered enemy airspace, only ours was functional due to hydraulic failure and one being sent out for recon earlier. It took a hit and caused a crack in the rotor blade. He gave the order we were going.

We did. We landed.

Things were fine. Until we were standing there facing each other...

Another knock interrupts my thoughts. "Enter!" I snap out, whirling around.

"I need to head to LLF to speak with Carys," Beckett informs me coolly. He doesn't step one foot past the jamb. But I can tell by the way his jaw is ticking, he's pissed at the less than respectable way I've just addressed him. Considering the amount he pays me to do the damn job, I'd be pissed as well.

Damn. I was so locked in the nightmare of the past, I didn't hear anyone come in. I hold up a hand.

Beckett, misinterpreting my actions as the beginning of another lecture about his protective detail, starts, "I tried to call, but no one..."

"I deeply apologize." The words rock him. "Something captured my attention. That shouldn't have happened."

"I don't mean to intrude, Kane, but it looked like it had you by the throat." Before I can say a word to contradict his astute observation, he goes on. "Take it from someone who knows. You have to purge whatever it is. Otherwise, you're going to have nightmares about it forever."

"That sounds like experience talking," I blurt out before I can hold it back.

He merely arches a brow before turning around. "Carys's? About fifteen minutes?"

"I'll have the car pulled around," I reply to his back, wondering, but knowing I'll never ask, what in Beckett Miller's past has him trapped in nightmares. I mentally flip through the file I have about him and come up blank. Well, the man's entitled to his own secrets. All he needs from me is protection.

And I better get on that before I get booted from this job as well.

A short while later, we pull up to the building that houses the law office of LLF LLC. I spy Erzulie making her way inside. The paparazzi are temporarily distracted from the SUV we're in as they blind the poor girl as she opens up the gilded doors. "She needs protection," I mutter absentmindedly as I place the vehicle in park.

"I've tried to convince her of that," Beckett replies surprisingly.

"To which she said?"

"After she stopped laughing? I believe the words were 'Over my dead body, Becks. Why don't you just leave security issues to my sister?' Then she skipped off like she normally does."

"It wasn't so funny when we were on tour." I recall a few incidents with fans I was certain were going to make headlines but shockingly didn't.

"No. Kylie doesn't worry about the press quite the same way the rest of us do. It's like there's a media angel on her shoulder," Beckett muses.

I open the door before declaring, "While the devil sits on yours? He seems to rest there with regularity."

Beckett gives me a thoughtful look. "You know, Kane, if you ever get tired of this bodyguard business, you could probably get a job as a songwriter."

I choke on air as I hold the door for the rock star before rushing him inside. Once we've finally made it safely inside the building, I accuse, "You did that on purpose."

"Completely. I mean, you come up with a few good lines, but nothing you should quit your day job over."

I use that as an excuse to do my job. "Remember, stay inside the building. And call when you're ready to leave."

He rolls his eyes. "Yes, dear."

Something he said earlier causes the hair on the back of my neck to rise. "And how about using some of your influence to get your tour partner to at least reach out to my boss to discuss protection—even if it's just for big events like premieres? The Grammys?"

Beckett frowns thoughtfully as we reach the elevators. "That's reasonable. I'll propose it to her. No promises."

Once he disappears into the elevator, I give some thought as to why I'm concerned about Kylie Miles. I know it has to do with the amount of time she spends around my principal, but there's something else nagging at me. And I learned all too well in the military not to ignore those feelings.

Not when people's lives could be at stake.

Leanne

Who knew Erzulie had a mole right there? Certainly we didn't until the pictures of her naked showed up in our inbox this morning. All we have to say, Erzulie, is wow! You may never be remembered for your vocal cords after this.

— StellaNova

It's a good thing I'm getting away from work. "Kylie better have my damn handbag ready, considering I just spent the better part of the night squashing that pipsqueak Hutnik?" I let out a growl when I think of the way he tried to photoshop our head onto someone else's body and pass it off to one of the biggest social media blogs in America.

Dumb-freaking-ass.

I feel the power surge through me as I speed my brand-new Bentayga down the Taconic. It has absolutely nothing to do with the fact I'm driving an SUV that purrs like a sports car and everything to do with the fact my sister's voice explodes through the sublime Naim sound system. When the song ends, the national DJ announces, "'Faith and Trust' has once again put Erzulie at the top of the charts. There's no stopping her as she soars with hit after hit."

Another voice declares, "It's hard to imagine that earlier this year, she was accepting the Grammy for Best New Artist."

"Nothing's going to stop her from reaching the top."

With an enormous smile, I reach over and pat my purse, where the card I received from her arrived before my meeting yesterday. My sister has the ability to pull me away from my computer the way no one else does. I burst out laughing at the two elderly women on the front before I read the preprinted *The sun will rise no matter what.* Then I read what my sister had sent to me via overnight messenger: *I'm so proud of you. I can't wait to see you. Once your meeting is done, get here fast. I have so much to catch you up on and this isn't the face I want to show you when I do it.* Then she drew an arrow around to the front of the card, making me laugh out loud in my light-filled office, despite how shocked I was when I read the postscript about her doing something we swore we'd only do together.

It was a vow. A promise. And my sister never broke them—at least, not to me.

Hopefully, we can use the weekend to catch up. In the last two weeks, our nightly calls have left me anxious just to get to her. Last night after she left a party early, the slightest noise had her leaping out of her chair. I frown in memory as I push my foot down on the pedal. "Don't worry about it, Leanne," I recall her laughing as she took another swig of a martini—something she rarely indulged in at home. "It's just something to calm my nerves before I go out and face the world tomorrow."

"You're you, Lee. You don't have nerves." Concern causes me to use our childhood nickname—each of us being Lee. A part of one another for always.

Her eyes unfocused before they bored through the video at me. "You'd be surprised at what makes me jump in shock these days. Or rather who."

Then I got her card. It was on the tip of my tongue to beg her to forget about her commitments, to leave the city, when the maelstrom of emotions settled and the dynamic smile I know better than any other would spread across her face. Then her voice hummed melodically, "I love you, forever, Leanne."

"I love you always, Kylie," I whispered back before she disconnected.

My phone rings over my Bluetooth. It's her. "Hey, I'm running late. I got yanked into a meeting with Ivan." I name my chief data scientist. She starts coughing uncontrollably. "Are you okay?" I demand.

"Good, fine. Couldn't be better. Should I just check in?"

"Let me call and add you to the room. I was certain I'd be there by now."

"Perfect. I'll see you in a few. If I get bored, I'll head down to the spa and charge it to you. I'm exhausted from a party I was at last night. In fact, you'll never believe who I ran into there. I thought his eyes were going to bug out when he saw what I was wearing."

"Who was it?" I ask curiously, wondering if Kylie ran into one of our mutual acquaintances from home.

"Nuh-uh. Not while you're driving. I want to see your expression on this one."

"That's just rude. Get me curious, and then leave me hanging."

"Well, curiosity is a bitch. You know what she did to that damn cat."

"Likely stepped on it with one of your shoes." We both laugh at my quick comeback. "Is this why you were so upset last night?"

My teeth clamp down at her obvious avoidance of the question when she blithely continues. "His only saving grace is what I was wearing wasn't sheer, otherwise he might have completely keeled over."

"Was it something scandalous?"

"You'd probably think so. The boots alone had so many crystals on them, I think I blinded half the guests. Or maybe that's because of where they ended."

We both chuckle. "As for the spa, I highly support this plan. In fact, get the works done for me."

"Consider it done."

I can tell she's about to press End, but my words stop her. "Hey, Kylie? I love you always."

I hear her chuckle, "And you know I love you too, Leanne. Forever. Never forget that."

Instead of settling me, her call causes my unease to intensify. I should have been in New York by now. I almost strangled Ivan when he dashed in my door at the last-minute meeting to discuss another request from Messenia to merge corporations. Infuriated because this is something that we've discussed many times before. It was absolutely something that could and should have waited. As a result, our conversation became heated. I ended up storming out to my Bentley after I reminded him not only am I the CEO of Castor Industries, Inc., but I hold the majority of the voting shares—all of which are held by Miles family members.

The meeting left a sour taste in my mouth after our team's success just weeks before. Now, more than ever, I want to spend time to celebrate with my twin and to listen to the news she wants to share.

But the closer I get to the city, the more something else pushes at me to press the accelerator down harder than I ever have.

By the time I'm striding toward the front desk of the Plaza a few hours later, I'm on edge. I'm even more delayed than expected due to an unexpected traffic jam. Plus, I had this odd onset of acid that made me pull to the side of the highway to vomit. *Damn, what the hell did I eat?* Mentally, I go over the takeout the team ordered last night and write them off the list. *Never having Yuck Truck again at 2:00 a.m.* Frustrated in line, I yank my phone out to try my sister again. I still can't get Kylie on the phone to tell her I'm here. Suddenly, I crumple to the ground, barely able to breathe. People milling around me look around in concern. Discreetly dressed security personnel begin to approach. One thought flashes through my mind. *Lee.*

I'm assisted into a sitting position. *Am I okay? Do I need medical assistance?* "No, thank you. I just felt..." *Like my world was coming to an end.* Where that thought comes from, I don't know. I have no idea. "... faint." Security moves me and my bag off to the side so other patrons can pass by in order to check in while I sit up, waving off their assistance. Frantically, I begin trying to get my sister on her phone.

I dial over and over, internally begging and pleading. But she's still not answering. At first, I try not to flip out. She could be with any number of people—maybe she's still in the treatment room in the spa. My fingers are shaking as I push Send again. I know I'm just lying to myself. *What's wrong, Lee? Why aren't you answering me?* I press Send for what must be the fiftieth time. I'm about to call over one of the Security team members, who is still hovering nearby, to call the spa.

But this time, someone answers. "Ms. Miles? My name is Dr. Jason Ross. I'm an emergency room doctor at NYU Medical Center. I've—"

I cut him off as I spring to my feet on legs that can barely hold my weight. "It's Lee. What happened?"

"Ms. Miles, how long will it take for you to come to the city?"

I swoop up my purse, ignoring my suitcase lying haphazardly nearby. "I'm already here."

He gives me the address and says something that gives me the fortitude to run outside. Ignoring the startled protests when I jump the line and get into the back of the taxi, I repeat the same words Dr. Ross said to me.

"Please hurry."

Then I begin to rock back and forth, terrified.

This can't be happening.

Leanne

8

I can't believe I'm IN at #Redemption! Now I can see what all the buzz is about with this #Kensington. Hey @CuTEandRich3 are you still waiting in line? Hahaha!
— **@PRyanPOfficial**

It shouldn't be like this. I stare at the broken and bruised body of my identical twin sister swathed in bandages, being kept alive only by the respirator moving her chest upward and downward. The doctors are outside, waiting for me to tell them to turn it off so they can begin harvesting her skin, her hair, even her eyes.

My eyes.

But they'll never have her soul. That was absorbed back into me the moment I slid inside this living mortuary. It was hovering in the air, almost tangible, making me believe for just a moment it could slide as easily back into her body as it did mine.

It might be my imagination, but I feel her desperation whisper on the fringes of mine through a bond that shouldn't exist because they told me it's only the respirator that's been keeping her alive since they wheeled her in not long before I handed off the keys to my vehicle to the valet. *Let me in one last time, Lee. Then let me go.*

I drop to my knees beside her bed, clasping her hand against my chest, shaking my head furiously. "I can't. Come back to me, my sweet sister. My twin. Don't go away!"

The door cracks open a bit, and I snap, "Get out!"

It quickly closes. "They're all waiting for you. They want to take you from me, piece by piece."

You have to let them.

"I don't have to do shit," I declare aloud.

Lee. There's a reprimand in her tone that's more like me than her. But when two souls are as deeply connected as ours are, it's not a surprise we've taken each other's mannerisms over the years. *After all, how many times did we manage to trick people into thinking we're the other?* I can almost hear her laughter in my mind. And it makes the pain that much more intense.

"I can't be the one to do this. Why did you make this my decision?" I cry out.

You know why, she chides me.

The answer skates along my spine. "Because I know you'd do it for me."

Not without feeling like you are. Now tell me you love me.

"I love you, Lee. Forever." I sob for long moments, holding her hand against my face before managing to stagger to my feet. Wrenching open the door, I call out to the ER doctor who contacted me a few short hours ago. "Dr. Ross?"

He's at my side in seconds. "I'm truly sorry, Ms. Miles. We did everything we could." His face is a mask of devastation. I barely manage a small nod. He hesitates. "Do you want to be here for this?"

"I'm not leaving my Lee."

He steps away and informs the doctor who informed me when I first arrived he was the pulmonologist on Kylie's case. Dr. Ross asks, "Do you want to know what happened to her now or..."

"Now," I croak out.

"She was strangled until she lost consciousness and then was beaten. Her heart stopped once, but we were able to resuscitate her. Then, she stopped breathing. An MRI confirmed internal bleeding, hence the respirator."

Oh, God. My Lee. Who did this to you? But what comes out of my mouth is a strangled sound of agony.

He reaches over and pats my shoulder. "The police..." But before he can say any more, the room is filled with far too many people who are changing the noise from serene beeps to noisy chatter. It's discordant to my ears because I can't hear her sweet voice over theirs.

Finally, Dr. Ross moves us to the end of the bed, closest to her head. Everyone else has stationed themselves at predetermined stations, ready to take action. "Whenever you're ready, Ms. Miles," he gently encourages me.

I want to tell him to go fuck himself. They have no concept of what it's like to be the person to extinguish the life of the person who you held wrapped in their arms before you could breathe your first breath on your own. And now, to be the one to take away her last one? To be responsible because of a stupid piece of paper we drew up years ago, assuming we'd never need it? Because I was late getting here, even though something compelled me after receiving a card to get here faster, to come see my Lee. She needed me, and I let her down.

We're connected by something far greater than sisterhood. We're twins. We share everything, from taste in music to sense of humor. Even our damn voice is identical, a curse or a gift from sharing strep throat back and forth too many years while sharing a room throughout our years of living together at home. And I don't know how I'll ever listen to myself speak another word. Not without knowing my Lee was being brutally attacked, out there being hurt somewhere I couldn't help her.

I lean down and press my lips to her forehead one last time. "There will never be a day I don't love you." *And I swear, I will find out who did this to you, Lee. Even if it takes the rest of my life.* My heart fills with a deep warmth. It's her. I know it.

I give the order, and the sound that emits from me when my sister's heart stops beating is terrible. It's a keening desperation I hope the gods take as the warning it is. Because everyone had better get out of my way.

Screw the perfect order I've spent the last few years trying to live my life by. War was just declared on whoever did this to me, my family. *They will pay. I swear it on our soul.*

"Time of death, 20:16," Dr. Ross announces quietly before turning to me and offering a simple "I'm so sorry for your loss, Ms. Miles."

I nod, unable to speak, not even if they forced me to.

"We can give you just a few moments," he begins, but I interrupt.

"She's gone. Nothing is going to bring her back."

His kind eyes harness mine. "No, Kylie, they won't."

I shiver when my sister's name slides from his lips, but I don't correct him. After all, nothing will change the fact I'll see her face in the mirror for the rest of my life. But when whoever crossed this line and stole my sister from me, they didn't realize death won't break a bond science can't explain, one that formulates when two bodies wrap around one another for almost ten months in a confined space, sharing the same food, the same nutrients passed through love by their mother.

Not just family, not just sisters, but twins.

Something stirs on the fringes of my mind, an ill-formed idea. Something Kylie absolutely would have approved of if I wasn't desperately clutching her dead hand.

"I have so many people to notify about my sister's death. I don't know where to start."

Guiding me from the chaos, Dr. Ross leads me into a private room. "Your parents?"

I can't fathom what my mother's reaction is going to be. What sweet hell is she going to endure when I call to tell her Kylie's gone? She won't make the same mistake the doctor did as soon as she hears my voice.

I begin to sob quietly. "What am I supposed to do?"

He guides me into a chair and offers me a box of tissues. I weep, "I don't know how I'm going to get through this."

"Do you want me to contact anyone for you?"

"She was the strong one, brave. And now she's..." I start to cry again.

He takes my hand and holds it while I cry into a mess of tissues. "A part of her will always live on in you."

Already I feel a gaping hole where Kylie lived starting to open, years of her being a part of me—of us—slipping away. For long moments, I fear I'm not strong enough to do this. Then I think about how Mom and Dad are going to handle this, and I feel something inside me crumble. "I need time to call my parents and then..."

Dr. Ross stands and hands me a card. "Please call me and I'll do whatever I can to help, Ms. Miles."

Pulling my cell out of my bag, I clench it over and over in between my fingers before I press the numbers to our family home in New Hampshire. It's picked up before it can ring. "Everything okay, Leanne? I thought you and Kylie were supposed to be twinning it tonight." My father uses his favorite expression for nights he knew my sister and I would go out and he didn't want to know what happened.

A choked sob escapes. I really don't want to say these words. "Daddy, she's..."

"What? What is it, Leanne?"

"Daddy." It's the only word I can manage. "Daddy."

"Hold on, baby. Renee? Pick up the phone! It's Leanne!" There's a muffled shriek before, "No, it won't wait a minute. Now!"

"What is so blasted important. I'm trying to pull a cake out of the oven," my mother snaps when she picks up the kitchen handset.

I sob even harder at the everyday byplay I'm about to destroy. Maybe forever.

"Leanne? Sweetheart? What is it?" My mother's voice changes immediately from annoyed to frantic.

"It's Kylie. She's...gone." And that's all I manage to get out before words become something none of us can manage through the shrieking and bitter tears.

Leanne

There's a universal pressure to be jubilant around the holidays. But don't forget the internal trauma many suffer amid your colossal need for twinkle lights. Some people feel they need permission to have an unshakeable place to completely disconnect from cheer. Be their place of normal.

— **The Fireside Psychologist**

The sun is up the next morning before I'm finished with the arrangements to move Kylie to New Hampshire to our small town for burial. I'm mentally and physically exhausted. If it wasn't for Dr. Ross, I'd don't know how I would have managed to handle as much as I have. My parents are understandably inconsolable and left everything in my hands. "You know Kylie better than anyone else in the world." I had to grit my teeth at my father talking about her as if she was still here, like she was just going to pop up next week.

When the only place I know she's going to surface is my nightmares until I can figure out what happened to her.

"I don't know how to thank you enough, Dr. Ross. You've been a complete godsend, you and everyone here I've come in contact with. I don't know how I would have been able to process all of this." The poor doctor has spent hours after his shift ended helping me make arrangements to have my sister's body transported to our family's home. I've been blindly signing paperwork, feeling with every stroke of the pen that it isn't ink but blood pouring onto the pages. *Is that how she felt when she wrote her music?* I wonder absentmindedly as I draw a treble cleft through the condensation on the glass.

We're standing side by side in a private family room next to a blacked-out window. The streets of New York appear lit with gold. To my analytical mind, it's watching tangible chaos between the speeding cars. Kylie would say that's just the dreams reaching up to grab hold. Bitterness swamps me. "She came to the city, and look at what happened. This isn't the city of dreams; it's pure fucking fool's gold."

I rein in my emotions. This poor doctor deals every day with life and death; he doesn't need my grief weighing him down. "I apologize. As I was saying, you and your staff have been nothing but supportive and professional."

He winces. "I'm not entirely certain about that, Ms. Miles." At my frown, he sighs. "Someone on the staff leaked what happened to the media. We've had to call in security for every entrance of the hospital."

I curse, my anger a welcome emotion. Frankly, anything is other than this overwhelming grief. "This is absolutely the last thing my family needs."

His face becomes more strained, if that's possible. "I agree. I know who I'd call in a situation like this, but I'm not certain if your people have someone different."

My people? A dawning horror races through me, and I stammer, "Dr. Ross, I'm not sure who..." I'm trying to string together a coherent sentence to remind him it was Kylie in that bed, hoping I didn't just sign a bunch of papers that declared me dead.

Me. Not my identical twin.

But he mistakes my confusion. "I'm sure your record label will be able to help."

Racking my brain, I try to recall the name of the executive Kylie dealt with at Wildcard Records when she left the Neo Agency and come up blank. The only name that comes to mind is her attorney. "Carys," I blurt out. "I just need to call Carys." I'm very positive my twin would have her lawyer's contact info programmed into her cell.

Dr. Ross gestures to the phone, but I'm already digging through my bag holding Kylie's personal items. "I'll give you a few moments' privacy." He walks toward the door and closes it behind him.

The moment it does, I'm frantically searching my bag for my secure cell. I press the only number in it and wait.

"This had better be important, *Qaza*. The kid is teething, and we've barely slept all night."

"I'm standing in a room at the NYU Medical Center. My sister's been murdered. I hope that doesn't inconvenience you too much, *sir*," my voice spits at him.

"What the fuck?" is shouted before a murmured "No, sweetheart. Go back to sleep. It's work."

"I wish I could sleep. I wish I could believe that closing my eyes would make it okay. If I could close my eyes and not see my Lee's body broken and bruised in front of me, I'd close them forever."

"Hold it together." Through the phone, I hear him close a door, and footsteps fall as he makes his way down a flight of stairs.

"It's going to be a cold day in hell before that happens." I already feel the dam waiting to burst.

"Talk to me. What happened," he urges.

His words, words I've heard from him in the middle of so many crises, send me into autopilot. I repeat the events of the last fifteen hours as if I'm telling him a report. Finally, I crack. I admit to the man who I've entrusted with my life for almost the last seven years, "Emotionally, I'm so lost, it's entirely possible I may have just signed my own death certificate. Literally."

He doesn't say a word for so long, I pull the phone away from my ear just to make certain we're still connected. "Hello?"

"I'm thinking."

"Think on your own damn time. I'm about to have a breakdown!" I screech at the top of my lungs. My capacity for his stratagems is at an all-time low.

"The first thing I need to say is I'm so fucking sorry." His breathing rasps in my ear. "I've lost too many brothers in combat for me to give you any platitudes; you know that, right?"

A sob wells up. "I know, but could you lie? Just this once?"

"No. Nor would you want me to." His voice is definitive.

I start to cry harder. "No, I wouldn't."

"The truth will come out, Qaza. Now *that* I will promise you."

I lean into the anchor he's offering me. I lift my eyes skyward in an effort to stop the stream of tears. "I have to figure out the truth."

"Of course you do because if there's even the slightest chance this wasn't some random mugging and they were after you—after us—I swear to you, I'll help you take them apart." It's a vow. And one thing I know about this man is he's shed blood to keep them in the past.

Something settles in my soul. "So, what do I do?"

He hesitates before shocking me for the first time since that long-ago day at MIT. "Stay dead."

"No, just no. Don't make this about work right now. I'm bleeding inside."

"If you don't, you could end up as dead as Kylie."

Hearing her name feels worse than the time I took a billy club to the chest by a high-tech company night watchman who caught me sneaking out with a handheld scanner clutched between my teeth. I can't get enough air into my lungs for long moments, but when I can, I hiss, "Do you understand? She's fucking Erzulie."

"And you're her identical twin," he shoots back. "You're the only one who can get answers. Do you want them?" Before I can lose my shit at him, he throws a bucket of ice water over my anger, leaving me terrified. Cold.

And alone.

"What happens if you are the target and they go after your parents next? Or would you rather give up and crawl into that grave with her tonight?" His words are downright cruel, but like they did the first time we met, they focus me in a way nothing else can.

They use my love of family to direct me to do the right thing.

A long gap of silence plays between us. He's letting my mind work through the preliminaries—doing what I do best.

Go dark.

"There's no way I can do this without people on the inside." I pace back and forth.

"Assess what you need. I'll get them cleared—if they can be." That's when he hangs up.

I squeeze the phone so tightly, my knuckles turn white under the pressure. Someone murdered my Lee. That someone will die. I'll personally see to it, or I'll join them in hell.

That's my vow.

Leanne

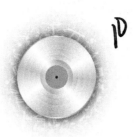

꜀ᴾ

Washington, D.C. Ivan Forfa, chief data scientist of Castor Industries, succinctly stated as of right now Leanne Miles is merely out of contact despite sources saying she was attacked while visiting her sister—the famed indie singer Erzulie—in New York earlier today. "Until we hear otherwise, Castor is still under Leanne's complete control."

— InfoSec Gov News

Scrolling through Kylie's texts with one hand—something I'll have to examine more closely later to study my sister's mannerisms with individual people—I find what I'm searching for. Pressing Send, I wait.

"Please tell me this is an emergency. It's the first day I've been home all week to put Ben down for his nap," a droll voice on the other end chides me. "What's going on?"

That's when I try to speak and can't. This friendly woman obviously is affectionate with my sister, and I'm about to blow her away emotionally once I determine if she can be trusted.

"Hello? Kylie?"

I decide to just go with my gut. "She's gone. Dead. Oh, God, help me."

"Who? What happened? Where are you?" is yelled at me frantically.

"Lee...NYU Emergency. Got the call. Last night." I don't have to fake the tears streaming down my face. The cold instilled inside me by my call melts away. I'm suddenly slammed in the chest with the pain I've been suppressing since her light extinguished.

"I'm on my way. Don't move until I get there. Do you promise?"

I naturally whimper, "Yes."

"Who do I ask for?"

I give her Dr. Ross's name. Carys's voice is both soothing and commanding. "Talk only to him. Don't say or speak to anyone further until I get there. Do you hear me? The last thing we need is press swarming the place."

Before I can correct her that it's too late—the press are already here—and strategize where to meet her, my sister's lawyer quickly hangs up the phone.

After getting myself under control, I yank out my computer. Some people need warm blankets and soothing drinks to pacify themselves; I need the feel of worn keys beneath my fingers. The melodic tip tap of doing something—anything—for justice. I can't just sit here helpless while my sister's body is cold in the morgue. Short of fighting my way to lie next to her, this is all I have right now.

And to give her peace, it may be all I can do.

I have to try to figure out why my sister was brutally beaten and left for dead blocks away from Fifth Avenue. I have no idea why Kylie had my lost driver's license in her pocket. But there's no way I can prevent the insidious thought trickling in that maybe this is her way of telling me I can use this to find out who might have helped my twin soar without the music that fed her soul.

None.

With that purpose, I yank my hair away from my face and go to work while waiting for the infamous Carys Burke to find me. Hopefully she'll give me some of the legendary fire Kylie told me about to see this storm through.

I'm going to need it until I can find some of my own.

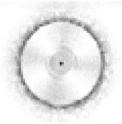

Hours later, I'm ensconced in an actual warm blanket at my sister's attorney's condo while her husband, David Lennan, makes coffee for all of us. "Don't worry about any of your upcoming show dates. It's times like this I'm grateful you signed with Wildcard. But that's business—the very last thing that needs to be on your mind. David and I will handle everything for you with Kris if you want us to. There's nothing you need to worry about. Nothing but healing with your family. If there's anything we can do to help you, Kylie, let us know."

My head pounds as sentences I don't completely understand are flung at me rapidly. The worst is the feeling that churns in my stomach every time this kind woman uses my sister's name. And after everything Carys took care of once she arrived with the press, I had a suspicion she's someone who would go to the mat for those she cares for.

My watch buzzes. I glance down. *Burke and Lennan clear. Proceed.*

I'm grateful I was right. Slipping into Kylie's life isn't going to be as easy as when we were sixteen and we'd go to each other's jobs. There's no way Kylie could do what I do without extensive training, and I sure as hell can't do what she does without some help. Once I come to that conclusion, I interrupt Carys's monologue of empathy and blurt out the truth. "I'm Leanne."

All movement stops. Carys, who had been dabbing at my tears, sits back—still holding the tissue—before whispering, "Excuse me?"

"I'm me...Leanne. They—the police, the doctors—they had it

wrong at the ER. Kylie had my ID on her when...when..." I gulp in a huge amount of air. "When she was murdered, Ms. Burke."

Carys is staring at my face as if she's unable to comprehend what she's seeing. My tears begin to flow again. "There's a few ways to prove who I am."

"How? You're her twin." Carys treads carefully.

"Identical." David joins the conversation as he places mugs of coffee in front of us. His eyes are compassionate. I understand why when he says, "Cream and two sugars?"

"Yes, how did you kn—?" My head drops to the side. Kylie took her coffee the exact same way. For just a moment, I'm reminded of the days we'd have cravings for the same food from hundreds of miles away. And then we'd call each other eating kung pao shrimp, strawberry ice cream, or our favorite snack: carrots.

Needing a moment, I take a sip of the coffee to steady myself. The trickle of heat is the closest to feeling warmth since the call I made to my parents. "Thank you," I say to David gratefully.

He nods and sits back with his own mug. "Honey?"

My head swivels to find Carys perched on the edge of her plush couch, like a coiled snake ready to strike. "And now I know why my sister both feared and respected you."

David tries to muffle his laugh with a cough. Carys's aqua eyes narrow on him before they turn on me. "And how do I know you're not Kylie? Police rarely make this kind of mistake."

"They found my missing driver's license in Kylie's pocket. Her purse wasn't with her. Her face was beaten but not badly enough that they couldn't identify her. Or so they thought." I reach down into my bag and pull out two items: the card and a small computer. The first I hand to Carys. "We're identical, but even with twins, some things are different. Fingerprints, for one." I don't mention mine are long gone, a necessary requirement to be eliminated long ago. Back when I was just an analyst, I thought he was just crazy. But since I began dipping my foot into fieldwork... I shove those thoughts away and instead nudge the envelope forward. "I received that from her yesterday morning before I went into a major meeting with a number of government officials. We had been planning on this girls' weekend for a few weeks, so I was touched when I first got it. Still, I couldn't leave it behind when I left my office in Saratoga around two. I had just walked into the lobby at the Plaza when I doubled over in agony."

Carys frowns. "Why?"

"Because that's when the doctor indicated her heart first..." I can't say the word *stopped*, but judging from the chalkiness of Carys's face, I don't have to.

It's an image that's already living in both of our minds. "A few moments later, I received a call from NYU's ER." Almost as an aside, I speculate aloud, "How am I going to get into my room at the hotel?"

"Leanne." Carys's voice snaps me back to the here and now. She nods at the card. "May I?" I nod. Carys grabs a tissue before touching the envelope—smart woman. She studies the outside of the envelope, frowning when she examines the postmark before setting it aside. "You said there were a few things. Does that hold something else?" She gestures to my small but very high-powered laptop

I open the lid and let my fingers dance across the keys, doing what comes second nature to me, much like songwriting came second nature to Kylie. Carys's brows arch so high, they practically disappear. A few seconds later, I flip the screen around and show her security footage from a tattoo parlor early yesterday. "If you read the card, you'll see she's apologized for getting this done without me. She went to a tattoo artist named Kitty and had this finished. The time stamp is yesterday at the same time I was in a final conference with my team preparing for that meeting. Do you see the look on her face? She's smiling." My eyes well up at the expression on Kylie's face.

"Yes, I see it." Carys's eyes are focused on my twin, who's doing everything I just described.

"The tattoo—it's something we always talked about doing... together." My voice breaks.

"Gemini. Twins," Carys murmurs as she studies Kylie jerking

when the needle moves back and forth over a particular spot, embedding the rich blue shade of our eyes onto her skin. Mine scrunch briefly as riotous emotions surge through me when I recall reading the postscript. If she'd lived, I'd be livid she went without me. Now? *I just wish you'd have been able to enjoy it longer.*

Setting the computer aside, I stand and lift my shirt to my ribs to demonstrate there's a thin scar along my midsection but no tattoo. It's the reason we were going to get the ink in the first place—to permanently hide a knife wound I'd sustained. Kylie gave me a knowing smirk at the bullshit reason I provided her for having it. I should have known better than to have believed she wouldn't have put it all together.

I should have protected her better. That's just the beginning and end of it.

I give Carys a moment to gape at my stomach before letting the shirt fall and sitting back down.

"You really are Leanne," Carys wonders.

"Yes."

Carys scoots closer and wraps her arm around my shoulders. I feel the pressure but no warmth. I'm not certain I'll ever feel warm again. "Leanne, I know what it's like to lose family members—close ones—but I don't know what to say to help..."

"Say you'll help me find out who killed my sister, Ms. Burke. Because this is too open-and-shut to suit me. Something else was going on with her, something she alluded to on the phone in the last few weeks and in this card." I pick up the card and slap it back on Carys's lap. That's not everything we'll be looking into, but I was advised to play up the shadowy parts of my sister's life I was one of the few people privy to while the investigation on whether one of my own cases became compromised continues. It feels wrong, so cold, but if I want answers, this is how I have to seek them out. *God, Lee. The agony of not knowing what truly happened is ripping me apart.* I swallow my nausea and continue. "The woman who sent me the extremely funny, yet completely inappropriate, card to my office to wish me luck on my meeting was *my* Lee. The question is, why is she gone? Was it a mistake? Should I be scared if they figure out they missed?"

David cautions, "Carys…"

And she holds up a hand to him while her eyes don't leave mine. "This is way outside my wheelhouse, Leanne. As your sister's lawyer, the best course of action I can recommend is for you to contact the police."

Frustration surges up inside of me. I'm about to grab my stuff and politely thank them for their time when Carys's hand briefly touches the top of mine. Her eyes are churning with the depth of emotions she's feeling. I easily recognize equal parts sadness and fury. "But I have a company on retainer who specializes in this type of investigation. If you're really interested."

"Yes," I whisper, even as David curses off to the side.

She nods before reaching for her phone. "You'll get your answers, Leanne. You just might not like them. Are you prepared for that?"

"I have to be, don't I? I have to know what happened to her." Without answers, I'll never come back from the dark places I live in. I just know it.

Carys presses her hand down. I feel warmth, that fire I need to absorb. "I'll make the call and see what they think but not until after your sister's funeral." Tears well in my eyes at the thought of burying my her. "That's the only thing you need to get through right now, Leanne."

And I have no idea how I'm supposed to handle that. I have no idea I've spoken aloud until Carys says with weary knowledge, "It will be the hardest thing you've ever done. And you'll never feel so alone as you do then."

A sob rips through me. "You do understand."

She nods, her own eyes damp. Then she stands, and her voice turns brusque. "Let's get you to bed."

"I have a hotel room," I protest, but Carys cuts me off.

"Tonight's a night you need to be alone, but you need to know someone is watching your back." She glances at her husband, who has risen to collect our mugs. "We cared for your sister. Let us help you before you have to go to help your parents navigate their pain."

I capitulate because there's nowhere else for me to go. Not tonight. And I need my energy for whatever tomorrow is going to bring.

Leanne

Crying in public is something that happens. Don't deny it; it's happened to all of us. We were not surprised to find some of the top places to do so being your car or at airports, but some people seek out the religious section of a bookstore. Really? Over self-help? I'm not judging; I just don't appreciate why one section versus another. What's wrong with self-help?

— **Beautiful Today**

I declared Carys insane when she came to the room the next morning carrying raggedy black sweatpants, a tank top that would hardly cover my midriff, and sparkly Ugg boots. She also has a pair of oversized sunglasses and a black cardigan in her hands. That is until she says, "Leanne, to get past the paparazzi that's camped out downstairs, you need to become your sister."

I immediately fly over to the window and find out she's not lying. They must be three deep. "What the hell are they doing here?"

"I am in no way surprised they're here." Carys's voice is flat.

"Why's that?" I ask suspiciously.

"You never left. The press was all over the hospital. You didn't go back to Erzulie's, and you didn't check in at a hotel last night. Someone must have trailed us here after we left from the loading dock because there's a picture of us slipping into the hired car at the hospital."

I try logic. "I could have used an assumed name."

She snickers. "Please. These people have a pipeline of their own. I guarantee there was a bounty for anyone hotel clerk or concierge who got a pic of Erzulie checking into a hotel last night."

I shiver in repulsion, though I'm well aware of the dark places these cretins lurk and the kind of bounties they'll pay for information. It makes the bug bounties I was paid in college look like chump change. "This is what my sister had to live with?"

"What she chose to live with," Carys corrects me. She shoves the clothes in my direction and points to a door I'm not even certain I noticed in my grief. "Bathroom if you want to shower."

I nod gratefully. I can still smell the stench of the hospital all over my skin. "Thank you."

"Do you feel like eating anything?" Carys questions softly.

I press my free hand to my stomach, and my body bucks at the thought. "No. I just can't."

She reaches over and rubs her hand over my arm. "That's okay, Leanne. Just promise me you'll try to get some fluids in."

"I'll try." That's when I notice she's dressed in all black from tip to toe. Tears begin trickling down my face. "For Kylie?"

"She was an innovative firebrand, and she'll be missed by many." Carys's simple words soothe something jagged inside of me. "I'll meet you in the kitchen when you're ready. We have to depart in about thirty minutes." She spins on shiny black heels when I call out to her. "Yes?"

"Thank you in advance for everything you're about to help me with but most importantly for who you were to my sister."

Her face softens before she shares with me, "Every time I called to lambast her about something, she said nothing I could say would be worse than what you were about to make her feel, even if you never saw it in the papers. How is that?"

I turn my head away so I don't soak my borrowed clothes with fresh tears. "It's a twin thing. We always just knew." And with that, I slip into the bathroom to get ready.

David jumps when I step into the room a short time later. "Erzu… Leanne. Sorry. The resemblance is startling."

I curl my lip a bit. "One thing that definitely changed over the years was the fact Kylie and I used to wear the same clothes."

A flash of a smile breaks out across his tired face as he hands me a cup of coffee. "Did you really?"

I confirm after taking a much-needed sip. "Through most of high school."

Carys's heels tap on their wood floors before she pokes her head into the living room. "David, I can catch you up later, but I really need you in the office this morning. Angie's already there, and she said she's under siege."

He nods. "That's my cue." He comes closer and holds out a hand. I take it automatically. "Leanne, we'll see you again."

I drop his hand without saying anything. The only thing my mind is capable of doing is screaming, *Lee? Lee? Where are you? You can't possibly be gone!* The impact of the lack of response has me sluggish. I think it would be easier if a limb had been severed from my body. It's David who gently nudges me back onto this plane when he murmurs, "Unless you're planning on a family-only event, Carys and I would like to attend the service. We would have been there for your sister even if…"

My shoulders droop. "I know she'd appreciate it. Somehow, I have to manage to drive to New Hampshire to make those arrangements." I have to bury my twin. *Maybe they can make room for me to lie down right next to her.*

"Don't worry about that. I'm arranging for a car," David says smoothly.

Confusion muddles my brain. A car, why? I have a perfectly good one. I voice as much. It's Carys who steps in. "Come on, Leanne. I'll explain it along the way."

Like a robot, I put down the coffee and grab my handbag after checking my computer is tucked safely inside. Carys said she'd have my clothes cleaned and sent to her office by the time we'd finished our business there. We step into an elevator, where we're the only two in it. "I can't thank you enough for being here for me, Carys."

"Of course. I hate that you're about to face what I had to after Ward and I lost our parents." She shudders. "There should be a law about the paparazzi giving you time to mourn."

We get off the elevator, and immediately, phones and cameras are stuck in my face. There are so many I'm momentarily blinded by the flash. I fumble in the pockets of the cardigan for the sunglasses Carys provided, along with the rest of my ensemble. Slipping them on, I mutter, "I wholeheartedly agree."

"Thank God for small favors," Carys mutters as we push toward the blinding lights.

"There's something to be thankful for?"

"Yes."

"What's that?"

Her face is ferocious. "You're more likely to listen to my suggestions than your sister would be. When we get out there, don't lift your head. Don't say a word, no matter how obnoxious the comment or question. Just head straight for the car. I'll be right behind you."

I feel my insides quiver. "I got it."

The doorman acknowledges Carys's nod before he opens the doors, and the muted shouts become full-fledged.

Erzulie, what happened to your sister?

Was she meeting someone to score some drugs to ease off the pressure?

Were you aware she was coming to see you yesterday?

What about her government contracts? Do you know anything about that?

Was she meeting a lover? Followed by, *Do you think she got involved with someone?*

Stock price of Castor has dropped by twenty percent; do you have anything to say? Oh, the urge to turn around and answer that one is real until I feel Carys's sharp nail poke my back. Right. Keep moving.

Was she jealous of your success?

I freeze up. Just behind me, I hear Carys mutter, "Shit. Don't do it."

But I can't let this pass. I whirl around and face the mob surrounding us. "I loved my sister. She was a part of my soul before we could comprehend what that meant. Since some of you don't even have one of those, you might not appreciate what that means. But I speak for me and for my family—we're in pain. Leave us in peace." With that I turn, yank open the door, and slide to the far side.

The paparazzi flashes try to swarm the far side of the car with their cameras, but Carys is too quick. She slams the door hard. I pray she got some of the maggots' fingers caught in the door. After I say as much, she quirks a brow. "What happened to not speaking to them?"

I burst out with, "Maybe I have a little more of my sister in me than I thought."

Her smile is slow. "Good. That might work well in our favor." Leaning forward, she directs the driver to Rockefeller Center before we both recover from that onslaught and prepare for the next.

We're safely ensconced in her office. Carys's receptionist—a knockout redhead named Angie—has already brought coffee and sworn no one will be able to get by her. "Not even Becks," she vows.

That draws a reluctant smile from Carys. "If you weren't aware of your sister's friendship with Beckett Miller, they are—were—close friends."

"During one of our calls in the last few weeks, when gossip started picking up about them, she said he was a mentor to her."

"He is—was. He's going to take the news of her death very hard. I suspect he's going to want to be there for her—you."

I shake my head. "I can't think that far ahead yet."

"Then don't. Focus on one thing at a time."

I lean forward, exhausted, wondering if I let the blanket of conspiracy theories I'm cloaked under suffocate me in my weakest moment. My voice is small when I question the path I've already stepped on. "Maybe I was wrong last night. Maybe I'm obsessing over nothing."

Carys doesn't say anything for a long while. When she does, I feel an immediate kinship with her. "My parents were killed by a drunk driver. It was my brother's birthday. Instead of celebrating together, my brother went out with some friends since I was held up with other priorities. We made plans to meet up the next night, only tomorrow never came. When the dust settled, the only thing I knew down to my soul was they loved me. Nothing else made sense. I felt like less of who I was, like I'd lost a huge part of my identity because they weren't there any longer."

"That's exactly what I'm feeling. I'm not certain I can handle it," I whisper.

Carys holds out her hand. "Go home, Leanne. Face the pain. Then, when you're ready, we'll do what's necessary to get you the answers you need to move on with your life."

I reach one with one hand and squeeze hers in return. The other is too busy wiping away the deluge of tears that just won't stop. "I'm not certain how that's going to be possible. I'm not certain how to exist in a world where my sister's not somewhere in it."

And with those words, I surge to my feet and dash out the door before I fall apart and am unable to do the last thing I want to do.

Bury half of my soul.

KANE

Our hearts go out to singer Erzulie tonight. Her twin sister's body was found murdered off a side street near Fifth Avenue. Police are calling it a mugging gone horribly wrong. There are no words to express the depth of our profound sympathy.

— StellaNova

"What are you talking about? How?" Beckett yells. He scrubs his hand over his face before whispering, "She must be fucking devastated." He begins chewing on the ankh on his middle finger.

We're sitting in the green room before he's supposed to appear live as a special guest on a late-night talk show. His face is pale despite the television makeup they spent an hour slapping on him earlier. I cock my head and mouth, *What?* but he turns his back on me. "Are you going to the funeral? Do I need to attend? For Christ's sake, Carrie. She's my friend. You of all people know that what's in the press doesn't mean two shits to me. "

To the funeral? I leap up from the couch and get right into his face. "Who?" I demand.

He holds up his hand to fend me off. "Yes, Kane's here. What should I... Of course they have it already. What do you want me to say? We both know I'm going to be asked about it." His frustration is evident. "Okay. Thanks for the heads-up. And Carys? I'm glad she was with you." He hangs up and just holds the phone without saying a word. His eyes are glued to the monitor, where the popular host is going through his monologue. Whatever Carys just dropped into Beckett's lap had to be huge because the host pauses during applause to lift his hand to his earpiece.

Beckett lets out a barrage of curses.

"Someone died?" I prompt him.

Beckett's eyes flick over to mine. In them, there's such sadness and pity that for just a moment, I want to ask him if he wants me to break him out of this joint, but if I know one thing about the man I've been protecting for the last few years, it's that he takes his commitments seriously. Defeated, he responds, "Erzulie's sister. It's all over the tabloids."

"Ah, Christ." Immediately, my mind whirls to the bare-bones facts Erzulie shared about her sister in the few conversations we've shared. For someone who was the twin of one of America's rising musical stars, she kept a low profile in her life. And while I can't immediately recall much, I do remember Erzulie saying her twin was older and they were close. Come to think of it, I recall with a frown, not many people know much about Kylie Miles's elusive sister beyond what's reported about her lucrative business in the news.

Beckett straightens his tie, his jaw tight. "That's a lot more politically correct than what I want to say when I'm asked about it." He strides to the door.

I call out to him. "You're her friend, her mentor. Tonight, tomorrow, your words may not matter, but in a few years, they're going to mean the world." *If she ever recovers*, I think to myself.

"That sounds like experience talking," Beckett notes.

I jerk up my chin but don't acknowledge anything else. He slips out of the room. Moments later, Beckett Miller is escorted onto the studio stage to screaming applause. And aloud, I whisper, "Don't fuck this up, rock star."

Seconds after Beckett's ass hits the chair, he's asked about Erzulie's sister. His face is serious. "I haven't had a chance to speak with her, but I hope she knows she has my support whether she needs it tonight, tomorrow, or a year from now. I can't begin to put myself in her place. I hope the world gives her an opportunity to grieve the way she needs to and isn't in her face while she figures out her world without someone who meant everything to her."

Perfect. Just as he finishes, I feel my phone vibrate. I slip it from my pocket and almost stagger when I see a text from Brit.

I know you loved him as much as I did, Kane, but I need more time. I'll call you when I'm able. In the meanwhile...

And attached is a picture of my goddaughter, the first one I've received since Gene died in my arms.

Maybe she's watching and heard Beckett? Maybe it was just time? But either way, my shoulders shake as I stare at Brit's beautiful smile just beneath my best friend's eyes staring up at me. There's absolution in those eyes. Absolution I'm not certain I deserve yet but I'll keep trying to earn.

By the time Beckett comes offstage, I've pulled myself together. "Do you want to go by Erzulie's?" I ask him somberly.

He shakes his head. "Carys said she's helped her escape out of the city. She's at her parents', but I do need to figure out how to get something to the funeral."

"We're not going?" Surprise leaks into my voice as we make our way out of the green room.

"No. There are days when I wish I could go back in time and make different decisions. Times when..."

"Yes?" I tilt my head, curious about the older man.

Beckett runs his fingers through his hair. "Never mind. It's too late to change the past. But no. We're not going. Apparently my showing up will cause too much of a media circus." He tosses out the words as if they mean nothing, but I know hearing them from Carys had to have stung.

I stop him. "If you want to find a way to go, I'll help find a way to make it happen."

His mouth falls open in surprise because typically I'm the one encouraging him to keep a lower profile. But once again, his thoughtfulness surprises me. "No, because if I show up, then it becomes about Ky and not about her sister. You know?"

"Don't I ever," I agree fervently as my mind drifts back to the funeral I attended just a few years before.

There's one thing I know for certain: I know I'll never be able to look at Kylie Miles in quite the same way I did before. There's something about death that binds people in unimaginable ways. Being left behind leaves you with a whole host of questions.

The most terrible being, why not me?

Leanne

Saratoga Springs, N.Y. Ivan Forfa has been named CEO of Castor Industries.

Amid overwhelming grief, Ivan Forfa has been voted to succeed Leanne Miles after her sudden death, effective immediately. Castor has announced they expect no delay in their recently awarded government contract with the Department of Defense.

— **Castor Newsroom**

Four days later, I can't remember a time I've been this exhausted. Not even in the early days of starting up Castor when we'd be pulling twenty-one-hour days and sleeping on our office floors to meet insane deadlines we'd set. *But at least you're alive*, I remind myself as I climb the small hill leading to Kylie's grave. I need to be alone with her for a while. Just us.

If the worst day of my life was watching my sister's heartbeat stop, today will be the night that replays in my nightmares for eternity. It wasn't a celebration of her life; it was about me. And above all, it was a goddamn farce.

I wanted to vomit on several occasions between listening to my coworkers, my supposed friends, alternately mourn my loss out of one side of their mouth and murmur they really weren't that surprised out of the other. "I always wondered if she was capable of running an empire of this magnitude on her own. Good God, you don't think it was drugs, do you? That she wandered off to score and got mugged?" I overheard Ivan exclaim as if he was the expert on my behavior.

Fortunately, Carys dragged me away before I could line up to ram my pointed shoe between his legs. That's when she guided me in the direction of my mother, who was in a catatonic state flipping through photo albums, touching pictures of my sister. And I felt like smacking every single person who told her, "At least you still have Kylie," because she'd just give them a blank stare. And they'd give her an empathetic pat, telling her her heart will heal with time.

Bullshit. A heart that's damaged can't grow back. It decays more over each day blood pumps through it. So, what the hell kind of good will words like those do anyone?

I somehow managed to hold up my family during the invitation-only service. It was the most impersonal service I could come up with. When I explained to my parents the reason why—that some reporter would likely try to sneak in as a guest—my father yelled, "Can't they just leave us alone? We just lost our little girl!"

I repeated the words Carys said to me in a whisper, "This is the life she chose."

My mother hissed, "No, this is the life you both chose," before she stormed out of the room, blaming me for my sister's choices. After all, if one of us got in trouble as a child, we both did. I guess we still are.

And if I'm right, I'll be contributing to her agony until I find out who did this to Kylie.

I pause for a moment in my climb, a snip of a conversation coming back to me.

"I'm so glad we set up the trust, Leanne."

"Why?"

"Because if it weren't for you, I'd never have this chance." Kylie hugged me hard. *"I wish you could feel what it's like to be up onstage when the nerves settle out and it's just you and the music."*

"I'd probably throw up," I joked. *"People would never believe I'm you."*

Her eyes stared off in the distance. "You'd be surprised."

Well, since I successfully managed that this afternoon after our estate attorney reviewed my trust with my family, there's no surprise left. Once Castor became profitable, I placed everything I had into a living trust—my home, my bank accounts, stock, even my car—unusual except for the fact it's worth a ridiculous amount of money. And once Kylie became music gold, she added her wealth to the same trust. We have codicil after codicil in the event something would have happened to both of us, but the biggest concern for me was Castor.

Right now, I'm not worried about my company since "Kylie" now holds the majority of the two hundred shares required by New York State law for any incorporated company, my parents holding the only others. Nothing about how my employees operate should change with the exception of Ivan taking over my role, a temporary appointment of one year in the event something happened to me or I became incapacitated in any way. My lip curls as I recall his comment this afternoon. I mutter, "Let's see how you do in the driver's seat, you schmuck," as I start walking again.

But insofar as the media, once the probate goes public, nothing unusual will surface about our finances. They'll keep reporting that Erzulie lost her sister. And in the eyes of the dark underworld of technology, I learned every corner, crack, and crevice of, pictures of well, me, will start surfacing with a vengeance. Bile rises uncontrollably when I realize I'm going to have to let some of the seedy tabloid reports come to light, otherwise this plan to flush out my sister's killer may never work.

"I hope you appreciate what I'm about to do for you, Lee," I murmur as I approach the freshly overturned dirt. I kick off my sneakers and kneel before the plethora of flowers. Reaching out, I drag my fingers through the rich, brown soil. "What happened? Who did this to you?"

But there's no answer, not in the air nor along the still-aching twin cord in my chest.

I lie down in the dirt and begin to sing the songs we listened to as little girls. Finally I end it with "I'll Remember," because Kylie and I swore no matter what happened, even if we were separated, one day we'd find each other again.

And we'd love each other all over again.

When I'm done, I lie sobbing on my sister's grave for an unknown period of time before the cold earth begins to register. I stand and whisper, "I love you, always."

Of course, there's no response. Not from her.

I hear a leaf, and I whirl around in fear, in fury. "If you want to kill me too, come out! Now's your chance!" I shout.

The man who slides out from behind the oak tree might as well kill me once I see the professional camera around his neck. He's tall, handsome, with a runner's build. But still, I sneer, "No, not a murderer. Just a parasite."

He flinches but doesn't apologize as I snatch up my shoes before turning and walking away as fast as I can. I get to the edge of the hill before I stop. My emotions feel violated, much as if he had run his hands all over my body. Yet my sister dealt with these cretins daily. My back goes rigid before I negotiate. "Just leave my parents alone. Let them grieve in peace."

"I can give you my assurance about that." My shoulders start to relax before he amends, "At least for tonight."

I whirl around to meet the man's eyes. His drop to the dirt where my sister lies, and his face is sorrowful in the shadows. It sets off a memory. There's something so familiar about him, I feel the urge to analyze him. But I force myself to turn and walk away. After all, Kylie wouldn't give the paparazzi the time of day.

And neither will I.

Later, in my childhood bedroom, being smothered by memories that are trying to steal me away to join her, something about the face of the man niggles at me. But with much weightier matters pushing at me from other sides, it quickly becomes a secondary concern.

I slip out of my bed and crawl into Kylie's. I grab her pillow and let tears flow when I realize there will never be another night we'll stay up talking. There will never be another night where she calls me randomly singing for no reason. I'll never be able to say goodbye because I never knew I had to.

It isn't until the sun comes up I'm able to close my swollen eyes.

And by then, I've remembered too much about the love that formed me to ever give up on finding out who killed her. No matter the cost.

Leanne

ㅕ

Kylie Miles shows her utter devastation for the loss of her sister, CEO of Castor Industries — Leanne Miles, in this heartbreaking photo.

This is one of those times when a picture speaks more than words ever can.

— **StellaNova**

"How am I supposed to survive?" I hear the wailing from my parents' bedroom and grit my teeth as I pass on my way down the stairs.

It's been a week since we buried Kylie, and every day feels worse. There's supposed to be something called closure, and I want to know when the hell that's supposed to happen. Because every moment I'm alive without my twin in this world feels like another day of hell. I feel like there's nothing left in this world for me. I wish with every fiber of my being someone would have just cut off a limb because it would have been less painful to my soul than the loss of her to my heart.

Even though I was there, even though I felt her spirit slip from her body, it's completely surreal to me. Family and friends have sent messages I've been fielding. There's nothing, no touchstone. And it wasn't until I lost my sister that I realized how much of my world revolved around her. Happiness, joy, balance, they were a part of me because she was. The real in my life has been stripped away. I can't fathom how I'm supposed to survive.

No, I know how. I'm going to find out who did this to my Lee. And I swear I'm going to make them pay.

Fueled by anger, I make my way into the kitchen just in time for Kylie's—no, I guess it's my—cell to ring. When I read the caller ID, I recognize Carys's name. My voice is dead when I answer. "Hey."

"I'm not accusing you of anything," she begins carefully.

"That's a great way to start a conversation," I drawl sarcastically.

"You'll understand why in a moment, Leanne. But is it possible you maybe, possibly mind you, were responsible for your sister not appearing in the tabloids as frequently as say, Beckett Miller?"

I don't even bother to deny it. "Yes." Quickly, I explain the bare bones of the automated script I have running under Erzulie's name.

There's a moment of silence before, "Then you'd better brace."

"Why?" I ask sinisterly.

"StellaNova has a picture of Kylie Miles—not Erzulie—lying on Ky's gravesite the other night." Her words tear through any modicum of disinterest I might have had in the conversation.

"Are you kidding me?" I shout.

"Unfortunately not. I always wondered how Erzulie avoided anything but positive press. The Neo Agency wasn't well-known for..."

"Not exploiting their acts? I'm familiar."

Carys puts two and two together quickly and whistles. "You're the reason your sister got out of her contract without any blowback."

"Oh, it was a pleasure to dig up the info on that piece of shit Hutnik. And if I find out he had anything to do with siccing the tabloids..." I choke back my words when my father steps into the kitchen. He appears to have aged twenty years in the last few days. "Daddy? I'm sorry for yelling."

"Is everything all right?" His voice is anxious.

"It's just..." I try to come up with an explanation, but my brain's too muddled to think. I give him the truth, apology in my voice. "Someone got a picture of me at Kylie's grave."

He pales. "Now they're going to stalk you. Please promise me you're going to be more careful, baby."

"Daddy, I prom—"

He shakes me. "No, I think your sister was killed because of some crazy, Leanne. You have to be careful now. You're all we have left."

Forgetting I've left the phone unmuted, I hug my father. "I love you, Daddy. And yes, I promise I'll be careful." He relaxes momentarily until I continue. "But you know I can't let this go. I have to figure out what happened to my Lee."

His arms around me tighten. "Please, don't do this. Don't let them get to you."

"I can't let them..."

"You *can*. It's not your responsibility. She's not your responsibility!" he shouts.

"You heard Mom. She is! She always was! She's a part of me! How can I go on if I don't *know*?" I yell right back.

He steps away, and I feel cold. Wrapping my arms around myself, I enter a staredown with my father. Finally, he sighs. "Just...don't make us lose you too." Then he turns and walks away, leaving me feeling anchorless.

For a few moments, I stand there immobile until a voice calling my name through the phone begins to penetrate. Shit, Carys. I answer dully, "Yeah?"

"Are you sure you want to pursue this? It's not too late for us to just go to the police," Carys probes gently.

"And do what, Carys? Wonder for the rest of my life when they blow off my suspicions? Make a token effort for the sake of saying they did because of who Kylie was? Who I am? No, I need to know. There is no halfway." She doesn't answer, which I take as answer enough. "I'm going to pack and head back to the city. It can't be easy for my parents to see me."

"Leanne, you're probably the only reason they're able to get through each day. When my parents died, that was my brother for me. Don't rush away because emotions are high. Now is the time when you need one another," Carys informs me quietly.

I explore my careening emotions for a few moments before

nodding. "Then at the very least, I need to get out of the house. I'm suffocating."

"Go for a walk, a drive. Get coffee, chocolate. Do something for you."

My heart breaking, I inform this kind woman who cared for my sister, "If I could do anything, I'd be in the lab at my office creating a time machine to bring Kylie back to us all." Then I disconnect the call.

But I take her suggestion and hunt down my father's car keys.

An hour later, driving up a twisting two-lane road near a local ski resort with coffee in one cup holder and a bag of chocolate on the seat next to me, I finally feel some of the suffocating pressure leave my chest. Despite spotting members of the paparazzi lingering around the streets of Silverthorn, I managed to dash into the local coffeehouse and escape unscathed. I ask my sister aloud, "Lee, how did you manage to deal with this?" Just a few days of the constant dodging of the media has me ready to scream.

Of course there's no answer, but it helps me to talk aloud to her. Even as I turn the wheel to navigate around another curve to climb to the top of the mountain, I whisper fiercely, "This is completely unforgivable, Lee. You're supposed to be here. We had too many memories we were supposed to make together. We were supposed to fall in love, be each other's maid of honor, be our children's godmothers. How am I supposed to get through a day without hearing your voice, let alone moments like that? Someone stripped us from having a future of loving each other." My voice cracks as I veer to the right.

"I forgive you for the tattoo, by the way. But I'm going to cry when I go and get mine—I hope you understand that. Even if it winds up being the most physically painful thing to happen to me, it won't be as awful as losing you has been. Nothing will ever rip my heart apart like that." I take a moment to swipe my fingers beneath my eyes to capture the tears that are trailing down my face.

Then guilt settles heavily around my heart. "I was supposed to be there. What if I had been? Would you have been killed? Or would you have been in our room telling me what was troubling you? I know you, my Lee. Something was wrong. What was it?" I slam the heel of my hand down on the steering wheel in frustration.

And I'll never know if it's pure chance or my sister watching over me that has me glancing in the rearview mirror. An SUV with no front plates is barreling toward me at a high rate of speed. Quickly, I press down on the accelerator, even as I'm reaching over to the glove compartment, where I stashed my government-issued handgun—another long-ago decree. *"Never leave home without it,* Qəza. *If you ever get into a situation, I'd rather clean up your mess and have you alive."*

Heart pounding, I'm suddenly grateful for the years of dictator-like mandates all the people who work for him have to subscribe to. Even as I wedge the gun between my legs and chamber the round with one hand, I can hear him bellowing in my mind over the noise-canceling headphones as we practiced, firing round after round, assuming we'd never have to use it in the line of duty—not doing what we did—then. "Carry the damn thing. You all are targets working here. It's a world where they will shoot first, people. If this gives you that split second to get out alive, I'm giving it to you."

My eyes avidly scan the landscape for the closest runaway truck lane—lanes trucks have the ability to veer off in the event they skid out of control during the winter months. I feel a jarring bounce as the SUV makes contact with my rear bumper. My heart skips a beat, pushing itself into my throat, as I stomp the accelerator all the way to the floor. I'm driving at a speed that is ridiculously dangerous on the twisty road, but I'm doing everything possible to avoid being hit. The heads-up display shows me I'm speeding up: forty-five, fifty. I glance in the mirror, and the SUV seems to gather speed as it makes another approach.

There! I quickly reach over and yank the center emergency brake, grateful for the defensive driving courses, he also mandated when I was in training, "Regardless if you're going to be sitting behind some machine or not, you get trained or you get out," he snarled.

"Who the fuck are you?" I shout. The instructor's words come back to me just as the SUV engine guns. *Avoid sudden braking. Turn into the skid. Don't accelerate out of it.* I'm grateful to hear my instructor's receptive directions on repeat in my head as I attempt to execute the turn easily ten miles per hour faster than any speed I trained at.

Fortunately, my mathematician's brain factored in the extra space runaway lane, so I don't crash into the side of the mountain. With a heart that hasn't yet started beating, I manage to straighten my damaged vehicle out as I bump and bounce on the gravel road. Removing the emergency brake, I press down on the real ones so I can be prepared to move in a second's time as I hear a wrenching metal sound that sends shivers clear through my soul.

My head pops out the window, just in time to see the black SUV attempt the first part of the turn. As the weight of the assault vehicle presses against the dulled metal, their rear end puts enough pressure on it to break through the knee-high guardrail.

I shiver as I put my father's car in park. Stepping out, still holding my weapon, I get a good look as the weight of the vehicle pitches and yaws. *It was supposed to be me.* The certainty of it slithers through me. I take a step forward, unconsciously wanting to pull the trigger to put an end to this nightmare for me, my family. *For Lee.* But before I can take a second to consciously make the decision to discharge my weapon in a fit of rage, a car coming down the mountain has to slam on its brakes, sending the acrid smell of dust in the air. I tuck my arm holding the weapon behind my thigh.

Whether it was the sudden movement of the other car vibrating the road, or fury from a force beyond claiming redemption, the black

SUV tips over the edge. I wince at the sound it makes as it pitches over the cliff because that was so close to being me. I lean back into the car and dig around until I find the cell on the floor. He answers on the first ring. "Qəza, what is it?"

"A black SUV with no plates just tried to take me out," I inform him flatly.

The only sound that breaks up the silence is the wind whipping through the line. "They're dead?"

"I haven't gone to check. The vehicle went over a cliff." I look at my watch and give him the coordinates.

"I'll deal with it. Qəza..."

"Don't say it." I hang up on him and stare at the broken rail.

Without a doubt, I'm in as much danger as Kylie was. Are they trying this quickly because they were out to kill her and believe they failed? Or they wanted to kill me and made a mistake? I'm not sure how long I have to figure it out, but I'll spend the rest of my life doing so.

However long that may be.

Leanne

15

Saratoga Springs, N.Y. Federal agencies struggle with implementing government mandates to store data in the cloud-first mandate. A new report released by Castor Industries shows staffing challenges and lengthy procurement makes it difficult to advance technologies at required speeds.

— **Castor Newsroom**

I located it early this morning when I couldn't sleep. I stood at Kylie's balcony door, imagining her sitting on her Adirondack chair with a cup of tea, when I spotted the padlock on the trunk.

Recognizing the lock as one we each had in high school, I dragged the massive weight inside, chills from the cold seeping past my already cold body. *Maybe there are answers in here*, I prayed fervently.

Instead, after I spun the ancient dial to 12-5-5, and it popped open as easily as it did off our lockers. *God, Kylie, did nothing I teach you about security penetrate.* I shake my head. Although not as bad as setting your luggage to 1-2-3-4-5, keeping our name as your padlock is a pretty simple password to crack.

Then I got lost in the treasure trove of the trunk's contents and forgot all about my training. At least for a little while.

Inside were boxes of photographs, yearbooks, mementoes of things Kylie and I had accomplished together—all carefully wrapped from the elements. Slowly, I unpacked each one, spending time reliving our childhood with one another, feeling her love comfort me in a way no one else's platitudes have been able to.

Then I found the pocket with her leather-wrapped journal. And the trip down memory lane ceased as I sat back to read about Kylie's life since she came to New York.

As the late-afternoon sun streams through the balcony doors, I flip back and forth between the entries. And I'm torn between an almost palpable anger and paralyzing pain as I read my twin's inner thoughts about what her early days in New York were like. I also suffer as she downplays her accomplishments to the point of self-abasement.

Clenching my jaw, I reread some of the passages I've marked.

There's no air here. I'm suffocating. If I have to ward off one more grabby-ass motherfucker who thinks he can "make me a star" by getting into my pants, I swear I'm giving it up.

Then another entry that's just a list of names before, *So many assholes at one party, not enough armor on this world.* I recognize a few of them and make a mental note to check them out.

It's like I fall through the cracks. Here, I'm not seen. What do I have to do? You were always seen, my Lee. Always.

What's wrong with me? Why can't I wake up and have it all? What's it going to take?

Screw my dreams.

Maybe Leanne had the right idea all along. She's turned into this mega success overnight. A sob emerges as this one comes into focus. *The right idea? Christ, Kylie.*

Finally, after having my heart torn to shreds, the entries begin to lift.

Tonight might be the turning point. From the stage, I spotted Carys Burke in the audience. After my set, she asked if I had legal representation. Since I'd just received a call from the NEO Agency to possibly represent me, I dropped that bit of info.

Blunt as I heard she could be, she pulled out her card and said, "Come see me first."

Leanne didn't understand when I exploded on the phone when I called, but she was happy for me. "I told you!" she screamed in my ear. I didn't realize until that moment how much I've craved her emotional support. It's bad enough I've been dependent on her financially. But one day, I'll be someone. And then I'll be able to be as generous as she is. Even if I'll never be as self-sacrificing.

God, I don't know how she juggles it all but if it takes the rest of my life I'll make her as proud of me as I am of her.

"I was always proud of you, Kylie. Always. There was never a day I wasn't," I say aloud to the empty room, praying she can hear me wherever she is.

I'm about to flip the book shut when my nail catches a page that's slightly worn. I flip to it and whisper, "What the hell is this?"

In her perfect penmanship is a page titled, "People I'd love to see run over by a New York City bus"

And there's a list of five names:

Owen Witt. I wince when I easily recognize the name of Mastadoon's drummer. Kylie's breakup with him was rough and very public. As hard as I tried, even I couldn't keep everything out of the press. And knowing how much she was hurt, I begin to understand this list more.

Kory Andrews. The power forward for New York's basketball team was head over heels for my sister. Or so the world thought. I knew better when I found those pictures of him with his side piece, Bunny, on vacation and gave them to my sister so she could prepare before they hit the media. *I agree. A bus would have been nice.*

Sebastian Tim. My brows shoot to the top of my head. *Our finance broker? Why? For what reason?* I don't know, but I'll damn sure find out.

Terrence Landon. "I know this name. Why?" Then I shout, "Snowy-T? I never heard a damn thing about you and my sister." I tap the book in earnest now. "Why are you on my sister's imaginary hit list. And why is someone like Hutnik not on here?"

Because I come to the final entry. It's an enormous "I" that's underlined and circled. I study it for a moment. "If she meant herself, she'd have said 'me.' Not 'I.' So, 'I' means someone."

Surging to my feet, I snag my phone and take a picture of it, forwarding the list to my handler. Then I decide to gather some intel the old-fashioned way.

I pick up my cell and place a call.

"LLF LLC. This is Angie. How may I direct your call?"

"Hey, Angie. It's..."

"Erzulie. Hey. Are you looking to speak with Carys?" Her immediate warmth wraps around me.

"Is she available?" I ask cautiously.

"She's actually on a call. I can interrupt if it's urgent," she offers.

"No. It's just...I just wanted...you don't even have to let her know I called," I finally conclude. I'm not really certain why I did except I feel like I need to be doing more to find out who did this. I can't possibly leave something of this magnitude to men who didn't know her. Didn't know us.

But Angie says something that jolts me. "Sometimes when the world's on fire, it's easier to find your way walking the same path you've already taken. Don't think any of us will judge you if you feel you're ready to get back to work. There are days it can be the only thing that might help you put one foot in front of the other."

Almost robotically, I wander out of the living room and enter the one space I haven't been able to breach for fear of it escaping: Kylie's room. I push the door open and enter her closet, filled with her style, her scent, her essence. Amid an explosion of Free People funk is enough sparkle to light up New York on New Year's Eve. And in many ways, it's my Lee's soul in designer clothing.

Realizing Angie's calling my name over and over, I murmur absentmindedly, "You're right."

"Do you want her to call you? She has a break in about an hour."

"No."

"No?"

"I'll come to her."

"Erzulie, the press..." Angie starts to remind me. As if I'm my sister and I need the quick briefing.

But she has no idea how aware I am of the maggots lying in wait outside the building. "I'll handle them." Closing the phone, I pull out a black sequined mini slip, a lush black cardigan that flows further than the hem, and a hat with a fur pom on the top of its head. Combined with black tights and my sister's motorcycle boots, it's exactly something she would wear.

And it's time to stop hiding and become Erzulie—my version of her.

Snatching up the clothes, I toss them into the guest bedroom before I pull out my phone. Quickly, I type a coded message before pressing Send. "That should keep them busy for a while," I mutter. Then I hurry to get dressed.

When I come out, every member of the paparazzi has departed, and I calmly stride from my building. Hailing a cab, I prop my chin on my hands before I pull out my phone and type, *Thanks.*

The almost immediate reply of *Yeah, yeah. Whatever,* causes my lips to tip up just a little.

But I do wonder how long it's going to take the media to realize I'm not heading for the Circle Line, despite what my cell coordinates are now showing. I'm certain the longtime boat operators are going to appreciate the additional income today, even without knowing why.

And knowing I won't have to face them here or at Rockefeller Center, I let out a relieved sigh before my stomach clenches in terror.

I'm about to do it. I'm about to give up my identity and become Erzulie.

The question is, for how long?

I enter the offices of LLF LLC about thirty minutes later. Angie's head snaps up, even as her jaw unhinges. "But the paps are trying..."

I offer her a wan tip of my lips. "It isn't much, but Leanne showed me a few apps before...before..." My throat closes because it's the truth. I did show Kylie how to mask her location with an app I'd helped write. While the use was originally for protecting our agents, my boss said to release it on a few of the darker coding sites with a few small modifications. "Let them think we can't track their movement, Qaza."

Angie continues to blink up at me, so I babble, "I don't always use it, but..."

"That's genius. Can we install it on Becks?" She points at her monitor. "There's twenty-six notifications for him and he just got back in town yesterday."

I roll my lips together before I ask seriously, "Do you think he'll remember to use it?" I'm not opposed to Beckett Miller having the public version of the app if it will help this small team as they're helping me.

"Who will remember to use what?" Carys asks from the door.

We both look her way. She gives me a head-to-toe perusal before stepping forward, hands outstretched. "It's good to see you, Erzulie."

I take them. "I appreciate all of the support you all have given me."

"Your ears must be burning. Kris said he was going to contact you about a couple of shows, see if you were ready." Carys turns and leads the way to her office.

I follow, my boots not making a sound on the lush carpet. "Was he?"

"Yes. If you think you're ready for it?"

I open my mouth to automatically accept but wait until we're securely closed behind her office door before I drop any pretense. "Do I have much of a choice?"

"You do, Leanne. You have the choice to stop this before it really starts," she reminds me.

Taking an enormous breath, I walk over to the window and ask her, "What if it was your parents?"

"That's entirely different," she dismisses my question.

"What if it wasn't. What if it wasn't a drunk driver but a murderer, Carys. What if they were still out there after all these years?" My head twists to the side to see her approach me.

For a long moment, she doesn't say anything. "I don't know."

Instead of feeling triumph at her honesty, I feel more of the same hollow ache I've endured since assigning myself this self-imposed mission. She goes on, "I do know I'd ask myself often if this is what they would want for me."

"I am. I do."

"And what is she saying?"

That's when my lips quirk. "That you should be glad I'm the one standing by your side. If it was the other way around, she'd likely have burned the city to the ground before apologizing for the damage. In case you didn't know, she was a bit impulsive."

Carys barks out a laugh. "Despite what you kept out of the spotlight about her, I am aware of Kylie's *leap before she looks* modus operandi. Now I know why she felt so comfortable doing just that."

My fist clenches at my side. "I just wish she had another lifetime to keep taking those chances."

Carys's hand clasps my shoulder. "Me too."

We stand there for long moments silent, both of us lost in memories. "Do you want to call Kris from here?"

"What do you think he's going to say?"

"This is completely new territory to me, Leanne. If I know him as well as I do? He's going to ease you back in—book you some practice space, open up discussions about any qualms you might have about playing publicly."

I nod. Carys moves behind her desk. It's time to dive in headfirst and submerge myself in my sister's life. "When we're done, I need to ask you about a list."

"What kind of list?" She frowns as her hand hovers over a button over her phone.

"A list of men. A hit list of sorts." Quickly, I explain what I found.

Carys's eyebrows wing upward. "Well, here's something else that's interesting. Snowy-T's having a party tonight. Angie just saw it tagged on his social media."

I feel my heart rate thud. "Really? How hard would it be for me to get invited?"

Carys gives me a daft look. "Just show up. You're now Erzulie." Just as the blood begins pumping in my veins, she warns, "But I'd check with Beckett. He's been to one and says they're nothing to mess with."

I scoff. "Seriously?" I whip out my phone and pull up my sister's last text to the infamous Beckett Miller. Carelessly, I type, *Snowy-Ts tonight. You in?*

His reply is immediate. NO! Ky, you are NOT going to that ass wipes.

Why not?

We've talked about this. He's a moral piece of shit and you're in a bad way.

My irritation flares. It's not like the megastar has checked in with me on a daily basis. We're not besties or something. *I think I know what I am or am not right now.*

Promise me you won't go.

I don't bother to reply. Immediately, my phone rings. And his face appears on my screen. I press Speaker before answering coolly, "Yes?"

"I swear it, Ky. Do not go to that asshole's," Beckett Miller demands.

I don't respond. My eyes meet Carys's, who is holding her tongue as well as her breath. "It's my life," I finally declare.

"You infuriating woman. You have no idea of the shit that goes on…I'm warning you, Ky. It's the worst mistake of your life."

The cold seeps through me and makes my tone pure ice. "No, the worst mistake of my life was not being at the Plaza on time."

"Shit. Ky…" Apology laces his voice.

I disconnect the call before he can say any more. I glare down at the phone for just a moment before I focus my attention back on Carys. "Is there anything else?"

"Leanne, if Beckett's that concerned, there might be reason to be," she starts off.

My teeth lock together. "It's not open for discussion." Carys starts to speak, but I cut her off. "I have to have answers."

"I'll let it drop on one condition."

"Fine."

"You let someone you trust know when you're going to be there."

Since that's a condition I can live with, and since I planned to do so anyway, I capitulate. "Done. Now, what else can you tell me about the other men my sister despised?"

Carys sits back, and we talk about men who made up the male presence of Kylie Miles—those the press knew about and those they didn't know about. And while we do, I realize something that breaks my heart.

My sister *did* have her own secrets.

I shove the emotions that come with that into a box. One day, I might be able to pull them out and deal with them. Right now, I'm gathering all the information I need to find out who killed her.

And then I can finally grieve.

KANE

Snowy-T is having a party tonight. Trust me, not even the god-like Beckett Miller could drag me to one of those parties again. No way, no how.

But don't worry, the pictures of who was in attendance will be front and center tomorrow. Just you wait and see.

— **Sexy&Social, All the Scandal You Can Handle**

"Do I look like a fucking Uber? I mean really. Is this what I do?" Beckett snaps from the back of the blacked-out SUV I'm driving through the streets of Manhattan around 3:00 a.m.

I don't bother to respond because the irony of him lounging in the back while I drive isn't lost on either of us when he takes a temporary break from ranting to twist his lips to form a semblance of a smile. But it's only temporary because he immediately goes back into bitching about Erzulie. "I feel like a parent going to pick up their errant child who's broken curfew."

I'm just as irritated as Beckett but for an entirely different reason. My principal wouldn't let me go pick up Erzulie; he demanded to come along. "You'll never be able to get to her without me," he declared arrogantly.

Despite my frustration, I can't prevent the chortle that escapes. Beckett is barely dressed in pajama bottoms and a shirt that has maybe one, two buttons done—max. When he got the text a few moments earlier from Erzulie, he must have rolled into the clothes he likely shucked next to his bed, electing to only cover what was legally required to prevent an indecent exposure charge.

His brows furrow. "I warned her, don't go to Snowy-T's party. She knows what the asswipe's like. And yet, she goes. Then, I'm asleep in my own bed for the first time in weeks with the killer schedule we're setting, and I get a text—a damn text, mind you—to come pick her ass up because she can't move. I swear to you, Kane, that girl needs help."

I don't disagree with his final assessment but am not in the position to voice my opinion. I compress my lips, because while I appreciate what the fuming tattooed man in the back is saying, his perspective is slightly different than mine about the warring emotions Erzulie is battling right now. Not since that first moment we crashed into one another as I followed a hell-bent Beckett do I feel such a connection with her. After all, I know what it's like to lose men and women who are your brothers and sisters. No, the people I lost may not have been my actual siblings, but on the battlefield, the enemy who shot us down didn't give a flying fuck. To them we were related in a more elemental way than that—as American soldiers who took a vow to protect against enemies foreign and domestic, we stood against them. And to them, the uniform mattered much more than the faces of the person wearing it.

But to lose an actual blood relative... I shudder.

"I seriously can't believe this shit. All I wanted to—" Beckett cuts off his wants just as we pull up at the building side entrance. "Praise the Lord. Is that what I think I'm seeing?"

"Yes." I slam the SUV into park, and we immediately leap into action. Mitch—who has been sitting quietly, listening to Beckett bitch as is his MO—and I scramble out of the car. He flings open Beckett's door as I scurry around the front of the car, scanning up and down the street. The three of us dash toward the empty side entrance, disbelieving there's no paparazzi lurking about.

The security guard recognizes Beckett and opens the door as we approach. "Mr. Miller. We didn't know you were attending, even though you know you're always welcome at any of T's soirees."

He spears him a heated glare. "You don't see me. I'm not here. You do, however, have five seconds to buzz me up to the penthouse."

He's about to argue, when Beckett yanks out his wallet and slaps several bills in his hand. "I need to find a friend. I'll be back down in ten minutes. They"—he jabs his fingers at me and Mitch—"will remain here."

I vehemently protest when Beckett aims that ferocious look at me. "There's a reason I didn't want her showing her face at this party. Sure as hell, I didn't need the two of you displaying yours to add fuel to the fire."

As the security guard makes his way over to the elevator, Beckett leans closer to murmur in my ear, "Snowy-T? The guy throwing the party? He's notorious for having, shall we say, extracurricular enjoyment available? He's openly propositioned her on any number of occasions. Kylie finds him to be utterly repulsive. She said the world would be better if someone would just run him over with a bus or something." At my implacable expression, he expounds quietly, "Drugs. Prostitutes. Getting the idea yet, Kane? God help me, I have no idea what I'm about to find, and I'd like to do as much damage control as possible. Carys will find a way for me to weather whatever happens. But sure as fuck, someone gets a snap of you, and that would be the exact moment the cops come prancing through the doors. Inevitably, it happens almost every time T throws a party." Then he flashes me a grin before tapping the side of my face. "I'd hate to find new bodyguards when I've just broken you both in just the way I like you."

I roll my eyes. "Like my bosses wouldn't deal with that."

Beckett's eyes become hard. "You don't understand. This asswipe is the kind who would throw you to the cops to save his own ass, and everyone there would swear to it just to get in his favor. Your bosses may have pull—these people will crush them." Beckett steps onto the elevator that opens behind him. "Wait here. I'll be back in five."

My fury mounts as I spear the security guard who steps in front of the elevator, blocking my following Beckett with a fulminating look. "If he's not back down in ten minutes, I'm going up after him."

"Who? Not sure what you mean, man" is the innocent reply that immediately makes me want to take out this fucker using the moves I spent hours perfecting during years of combat training.

Six minutes later, the elevator opens. Mitch and I go from alert to static when we see Erzulie cradled high in Beckett's arms. I can't see her face clearly. But what I can see is Beckett's laced with utter disgust. "Let's go. She's breathing, which is more than I can say for what's going to happen after I'm through with her," he bites out.

"Uh, Beckett, you know I can't let you out the side. Take the front entrance," the security guard urges.

I hold up a hand and lean partially into the foyer. A million cameras begin flashing. "Yeah, I think not. We'll stick with our original plan."

He looms over me. "I really have to insist."

I drop back and turn my back on him deliberately. "You do?"

Mitch mutters, "Shit," just as the security guy slams both of his meaty hands on my shoulders. "Yeah. I really fucking do. What the fuck? You're going to come in here and disrespect my boss by—"

He doesn't get another word out. I wrap my left arm around his elbows before throwing a few punches just beneath his ribs and strike with my right elbow across his nose. Stepping over his feet, I trip him down before dragging him out of Beckett's way. Then I growl, "Let's move."

"Right." Mitch has the door open. Beckett is already easing Erzulie through it with me coming up on the rear. In unison, Mitch and I take flank on either side of Beckett, helping him ease her into the back of the SUV. None of us says a word until we're all safely inside. Gunning the vehicle, I calmly ask Beckett, "Where do you want to take her?"

He frowns down at the woman who has curled in a ball away from him. "Home. She'll be best sleeping this off."

"Do you know her address?" Beckett rattles it off, and I wheel us toward Tribeca.

"Kane, nice moves with the security guy," Mitch pipes up.

"That reminds me, call Sam and tell him to wipe the security footage. We don't need that asshole selling it," I remark, even as Beckett curses. "We'll add that to your bill."

"And I'll make her pay for it," Beckett begins before Erzulie starts calling out her sister's name in her sleep. But his voice softens when he whispers, "God, is she ever going to recover from this?"

I want to reassure him that yes, she will. But since I haven't, I can't make him those promises. So, I just drive.

It's almost four by the time we make it back, and I manage to write up my notes before crawling back into bed. At that point, all I can do is stare at the ceiling, empathizing with Erzulie.

She had devolved to a confused, slurring mess of tears, asking over and over, "Where's my Lee? She's not here. I need to go find her."

If Beckett hadn't wrapped her up in the blanket and practically sat on her, I suspect she somehow would have escaped and harmed herself or—worse—someone else in her quest to solve the unsolvable—the open, unexplainable, and tragic case of Leanne Miles being killed when she was mugged. It's eating away at her heart to the point she's becoming dangerous.

And it's a feeling I understand all too well.

It's been years, and even then, if it wasn't for the team supporting me at Hudson, I'm still not certain I wouldn't have found my way back to active duty. I was looking for a way to die—preferably with the honor I felt I'd lost by trusting the wrong person. I have no illusions about the kind of man I am. If it wasn't for those last-minute changes I let Gene convince me to make…

The deaths of my team weigh so heavily on my conscience. I broke the cardinal rules of spec ops—keep it simple, and follow the plan. Even with the last-minute intel I received, I knew we were supposed to abort if two choppers couldn't get into the Azerbaijan airspace because we'd only have half the team to secure the perimeter. Instead, Gene convinced our commander we needed to push on because the target we were retrieving was too valuable. This was our only choice, and after listening to his reasoning, I convinced our team to go in.

We were given the green light and pushed on with the mission.

We lined up a new plan. With strength and courage, three men and one woman, not including the flight team, were going to get into the compound. We quickly reviewed the intel we'd trained with inside the kill house and came to the same conclusion. We could still do it.

Who the fuck could have predicted the son of a bitch would disable the chopper so we'd be forced to land away from their target? Even with the intel from an unexpected source, there was no way I could have predicted that. I've turned the mission over and over again in my mind.

It was one moment in time that changed the course of my life forever.

As I slowly drift to sleep, I rub my hand over my over my heart, where each of my team still lives. I know since their bodies were recovered, they're not wasting away in Azerbaijan, but I just wish there was some sign they made it past heaven's gate. But the reality is there's just this empty hole that I know can never be filled.

So yeah, I appreciate Kylie Miles is searching for some kind of order in her life. Because even the best-laid plans can blow up in your face. And if half the stories the media reported were true at the time of her death, for Kylie Miles, those plans were as simple as a weekend with your kid sister.

I only hope Beckett doesn't push her further away by trying to teach her a lesson about her safety. On that last thought, I fall asleep for the few moments of sleep I can manage before the day begins again.

Leanne

1

If you can't take time to enjoy the scenery while you're dining, well, you're not opening up all your senses. Even if you are simply reheating leftovers at home, make every meal an experience. Pretend your favorite celebrity is dining with you. Set the table. Interact with one another. Embrace the experience.

— **Fab and Delish**

The first inclination when I come to is to vomit.

The second is to reach for the knife I had strapped to my thigh before I sauntered into Snowy-T's dumpster fire last night. I find it missing.

The third is panic because I don't remember how I got back to Kylie's, nor do I remember someone unzipping the leather boots I was wearing which have a stiletto hidden inside. Blindly, I slide my fingers down and reach for the quick release. The thin blade pops into my hand like it was custom-fit to be there. Which it was.

How can I get so sick from drinking a club soda with a twist of lime? The thought passes through my mind quickly as I hold my hair back before retching again.

After having relayed the information, it was agreed I should attend, but, "Use caution, *Qaza*. I'll have you passively monitored through your personal cell. Authorization?"

I immediately recited my authorization code, bypassing his need to get a warrant. Ah, the freedom we enjoy that is in no way free. How many citizens would be horrified to know the handy little devices they carry to make their lives simpler actually can be used not only to track their every movement, but can be flipped around to actively listen in? Computer cameras that can be turned on with a few keystrokes?

I can only pray that's how I was extracted.

Feeling marginally better, I rinse my mouth. I crawl back to bed and reach for my phones.

The unsecured one has a million texts. I don't focus in on them other than to determine the majority of them are from an enraged Beckett Miller. "Later," I whisper, feeling dread in the pit of my stomach when I realize somehow "I" texted Beckett to get me out of the party.

Because I didn't.

I fumble around to unlock my secure one. Choosing each letter with precision, I type, *Tell me it was you.*

Seconds later, it buzzes in my hand. I answer immediately. "I have a doctor on standby. She'll be there in minutes to take a blood sample," I'm informed brusquely.

"All I had was a club soda!" I exclaim.

"Do you think I don't know that?" His fury, barely leashed, explodes. "I turned on the camera when you didn't respond. Screw authorization. And there you were—just lying there. I thought you were... You were just lying there." His lack of words makes me appreciate his anger more.

I open my mouth to speak, but I end up racing back to the bathroom. I toss the phone on the counter while I dry heave over and over. Finally, I sink down onto the cool tiles and whisper, "I'm okay."

"For the first time since your sister died, I have zero doubt which of you they were trying to kill."

His words send a shiver down my spine. Before I can answer, a peal rings out. "That will be Chief Petty Officer Orhan. Let her in once she verifies where her sister's husband's restaurant is located at."

After validating the response with both of them, I fling the door open. The young woman of Irani descent nods efficiently before stepping over the threshold. "Just a quick blood draw, Ms. Miles?"

"Yes. Thank you." Keeping the line open, I let her draw the blood and show her out. The moment the door closes, I sag against the door. "How long until we know?"

"Just a few hours. Get some rest and some fluids." The call is disconnected in my ear.

A few hours later, I almost want to find a rabbit hole to hide out in. *It was gamma-hydroxybutyric acid. GHB.* My eyes pop when I see the amount per blood volume. The odorless, tasteless concoction was just short of enough to kill me. And I still don't know who the target was—Kylie or me? I keep scrolling through the rest of his message, my insides chilling with every word.

They likely thought you were drinking, Qəza. Had you been, you'd be dead. The fact you didn't have alcohol in your system was the only thing that saved you.

I quickly type, You trained me better than that.

At least you listened.

His response would normally draw a reluctant smile, but I can't even work one up. A shiver racks my body. I tuck my knees beneath Kylie's Vanderbilt sweatshirt and type, *What the hell am I supposed to do now? Track down everyone at that party?*

Leave that to us. You do what you do best. Go hunting.

And what will that do except expose me more?

He doesn't answer for a long moment. When he does, his words don't reassure me. *Then we'll deal with that when it comes.*

That's when a trickle of fear begins to seep into my mind. What if it's not an enemy who's out to get me, but someone who's supposed to be an ally?

Or possibly worse, a friend?

I need to find out.

I slip my secure laptop from my bag and go cyberhunting until the sky turns blush pink. When it's done, I have a whole lot of nothing for it other than a crick in my neck. The shadows are hauntingly quiet, which is terrifying unto itself.

If I've learned nothing over the last few years working in the world of black ops, it's that the biggest disasters occur when no one expects them. I've been called upon to discuss examples of everything from arms deals, to hostage rescues, to other greater threats to our nation. In all of these instances, public chatter disperses, and the individuals pulling on the reins bury themselves deep in the darkness to exploit the powerful lack of principles available, if you know how to get there.

And I'm more than an expert at it. Since I was in my early teens, I've helped dominate it.

As Leanne Miles, I first earned a reputation as a black hat, a ne'er-do-well available for the highest bidder when things went tits up. Eventually, I let my black turn to shades of gray as I laconically told people I could use my skills to make a few bucks legally. They all thought my founding of Castor amusing—another way to operate right under the government's nose.

But few people on the planet know me as *Qaza*—the high-powered intelligence broker for the US government.

"Who is it they wanted to kill, Kylie? You, me, or her?" I refer to my alter ego in the third person as I watch the sunrise. "And why can't I figure it out?"

Stumbling to the couch, my eyes drift shut. In my nightmares, all I see is my Lee. And nothing she's trying to tell me makes sense.

I wish it did.

I'm woken hours later by a phone ringing. "'Lo," I yawn when I answer.

"I am going to do everything short of murder you. You're too talented to be dead. I told you not to go to that frigging party," a very angry male shouts in frustration.

I yank the phone away and check the caller ID. Shit. Beckett Miller. "Uh, Becks? What's the problem?"

"The problem, Ky, is the fucking paps got a picture of me carting you out of the hotel when you called me drunk off your ass. And do you want to hear the caption on this one?"

"Umm..."

"Rock God and the Indie Goddess? Is this a match made in heaven or someone's idea of a sick hell. In this case, the daddy/daughter dating doesn't do it for us."

"Oh shit. Tell me it wasn't..." Please, oh, please. Just not...

"Yes, little girl. Your favorite of the bunch. StellaNova."

I let out an ear-piercing scream.

Beckett shouts, "Do you get it now, Ky? Do you? I get you're suffering. Believe me, I understand that. But you know the rule I taught you to live by—nothing to excess."

Suddenly, everything comes crashing down on me—especially the disappointment in myself. I've solved international skirmishes in this amount of time. How hard is it to find out who killed my sister? A sob wrenches from me. "It just hurts so damn bad. Nothing makes the pain go away."

Why am I surprised when he displays no emotion other than that of his own image? God, what did Kylie see in him as a friend? He is unsympathetic when he lectures, "Take your emotions out on the music, Ky. Now, I have to go have Carys deal with this for both of us. Do you realize how pissed she's going to be?"

"Oh, God. Becks, no. It can't be that bad."

"I suggest you haul your ass up out of bed and check your phone. You aren't in school, and this isn't playtime anymore, little girl. Your whole life is a damn business. And next time, figure out some other way to deal with the pain. Just like I told you after the Grammys when I had to hold you up when we got out of the limo and we dealt with these rumors then."

I pull the phone away, and the lick of anger begins to fire in my blood at the disrespectful way he's talking to my sister. "I swear if it's the last thing I do, I'm—"

I hear the beep signaling he's hung up on me. So, I let out the primal scream I've been holding inside. I immediately dial Carys and begin pacing.

"LLF LLC. Hold on, Erzulie. She's waiting for your call."

I hear the line connect, and before I can say a word, Carys says, "Tell me two things."

"Okay."

"Was it as bad as Beckett says?"

I'll give him this. "Worse." Quickly, I inform Carys about my suspicions I was drugged. "I swear, I didn't have anything to drink."

I can hear her fuming over the phone. "Then that answers my second question."

"Which was?"

"Whether you still want to meet with the investigators. If so, we have an appointment for a week from tomorrow at 7:30. I'll pick you up."

My lips curve upward. "Is that a.m. or p.m.?"

"In the morning. Be ready—these aren't the kind of guys you mess around with." With that, Carys disconnects the call.

"I sincerely hope not." I wish Carys had left me the name of the investigators, but I'm certain I'll know who I'm going to meet with before that meeting. In the meanwhile, I have some work to do.

It's time to find out what I can dig up on Snowy-T to let the media hounds gnaw on for a while.

150

KANE

18

December

Jack Daniels or Cristal? Rumors of a party at Beckett Miller's are surfacing, but the details are unclear. All I know is I wish I was invited regardless of what was served.

— **Viego Martinez, Celebrity Blogger**

December

My hand is slapped with a spoon as I try to reach for another freshly fried piece of chicken, just like it would be when I was a child, then as a teen. I wrap my free arm around my mother and kiss the crown of her head. "Ma, give me a break. You're frying enough chicken to feed twenty. And besides, how often do I get home to have any?"

She doesn't look impressed with my logic, despite the fact this is the first time I've stepped foot on the farm in years, though I've paid for her and my father to meet up with Beckett's entourage whenever they can spare a few days away. While she doesn't particularly care for his music, being a country lover her whole life, my mother adores the people I work with. It's obviously mutual, with Beckett sending me off with a crooning "Tell your family hello. Be sure to give your mother a huge hug from me."

So I'm surprised not in the slightest when she declares, "These are for you to take back with you. Beckett needs some meat on his bones. He's looking too skinny."

"I guarantee you, Ma, you're the only woman in America who thinks that."

She rolls her eyes as she uses a wire contraption to shift more chicken to the growing pile before salting them and adding more to the scalding hot oil. "It won't be that many. Especially after your sister and her brood get their fingers on them."

I eye the pile of chicken left to be fried warily. "Are you certain? Do we have any chickens left on the farm, or do you need money for more?" I whip out my phone and snap a picture of the chicken production. I quickly text it to Beckett, who is with a backup team provided by Hudson in Memphis this weekend. *Your number one fan is sending me back with gifts.*

His response makes my shoulders shake. If you eat any before I get some, I'm firing you on the spot.

I quickly type back. We're having it for dinner.

His I wonder if I can make it there in time? makes me laugh aloud.

Immediately, my hand is tapped with the wooden end of the utensil my mother is using to flip the chicken over for the golden crust. "Stop making fun of your mother," she admonishes me.

"Yes, ma'am." I step away and move over to the refrigerator. Pulling out a pitcher of lemonade, I catch sight of the big blue enamel bowls overflowing with potato and macaroni salad inside. Quickly closing the door so I don't receive a lecture about letting the cool air out, I declare, "They remind me of all the times we'd bring casserole dishes to funerals."

"What do, sweetheart?"

I pull down two glasses and begin to pour. "The huge bowls of food. I remember when someone would pass away, you'd cook not just for the service, but weeks later." I set her glass next to her before returning the pitcher to the refrigerator.

"Grief isn't something that's immediately handled, Kane. You appreciate that. People who are left behind need to know they're being thought about long after the initial blow of death has occurred."

I deliberately drag up the feelings about Gene: the guilt, the sadness, the despair. I still feel all of these emotions all of these years later; how must Erzulie be feeling about her sister? Her twin, no less? I swallow the oily bile that tries to rise up with the cool, tart taste of my mother's homemade lemonade.

"What made you bring it up?" she wonders.

"A friend of Beckett's lost someone close to them. In addition to the fact they're close, the media's a bitch. I never realized before how difficult it must be just to have an honest-to-goodness friend at a time like this," I tell her honestly. There's no need to go into my lingering emotions. I probably don't have to. After all, Brit and Maddie live only twenty miles away as the crow flies. And in this part of the country, that's practically next door.

I could be at their front door in an hour, but I won't be.

They need time and space.

So, I'll continue to give it to them.

She whirls around, shock on her face. "Why, I never thought about that before. Oh, honey, was it someone you knew as well?"

"I know Beckett's friend, not her sister," I explain, hoping she leaves it at that.

She studies my face before turning back around to fry her heart out. I let out a relieved breath. Turns out to be too soon when she probes, "And it's not bringing up anything I need to worry over?"

Damn, my mother sees too much. Part of me would resent her for it if it wasn't for the fact it's completely out of love. "She reached out—Brit did."

My mother's arm, lifting the next batch of chicken out, stills. "Oh? When?"

"The night Erzulie's sister died. Said she needed more time. Sent me a picture of Maddie."

"She's healing as well." She pauses before announcing, "She's dating. Local man. Widower. Zak Johnson. You might remember him."

I do. And I don't feel the punch to the gut knowing Brit's moving on with her life. She should. She and Maddie deserve all the happiness out there after their lives were destroyed, and the extent to which they were. "Good guy, as I remember. Though now I feel like I have to run him." The second I mutter as an aside.

That earns me another smack on the hands by the wooden handle. I grin.

It's good to be home where the good, the bad, even the hellacious never affect the love. And I soak in every ounce of it before I go back to New York, knowing exactly how precious it is.

And how quickly it can change.

Knocking on the doorframe to Beckett's penthouse a few days later, I wince. Christ, no wonder Mitch sounded so pissed. The place is completely trashed. "What in the fuck happened here?" I demand.

I've come straight from the airport. Beckett is en route from Memphis. Mitch—who was also off this weekend and spending time with his family—happened to see a social media post. "The alarm went off, but it was shut off in a matter of seconds."

"That's supposed to be impossible. We installed a server room to lock up his security equipment," I reply hotly.

"That isn't even the worst part," Mitch says forebodingly. He steps over broken pieces of art to hand me a tablet.

I unlock it and find the police report. I'm incredulous. "The cops were called?"

"Yes."

"And as the head of Beckett's detail, no one saw fit to call me?"

Mitch opens his mouth and then smartly closes it. "That was a mistake."

"A huge one. There's nowhere on the planet where I'm that unreachable."

"Understood. That was an error. We thought we had things under control."

"A huge one. Has anyone called this in to Keene or Caleb yet?" I'm sorely tempted to hurl the device in my hands, but I'm going to need it to take pictures, and I'm not certain if I can rely on the servers in Beckett's place to still be in working order.

Mitch winces before rubbing the side of his head near his ear. The corner of my mouth lifts just a bit. "Got an earful didn't you?"

"That's an understatement," he admits. Then his face turns chalky. "Oh, God."

The tension in the room goes electric. *Honey, I'm home.* The old whimsy floats through my head as I turn to face an enraged Beckett Miller. His voice is eerie. "Tell me I'm hallucinating from drugs I've never done."

"I wish I could." My eyes sweep the room. God, what a disaster.

His eyes lock onto mine. A muscle ticks in his jaw as his phone rings. Slipping his phone from his pocket, he answers it. I use the reprieve to check out the door to the server room. I hear his furious voice and a feminine one I recognize as Carys Burke's responding. Despite the disparaging comments he's making, I'm grateful for it. She's deflecting the anger he'd be justified in tossing in my direction, but it's freeing me up to help the team figure out the how and why.

I slip a pair of gloves out of my wallet and make my way to a closet. Along the way, the stench of the party permeates my nose, but it isn't until I spy the broken handle of the server room door that I feel nauseous. Because lying next to it is the broken pieces of Beckett's Grammy.

And when I line them up, the bell and base match the gouges next to the keypad perfectly.

I step into the room and find not only the primary server equipment destroyed, but the secondary equipment—something only someone from Hudson should know about—disabled. "Oh, holy hell." The implications for this cause my head to reel. Not only would someone in the building have to be involved, but someone in Hudson was here as well.

I step out and prepare to face Beckett's wrath.

He's in the middle of shouting, "Are you kidding me? I wasn't even here! And we'll be able to defend that once the security team..."

I shake my head.

"You've got to be fucking joking, Kane. What did they do? Use a kitchen knife to pick the..." His face flushes when I lift my arm and he sees his broken Grammy in my hands. Before I can speak, he grinds out, "Are you telling me that whomever was in this place used one of the crowning achievements of my career to smash the keypad lock your team installed on the server room holding the data we need to prosecute them?"

"Yes."

"I suggest you get building security to figure this out before I call Hudson and get all of you fired for oh, say, gross incompetency?" he drawls sarcastically.

I frown, thinking of the backup server loss. "Someone has to stay with you."

"Someone has to come with me because I'm sure as hell not staying here. One more minute in this place and I'll be arrested for murder."

A few minutes of him and Carys discussing where he's going tonight, I declare, "We will figure out who did this, Becks. That's a promise."

"It'd better be." He ducks inside the elevator and heads downstairs.

I bark out to Mitch, "No one leaves until I get Beckett secured."

"Secured where?" he asks.

I don't bother mentioning that's going to be need-to-know until I get ahold of the two people who might lose their minds more than Beckett has. And if I still have a job after being lambasted by Caleb and his partner, Keene Marshall, then they can give me direct orders about how to handle this situation. Because the first order of business is protecting Beckett, not the feelings of my team.

Protecting Beckett is the only thing that matters, and even though I wasn't here, I still failed abysmally at it.

Leanne

If I see one more ad pop up after I've been having a conversation in the privacy of my home, I swear I'm going to move to a deserted island. Well, let's get real—we all know I won't. But I just might use the Wi-Fi at Niemies to write this column. At least I'll get higher-quality dresses in my feed instead of crap that will fall apart after one use.

— **Moore You Want**

I was briefed thoroughly about the men I'm going to meet this morning, but still I'm paralyzed by the unexpected one who shoots me a sympathetic smile after he ducks behind a closed door. When the doors snaps shut behind him, I whirl on Carys and gape. "That was Sam Akin."

Her face lightens for a moment with amusement. "I know. He introduced himself."

"My junior year in college, I completely crushed him at Defcon. At first, I was in shock. Then I couldn't stop crying after it hit home," I whisper. Sam Akin. He has no idea how he changed my life. I'd hoped we'd one day have the opportunity to meet again now that we're both professionals so I could openly admire his work face-to-face, but today isn't that day. Hell, if someone succeeds at killing me, I may never have it.

We stand as a ridiculously gorgeous man steps from the same office Sam disappeared into. Following him, Sam hangs up his phone and nudges him. The dark-eyed man's question immediately alerts me to the fact the outer lobby is bugged—not that I'm surprised. "The question, Ms. Miles, is were you happy about it or upset?"

Even though I know exactly who he is from my briefing, I cut a quick glance to Carys as if I'm clueless to his identity. After she nods, giving me leave to speak freely, I respond openly to the first man as she holds out her hand to the other. "I was stunned. I went back to my dorm room and began writing what became my senior project based on the experience."

Sam throws his head back and laughs. "Best news I've ever heard."

The dark-haired man chuckles. "If Sam had more time with you here, he'd be dragging you down to his lab. As it is, he's been all up mine and Keene's asses for years for IT upgrades we haven't given him budget for." Sam immediately begins nodding frantically, lending credence to the other's words.

I blush. "You flatter me."

"I didn't think that was possible with your reputation. Oh, I apologize for not introducing myself. I'm Caleb Lockwood, co-owner of Hudson Investigations."

Temporarily forgetting my grief and fear, I hold out my hand to shake his. I recall what was said about him. "Caleb is cleared, but not at your level, Qaza. Still, if you interact with either Lockwood or Marshall, they're completely on our side. Implicitly. You have no reason to question their loyalty."

Caleb takes it. "Welcome to Hudson. I must say, it's nice to put a name to the face after the last few years."

I immediately slip into my CEO guise. "The lawyer who leads your contracts team is a pain in my ass. He's an arrogant, royal prick. Completely autocratic, demanding—" Then I clamp my lips together, remembering being told Keene Marshall saved his best friend's life by walking straight into a hail of gunfire.

Caleb, obviously, isn't that impressed with the long-ago act as he encourages me, "Don't let that stop you from enumerating Keene's high points, Leanne. So often, people try to tiptoe around him."

Sam rolls his eyes. "You know, Caleb, if you went up against the proposals team from Castor on a regular basis, you might feel a bit more sympathy for Keene."

Carys wisely steps in to stop the verbal clashing. "Caleb, Sam, perhaps we should take Leanne into the conference room before anyone else overhears us?"

A feeling of nausea over the events of the last few weeks overwhelms me, and grief descends when the reason I'm standing here smacks into me like a 2x4. "Please."

Caleb guides me forward. "Grief is a journey no one wants to be on, Ms. Miles. One moment, you feel anger so severe you feel nothing but the need for retribution. Then there's the pain so debilitating it's almost crippling." He pauses temporarily by a door that's partially open. His eyes are drawn to something before he continues. "There are times when it feels like you'll never remember the times of joy."

Just before Carys and Caleb join us, I probe, "Did you lose a family member suddenly, Caleb?"

His chocolate-colored eyes stare down at me so hard, I feel like twitching. He doesn't give anything away verbally, but as I stand next to him, he emanates the same energy swirling inside of me. I sense it. My voice drops to a whisper. "Then you understand my need for vengeance."

Suddenly, Caleb Lockwood's face sharpens. The gregarious lines of his face become lethal when he growls, "Absolutely." Then he morphs back into the calm businessman as he swings open the conference room door for me and the others to pass by.

Carys whirls on Sam and Caleb. "I can't believe you both are listening to her half-assed idea."

"When you're trying to flush out a perp, you have to take drastic measures." Caleb's voice is calm, even if his eyes are sparkling with malice. Okay, it's confirmed. He's on the list of my new favorite people.

Sam is a bit more reticent. "The best thing to do is to announce to everyone that Kylie is dead and Leanne is alive, Caleb."

Bickering ensues. While the three of them go at it, I whip out my computer and quickly hack into Hudson's mainframe. *Sorry, Sam,* I apologize to my idol for breaching his network without a by-your-leave. I cover my tracks and throw data up onto the screen. "Let's look at the facts," I announce calmly.

Sam's jaw falls before a wide smile breaks across his face. Caleb smirks. And Carys's head falls into her hands before she asks, "How many laws did Leanne just break in under fifteen seconds?"

Caleb waves away her concern. "And what are the facts as you see them?"

I rip the card out of my bag and toss it onto the table. I go through everything I've unearthed recently about my sister—including the hit list of men, Carys's assessment of them, and my own encounter at Snowy-T's party. I conclude with a heartfelt "If you had been on the phone with her the way I was, you'd know there was no way she was planning on leaving the Plaza."

Caleb's suddenly intrigued as I flash the police report on the screen. As an aside, he reveals to Carys, "Now, we're looking at some serious jail time if anyone caught her. Though, I don't think Leanne gets caught often."

"I haven't yet," I drawl. Besides being the truth, I don't bother mentioning my all-purpose get-out-of-jail-free card.

Carys begins banging her head on the table in front of her but still manages to get out, "Shouldn't the police have pieced this together?"

Sam's scanning the report. "Best- or worst-case scenario? Despite the notoriety of the victim, unless they receive a tip or something's fenced, there's little hope of finding the killer in this type of case. They have no suspects, no leads other than the obvious. They had a body—sorry, Leanne. Your sister. She was there with her identification in her pocket. It matched. Plus, she was still alive at the time. And from what you told us, you call her Lee?"

"Yes. Ever since we were children or in times of extreme emotion, that's what we both called each other," I confirm.

"Kylie and Leanne," Carys murmurs. She turns her face away, her throat working.

"If I was the kind of man who made assumptions—and I like to think I've learned not to be—I'd bet they assumed 'Lee' was 'Leanne,' not just a treasured nickname you gave each other," Sam concludes.

There's silence around the table while everyone absorbs the mistakes in identifying my sister. Then Carys questions, "What about an autopsy? Why didn't this come up during it?"

"Because one was never performed," I say dully.

Sam scoffs. "Are you kidding? We're talking about a newsworthy death. I mean, we're talking about 'Leanne Miles'?" he air quotes.

Caleb interjects. "Statistically, only about five percent of the deceased bodies in the US are autopsied annually."

"Including deaths arousing the family's suspicions?" Carys is incredulous. She whirls on me. "I can't believe you didn't ask for one."

"Sorry. I was too destroyed over Lee's death and subsequently in too much shock I didn't recognize I was literally signing my own death certificate to remember to ask my parents if they wanted to have their daughter sliced and diced to add to the media swirl we were all about to endure. Let me be sure to add that to my list of items to correct once I get back to my lab. Right after I build that time machine and somehow manage to save my sister's life," I bite out.

Carys has the good grace to look abashed but still presses to ensure there wasn't a mistake. "Caleb, seriously? It wasn't mandatory?"

Caleb shrugs. "New York doesn't require it. Suspicious deaths are required to be investigated, but it's up to the ME on whether one needs to be performed. Since Kylie died under the hospital care, why waste the money when they had a cause of death certified by a medical professional?"

Why indeed? Bitterness crashes over me like a tidal wave that in my grief I didn't ask for that—that there could have been some physical clue I missed—but I dive through it.

"Leanne, what did the final report from NYU list as cause of death?" Sam asks.

My fingers fly as I access NYU Medical Center's records, and both men become very quiet.

"Is that the same Dr. Ross, Caleb?" Sam worries.

"It is," Caleb confirms.

"What? Is there a problem with the way she was treated?" I ask frantically. I never even thought of that angle.

"Jason notes broken bones and contusions. He also notes defensive wounds," Caleb responds carefully. His fingers are clenched in a fist so tight, the knuckles are white with strain.

Sam leans over and studies the report. "Being as thorough as he always is, he still ran a tox screen. Though the final results are still pending, he was still able to rule it officially as a homicide the day of the attack because of the head trauma and suffocation. Open. Shut. Really, the tox results are superfluous. That's why he didn't flag it as a priority. I doubt it will find anything to affect the detective's report unless your sister was doing illegal substances, at which point, every tabloid on the planet will be reporting it."

My hair flies back and forth as I shake my head. "Not recently. And even then, it was a few joints maybe in places it wasn't legalized. Nothing more significant than that."

"Like that isn't half the known world," Caleb scoffs.

"You speak of him like you know him—Dr. Ross, that is?" My voice is anxious, wondering if I've made an error coming to Hudson with Carys.

"He's my brother-in-law," Caleb explains.

I study the precise report carefully, noting all the different life-saving techniques he used before he ever made the phone call to me. Concluding he did everything possible short of lie in my sister's place to save her, I murmur, "He went far and above what was expected."

Caleb says quietly, "He always does."

For a moment, we're all silent until Sam's determined voice asks, "If your sister willingly left the Plaza, where's their surveillance? The streets surrounding it?"

Jolted back to the business at hand, I draw out my words even as my fingers fly. "Well, Sam, wouldn't you know there was a four-block outage—including internal Plaza security footage—for hours surrounding her death." I pull up an eight-screen divided view and let the video play just before the cameras go out, and then I speed it up to when they come back on. Which is when you can see security approaching me.

Sam sits back in his chair and folds his arms behind his head. "Accidental death, my ass."

"Both our asses," Caleb chimes in grimly.

"I think we're all in agreement about that." Carys's voice is laced with fury. "The question is, what do we do about it?"

I don't know what makes me do it, but I begin to sing. What comes out is an old country song Mom used to play about being unable to live without someone. It touches on the person being their heart, their soul. She used to dance with Dad in the kitchen while we watched. He used to tease it was all of our song since we couldn't live without each other.

I'm beginning to realize he was right.

Carys gapes at me. "Christ, you even sound like her. If it wasn't for the tattoo, I'd never have known the difference."

I don't bother to acknowledge her words—it's something I already know. Instead, I press my agenda with force. I'll use these and any resources I have to. Screw country first—finding Kylie's killer has become my primary objective. Hotly, I list the facts. "After what happened in Silverthorn, then at Snowy-T's, I don't feel safe. They killed my sister, and now someone is trying to kill me. Maybe it's a crazy who hates her, someone from our past who hates us both. Or maybe it's someone not so insane. Either way, I feel like I'm next."

Carys tries one final attempt at reason. "It was the police's mistake in identifying her."

"Something we'll point out when we're good and ready in the event they try to bring charges against Leanne for falsifying her sister's identity. I don't care if they had her license; they should have checked the fingerprints. It's one of the few things not identical on twins. Their mistake. We'll use it to our advantage to keep our client alive," Caleb bites out.

"Leanne came to Hudson and was honest from the beginning. She doesn't feel safe. She won't go down for impersonating her twin so long as we keep records of her activities." Sam's penetrating glance bounces off mine as he outlines the plan.

He's right. I won't go down for this, but his reasoning is a bit off. It's not often agents of covert agencies of the US government are punished for doing their jobs when they're sanctioned. It happens, but it's rare. I just can't share that truth with them without authorization. But chances are if the person was trying to murder me, they'll come after me again, and we'll have them. I just don't have enough eyes to cover every angle. I grit my teeth in silent supplication once again about his being right. *"No, it won't hurt to have someone with the reputation of Hudson checking out the unclassified side of things. In the meanwhile, focus on your perimeter, Qaza."*

He's not wrong. I have no problem with staking myself out. Nothing's more important to me than finding out who hurt my Lee. Even if it means my own death.

"Then I have one last concern," Carys declares.

"What's that?" I ask.

"We have to loop in Kris." I'm about to protest at the idea of *another* person—especially another civilian—being brought in on this when she stops me by lifting her hand. "None of this can happen without his awareness. He has to know for her—your—career's damage control."

I think for a long moment before ceding the point. "I have a request as well."

"What's that?" Sam asks.

"Stop calling me Kylie."

Everyone appears distressed. "Your sister went by her first name with friends," Carys reminds me.

"I guess I'll have to get used to it, then." Though, privately, the idea of being called Kylie nauseates me. I've been called her name by mistake over the years, sure, but deliberately being called my dead twin's name? No. Just no. My wounds are too raw for that.

"But it's going to hurt too much," Caleb observes perceptively.

"Just...call me Lee. We both responded to it." Deep inside, it's who we always were to one another despite our lives branching off in such wildly different directions.

"Okay, Lee. Here's your first assignment," Sam drawls. "Send me those files, and then get your precocious little fingers out of my network."

Unable to stop the small curve of my lips, I erase the screen. Immediately after I do, Sam's and Caleb's phones ding. "I set you both up with a special email address for this. You won't be able to admin it, Sam, so I'll have to be in your network for a little longer."

"Well, since you're my newest lackey, set one up for Keene Marshall—Caleb's partner. If Caleb's not available, he's your point of contact here at Hudson," Sam directs me.

A few lazy strokes of my fingers later and Keene Marshall has a new email address as well. "Done."

After he jerks up his chin, Sam threatens me, "When this is over, you're going to close every security hole you're punching, *Lee*."

"I promise." And I mean it.

I just hope nothing happens to cause me to break that promise.

Leanne

Saratoga Springs, N.Y. Castor partners with Sky Harbor Cloud to accelerate its Managed Detection and Response cyber capability, a cloud-based cybersecurity threat monitoring and incident response solution.

— **Castor Newsroom**

Carys and I spent some more time with Caleb and Sam in our client conference. "After all, it makes complete sense you'd be interested in protection after the death of your sister. Sam's just here because Keene's at the other office this week, and I wanted another partner around," Caleb is unperturbed when I worry aloud.

Sam scrawls his name on a form before flipping it around to me. He says cheekily, "This way we can bill you for our initial meeting."

I don't even blink at the amount before I scrawl an unreadable signature to the bottom.

During the time we established my reason for being at Hudson, I find out much more about the primarily veteran-operated company. A knot deep inside of me slowly starts to unwind as I receive even more information that was able to be unearthed about the missions Caleb took on behalf of our country. And while it was offered to send info over about Sam, I tell my boss to forget it. *I know so much about Sam Akin, I might be able to write a book about the man.*

Still, he reminds me, If you'll feel more comfortable, we can always formally loop in my contact at Hudson.

Why am I not surprised you have one here? Before he can respond, I quickly type back, If it becomes necessary, we will.

Let me know.

Just after, more information flows to my computer to get me up to speed on the rest of the players in this game I will likely interact with, including Keene Marshall and Kristoffer Wilde. I'm understandably quiet as the three carefully plan the next several weeks including Erzulie's public appearances, but the reality is I'm scanning data to learn more about the people I'm trusting my life to.

These people are as solid as they come.

I'm jarred out of my reverie when a knock on the conference door startles us all. Caleb presses a button on his iPad before calling out, "Come in!" A man strides in with a stack of files requiring a signature, which is when Caleb hands him the form I affixed my John Hancock to earlier. After he departs the room, Caleb reengages the sound-proofing. "Tony's our personal assistant. He's our go-to guy for dealing with red tape of any kind."

My laconic "Is he interested in a different job?" isn't appreciated by Caleb, who throws a wadded-up ball of paper at my head.

It bounces off and hits Sam, causing us all to chuckle. Sam's frowning at something on his screen. "Speaking of cars, how is it possible Lee was driving up in hers when her sister was..."

There's a long silence before Carys points out. "Sam's right. How could she have been mugged and parking her car at the Plaza at the same time?"

"One of the many, many questions we'll be researching. But I have one for you, Lee." Sam turns his penetrating stare on me. "How did your sister have a copy of your ID?"

"I've been twisting that around in my mind. The only thing I can think of is I know I lost it the last time I stayed at her place—a few months before her tour. She must have found it and was bringing it to me. It's been a while, but she promised she'd send it to me if she found it. I had a replacement ordered even before I left to go back to Saratoga anyway." I don't mention I reported it missing to my handler, nor do I miss the look the two men exchange. "Why?"

"How blunt do you want us to be?" Caleb asks gently.

"Oh, just tell it to her straight. Lee, your sister died with your ID. There's a reason for it. Now, it might be as simple as she found it and had shoved it in her pocket or something else. It's our job to look at all the angles. The first step is to investigate Kylie. And that means everything about her: her habits, her lovers, the hit list you gave us, her finances. There won't be a damn thing you don't know about your sister. Is there anything you want us to know before we start?"

I push to my feet and hiss, "I loved her more than anything or anyone on this planet. There are secrets about her I've held for a long damn time because I didn't want my parents hurt. I'll share them all with you if you think there's any chance they might lead to her killer."

Sam frowns. "What secrets?"

I shake my head. "Please. I made her look like an angel. Carys can tell you she definitely wasn't."

"That's the truth," Carys mutters.

"How quickly can you have a copy of that information to us?" Caleb prods me.

I think about the footprints I'm going to have to bury inside my own software to get to the core of Dioscuri. "It could take me a while. Can I work from here?" Despite how quickly I accessed the Hudson servers, they are much more secure than the average internet connection. Then there's the part of me that wants to just work in Sam's office, to be near my idol, absorbing more of his mojo. Plus, I'm just plain hurting. I want to be somewhere I know I can lose myself in the work and not worry about watching my six.

"It wouldn't be a good idea for you to be seen around here, Lee. After all, you're not Leanne Miles any longer. You're Kylie," Sam reminds me.

Caleb is more blunt. "Be very certain you can do this. Love can drive us to be a lot of things, do a lot of things. It doesn't prepare us for this."

I swipe up my bag. "We breathed each others air, protected each other, for almost a year. It created an unbreakable bond. It prepares you for a hell of a lot. Everything, except death." Caleb winces,as I continue. "But I get your point. I can't be seen here. I can only go where Lee would."

Skirting the conference room table, I make my way to the door when Carys calls my name. I stop. "Yes?"

"Call me when you're settled. We'll discuss your schedule and do everything possible to ward off the press," she reminds me.

Fucking hell. The paps. For a moment, pure emotion trickles in. I have to blink rapidly to clear the tears that want to clog my vision because that's something I know my sister would say. Still, I manage a nod before I slip out the door before striding to the elevator to get the hell out of the building.

But is it so awful that when I reach the street, all I want to do is escape into the crowd and disappear? I just want to go somewhere I can't be found and mourn the loss of my twin for an appropriate duration.

Eternity.

KANE

Did Beckett Miller sleep in his clothes, or were they strewn about someone else's floor? He was without his usual flair this morning outside Rockefeller Center.

— **Moore You Want**

"Kane, when you have a moment, can you head up to Caleb's office?" Tony informs me before disconnecting the call.

My lips curve into a brief smile before I push away from the desk I so rarely use in the offices of Hudson Investigations and head immediately to the elevator. It's easy to translate the shorthand of that message from the co-owner of the company to mean *Get your ass up here. Pronto.* Fortunately, Tony has more diplomacy on the phone than Caleb does. Though any of us who have ever worked for him can certainly attest to the fact the man has mellowed significantly in the last few years.

I pass the reason for the smile that occasionally graces my boss's face when I step out of the elevator. "Mrs. Lockwood," I greet Caleb's wife politely as I hold the elevator for her.

She flashes me a brilliant smile, though I doubt she'd be able to pick me out of the hundreds of employees who work for the firm her husband built out of a determination to set his part of the world right once he left the military. Fortunately, he elected to—and continues to —bring a number of us in to do just the same.

Smoothing my hands down over my custom-made jacket to hide the weapons I conceal, I never imagined I'd transition from putting my life in danger working on the front lines of HUMINT to being the lead bodyguard of someone like rock star Beckett Miller. But as Caleb said when he convinced me to take the assignment, "Beckett is more than he appears. You're going to need every ounce of your training to keep up with him."

Damn, if he wasn't correct. To date, it's the break-ins of Beckett's supposedly rock-solid fortress in the sky that involve every skill I've learned, with the exception of lethal force. I wince remembering the first interrogation I was called in to give the doorman who accepted a $50,000 bribe from a spoiled girl who believed Beckett would fall in love with her immediately upon sight. That was three years ago.

Now, I suspect I know why I'm being called up to the executive floor. I screwed up. After last night's debacle, a picture of Beckett appeared in the media he's already sicced Carys on. Just before he did, he made an off-the-cuff comment about it being good to have us around. *Shit. What did you get me into this time, Beckett?* I wonder wearily.

I jerk my chin up at Tony before I point at Caleb's door. Tony remarks, "He's waiting for you."

"Do I want to know?"

For a brief moment, amusement breaks out across his face. "Why does everyone come in here expecting one of the bosses are going to execute them?"

That stops me in my tracks. I counter, "Have you ever screwed up under them?"

He lifts a phone and asks the caller to hold. "Can't say I have."

I roll my eyes. "Try it. You'll have a better understanding that way." I move forward to knock on Caleb's door to the guffaws ringing out behind me.

Caleb barks out, "Enter." Flinging the door wide, I'm—as always—immediately enraptured by the view behind his mammoth desk. It causes my footsteps to falter.

And the lips of the man behind it to curve. "You and my wife," he murmurs.

"Excuse me?"

"Both of you have the exact same reaction every time you walk through those doors. Come on in, Kane. Close the door."

Before Caleb can launch into the story of what happened with Beckett at Snowy-T's that hit the media, I go on the offensive. "I was with the principal up until the point he went to get Ms. Miles. Then he decided to try to protect us."

Caleb sneers at that comment but makes no comment. I plow on. "Other than those few minutes, at no time was he alone from the time he left his penthouse to the time we returned Ms. Miles to her condominium and returned to his residence."

Caleb leans back in his chair and stares thoughtfully at a painting that hangs over his couch. He doesn't say anything for long moments. "It's not Beckett I want to ask you about. I need your opinion regarding another matter related to what happened."

"What is it?"

"Do you think Erzulie was truly that drunk, or do you believe she was drugged?" Caleb's quiet question causes my body to jerk as if I've just been shot.

I surge to my feet and begin pacing as I recall the events from the night before. "Erzulie, given name Kylie Miles, often known as Ky by close friends, has been through a serious trauma recently. Her older sister—her twin—was found mugged and barely alive."

"She prefers to be called Lee, but yes. So far, your report is correct. Carys obtained the originals of those photos from the social media site, StellaNova. I want your opinion of what you saw, Kane. Do you think she was just drunk?" Caleb sits forward and steeples his fingers together.

I stop moving and brace my arm against the glass. I squint against the sun flooding the room as I recall Beckett relaying the scene he walked in on after we peeled away. Erzulie passed out in the bed. Her clothing rumpled, but not unusually so. Not moving at all, not until she started talking about her "Lee." I murmur aloud, "Drugged? How the hell did she text him?"

"Exactly what I've been wondering." Caleb shuffles the papers on his desk for a moment before he finds a file and slides it down toward me. I snatch it and flip it open. There's Beckett, wearing loungewear pants and a hastily thrown-on shirt—unbuttoned—looking for all intents and purposes as if he'd just rolled out of bed. Which, I know for a fact he had been since he called me to tell me we were going to get Erzulie, and I insisted on going.

But being in the moment and staring at the picture, I take in details I didn't notice. Erzulie's not holding on to Beckett as much as he's forcing her against his chest. Her head's lolled back against his shoulder, blonde hair streaming down his arm haphazardly. It's the look on her face that draws me in.

It's completely blank. There's nothing there. Not even a mild recognition of who has her. I glance to the side and catch the hard edge to my own face—the irritation because the individual I'm supposed to be protecting is putting others ahead of himself again. And I realize I missed all of this in the moment.

I screwed up huge.

"No, that's not someone who's just passed out. That's someone who has no idea where she is. There's something else in her system," I say slowly. "I FUBARed. I put people at risk." *Just like you did the day Gene convinced you to continue the mission, you ass.* The taunting words float in my head.

"So did a lot of people, Kane. You did your job, which is to protect Beckett. You're the head of *his* detail, not hers."

"She doesn't have one."

"Carys is working on that."

I snort. Convincing people they need to have protective services is next to impossible until it's too late. "Good luck with that."

Caleb holds out his hand. "These will help."

I hand him back the photos. "Did you just show them to me because of the screw up?"

He hesitates before answering. "They're friends. You may be in a situation where you notice something. Your primary job is to protect Beckett, but..." His voice trails off.

"But neither of us would feel great about ourselves if something happened to an innocent when we could have prevented it," I conclude.

He relaxes. "Exactly. It's difficult to express that to someone who just doesn't understand that. And yet, I wouldn't want them to."

"I completely understand." I hesitate before asking him a question I've always wondered the answer to. "How did you do it, Caleb?"

"What?" His penetrating green eyes don't flicker as they stare at me.

"How did you go on every day after everything that happened to you?" I ask him bluntly. Caleb's past includes a military background that's shrouded in darkness, on top of which he's fought through personal trauma to form a loving family. "Between my own issues and having a front seat to Erzulie's trauma, I feel like I'm going to be sick."

He rubs his hand absentmindedly over the back of his neck. "What makes you think I do?" Before I can clarify my question, he goes on. "It took a long time to accept—and remember, not everything we fear is something tangible. As soldiers, too many of the battles we face are in the dark, alone."

"I'm glad you found your way," I remark as I stand in front of a man I briefly worked with in my early days on a joint task force overseas right before he left the Army.

His eyes drift to the Manhattan skyline. "So am I, Kane. Anyway, if you notice anything unusual, raise it up. I'm code wording both Beckett's and the file I've started on Erzulie, so you'll need to come to me or Keene for access."

I arch my brow but don't contradict him. Something big must be going on, but since Caleb doesn't offer more, I don't ask.

For now.

Hours later, I'm working out in the gym in the building where Beckett bought a condominium for the team for Hudson to crash when we're not on duty. *Benevolent motherfucker*, I think ruefully. He drives us insane on a daily basis with his arbitrary requests to bounce from one side of New York to the other but drops millions of dollars to ensure our comfort.

I groan aloud when the heavy metal I'd been listening to changes to the Backstreet Boys. I don't even bother to hide my irritation. "For real? The Backstreet Boys?" I drop the free weights to the floor with a thud.

And the man known around the world for his lyrics that bring both men and women to their knees pops his head around the corner with an enormous grin. "I'm expanding your musical knowledge, Kane."

"You're trying to send me into a diabetic coma." I snatch up my water bottle and drink while glaring at the tattooed megastar.

"Listen to these lyrics. They're ridiculous."

"That's the truth," I mutter.

"You have no soul. This is..."

"Crap. If you want to listen to '90s music with soul, put in Dave Matthews. Hell, slap on Ani DiFranco, but turn this off."

Beckett's eyes light up like I've just told him Christmas has come months early. I hold up a hand to stave him off. "Not now. Right now, since you're here, I have a question for you."

He frowns. "What's wrong?" He slips the remote from his pocket and turns down the music.

I straddle the weight bench. "Have you noticed anything out of the ordinary with Erzulie recently?"

"Other than her stubborn determination not to listen to a damn word I've said?" Beckett's frustration is palpable.

"Sure." I've learned in interrogations to let people just talk. I'll eventually get the answers I want.

He runs his hand over his jaw. "It's since she lost her sister. I... appreciate...what it means to have loved and lost someone you're soul bound to."

It's a good thing I'm trained at this, otherwise I might have choked on air before asking, "Oh?"

His face goes blank. "There are just some mistakes you don't get a second chance to fix, Kane."

Don't I know it. "So, you're not concerned she's going to be pulling any stunts like this again?" I ask casually. Beckett shoots me a confused look. "Look, man, it's my job to walk in the room before you. I need to know if I need to add Erzulie to a proscribed list—at the very least screen her shit before she gets through to you."

Beckett's face breaks into a wide grin. "Aw, Kane. You care."

"Yeah—about not getting shot. I'd like to think you'd appreciate that."

Beckett acknowledges my statement with a tip of his head. "And I appreciate you thinking this through with a calmer head than I did. I don't think there's going to be a problem with Kylie though. I tore into her pretty good after it happened."

I bite my lip to hold back my initial reaction, which is to defend her. Instead, I remark, "Well, that must have been enjoyable for her if she had a hangover."

"I'm sure it was." Beckett's eyes turn hard. "We've all lost people who have meant the world to us. I told her to put it in the one safe place she can—her music." He pivots and heads for the door.

"Beckett," I call out. He pauses. "Are you going to change the music back?"

His wicked smile amplifies, and he turns up the Backstreet Boys before he saunters away. I wince as I let the atrocious music wash over me. Then I jog over to my gym bag and pull out a second remote before I switch back to the hard rock channel and jump on the treadmill.

After all, it's my job to be prepared for anything. At least when it comes to the person I'm protecting.

KANE

Erzulie broke down on stage last night during her show when she was singing a rendition of Stevie Nicks' "Landslide." According to a member of her crew who gave a quote, it was "uncomfortable. She's been getting progressively worse." Apparently, the indie goddess is beating back some serious demons.

— **StellaNova**

"I quit," I tell Colby Hunt after getting him on the phone a week later after Beckett Miller storms into the law offices of LLF LLC and ordered us to lock it down. This after jumping out of the secure car he was riding in that was slowing so we could escort him safely inside. Instead, the schmuck leapt out and chased a random woman down a city block before detaining her until she took off running in heels so high, I thought she might break an ankle.

Colby—one of Caleb and Keene's partners who worked protective details, almost dying in one situation—doesn't laugh. He immediately asks, "What happened?"

After recounting Beckett's reckless stupidity, and my enjoyment in reaming him out as I dragged him inside the building we're now standing in, Colby sighs. "Impetuous bastard."

"There's about eight different ways he could have been harmed, Colby! In the time he was out of my sight, he could have been shot, stabbed, at the very least kidnapped," I shout.

A weak mew causes my head to snap up. In front of me is Angela Fahey, legal assistant to Carys and Ward Burke—the sister-and-brother team who own LLF. Carys started LLF when she left Wildcard Records as their general counsel years ago, bringing with her Angie and her then senior paralegal and now husband—David Lennan. "Excuse me, ma'am," I apologize.

"No, it's okay. I..." She turns and flees back inside, causing me to curse in Colby's ear.

On days like this, when controlling Beckett is like corralling a rambunctious child, there's a small part of me that almost longs for the rules and regulation of the military. Then I sneer when I recall I wasn't given much of a choice when I was presented with the choice of hiding my ass inside the Pentagon for the rest of my career or accepting the early retirement with full benefits.

"Your service to this country has been exemplary, Captain McCullough. However, fieldwork is no longer an option. We would be enormously pleased to have your skills at headquarters..."

I interrupt the committee to say, "There is nothing physically or mentally wrong with me. I passed all of your tests."

"The mission failed under your command, Captain," one senator states.

I stare at her. "The mission failed because there was a mole. We eliminated the mole." My stomach twists because I held that mole while he died in my arms.

"Yes you did. He was your best friend, wasn't he?" she counters.

"And I still did the job. Because that's what I trained for. If he was standing right here, and our situation was reversed, I'd expect the same of him." At the confusion on their faces, I clarify through gritted teeth, "I'm a soldier. I love my country. I was trained to support the mission of protecting the United States against all enemies—foreign and domestic."

"Which we feel you can still do," that same senator reiterates.

I listened to them give me my options before turning the desk job down and walking out of the subcommittee chambers.

It was about a month later before my phone rang and Caleb's cool voice asked, "Are you done being bitter yet?"

"Hardly," I replied caustically.

"Good. Report for work at 0800 at this address." And he rattled off the address of Hudson Investigations, not far from where I'm presently standing on the phone. It was the best decision I'd ever made in the last three years until twenty minutes ago. "This is after the party where someone broke through his security the other night. Beckett is on a rampage like I've never seen."

Colby begins chuckling. "I've decided we're having the management company reassign all of the people in his building, and we're placing our own people there."

I close my eyes. Beckett's place was ransacked, a party so loud, so obnoxious, the cops were called. He's getting slapped with a disturbing the peace charge his lawyer, Carys, has to defend, and, "You're telling me it was another guard who let people in?"

"Through the fire escape. He was paid a hefty sum for his assistance." When he tells me who they traced the money to, my jaw falls. I would have laid money on it being a rabid fan or Snowy-T out for retribution. "If we tell him who it was, he's going to declare war."

"As his lead agent, you get to make that decision."

"Thanks." For nothing is left unsaid.

Colby continues. "As it is, the guard faces breaking and entering charges since he technically had no cause to enter Beckett's residence, though I have no doubt his lawyer will try to say there was an emergency."

I sigh, knowing Colby's right. My eyes fly open. I stare down at the lush carpet, feeling something akin to relief. *That's at least something positive I can share to bring Beckett's mood under control*, I think.

"Plus, I found the person in our monitoring room. They...let's just say no longer with us. Keene's out for blood. He's demanding everyone come into the office for a briefing on their responsibilities toward Beckett," Colby informs me.

"I really quit. I am not standing outside Beckett Miller's fire escape in the middle of a New York winter. In no way am I paid enough."

Colby begins laughing. "Sam already figured something out."

I close my eyes in relief. "Bless him." It's something we've all said at least a half a dozen times a day since the company Sam Akin worked for merged with Hudson.

"Think of it this way, Kane. Part of your salary goes to paying for Sam's toys," Colby reasons.

"That I can live with. Beckett Miller not on an electronic leash where I can zap him back in place, nope."

Colby is pounding his desk in hysterics at this point. "You mean like in *Loki*?"

"Think Sam can build that for us?" I ask hopefully.

"I'll get him right on it once he finishes trying to fix a glitch he noticed with our firewall."

"That's much more critical."

"Feel better?"

"I do, but more importantly, you should. I'm not going to strangle your highest-paying customer," I retort. Then seriously, I ask, "Did you struggle when you took on civilian protective details?"

"Sure. But I found a way to fix it. Huge stress reliever."

"Enlighten me."

"Oh, I'm not so certain you want to know." Colby's voice turns serious.

"Why not?"

"Because it involves falling in love. Are you ready to do that, Kane?" Laughing himself sick, Colby disconnects the call.

"Asshole. I work with a bunch of assholes," I mutter.

"I'm wounded, Kane. And here I thought we were getting along so well," Mitch chortles. Rumors circulate his uncle was fairly high up in Hudson Investigations before he retired, adding to the speculation about how he was selected to join the firm. But since I had an opportunity to review his file before we started on this assignment and I didn't recognize his last name, I wonder at the validity of that.

Whatever. He's a solid guy with good instincts about people and a good attitude. "Well, Clifton?" I turn to face Mitch. "What's your take on Beckett's little stunt?"

Mitch is thoughtful for just a moment. "Well, there's a few ways to look at it."

"Which are?"

"No one's hurt, and no one's dead. At the end of the day, I'd call that a good day."

"Good theory. Did you learn that on the force?"

His face hardens. "No. At home. My brother, Trevor, and I didn't have the greatest living situation at home. A family member..." He's about to say more when the door opens and out comes Beckett with a number of people following him.

Before I can say a word, Beckett immediately apologizes again. "I'm sorry, Kane." Then he turns to the dainty brunette with multi-hued braids and squeezes her hand. "We'll talk soon."

She nods. I recognize Carys Burke, who wraps her arms around the girl as Beckett sweeps from the suite of offices. There's a hard look on Mitch's face that I can only hope isn't reflective on my own.

Who is she, and what kind of trouble should we be bracing for?

Three days later, I know the answer to both as we're ensconced in Beckett's private jet on our way to Austin, Texas. And I'm simply flabbergasted by what I'm hearing from a few seats over.

The woman seated nearby with the long, colorful braids is Beckett's daughter. And the woman he leapt from the car to chase was her mother. As discussions between them continue, more about Beckett Miller is becoming clear. He isn't this cavalier man gliding through life—he feels too much. And much of it about the woman we're chasing after.

I'm furiously typing up a report to send to headquarters about what's happening when Beckett's phone he had forwarded to mine for the duration of the flight buzzes with a text. I flip to my text app and read a message:

Kylie: Hey. Are you there? I think it's time for us to talk.

I respond on his behalf. This is Kane. Beckett isn't available right now.

The dots move for a few seconds. Oh. Okay. Thanks. No need to tell him I texted. Thanks anyway. I just wanted to apologize, well, for everything.

I don't know why, but my heart pounds after seeing that. Beckett wouldn't hold a grudge, and seeing her apology triggers something in me. Gene never apologized, not even at the end when I held his bleeding body. He just kept repeating over and over he'd done it for Brit. Erzulie isn't cut from the same cloth. She's hurting, she's in pain. She's just trying to find herself in a world where's she's as much the victim as I was. Then I recall what Caleb said about what she prefers to be called. My fingers fly. *Lee, this is completely not my place, but if you just need someone to talk to...* I hit Send.

Immediately she replies, *WHAT DID YOU CALL ME?*

Um, Lee? Someone mentioned you like being called that.

I do. It's just...few people do anymore.

What the hell am I supposed to say now? But I don't have to guess. She texts again. *Kane?*

Yes?

Thanks. I think I just needed to be reminded deep down of who I really am.

How unusual, I think. But moments later, the pilot is telling us to buckle in as we're getting ready to touch down. And with no idea of what we're about to face once we leave the sanctuary of the plane, I shove the conversation with Kylie Miles to the back of my mind.

For the moment.

Leanne

However you celebrate and whomever you celebrate with, may you find peace tonight.

— **Beautiful Today**

I slip out of the car and am practically swept away by the cold air pressing me forward to the last place I want to go and yet the sole reason I'm here. Quickly, I grab the bag I slipped into the trunk before I change my mind. After all, what news do I have to share with my Lee? I sure as hell haven't found the person who caused her murder.

It's anger over that which pushes me forward down the snow-covered gravel until I'm standing in front of the stone my parents tearily informed me was laid earlier in the week. *Months—it's been months she's lain beneath this cold dirt. Alone. Unacknowledged.* My head is down as I recall the number of times she pleaded with me to move to the city but I wouldn't. And as the business took off, I couldn't take time. No, I didn't make time. I thought we were making do with nightly phone calls.

"Lee, I've got a critical meeting tomorrow. I can't drive down to the city tonight." I scanned a tablet with a multimillion-dollar contract and struck through a clause I didn't agree with.

"But there's so much happening." My own face pouts back at me over FaceTime. *"Too much to share over a call."*

"Is it important? Why can't you share it with me now?"

"Because now you're busy. And as for it being important, well, it's just my whole life."

I can still hear her laugh after that comment as I fall to my knees at the base of her, our, tombstone etched with both our names as this plot was purchased to hold both of our souls when the day eventually came to lay our bodies to rest. A mournful wail escapes me when I read what my parents decided to inscribe it with:

I'm half a heart without you.

"God, Lee. I'm so sorry. I'm sorry for not getting away sooner and letting something come between us. I should have known. Then you wouldn't be gone. I could have done something. Anything."

The wind picks up as I pull a sleeping bag out of my bag. Then I pull out a small Christmas tree powered by a battery. "Every year, no matter where we were, you and I stopped what we were doing to wish each other Merry Christmas at midnight." A watery laugh bubbles up. "Mom and Dad swore we didn't even care about Santa, we just cared if we said it to each other. Don't think I'm letting that tradition go just because you're not able to say it back.

"If I could have anything for Christmas this year, I would ask for more time with you. All the years we were each others Lee. I never expected that to change—for us to become Leanne and Kylie. For you to become Erzulie and my life to go the way it has. I read your journal. Vut God, Lee, the more I've gotten to know you by stepping into your shoes, I understand you even more. Why didn't you tell me about any of the pain you were feeling?"

The wind whips through my jacket, a reprimand. I bow my head. "I had to do it. I have to know everything about you so I can find out who harmed you. I have to set your spirit free, my Lee. Maybe then, there can be peace.

"I never told you I did some research when you first announced your stage name—Erzulie. At first, I thought it was just a play off our name, Lee. But it was so much more than that, wasn't it?" I press my hand right over where Lee's ashes are buried. "The loa spirit's

Erzulie's symbol is her heart, and that's you. I've never known another person with a bigger heart than you. You embody femininity and compassion, just like the name you assumed. I just wish I'd given it this much thought when you were alive.

"Ah, Lee, you were right when you chose your stage name—Erzulie. Erzulie Fréda Dahomey, the Haitian African spirit of love, beauty, jewelry, dancing, luxury, and flowers. She is the Erzulie that's you, my beautiful twin. I'm certain she likely told her stories through song, seducing her lovers with her mysterious voice and tales as you so often did. But did you know there's more than one Erzulie, just like there were two of us?"

I draw my fingers through the snow around the tree and draw a heart with our initials on either side before going on. "Erzulie Dantòr is considered to be the loa of vengeance and rage in Haiti and the Dominican Republic. And that's who I am. That's the Lee this has made me."

A jagged line is placed in between our initials, and I whisper, "Beneath me lies half of my whole. Until I know for certain what happened to you, I can't move forward."

My phone beeps, letting me know the hour. I lean forward and press my lips against the ice-cold marble and whisper, "Merry Christmas, my Lee. I love you. Always."

As I gather my sleeping bag and shove it into my bag, my insides are filled with sharp icicles because I know even if I were to hear the rest of what should be said at the end of that sentence, I'll never believe it.

Love isn't forever. It can't be.

The next morning is dark instead of light. My mother ignores us, immediately splashing liquor into her coffee, while my father tries to ask me how I'm handling things in New York. When I respond, "Slowly," she immediately whirls around and accuses, "Why? Now you have time for your sister you didn't have before?" It shoves the knife of guilt even deeper.

"Mom, if Lee had let me know anything was wrong..." I begin.

"You're twins," she yells. "All your lives you had this 'twin talk' I could never understand. Yet, when it came down to it, you couldn't save your sister? Instead, you just happened to be there in time to watch her die?"

I stumble backward. My eyes dart to my father's, finding no accusation but no support. I get his lack of intervention on some level—he has a job to get my mother past her devastation. And me? Well, I have a job to find the order in something that has caused such devastation to our lives despite the fact we will never recover to be the same way we once were.

Pushing aside the gifts that were bought for me either before Lee died or were half-heartedly selected, I get to my feet and make my way to our old room, where I dumped my bag after I left the cemetery last night. Sitting in the middle of the space, I surround myself with the physical evidence of memories to sustain me long after I'm gone. Because it's obvious I can't stay.

Lee and I as babies, wrapped around each other in the same crib.

The two of us swimming together for the first time, trying to hold hands.

Running through the backyard. Falling down on the sweet-smelling grass. "All I wanted to do was be with you. Even when we were apart. What changed?" My voice is hoarse with unshed tears.

"You both grew up. It's natural that your personalities developed, sweetheart." My father's voice is a balm.

"Mom's right; I let Kylie down, Dad."

"You did no such thing. Your mother is grieving. If anything, you're going above and beyond to try to find answers. Leanne, look at me." Just like the text from Beckett's bodyguard, it's having someone call me by my name that jolts me into action. I whirl around and face him. "What are you doing? I see her name everywhere."

"I..." But before I can speak, he interrupts me. "You're trying to find out who killed her. That's why there's been no retraction. That's why you haven't had a press conference taking Castor back over."

I nod, able to give him this, believing it a gift. What I don't expect is the explosion that erupts. "Are you fucking crazy, Leanne? She was murdered!"

"I can't let it go, Dad! I can find out who killed her," I shout back.

"With what? A little hacking here? A little dipping into people's lives there? What is that going to do to *you*—your life? Your business?"

"What does it matter?" I scream, shocking him. I fling out my arm. "Seeing my face just causes you both more pain."

"No, Lee..." Then almost as if his mind acknowledges what he's subconsciously called me, a ripple of agony destroys his composure.

For long moments, there are no words. The only movement is the flickering of holiday lights from the neighbor's house across the street. Suddenly, fiercely, I'm glad they strung them up. "She deserves to have her killer caught."

"So, what? You're giving up your life to finding out what happened to your sister? In your heart, do you think Lee wants you to do that? Do you think in your heart your mother wants you to?"

Without hesitation, I answer, "Yes."

"No. All we'll have will be different answers. We still won't have her back."

"But we'll have closure, Dad. And from there, maybe she can find a way."

"Leanne, don't do this. You can't possibly know how dangerous the game you're playing is," he tries to warn me.

I open my mouth to tell him about the attempts that have been made on my life already—that the accident the week Lee died wasn't merely that—but close it when I see how haggard his face is, how the strain of the last few weeks has aged him.

For long moments, we stare at each other before I nod, breaking the eye contact. "Is there anything I can do for you before I go?"

His harsh sigh fills the room. "Why did I know you were going to say that?"

"Because seeing my face is just causing more pain. And maybe when I can give you both some closure, you can..." *What, Leanne?* I mock myself. *Look at me? Love me? Or is it maybe I can love myself again.* But I keep those thoughts to myself. "Is it okay to take a few pictures?"

His hand comes up as if he's going to touch me. It drops before it comes close. "Take whatever you want. And regardless of how you're feeling today, this is your home." Tears fill his eyes as he speaks the words.

I don't bother to acknowledge this will never be my home again. If the expression on his face is anything to go by, he already knows that. It stopped being home the day Lee died. Right now, the closest thing I have to a home is spent with a battery-operated Christmas tree. And that's okay. I never needed much to be happy, despite all of my gung-ho efforts to build my business to incomprehensible levels.

I just need the other half of my heart to share it with. And for a while last night, I had that.

KANE

What's the best gift you ever received? For me, it was a second chance.

— **StellaNova**

It's Christmas Day, and I've just uploaded my report, including the unusual text message I exchanged with Kylie Miles, to the server at Hudson Investigations. I kick up my legs to unobtrusively enjoy Beckett Miller's family Christmas when my phone buzzes with an incoming call from Caleb.

Stepping outside to take it, I growl, "Merry Christmas. Do you ever take a day off?"

"You've known me for years. Want to answer your own question?"

"You have three kids and an enormous family. Go do some family crap."

"Cassidy has already given me the stink eye, so I'll make this short. You called her 'Lee' in your text with Erzulie? Why?" Caleb demands.

"You mentioned she prefers to be called that in the office. I used my gut because it sounded like she needed a friend," I defend myself, wondering where this is going.

"She needs one more than you know, Kane. She needs to unburden on someone she can trust, and she can't even do that with the people closest to her."

I frown, because Caleb's words make no sense. Then the phone in my pocket buzzes. My hand automatically slips into my pocket, and it's a message from Beckett. *Merry Christmas, Kane! Hope you like your gifts.*

My lips part. If Beckett is texting me, then Caleb is calling me on the secure sat phone, which means we're running hot at Hudson Investigations. "What is it you're not telling me?"

"Do you feel like you can be read in and keep this data from your principal?" is his only response.

I ask the only question that matters in the moment. "Is it going to endanger his protection?"

I can practically visualize his lips curving across the line. "Merry Christmas, Kane. I'll call you back tomorrow at 8:30 your time. Be somewhere alone." Then Caleb disconnects the call.

I pull the phone away from my ear and press End. "Yeah, Merry Christmas. What the hell kind of present are you about to drop into my lap?"

But I know Caleb's a man of his word. There's no way I'll get any information before 8:30 tomorrow morning.

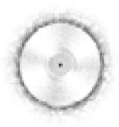

"There are no leads." Caleb's voice is filled with the kind of frustration that shouldn't be there for a man who just celebrated Christmas with his wife, his children, and a family crazy enough to plot taking over the world and actually manage it. "It's been two months of Lee living—no, I'd say surviving—her identical twin's life."

My eyes drift unfocused on the Texas landscape. "Maybe you're going about this the wrong way. Maybe someone isn't looking for Erzulie to appear, but..."

"For Lee to step forward and declare she's gone," Caleb says slowly. "If that's the case, then Kylie was trying to leave a clue when she had her sister's ID on her."

I've seen a lot of death. I've even had to kill, to protect my team, but the idea of a young woman in the prime of her life being brutally murdered still makes my stomach churn. "What do you want from me, Caleb?"

"I need you to do your damn job."

I frown. "What the hell does that mean?"

"Protect the principal. Keep Lee away from Beckett. She's a powder keg ready to explode. Intercept his next message from her."

"And do what?"

"And friend her."

"You're talking outright deception," I declare flatly.

"I'm saying your instincts were spot-on. And right now, I need them. Kane, Keene knows, Colby doesn't. Sam knows, Cal is locked out." He rounds out the list of partners. As the implications of his words penetrate, Caleb continues. "If it makes you feel better, tell her you're responding because Becks is too busy falling in love."

"There's a small fault in your plan," I inform him.

"There is?" He's surprised.

"Becks is already in love." I hang up on the sound of Caleb's laughter, thinking about everything he just shared and what it means for my charge.

And for the woman I exchanged barely a few words with the other night that has to be hurting.

Ignoring Caleb's edict, I pull out my own cell that's cloned to Beckett's. Before I can stop myself, I use my sat phone and type in the number and save it under "Lee." Then I send her a brief message. *Yesterday must have completely sucked. The firsts always do.*

I shove my phone in my pocket and wait, knowing she's likely running the number through Caleb, Keene, or possibly Sam. About thirty minutes later, I get a message back. *You know, Kane, stalking's really not a way to move ahead in your line of work.*

My lips twitch. Am I going to be spanked by my boss?

I know they're all married, but really? Is that such a punishment? she wonders.

I bark out a laugh. *You've met them?*

Some, yes. And stop trying to distract me. Why are you texting me?

It's easy to bring up a picture of the woman I knew as Kylie Miles in my mind. There's no doubt she's incredibly beautiful, but in a short conversation with her and one with my boss, I've learned Leanne Miles has the heart and courage of a warrior. *I could tell you it's because my boss wants me to friend you as well as make sure Beckett's protected while you're on your quest.*

She sends me an emoji with a scrunched-up face in return before typing, *Is that what you plan on doing, Kane? Because right now I'm doing okay.*

No you're not. I hit Send. Then, I keep typing. *I refuse to lie to you, Lee. I think you could use a friend.*

There's no response. Then, *And why should I trust you? Because you're telling me I should?*

Smart lady. No, because your instincts have led you this far. I've been ordered to curtail your visibility to Beckett.

There's no response.

I provoke her into doing so. Would your sister want you to live with her ghost?

HOW DARE YOU? You have no idea what it was like between us. If you don't want me speaking with Beckett, that's fine but you don't get to question my actions. You don't know me.

I type out a message. *I know the pain that lives inside you, Lee.* But when I hit Send, it comes back Undelivered.

And I stare down at the message in disbelief. "The little minx blocked me." Then a smile breaks across my face. "Good for her."

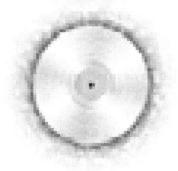

A few days after New Year's, I receive a stilted message from Lee. If Beckett hasn't received a call yet from Carys, he's going to. I'd appreciate if you'd pass that along.

Uh-oh. I pull my principal's cell out but don't see any missed calls. I flick the ringer on and quickly respond back while I have the opportunity. *Anything I should know?*

I'm certain you'll find out. Have a lovely day.

How are you?

Fine. Goodbye, Kane.

Wait. Please let's talk, Lee.

Stop. Just stop.

Stop what? I stop moving to where I hear Beckett talking with the mother of his child on the lanai to hand over his phone. The dots move furiously.

You don't know what it was like for us. We were one soul. We shared one lifeline. And I was late. Because of it, she's gone. I can't shake that feeling.

You're wrong. I do understand.

Were you a twin, Kane? she fires back.

No, I was a soldier. The lives I was responsible for may not have shared my own blood, but their blood is still on my hands. This time I'm pissed enough to be the one who blocks her, just as Beckett's phone rings. I see Carys's name on the caller ID and answer it. "Hello, Carys. Let me get Beckett."

"Please don't interrupt him if he's in the middle of something." Her voice is droll.

"Do I look like I have a death wish?" I mutter aloud.

"Fortunately, no. And if you value your hearing, you may want to take cover. He's not going to be happy."

"Thanks for the warning." I bound up the stairs to the back of Paige's lanai and knock. Beckett's rude "Go away, Kane" doesn't deter me. "It's Carys. She says it's important."

"Crap, Paigey. I need to take this." Beckett reaches for his phone.

Paige shifts in his arms but doesn't move out of them.

I slide out of their view and head back toward the side yard to ignore the ache of my conversation with Lee.

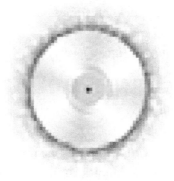

Later that night, an email from an address I don't recognize from the Hudson server appears in my work inbox. It's titled *My Blood*. After running it through the normal checks, I open it and swiftly inhale every ounce of air in the room.

The first picture is two babies swaddled in matching pink outfits.

The second is blonde toddlers dressed for a birthday party.

The third is two little girls lying together eating carrots in the grass.

More and more photos of two girls identical in every way until they got older and began dressing differently. It suddenly becomes easy to pick out Leanne from Kylie. And I ache when the last image is the blogger StellaNova capturing Lee singing over Kylie's grave long after the funeral service is over.

The message is simple. Every time I close my eyes, this is what I see. She was the other half of me. She died and I know there was something she needed to tell me. In that, and in so many other ways that have been pointed out to me, I let her down.

I have to live with that.

But I owe you an apology, Kane. I'm so deeply sorry for those you lost, soldier.

I hope you know, that you believe down to your soul, there was likely nothing you could do to have changed the outcome of his death. You made the only call you could. He was a traitor to everything you were fighting for. How dare he betray everything you stood for, bled for? You did everything by the book. What was the alternative? You could have died yourself if you didn't take the shot.

You were right, and I was wrong. I guess we all have our own ghosts. They pop up everywhere, don't they? Shadowing us no matter how far we try to disperse them.

It almost makes a person wish they could become one to escape the pain.

Terrified I drove this woman into doing something drastic, I immediately reply to the email, only to find the email address doesn't exist. Frowning as I begin to dial Caleb, I wonder how she obtained my work email. The minute he picks up, I'm royally chewed out, ending with "I said friend her, not lecture her."

"Is she okay?"

"She's fine," he reassures me.

"She's holding on to guilt she's likely to make a mistake," I press.

"That's not in question, Kane. It's why I read you in. But the game is already in play. It's too late to pull her out now. Especially since she now has to be in the headspace to perform in front of millions of people at the Grammys."

"The call from Carys," I surmise.

"You got it. I don't know what you said to her, but way to go, hotshot. She said for now if we have anything to share about the case to work through Carys. She doesn't want to speak with any of us."

"Caleb, did you give her my email?" I question.

There's a moment's pause before he bellows out a laugh. "No, and neither did anyone else. I think I'll leave you to wonder about that—and her—for a while." He disconnects the call in my ear. I'm certain if he was at the office, he'd have slammed down the receiver.

As I sit on the couch I've been bunking on since we landed in Texas, I wonder if it's too late to make a resolution for the new year. If I could, I'd take the words I harmed this woman with and fling them out. Instead, I'd ask her if she needs help to make some order out of the mess she presently finds herself in.

It's something I wish someone would have offered me in Azerbaijan.

With that last thought, I toss my cell on the table and fall back against the cushions, frustrated. Then I shoot straight up as Caleb's words penetrate.

Who is Leanne Miles?

Snatching up my cell, I begin with a simple online search, and once I get past what I now know are the fake obituaries, my eyes widen even as my lips curve upward. "No fucking way."

KANE

 84

What the hell does a guy have to do to get tickets to the Grammys? Beg? I'm good at begging. Just ask my ex.

— @PRyanPOfficial

Now don't you wish you were nicer about those Brendan Blake tickets? @PRyanPOfficial #HereICome #LA #Grammys

— @CuTEandRich3

"Leanne Miles, CEO of Castor Industries Inc., was considered by many to be one of the most brilliant software developers on the planet," Sam Akin confirms the next day when I call him at the office. "Her death was mourned. Every year at Defcon, from the time she was eligible, she and the core team she assembles from Castor actively compete for the Black Badge."

"Stop speaking computer, Sam," I order. "Talk to me like I'm three."

"Okay, wrap your mind around this. Leanne Miles is considered by most to be one of the most brilliant artificial intelligence developers on the planet. And the contract they announced she won with the DoD wasn't her first stint with the government. She's likely supported missions the public isn't even aware of all from her mountainside office."

"So, you're saying someone like her could get into our systems?" I question sharply.

Sam laughs. "With one hand tied behind her back and possibly her eyes closed. Are you kidding me? If I could, I'd get down on my knees and beg for Caleb and Keene to approve her to upgrade every aspect of our network I don't have time to work on. She's the best of the best, Kane. She wrote the encryption software we use today to protect Hudson's data as her senior year project at MIT." Sam is so enthused about Leanne, he doesn't realize he's speaking about her in the first person to someone who shouldn't know she's alive.

"I thought you were the best of the best," I challenge him. I know for a fact Sam Akin has a resume that's easily a mile long with accolades from the president himself.

"I'm a *think on my feet in the moment* kind of guy. Leanne Miles is the person you want at your back making sure your tracks are covered. I swear, the day they announced she died, every cretin on the Dark Web held a memorial for her. I attended a few, and no joke, there was some serious mourning going on. Granted, the tears were black, and they led to some awful shit happening... Hey, why all the questions about her?" he regains himself to ask.

"Her sister is friendly with my principal." I mean, it's not a lie.

"And you want to see if they have the same skill set?" Sam jumps to a logical—if erroneous—conclusion. "No, Kylie Miles took her degrees in math and parlayed them to music. Same principles if you think about composers writing in patterns and rules. Plus, she had courses on music theory—"

"Sam," I ground him in reality. "One last question?"

"Sure."

"If Leanne Miles were alive today, would you ever know if she were in Hudson's systems?"

"Nope. I'd never have a clue," he admits cheerfully. "She is seriously that damn good. In fact..."

Great. Just great. I interrupt him before his enthusiastic loose lips can get us both in trouble. "Thanks, man. We'll have to grab lunch when I'm back in the office."

"From what I hear, you're heading to LA soon. I have to tell you, Iris would come out of retirement in order to join Beckett's team."

Sam names his wife, a notorious linguistics specialist who now only does special assignments with foreign dignitaries.

"No dice."

"Tickets to a show?"

I hesitate before admitting, "I don't even know when Beckett's touring next."

"This phone call has been completely depressing, Kane. First, you bring up Leanne Miles, and then you're going to force me to tell Iris her persistent refreshing of Beckett Miller's website is fruitless. I think I'm going to go beg my cousin for a coconut cake to cheer me up."

"Life sucks. Beg hard," I tell Sam right before I hang up, and an insidious thought pops into my head. *What if whomever killed Kylie wasn't after her but after Leanne?* Pulling out my sat phone, I send that quickly to Caleb.

Seconds later, it rings. "Talk."

I repeat to him the information Sam told me. "Caleb, you know as well as I do that means government contracts. That means domestic and international terrorists. That means—"

"You're doing your job," he cuts me off quietly. "Leanne has had us so focused on her sister's life, spouting off about things that were hidden from the press about Kylie, we've barely had the chance to skim the surface about her own past. And trust me, I'm not a fool. I'm well aware of the mind in that woman. There's way more there than what she presents to the world than a former world-class hacker turned government contractor. The question is, how did you connect A to Z so fast?"

I inform him with great relish, "She hacked Hudson last night."

His frustration is palpable. "Again? What did she access this time?"

"How the hell am I supposed to know? I *know* she sent me an email from an address that didn't read an external sender." The cursing on the other end of the line would be amusing if I didn't have to admit, "She sent me pictures of her and her sister. At first I thought it was because she was telling me I was a jackass." I leave off the rest of the email about which I'll discuss with Leanne when our day of reckoning comes. I have to find out how she knows about Gene, but that's between me and her.

"You are a jackass, but you're one that might save her life," Caleb candidly agrees.

"Thanks," I grumble.

"Let me call Carys. We're going to have to refocus the investigation entirely. I was getting ready to tell her we'd hit a brick wall, but you might have just shone a new light on this." He hangs up.

I pull up the email once Caleb hangs up, and I reread the words Leanne sent me for the millionth time. I hope you know, that you believe down to your soul, there was likely nothing you could do to have changed the outcome of his death. You made the only call you could.

And more than any words of comfort my family has tried to drill into me, than fellow soldiers, her short message causes the first pinprick in the bubble of guilt I've been living with since I had to pull the trigger to stop my childhood friend from selling military secrets in the war-torn mountains of Azerbaijan after he'd shot and killed two other members of our unit. "For more money than you can wrap your mind around. It will set me, Brit, and Maddie up for life." Gene tried to convince me as his hand held the small drive containing the specs of our warfighter out to the foreign agent.

That's when I heard the snap of the twig behind me. And without hesitation, Gene lifted his service revolver from where it was resting at his thigh and pulled the trigger twice. It wasn't until after I pulled the trigger once, twice, ensuring the operative dropped, that I whirled around to see Adams had hit the ground. Right next to him lay Baldy. I whirled back to find Gene's barrel trained directly on my head.

A perfect shot. A kill shot.

One to be delivered by my best friend because of fucking money. Greed—inexhaustible in its need to be satisfied, including the need to be fed by blood and tears. Gene certainly had both of mine to pay the price for his deeds. My finger was just a little bit faster, but I damn well know he would have pulled the trigger to have ended my life. The wetness on my cheeks mingled with the blood that flowed down his face as I cradled his limp body in the wet snow until a chopper arrived to evacuate us all. And inside, I felt as dead as the three other bodies surrounding me.

That is until I bumped into the woman I assumed was Kylie Miles on the street.

Now, as I clutch my phone in my hand, the words of a practical stranger send a strange ripple of peace through me. The dam I've kept around my heart bursts, and I feel a geyser of emotion rush back so fast I'm worried I might drown. As the painful pounding settles down, an insidious thought works its way into my mind.

Was it Kylie I crashed into that long-ago afternoon I was following Beckett in those early days from Carys's office?

Or was it Leanne?

KANE

January

Saratoga Springs, N.Y. Cybersecurity attacks can happen anywhere! Even e-readers can be hacked by just opening a single e-book infected with malicious content, according to research published at Defcon. #defcon29
— **Castor Newsroom**

A few days later, we've flown back to New York amid a million and one protests from Beckett. I've never been so grateful to have dumped him with Mitch so I can get some peace and quiet in the office, poring over paperwork just so I can escape from Beckett's persistent black mood.

Once I've completed the normal assortment of reports, expenses, and documentation of Beckett's antics, I begin tackling some of the legwork Caleb assigned to me regarding Leanne Miles. Since this work is still code worded, Caleb had Sam grant me access to Keene's office on the executive floor while he works from our Norwalk office.

It's well after hours, so no one is around to disturb me while I dive into Leanne Miles's business ventures. I'm recovering from the shock that anyone her age could have built an empire so complex as I keep running into dead ends, shell corporations, and enough government contracts that make me grateful that someone else handled all this nonsense when I was in the military.

I'm in the middle of reviewing a contract between Castor and a friendly government when a message from an unknown sender pops up on my screen. Contracts are so boring. That one was particularly more awful than most others to negotiate. Don't you have anything better to do with your time, Kane?

Heart pounding, my gut tells me this is Leanne. I bank everything on being right and type back, *Aren't you supposed to be practicing things —like learning to sing?*

It's not the singing part that's the problem. We've been able to do that since we could talk. It's the part where I have to do so in front of an audience of people who believe I'm her.

Bingo. I focus on the small text box, and my fingers tap out to trust but verify, *How do I know this is you?*

Simple, I'm bored watching Beckett being an ass at rehearsals. The guy you left with him—tall, dark, tattooed?—is justifiably amused and not trying to hide it. As a bonus, it's possible Mick and Carly are going to rip his head off soon if he keeps snapping at them.

What's he wearing? I reach for my cold coffee and take a sip, grateful for the caffeine if I'm about to go head-to-head with one of the smartest minds in the world.

Who, Beckett? Before I can answer, she continues. *Well, his shirt is buttoned for once. Are you sure* he's *not a pretend Beckett Miller? A Beckett-bot maybe?* I start coughing as I choke on my own laughter as I had that exact same thought when we left the condo earlier.

Beckett's been like a zombie since we left Texas, I inform Leanne.

Ahh, is that what the problem is. I thought it was...

What? I ask when she doesn't say any more.

Just something Lee used to say—that there was something wrong with Beckett deep inside. That he had a sad soul.

"Holy hell. I've been living in the man's back pockets for years, and it hasn't been until recently I've noticed how he is without Paige." To Leanne, I reply, *He's temperamental.*

You don't have to tell me that. One simple misstep going to that party and phew. I haven't had a royal ass chewing like that since I was sixteen.

Why did you go?

Because I found a journal where Lee declared Snowy-T as one of five people she would like to run over with a bus. She had a smart mouth, but she wasn't vicious like that.

Huh. I never thought of that angle. I probe a bit deeper. *Did you think he'd try to drug you?*

She shoots back, No. Not until I woke up the next day. And honestly, I'm not entirely certain it was him. Snowy-T's a piece of slime—trust me. But if he was anything like Hutnik I'm fairly certain he'd have tried to take advantage of the situation, not allowed Beckett to haul my ass out of there. I'm still trying to comb through the elevator footage to determine who might have had a beef with Lee. Why do so many people want to attend a slime ball's party?

Because they want to be famous for no reason other than being famous? I suggest.

Lord deliver me. Don't we get enough of that with reality TV. Her response causes me to crack up. She's a damn firecracker.

How long will it take you to scan the footage? I almost reluctantly bring us around to work.

Who knows? There's this singing thing, you know.

I smile briefly before scrolling up and focusing on another name she mentioned leaps out at me. *Who's Hutnik?*

Lee's former agent before she signed with Wildcard. SOB liked to get his acts in compromising positions by drugging them. Who do you think released the pics of her half-dressed to StellaNova?

You're kidding?

Not even close. A series of angry faces appears.

I try to do the same but realize I have no idea how in this unusual chat window Leanne's created. Instead, I go low-tech and send her a colon and shift+9. The frown face is quickly mocked by the woman on the other end of the line. We really need to up your keyboarding skills if we're going to continue chatting like this, Kane. Since I know you're using a Mac right now, hold down your Command, Control, and Space bar keys at the same time. All these pretty pictures come up for you to play with, she taunts.

Considering she's hacked through my company's firewall with the ease of a baby taking their first steps, I give her that play before sending her an actual frown.

She sends me back a pair of hands that simulate applause.

I probe gently, You seem better.

Her dots move furiously before I get a message that rocks me. I'm certain you know the hardest things to give up on are hope, faith, and trust. Once you've lost those, it's impossible to go on believing. You just feel like you're perpetually sinking. I don't know if you're onto something or if I'm going to sink right back down into wondering if I'll ever find the answers—which is where I was spiraling to. Let's just say it's nice to have someone with a different perspective on the team. It helps battle back the despair for now.

Leanne, I start to type, but another message of hers pops up. And what it says lets me know that Caleb shared enough about our conversations with her to rebuild a tentative truce and possibly a modicum of trust.

Two things. First, this contract was never executed. I yanked the deal at the last moment because the terms and conditions couldn't be met by my team. Second, Sam Akin is one of my heroes. What he did... Anyway, when this is over, you all will be secure. For as long as I can keep you that way.

The message box disappears before I can reply. "Holy crap, did that just happen?"

Then my phone buzzes. When I glance down, there's a text from Lee. All it says is Yes. Oh, and you know people with certain skills can turn on your computer or phone mic whenever they want, right? Really Kane, you're a smart guy with great instincts. How were you that obtuse about Beckett's emotional state before? BTW who is Paige?

"Leanne," I warn.

Nighty night pops up on my phone's text message. I flip over to Settings and see I haven't unblocked her number. "I guess she took care of working around that little problem." I wheeze out a shaky laugh.

Leaning back in my chair, I realize how completely over my head I really am. Truth be told, I'm not certain if it's excitement or fear that causes my heart to pound when I come to the conclusion she'll be back.

I just don't know when.

Leanne

26

It's Erzulie's twenty-sixth birthday. I suppose I should make some smart-ass comment on the obvious fact she ran to the local baker picking up a dessert to dine at home, but it just seems wrong in light of what happened to her.

Try to have a happy one. If you can.

— **Moore You Want**

"Happy birthday to us. Happy birthday to us. Happy birthday, my sweet twin, happy birthday to us." I whisper the song as I sit on the floor of her condo, a single candle burning amid the circle of twenty-five of them around me. I scoured her place to find just enough. And since not a single one would fit on the small cupcake I bought to celebrate with my sister, they're just setting off enough light to make me believe it's possible Lee's going to walk in the door any minute with her boisterous laughter, asking me, "What the hell are you doing?"

God, I wish that were the case.

"There's not enough space in my heart for this pain, Lee," I whisper in a hush. All day long, Lee's cell pinged with good wishes mingled with concern. My secure phone had a single text that made me want to drop it off Lee's tenth-floor balcony. *Another day, another year. Keep moving and it won't hurt as much.* But at least my boss acknowledged the date in his way.

My personal cell sat still and quiet. Nothing. Not a peep from my parents, but they're likely pissed I didn't make the drive to New

Hampshire. After the debacle at Christmas, that's the last thing I would do. I tried to explain that to my father the other day, and he simply hung up the phone.

"God, Lee, there are some days the pain I feel is killing me. I've done everything I can think of to solve this, and all the signs are pointing to one of two things—a random insanity or me." My breath shudders in my chest. "What if I got you killed? It's too late to hide things from you now. You suspected before, but despite your best attempts, I'm certain you're in Heaven, causing a riot."

I reach forward and trail a finger through the mounds of butter-cream frosting. The idea of tasting it makes me nauseous, but Lee would expect it. I pop my finger in my mouth and suck down the sweet cream cheese flavor. Knowing I have to, I lift the carrot cake to my lips and take a small nibble. Afraid if I taste much more, I'll be sick, I set the cupcake back down. Gasping for breath, I manage to control the rush of emotions to hiss, "You know now. You know who I am, what I've been doing. There was so much careful planning that went into constructing my cover—the prodigy hacker. But how could I say no, Lee? How could I turn my back on helping to save lives—particularly when I was shown evidence that me, you, Mom, and Dad were already on people's radars? What was I supposed to do? Let one of you be kidnapped with no protection? No one to turn to if shit hit the fan?" I scrub my face against my knees. "And look what happened. Was I not careful enough? Did I make a mistake? Not cover my tracks? Did I get too arrogant?"

A rush of wind flows through her condo from the cold January air, threatening the light of the candles. "I know, talk about arrogance. It could easily have been you. But I've had your 'bus' list checked out. Let me assure you, if I'd known Sebastian Tim had pawed you, we'd have exposed him much sooner. Oh, didn't think I'd find that out?" I tell my twin sweetly. "Asshole recorded everything. I enjoyed going through his drive. I dropped a copy of all his videos on his boss's work cloud. Consider that a birthday gift."

The breeze rushes through again. I imagine it's Lee's laughter.

"As for Snowy-T, well, there's not enough words for the way he's a complete douchebag. I had a hard time preventing my eyes from bugging out. And, well, someone ended up drugging me." I feel the same sickness that crawled up over me the next day begin as panic begins to surge. "My training included the ability to resist most drugs, Lee. That was another attempt to kill you, me, us. Damnit, which is it? Who is it?" I shout.

Forcing myself to calm down because this isn't what we're supposed to be talking about on our birthday, I change the topic. "I don't know how you deal with Beckett Miller. He's an interfering goat."

I can practically hear Lee roaring with laughter. "No, you don't get it. He has a daddy complex. He lectured me worse than the time we borrowed Dad's car for going to Mackie's party. Then again, that might have to do with the fact my handler cloned my phone and texted Beckett to get me out of there. And, of course, StellaNova got a picture of the whole debacle. Not your boy's best look. But now he sees it as his mission to drag me from my sadness. Doesn't he realize that's never going to happen?" The last is whispered but no less heartfelt.

To stop myself from drowning in tears, I jam my fingers back into the cream cheese icing and shove them in my mouth. "Secrets are dark and dangerous, which is why I never shared I had any. Even when I couldn't tell you what I really did, you always had this certain look you used to give me when I talked about Castor. I loved it because you alone understood me. I knew it without words. There will never be another person who will measure up."

At that a gust of wind comes in and blows out all the candles except one. I give a watery laugh. "Time to make a wish? Okay, Lee. Here goes."

I want Lee's death to stop shadowing my dreams, I think fervently. Then I lean over and blow out the last candle. Standing up, I move over to the double doors leading to the veranda, and I'm hit with a blast of cold air quite unlike the others. "Well, what did you expect me to ask for? To fall in love? To have a happily ever after? Christ,

Lee. How am I supposed to live with myself if I can't figure out who did this to you?"

And on that, I shut the doors on the first birthday I've spent without my twin.

The next night, I tell Kane about what I did to celebrate while he's reviewing a contract that's about four layers deep. Part of me feels a little bad, but he'd need access to a classified proposal system to read the actual agreement. The placeholder agreement he's struggling through has enough legalese and references to confuse the average person seven different ways from Sunday. *No, I just miss everything about her. For five minutes with her, I do anything. I'd take the good, the bad, the annoying.*

I understand that all too well. There are so many unanswered questions because of the suddenness of his death, he replies.

Yes! There's times I feel like I'll just walk through her door and I expect her to look up from the couch. Or my phone to ring.

The key logger captures words as he types and then backspaces them. And my heart melts a little as he struggles with trying to find the right words to comfort me. This is a good man—Captain Kane McCullough.

I quickly send a text using my phone. *He was completely screwed over.*

Seconds later, I get one back. *Agreed, Qoza.*

I hesitate for a moment before typing, Make certain he's okay if something happens.

Qəza...

Promise me.

He hesitates, but I get what I want when I see his *Promise.*

I accept his message as my due. Besides, Kane finally found his words. And sometimes you just wish it would ring one more time so you could get the answers to the questions you never got a chance to ask.

Before I can type anything in response, Kane asks me a question that startles me. *You never said—did you make a wish for your birthday?*

Yes.

Then, I hope it comes true, Leanne. I hope everything you wished for comes true.

A warmth I never expected fills me. Thank you, Kane. That means...everything.

You're welcome.

Leanne

Rumor has it that indie goddess Erzulie—a.k.a. Kylie Miles—doesn't have to work another day in her life based on the amount she inherited from her sister, Leanne. That amount was made public with the final filings of the stock transfer on behalf of the Castor Trust. However, Erzulie continues to dedicate herself to her music. The real question is which Erzulie will be showing up at the Grammys? Will it be the seasoned performer or the woman rightfully still in the throes of grief?

— StellaNova

"Let's take it from the top," Kristoffer Wilde suggests kindly.

I sit with Lee's guitar strapped over my shoulder, and I strum the opening bars to her current hit—my song!—before I falter. "I can't." I swing the guitar strap over my neck and lay the precious instrument in the stand.

Unlike many other people of his ilk, he doesn't launch into a tirade that this is what he's paying Erzulie for—though he is. He simply steps up next to me and offers me his silent support before questioning, "You've played before a large crowd—albeit with some hiccups."

I can't help but press my lips together to prevent laughing at the understatement. "Albeit with that," I manage to agree.

"Then it must be the song," he concludes as if I haven't spoken.

I run my hand through my hair before admitting, "She wrote it for me, for us."

"Ahh." His hand comes up and pats my shoulder. "If she were here instead of me, what would the two of you sing to one another?"

At that, I begin to sing a cappella an old, classic love song. When I finish, there's silence between us. I finally break it by whispering, "We always said that song captured our ideal love story."

"I think that's beautiful."

"Me too." We lapse back into silence. I feel Kris shift and prepare myself to sing another Erzulie song until Kris shocks me to my back teeth.

"Let me speak with a few people, but I don't see why you couldn't sing that the night of the Grammys. They're already willing to bend over backwards because you agreed to play," Kris considers.

"I don't want to make this more difficult for you. I can do it," I say carefully.

"But would she want you to, Lee? That's the question I've been asking myself. And I keep finding my answer to be 'she wants you to be happy.'" Turning me back toward my sister's guitar, he asks, "Do you know the music to accompany it?"

Feeling a bit lighter, I answer, "I do."

"Then let's get back to work. From the top."

And I begin to do exactly what Lee would do in this situation—I lose myself in the music. At least, just for a little while.

When I finish, Kris smiles. "Now, let's work on your walk."

I balk. "My walk?"

And that's when the esteemed Kristoffer Wilde causes me to fall backward off the stool when he does more than a fair imitation of the combination sashay and saunter my sister glided everywhere with. "Talk about wishing I had a video recorder to show Carys," I murmur.

He abruptly stops and pins me with a hawkish glare before announcing, "Now, it's your turn."

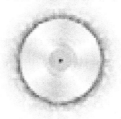

Later that night, I type the same words I said to Kris after he wanted me to walk the walk. *Nope. No way. No how.*

"Why not?"

I run my fingers through my hair in frustration. Because. Watching movies about clowns is creepy. I don't care if it is It and the book is freaking brilliant.

Kane bursts out laughing, which I can hear through the microphone I turned on. I asked if he minded this time, to which he drolly replied, "What? Giving me advance warning? Go for it."

To which I typed, Well, I could have just done it.

"True."

Besides, this way you don't have to type as much.

"And I appreciate that more than you know. Some of us weren't born with a keyboard in our hands."

Hardy har har.

So, in the process of bantering back and forth, we've been reviewing more contracts that were dumped into a file. What Kane doesn't know is I've accessed a drive where my boss backed up all of my contracts. When I'm not practicing singing and getting ready for a very public humiliation I'm enduring in hopes of bringing Lee's killer forward, I'm reviewing them based on a risk-rating system I established long ago: interest to national security, client, asset, activity, information, volume of data—the list goes on. With a few clicks, I dropped a bunch in Kane's hands and have focused on the higher higher-risk ones myself—the ones some of the other agents would be obligated to shoot me—or the big man himself wouldn't hesitate to toss me into a cell—if they were ever read by someone outside the agency.

But after I called the deputy director of operations an ass clown and Kane mimicked some of the movie's most famous lines, I typed, *No, no clowns. We don't do clowns in this house.*

"What do you like to do?" he asked casually.

I thought about the answer before typing, I don't often have a lot of down time but I love sitting out on my deck in the morning.

"Even in the winter? Wait, where do you live?"

I ignore the second part of his question for now. I'll take my morning coffee with me, even if I'm seeing it from the other side of the night. Watching the sun rise is incredible.

"Are there a lot of nights where you do that? See the sun rise from the night before?" His voice has a forced casualness to it I'd have to be deaf not to hear.

How do I explain this without telling him everything about who I am? Finally, I give him a good portion of the truth. There's a vulnerability when the world's asleep. It leaves our hearts and minds open to so much— including new ideas. And attacks, but I don't share that. But there are nights when my eyes just won't close. I can't lose that energy. A shapeless idea in the darkness that sparks in the light of the stars illuminates into something magical under the first rays of the sun.

He doesn't say anything for a long while, but when he does, I have to fight the urge to flip on the camera to see him. I have to wrap my arms around myself not to hack into Hudson's system to pull up a picture of his face. I fight hard not to dig deep in the murky shadows of the internet so I can learn more about Kane McCullough. His voice is tender when he murmurs, "I thought you said you didn't write music, Leanne."

My fingers hover over the keyboard to take that next step, but finally, I just type, *Maybe I'll be able to see it again someday.*

Then to get us back on topic, I drop a file into his folder and ask him to look into it. Kane quickly agrees. And we stop our banter to get back to work.

KANE

28

I went to a joint bachelor/ette party last night. Instead of strippers, we sang karaoke. Why? Will someone just give me a good reason? Was the intent to induce projectile vomiting? If so, mission accomplished. My apologies #mtasubway

— **@PRyanPOfficial**

"Just because she hasn't been at *your* practice doesn't mean she hasn't been practicing, Becks," Carys's exasperated voice comes through the line as we ride with Beckett to the studio located in an old warehouse in Tribeca.

"I booked enough studio time for all of us to practice, Carrie. It's ridiculous she's not using it," Beckett counters.

"No, you're just a cranky ass because Erzulie is doing what she needs to do without your omnipotent presence."

Riding next to him, I have the pleasure of catching him opening and closing his mouth before he presses the button to disconnect the call. "She's such an ungrateful wench," Beckett declares to no one in particular.

Mitch, of course, eggs him on. "Erzulie?"

"No, Carys! Here I am calling as a concerned friend, and she doesn't take me seriously." Mitch steers the vehicle down the small side street where I know the entrance to Erzulie's building is located.

Beckett perks up. "Hey, maybe we should stop in and see if she's around?"

I quickly squash that idea, knowing Leanne is likely reviewing another set of contracts in advance of our rendezvous later tonight. I suggest, "How about we get you to your bandmates on time so they don't swing for your head?" reminding Beckett of his drummer, Carly, flinging drumsticks off his chest during yesterday's rehearsal despite his massive apologies because he was over half an hour late since he was FaceTiming with Paige.

"Which head? That does make a difference," Beckett wonders.

I manage to keep a straight face, even as the rest of the car snickers. Fortunately, we pull up to the entrance of the studio right then. I slide out before I lose my composure. It really doesn't do well to give Beckett the upper hand in any situation—something I need to remind his team of.

But I do allow myself a quick grin as we reach the elevator. Though I suppose it is a valid question in his case if what I walked in on between him and Paige is a regular thing.

You did what? Leanne's comment comes back so fast, I'm in shock. I've never met anyone who can type this fast.

"What the hell was I supposed to do? I couldn't just forget I saw her there," I reply indignantly.

Umm...

"Exactly. She was naked, Leanne. Head-to-toe naked. And she

was lying across the entrance to Beckett's dressing room backstage like a pagan sacrifice."

That's so—

"Don't say it," I warn her.

—sweet. Not many men would have taken their custom-made jacket off to cover a groupie.

"She lost the coat when she was arrested. Made for some interesting tabloid photos. And her father a congressman? Yeah, that went over real well." I take a drink of the bottled water next to me.

Oh, I bet. Forget whatever bribe he was offering, they had newspaper gold right there. I mean, she'd just hussied-up and got shot down by the Beckett Miller and was arrested in the buff? That's worse than... Leanne names a recent computer scandal involving classified documents and overseas escorts.

But it's her phraseology that causes my lips to curve up in a smirk. "Up until you used the phrase 'hussied-up,' I thought you were some sort of badass."

You can take the girl out of the small town...

"I guess so. But in any event, I told you the story because I was trying to show you there's more to Beckett than meets the eye. And maybe demonstrate there's more to my job than simply following him around," I grumble.

Why do you need to? If you like what you do, who do you have to justify it to but yourself?

There's no way for me to express how her words make me feel, so I don't even try. I just let my lips curve and keep on telling her stories about some of the more interesting experiences I've had working with Beckett since I've left the Marines.

KANE

29

Online dating is not for the faint of heart. First, there's a profile so detailed it makes your annual physical almost amateurish. Then, let's talk about sex, baby. Do you or don't you? And if so, with who and how many? Do you want hearts and flowers or a 'wham-bam-thank you-ma'am'? By the time I get around to meeting the individual in person, there's nothing to say.

If any of you have any suggestions, please share them.

— Sexy&Social, All the Scandal You Can Handle

"Team of twenty down the red carpet. Team of fourteen inside. When he's onstage, ten in the wings—five on each side." I lay the plans on the table and point to the sides of the area layout where I want our people stationed.

"What about this spot right here?" Mitch points to the one area where we don't have coverage on the red carpet. It has a big X marked through it.

I shake my head in frustration. "Stationary cameras for the live broadcast. I tried everything to get a person up there, but unless Beckett wants to buy a news station in the next twenty-four hours, it's a no go."

"Shit. I hate blind spots."

"Me too." My finger taps at the spot before I make a mental note to point out the problem to Keene later. He's sending people down the red carpet with Leanne. Thankfully, she finally capitulated after we had an intense discussion about it, where I yelled and she finally typed in all capital letters, "I CAN TAKE CARE OF MYSELF!"

I informed her, "I don't care what you think you can do. You're a computer whiz. These people killed your sister, and I couldn't bear it if you're next."

I don't know if it was those words or her own logic kicking in, but she finally typed, *Fine. I'll arrange security.*

I don't know who is on deck, but they need to be aware of this spot and keep her out of range of it. In fact, I take out my phone and send him a message. *For Erzulie's team. Blindspot.*

Roger that. I'll pass it on, comes his reply a few minutes later.

I want to ask him who is covering her for those long minutes as she glides over the red carpet. The urge is so strong, it causes my hands to shake, but I can't. I have to focus on my principal and his safety. With that in mind, I tune back in to Mitch. "We'll have an extra team in LA, so when Beckett's in residence, we can arrange for some time off."

His lips twitch. "Have you shared this with the team yet?"

"Do I look insane? I'll set the schedule, and then I'll announce it."

"Smart man. Any special plans?"

I'm about to give him an immediate no, that I likely won't take any time off at all, but what comes out of my mouth is "I don't know."

"Well, if you need to work around someone's schedule, let me know." My brows raise in question. He just shrugs, causing me to ask, "Are you feeling okay?"

He opens and closes his mouth before huffing. "Ask me that at another time. I'll let you know. Are we good for now?"

"We are."

"What's the worst date you've ever had?" I ask her later that night.

I could pick out any of the ones Kylie sent me on, comes her immediate response. Leanne begins telling me all about how Kylie created one dating profile for the two of them. She'd then screen the guys on it by going out with them to vet them first. But only to check them out, you see. She was just making certain they were good enough for me. I'd have no clue. Then on the second date, they'd all look at me strangely like why don't you remember where we went or what we said? Or if we even kissed. The facepalm emoji follows that litany.

"Oh, come on. You're twins. You're not supposed to do that to each other." And immediately, I want to punch myself for not taking more care with my words. Here we are trying to find clues as to who or what may have led to her sister being killed and I refer to her in the first person. "Such an ass, McCullough."

"Don't beat yourself up, Kane. It's next to impossible for me to believe she's gone as well." Her voice comes through the computer, causing me to roll my chair back and knock into the L-shape of Keene's desk. It's dark, raspy. Familiar, yet it sends chills up my spine in ways her twin's never did. It's unique like the woman herself, despite the fact she had a mirror image for her entire life.

And between us, despite our online banter, falls an awkward silence. Just like a real first date, I recognize with startling clarity. My shoulders shake, trying to suppress my mirth at the image of two computers facing each other over a candlelit table in a dimly lit restaurant. "Well, if I knew my faux pas could cause this kind of drop-in, I'd have done it long ago."

"I don't know. You don't give the impression of a man who likes to make mistakes," she observes.

"That's because I've made more than my fair share."

She hums in the back of her throat, and everything inside me clenches in awareness. The fiery lick traveling up my spine is welcome. Deep down, I knew it. The moment our visions clashed a few years prior wasn't mere chance; it was a beginning. It wasn't our time then, and maybe now isn't all that better, but I know who she is.

And this time, I'll find her again.

Leanne

30

New York, N.Y. The Erzulie you'll see on stage at the Grammys has changed, yes. She's still the starry-eyed dreamer, but she's been dealt a harsh blow of reality, which I hope you all consider. Her voice will reflect all of that and more. I refuse to answer what she will be singing.

— **Wildcard Media Representative, Paula Stone, during a press call about the upcoming Grammys**

"Hey, Dad."

"Leanne." He doesn't say anything more, and for long minutes, neither do I.

Finally, I break the awkward silence. "How have you been?" Then I mentally kick myself in the ass. How the hell is my father supposed to be other than a complete wreck?

His answer pretty much confirms that. "Surviving."

I open my mouth to let him know I feel the same when he bites out, "You seem to have slid into your sister's shoes without much trouble."

"Dad, no. It's not like that," I begin. But he doesn't let me get any further.

"It appears to be just like that, Leanne. Your mother wonders if that's the real reason you made Kylie look like such an angel over the years—so you could just move from your life to hers."

"You don't mean this." My voice is barely a whisper. I feel a trickle of wetness down my cheek, and I impatiently wipe it away. "You don't understand..."

"I understand everything! It isn't Kylie getting on stage in a few weeks to sing at the Grammys—that's you! Do you think your sister would do that to you?" he yells.

"I think Lee would do anything..." I start.

He hangs up before I can finish telling him, "Anything to find out who killed me. Who destroyed our family. And that's what I'm doing, Daddy. Even if it makes you and Mom hate me."

Slowly, I replace the receiver and reach for the picture of me and Lee on her end table. "You would, wouldn't you? I can't rest until I know for certain, Lee."

Her image blurs, even as an insidious thought races through my mind. I have to protect them if you died because of me. Even if that means separating myself permanently.

"What's your family like?" I reach over and drag the bowl of popcorn next to me. I don't dare tap into the video in the office Kane's using. Not yet. If I did, I'd be down there instead of sitting in Lee's condo running scripts to suss out some of the people who are sniffing around her hard drive. *Idiots. Do they think she didn't have me watching her six? Just because I'm supposedly "dead" doesn't make her an easy target. Asswipes.*

But I tune in when Kane's smile infiltrates his voice. "They're a hoot. My sister and I believe our mother should have her own television show. She's a trip."

"Really? Tell me about her."

I listen as Kane tells me a few stories about his mother and almost upend the bowl laughing when he shares about his mother, cocks, and the day he met Beckett Miller. "Stop it. She can't be real," I manage to gasp.

"Completely, one hundred percent, no lies. That's my ma." And in his voice is so much love, it's palpable.

"She sounds amazing." I hear the wistfulness in my own words.

There's a pregnant pause. "You're not close with your own folks?"

I shake my head before realizing he can't see me. Too often as of late, I've forgotten we're not in the same room together. It's something I want to rectify soon, but I need to focus on the mission at hand. And that includes what I'm about to share. "We were. We *all* were. And then Lee died." I pause for a moment, gathering myself before I try to give voice to some of my innermost thoughts. "My whole life, I shared my soul and face with someone I loved more than any other person in the world. Now, she's gone." I take a few deep breaths to control the tears threatening to pour down my face. "I just never knew it would become my fault I died before she did."

Long seconds go by where the only thing keeping time are the beats of my heart. Finally, Kane speaks. "They blame you for your sister's death?"

"Maybe? I don't really know. I know my mother can't bear to look at me, and my father has to care for her."

"That's not how it should be," he declares hotly in my defense. It makes me want to race down to Hudson and throw my arms around him and pepper his face with kisses.

And yet, I still don't know what he looks like. Maybe for me it's meant that I fall in love with a person's soul before their face. After all, that's what happened with my Lee. And with her, we never exchanged a word for it to happen. With Kane, all we're doing is exchanging them, and I'm already feeling the same bonds snap into place, locking me to him. "It will work out the way it's supposed to," I whisper philosophically, though I have no idea if my mother will ever be able to look me in the face ever again.

I feel a small buzz against my leg. Swiping up my phone, I frown at the message. *Less flirting and more working.* I growl and lift my middle finger, waving it around the room. I'm not certain if he turned on my phone—something I taught him, ugh—or if he arranged to have my place bugged, but either way, let him deal with my very visible answer. I mumble under my breath, "You have no idea what my flirting would be like."

"Oh, I don't?" comes the amused voice on the other end of the line.

Christ, I wasn't muted, and Kane thinks the comment was for him. I drag air into my lungs before I return, "No idea." I pop some of the salty, buttered goodness into my mouth, chew like I don't have a care in the world, and wait for his rejoinder.

But in no way am I prepared for his voice to drop and his "Neither do you, Leanne. But I'm game if you are."

I promptly choke on a kernel. "Oh, holy hell."

There's lazy amusement dripping in his voice when he asks, "Are you all right? Do I need to send paramedics?"

"To get my heart started again, maybe," I admit.

His sexy laugh causes parts of me that have been dormant to rise. Hell, even the hair on the nape of my neck feels like it's floating independent of my skin. There's a fire burning in my blood caused by a maelstrom of emotions, none of which is vengeance. But sorting them out is for another night when my heart isn't jumping because it's just run the gamut of emotions from today's earlier castigation to a ridiculous longing for the faceless man on the other end of the line.

Leanne

Get a look at this fabulous picture of Kylie Miles one of our dedicated fans snapped today as she dashed out of a SoHo loft. This isn't a woman feeling nothing; she's feeling too much. And all I have to say is, welcome back, Erzulie. You've been missed.

With this picture, maybe I'll need to stroll by. After all, the photog told me he saw my dream man slipping in not long before Erzulie dashed out—Beckett Miller. I'd love to bump into him, if you know what I mean.

— Sexy&Social, All the Scandal You Can Handle

There's a small storm outside that caused the studio to cancel my solo time for today when all I wanted was to escape my thoughts. I wander around aimlessly searching for something, longing for something. Needing more. And I know this emotion well. It's a prelude to trouble, the kind of trouble that could tumble this house of cards I've precariously balanced amid a windstorm.

It was my choice to surround myself with the essence of Lee, but after yesterday, I need to escape. "What the hell is happening to me?" I shout aloud.

I'm certain one of the agency's shrinks would have some psychobabble about the stress of being undercover as my sister finally getting to me. And they'd be right. I was barely given a moment to grieve her loss before I was swept up into this quest for vengeance. For what? "To be abandoned by the same people who I was hell-bent on getting answers for?" I yell. Well, to be fair, my father knew I was going to be investigating Lee's death, but to this extent...

I'm so far from the sane, stable woman who fearlessly negotiated the hell out of a contract inside a windowless room for days with nothing but my mind and my fingers as the primary commodities.

My phone buzzes. *Go over the facts. From the beginning.* "Fuck you, you ass. Get the hell out of my devices!"

When we're done, comes his lightning-fast reply. My phone clatters to the coffee table as I drop it. I shove my fingers through my hair and yank sharply. "What the hell were you trying to tell me, Lee?"

You were going to the spa. The Plaza has no record of you—or me—checking in. That was confirmed by the police.

You were found blocks away from Fifth Avenue. "Why? What or who could have lured you there?"

You had my ID on you. "I still don't get it. If it was a regular mugging, they would have patted you down. Stolen your purse. But that was recovered. The cops wrote it off as you had a different bag. I call bullshit."

Even as I recant the facts as I know them, my gaze lands on the shelf over her desk. On it is a framed picture of me and Lee at her graduation from Vanderbilt. Next to it is the one of mine taken just a week later from MIT. My gaze is dragged down to the mixing equipment plugged into her laptop. I haven't disturbed any of it, thinking if something—anything—would have turned up by now through the Hudson investigation. But what about that odd "I" on the hit list in her journal? And since I know damn well Lee truly suspected what I really did for a living, she was certainly smart enough to find her way into the top-level parts of my world without detection. "Is it possible she left me a message there?"

Almost in a trance, I move over to her laptop and turn it on. After booting her computer with a terminal interface, I quickly bypass the operating system login, and my fingers begin to dance as scripts I've written to lead me into the dark pop into my mind like ancient chants. "Where would she have gone?"

Immediately, I think about two companies—Wildcard Records

and LLF LLC. "Lee trusted both of them. But did she trust them enough to leave me a message there?"

I dive beneath the surface of the web to find out.

There's no gray area about what I'm doing. The waters I'm diving into are completely black. And I don't care. Let the government strip away the credentials so I can no longer augment what they begged for me to build for them, I think ruthlessly as I plunge deeper and deeper into the murky cesspool, searching for any byte from my Lee. Because if there's a message from her, I'll find it

While I'm there, I do my own quick search for all of the players in this game. I ignore every image file since I don't have my team here to tell me if they're safe and focus on the lines of data scrolling past my eyes as fast as my fingers can make them appear. My jaw becomes unhinged at some of the information I'm able to find—information I'm infuriated my bastard boss hasn't shared. "I'm going to shoot him with his own gun after I'm done shooting him with mine."

I get a text at that point. *What did you think of?* I ignore it, him, and keep digging.

I spend hours picking and poring over every bit of data I can find with a clear reference to Lee's and my real names, but I don't find anything that sparks my interest. I also stay far away from the traps the agency set with my government handle. Another text I haven't yet responded to warned me a number of these were floating around to see if there were any bites. *If we get a nibble, we might have a lead, Qaza.*

Still, I study the bait they selected carefully. And as a pattern emerges despite the lack of responses, it chills my blood. *They're using data from my missions.* No, it's more than that. I carefully study the timeline and realize the hints start as far back as when I first joined the team as an analyst.

Why? Why go that far back.

Without hesitation, I slip into the hole I built into the agency firewall long ago to reread my files.

What the hell are you doing?

Pretending ignorance, I take my time reading in reverse chronological order. I scan the mission files I submitted and the notes that were augmented as each case was completed. Then I go back to my time as an analyst. My persistent digging where the knowledge I unearthed was passed along for someone else to act upon.

And that's where I find a link that sends me surging to my feet. "No. It can't be."

A message pops up on my screen. *Speak, now. What did you find?*

I ignore him. He'll make me pay later, but I don't give a fuck. "You should have told me, damnit," I snarl. And before he can call me, I reach for my secure cell and pop out the battery. The personal cell I'm using begins ringing immediately. I ignore it because he's had his time to calculate his moves. Now I need time to think about how they impact my life.

I take my time backing out of the database, using enough code to send someone subpoenaing an internet provider in Des Moines before they'd remember to hunt me in New York. As a precaution, I also scramble the IPs I borrowed through varying cable providers and reset Lee's network. I'm shaken when I realize the implications of what I've found.

"I'm going to have to tell him everything. I can't put him in danger."

But how? How can I break the trust placed in me when I took my vows to uphold and protect the United States against all enemies, foreign and domestic, for the duration of my life?

I move away from the desk and drop onto the couch. Wrapping my arms around my legs, I stare out the door and think. Then jumping up, I grab my secure computer instead of Lee's, which I left running with a bunch of defend and destroy scripts. Within moments, I have my answer and close my eyes in relief. I quickly close the hole I punched in the agency clearance database with a massive mental apology to confirm what I already suspected.

I still don't know what he looks like, but I know I can trust him. And I know he has the same level of clearance I do. And Kane of all people can appreciate what it's like to be responsible for someone's death.

Fuck, it has to be my fault Lee was killed.

On that thought, I begin to sob harshly.

Pacing back and forth the next night, I'm antsy. I really want to get this joint rehearsal Carys insisted upon over with so I can connect with Kane, but Beckett's an hour late. Finally, my patience snaps. "Ah, screw it."

I stomp over to the piano and lift the lid. My fingers come crashing down in an introduction before my voice belts out Lady Gaga's "Shallow." As I belt out her soulful words, they pierce the thin shield I have around my heart: void, longing. Fear.

My head falls forward as tears clog my voice temporarily when I hit the refrain. My right hand begins slamming on the keys just before I toss my head back. I let loose with the frustration and anger of Lee being gone from the depths of my soul. Eyes closed, I finish the song, and my breathing is heavy in the quiet room.

Until the clapping and whistling begins.

Frightened, my head snaps to the side to find Beckett with Mick and Carly standing next to him. "You're late," I growl at him.

"And you made good use of the time. It's like I told you, put the emotions into the music, Ky," he congratulates me.

"Lee!" I shout, unable for one more second to hear my sister's name fall from someone's lips. "She called me Lee!"

Mick and Carly quickly take a step back. As his blue eyes light up, I think, *Uh-oh*. Lee forgot to mention Beckett Miller apparently thrives on confrontation. "Bring it on, little girl," he challenges.

"Hard-ass Beckett Miller," I goad, pushed beyond caring.

For just a moment, his lips soften, but I think I might imagine it when he leans forward and declares, "You want to know what I think? I think she'd say, 'Live your life, Kylie. Love for both of us.'" He folds his arms.

Chest heaving, I open my mouth and say, "You don't know how wrong you are."

His brow quirks. "Oh?"

"Yeah. Because if she knew the way I was living, she'd be terrified about me dying more than what happened to her." And with that, I race out of the studio, ignoring the calls of Beckett, Mick, and Carly. I race past Beckett's ever-constant guards, not even noticing which ones are with him today.

All I can think about is getting to a safe place and texting Kane. I need to tell him everything about who I was.

Who I am.

Who I guess I'll always be.

KANE

Conversation starter: If you know exactly what's going to happen when you do something, why do it? — **Viego Martinez, Celebrity Blogger**

"What the hell just happened?" I demand as Leanne streaks past without a word. I'd hoped to intercept her at some point tonight to introduce myself—finally after days of exchanges about her company entwined with flirtations. I've never been so anxious to put in over-time, but knowing I have her to interact with at the end of the day, I've been feeling a sense of anticipation. We're on the precipice of more, something I thought I could nudge along tonight, but obviously there's no chance of that happening, as evident by the tears falling down her face.

Beckett looks years older than his late thirties when he admits, "I pushed her. Too hard, it seems. But..."

"But what?" I snap, ignoring the fact he's the one I'm supposed to be protecting. Something indefinable is drawing me toward Leanne Miles the more I get to know her.

I just want her alive to figure out what it is.

"When I heard her sing, I thought it was time to prod her away from her grief. She didn't take it well," he admits. Out of the corner of my eye, Mick and Carly are nodding frantically, supporting Beckett.

I lean in so only Beckett can hear me. With a great deal of reluctance, I say softly, "The kind of grief she's feeling isn't going to just go away, Beckett. It's the kind you carry until you join that individual in the grave beside them."

Beckett gives me a sharp glance. "You sound like you're talking from experience."

I don't bother responding before I turn and walk back to my post. The rock giant isn't an uber-millionaire who once declared he'd join the ranks of Andrew Lloyd Weber and Sir Andrew McCartney as billionaires because he's an idiot. I just slip my hand into my pocket as unobtrusively as possible and hope like hell Leanne reaches out.

Because I'm now certain it was her that day. Tonight I wanted to run after her just like I wanted to stay with her when I first saw her years ago. And it's my responsibilities to Beckett that's prevented me from doing both.

Damnit.

Hours later, I'm logging into the file Keene's been filling up with data about Leanne and Castor while sitting at his desk at Hudson. Mitch gave me a face because Beckett was bitching nonstop until he received a call from Texas. Then he was glowing like a damn bluebonnet.

I wish the rest of the problems in the world were that simple, I think sourly as I pull up a communication exchange between Leanne and her chief data scientist.

Almost as soon as I do, a text pops up. *I need to talk with you. Are you alone?*

Thank God. It's her. *Yes. I am.*

Where are you?

"Where am I? I'm at the office, Lee," I respond aloud, certain she has my computer microphone on.

I'm proven correct when she responds, *I mean, whose office?*

"Is this supposed to be funny? Are you going to walk in any minute?" I joke.

It's not a joke. I need to know. Now.

Her emphasis on the word causes my heart to leap. My voice comes out rusty. "Keene's. I'm in his..." Before the word "office" can escape, I hear the door latch click. The view that so enthralls me begins to disappear as metal shutters begin to drop and lock into place. Before I can utter a sound, a light over the desk comes on. "Nice parlor trick."

I jump when her voice comes out at me. "Every office on the executive floor has this capability." Her voice is cool, certainly not that of the emotional woman who ran out of practice earlier.

"Lee, about earlier. Are you all right?" At her silence, I hastily continue. "I was there at practice. I wanted to talk with you."

"You were?" The confusion in her voice is better than the flat ice from just a few moments ago.

"Yes. Lee, Beckett didn't mean..."

The cool filters its way back into her voice. "I don't want to talk about Beckett Miller. Not right now."

"What do you want to talk about?" I immediately reply.

"Your clearance is still active." Before I can formulate a reply about how she came about that information, she muses, "I wonder if mine is. I mean, technically, I'm dead. So, who knows if my boss some strings and kept it active. Then again, regardless if mine is, my sharing what I'm about to might be considered by some to be violating all kinds of laws. For certain once I announce I'm still alive after I find out who killed my sister, I would go to jail if yours wasn't still active, Captain McCullough."

I stiffen at the use of a title few have referenced since I departed the Marines. Then I start coughing when she airily declares, "Oh, what the hell am I saying. I can double check by hacking back into..."

"Don't!" I shout. "Swear to me, Leanne. You haven't hacked into any sort of agency database."

There's a dramatic sigh before she grudgingly agrees, "Fine."

My eyes narrow. I'm pretty damn certain she's crossed every limb and appendage while saying that. "Turn on the damn camera. I want to see your face when you make me a promise that was the last time you'll do something like that."

"You're no fun," she pouts. But within seconds, the light above my monitor turns green. A small box appears in the upper-left corner.

And there she is.

It's obvious she's been crying. Her deep blue eyes are swollen, makeup streaked. Her hair is haphazardly twisted into a knot. Tissues are scattered around the desk she's sitting at. But she's never looked more real, more beautiful, than I've ever seen her. "Hi," I murmur. "It's good to finally meet you."

But Leanne must think differently. Her hands fly to her cheeks. And when she finally speaks, she only manages to gasp, "You!"

I jerk my head from side to side before my eyes return to meet hers. "Me what?"

"You're the one who..." And she blushes bright red.

Like lightning, her words slam into me, sending every nerve ending sizzling. I finish her sentence. "Who crashed into you."

Her lips part slightly, giving me more than words could. I know now I wasn't the only one who felt the pull in the few seconds we collided. I don't say anything, hoping the intensity of my expression conveys my emotions.

I click the button in the corner to expand the chat so Leanne's face is the only thing filling my screen. For long moments, I memorize the features of her face, committing them to the recesses of my memory. The hints of gold and brown that weave through the lighter blonde in her hair. The shades of different blue that make up the fathomless color I wanted to lose myself in that afternoon on the street. Her naturally plump lips are still parted in shock. *What would they look like after I kissed them?* I wonder.

"All these years, and you're finally here. There were times I started to believe I dreamed what happened."

Her soft sigh jolts me back to reality. Leanne's holding me captive in Keene's office with a swipe of her delicate fingers. "As much as I want to explore that comment, you have me trapped in here, Leanne. The question is why?"

Her face pales. Then she says words that send me reeling back in time. In my mind, I'm standing in uniform, listening to the intelligence subcommittee replay each moment of my last maneuver minute by minute. "What made you trust the intelligence from *Qəza* on your final mission?"

On automatic pilot, I reply, "Because *Qəza's* intel had never let us down. It was the best we had in the region." I surface from my trance and give voice to my suspicions that began at Christmas. "You hacked the DoD."

"I didn't have to," Leanne sniffs.

"There's no way you'd have the name of my unit's informant otherwise," I snarl.

For a long moment, she doesn't say anything. All Leanne does is regard me with the saddest eyes. Then finally, she asks, "Do you know what *Qəza* means?"

"Crash. I looked it up once." A horrified thought lances through me. I begin to shake my head back and forth. "No, it's not possible..."

She folds her hands behind the keyboard. "I was recruited right after I kicked Sam's ass at Defcon. I hadn't been caught, but long before I went to MIT, I was suspected of peeking into several mainframes I shouldn't have been able to access. My now handler propositioned me on campus. He frankly bullied my ass." If her voice didn't hold a hint of affection despite the fear pumping through me, I'd be enraged. "Even tried to allude to the possibility of jail time. I laughed him off. Then he flat out appealed to my sense of protecting Mom, Dad, and Kylie." I can't tear my eyes away from her as she buries her face in her hands. "God, the last thing I wanted to do was live a double life, but what other choice did I have but to say yes?"

"Who is he? What agency, Leanne?" My hands clench the edge of the table.

She gives me a pitying look, as if I can't already guess her answer. "For years, I cultivated a hard-core reputation as a for-hire hacker to maintain my connections. But that's how they wanted it played. Our government would 'hire' me publicly when their own analysts couldn't handle the work. The reality is I was already on their payroll, being trained for more difficult missions. When I wasn't in use, I prepared their systems against outside attacks from our enemies."

"You're an operative." It's a statement, not a question.

"Not at first. At first, all I did was gather intel. I was damn good at it." She quickly outlines what she did earlier, hoping to find a message from her sister in the darkest corners of the internet. In light of everything else, finding out Kylie Miles did have some of the skills as Leanne doesn't shock me as much as realizing Leanne was one of the people passing along intel to me for years. Including the last piece of information that saved my life but caused me to pull the trigger on my best friend.

Shoving the memories aside, I demand, "So, Crash, what you're saying is there are new messages for you in your drop spots, waiting for you to access them?"

She nods. "Job assignments since I 'died,' Kane. Either my old contacts didn't get the news, or they know I'm not the one whose ashes are buried in that plot. My handler should have shut these down—assigned a new operative. Whatever's waiting for me shouldn't be there."

"Who's laying the trap?" I wonder.

"Got it in one." In her voice is a note of weariness that leads me to believe she's relieved to share this burden.

My mind is whirling a mile a minute. "I want to ask you a million questions."

"I figured that."

"But I need to bring Caleb up to speed."

"You can't," she states flatly.

"Why not?" I demand.

"Because his clearance isn't the same as yours. And..." Her voice trails off.

"And what?"

"So many times, our lives have intersected in ways no one else can understand: me, you, chance, each of us protecting the other because it was our job. Now, it feels...different. Plus, I don't trust him the same way I feel like I can trust you."

"Christ, you can't say things like that to a man." I run a hand through my hair, hoping the shaking doesn't show on video.

"Why? It's the truth." Her confusion is obvious.

My lips quirk up into a smile. She might be her sister's identical twin, but it isn't difficult to tell the two women apart. Despite the murky world of covert intelligence Leanne's been mired in, there's an air of innocence cloaked around her, whereas Kylie had a wild wariness.

Whoever killed Kylie either made a drastic mistake, or was she deliberately sacrificed to draw out the other Miles sister? The thought careens through my mind. To Leanne, I wonder, "How did you run a legitimate business and still fulfill your obligations as Qaza?"

"I don't require more than a few hours of sleep a night. But I also have a crazy-intelligent staff that sometimes puts me to shame."

"Uh-huh." I wait for the other shoe to drop.

Her smile turns smug. "It also helps there are several secured facilities in the Castor office up in Saratoga Springs. My office converts into one, just like the one you're sitting in. With the kind of work Hudson has bid on, I figured either Keene or Caleb would have one. The building specs weren't difficult to access."

"Of course, because that's what every good office has—a qualified hacker to download their building specs after hours."

"Hey, you guys have Sam. He's better than I am in a lot of ways."

"I'm never going to feel safe using my phone again."

"Just remember to reset the password for your social media accounts. Sorry, but they're for sale on the dark web."

I immediately begin banging my head on the desk before I meet her eyes. "I'm going to live in a tent."

Humor at my reaction is chased away by sadness. "Lee wanted me to build in the city to be closer to her. Maybe if I had, I could have protected her better. Then maybe this wouldn't have happened to her. Listen, I have to lift the filter on my side before someone gets suspicious I read you in." She hides her face as her fingers begin tapping away.

Even as I try to find the right words to say, Leanne lifts the security lockdown. I know I'm in deep trouble when I find intimacy in what should be a work meeting. Yet, "I like the idea of upstate New York. The idea of your fingers flying over a keyboard with the mountains in the background, the moonlight gleaming over your skin, is incredibly enchanting, Leanne."

Her head whips up, eyes as big as an owl's. "Excuse me?"

"Oh, I'm sorry. I thought we were done talking about work and had moved on to personal stuff."

"I...we...personal?"

"Oh, wait. Did I misunderstand all the flirting, not flirting conversations?" I try to tease away her sadness and fear. But then I get serious. "Are you ready to talk about us now?"

"Us? What us? I mean, I never expected after I told you about..."

"About what? That you were the individual who fed me the intel that saved my life? The lives of how many others by stopping an arms deal?" This woman was in no way responsible for what happened in Azerbaijan. All she did was give us the final nail to find the mole in our unit. "Did you really believe that dims you as a woman in my eyes?"

"Yes," she declares bluntly.

"You are very, very wrong, Crash." I reach up and drag my finger down the screen— tracing her cheek without touching her through the bits and bytes of technology. Her cheeks flush as if we were skin on skin, and my heart accelerates accordingly. "All you did was give me another angle of you to process."

She weighs that in her mind. I hold my breath until her body visibly relaxes. "So, tell me this, how did you never know who I was with those mad hacking skills of yours? Or are you just getting rusty?"

She aims a lethal look at me. "I prefer to access plain text. There's less of a chance of fending off a cyberattack as there is through steganography."

"Stegasaurous-what-ophy?"

"It's the use of hiding malicious code within an image file. It's being used more and more frequently these days. I leave that to others who specialize in its use to examine the pixels within the images to see if there's coded messages—things like that." She shrugs. "That's why I never put two and two together. Your file had an image file referenced, but sure as the devil, I wasn't going to open it. The only thing I do to images is blast them."

"Christ." I scrub my hand over my face.

"What about you? How did you never put it together? It's not like you didn't meet my mirror image," she challenges me.

"I wasn't protecting your sister day in and day out, so I never got to know her well. And yes, she mentioned an older sister, a twin. But never an identical one." A wrinkle of pain ripples across Leanne's face. I continue. "I suspect she assumed most people knew she had one, especially if you were at most of her shows."

Leanne's face brightens. "That makes sense."

"Why were you upset?" I probe gently.

She chews her nail. "Something my mother said. She said I didn't have time for Lee anymore." A harsh laugh escapes. "I'm certain you can guess she hasn't taken this well."

"And since you look just like her..." I don't get to finish the thought.

"I've spent maybe a few hours at home since the week of the funeral. I'm persona non grata there. And God, Kane. If this has to do with the things I did, I'll lose them all." Tears fill her eyes.

"You won't. Despite everything, they love you. It takes time."

"That sounds like experience talking."

I nod sharply. But instead of pressuring me, Leanne holds up a hand as if to run her hands over my hair. "I'm here if you want to talk about it."

Her simple words cause my heart to shift inside of me. If I'm not careful, it's going to fall right out of my body and land at her feet. *Crash.* In so many different ways, her code name was appropriately chosen. I recall after a few missions when my commanding officer used to tell me about *Qəza.* I didn't know until he informed me that the intel agent had disabled certain enemy systems so we could access our targets and recover weapons, intel, hostages. Or about the time *Qəza* had alerted us to nearby bogeys unidentified by command all because she'd won a high-stakes game online. But it was me *Qəza* contacted when Gene tried to sell the weapons for cryptocurrency. She'd documented everything in the event lethal measures were necessary.

I owe this woman not just my life but my freedom. And she thought I wouldn't look at her the same? Well, in some ways, she's right.

For the rest of the night, I can't prevent my lips from curving every time my eyes meet hers. As we spend the next few hours going through additional Castor contracts with one another, it's different. This time, with location being the only distance between us, everything's different.

KANE

February

Poll: How many of you dress for yourself and not to impress for someone else? In the comments below, tell me your go to outfit if you knew no one was watching.

— **Eva Henn, Fashion Blogger**

"Lookin' good, Kane. Big date?" Mitch stops me as I head out of my room and make my way past him and the other members of the day team.

I glance down at the shirt and slacks I've donned. "Just have to do some work at the office."

He smirks. "Right. If that's what you want to call it. I take it you're not eating with us—again."

I roll my eyes and reach for my wallet. Tossing some money on the counter, I declare, "Pizza on me. I'll see you guys later."

Just as I reach the front door of the condo, Mitch pitches his voice into a falsetto. "Oh, isn't Kane so sweet. He bought dinner and everything."

"Assholes," I clearly call over my shoulder as I snag my leather jacket off the tree before I disappear amid the team's laughter into the hallway. It's only then I glance down at my freshly showered body and realize, *Crap. I did dress up for Leanne.* I debate for about a half a second over ducking back inside to change before I realize if I do, I'll have to put up with a dumpster full of shit from the team.

After all, there's no harm in looking professional when I'm meeting with her anyway.

An hour later, I realize I've been lying to myself. I no longer see Leanne Miles as a client. As she reaches over and grabs the box of Chinese without breaking eye contact from the contract she's reviewing, I realize I have a major problem. It isn't the work I'm focusing on.

I can't drag my eyes away from her.

Her eyes dart back and forth as she reads the screen, her lowered brows causing the skin between them to pucker slightly. She lifts the chopsticks she's using to her lips, and I catch a glimpse of her pink tongue as it darts out for a bite of shrimp. "Yes...yes. Right." And she laughs softly.

I groan aloud. Fucking hell. If she says "right there," I'm storming out of this office and heading to her place. Screw whatever security protocols she's been warned about.

"Is something wrong, Kane?" She's just lifted another bite of food to her mouth, but it's suspended in midair.

I grab my own box and shovel in a bite of General Tso's. "No, I'm fine. Just hungry."

"Have you found out anything?"

Just that my mind can't focus anymore. Then I decide, to hell with it. "What were you laughing about just then?"

Her lips form the first full-fledged smile I've had the pleasure of witnessing since I almost barreled her over. She drops her chopsticks back in the box and waves at her screen before chortling again. "This contract. It reminded me of Lee."

"Why's that?" I ask, anxious to keep that look of happiness on her face.

She crosses her legs and then tucks them beneath her. When that happens, it pulls at her oversized sweater, yanking it to the side and exposing one creamy shoulder. I swallow hard, trying to give her my full attention, not just the attention of certain parts of my anatomy. "When I first bought the building that Castor is located in, I had a certain budget. And—as I'm certain you're aware—we had to meet the security protocols for everything from the ceiling tiles to the flooring. Lee was less than impressed when I began running out of money and bought this ugly-ass carpet tile."

"You were walking on it, not decorating your home with it." I understand her logic completely.

"Exactly! You get it."

"Totally." I shove another bite in my mouth and chew.

"But to Lee, this carpet was unacceptable. After all, I was presenting an image." Leanne strikes a pose of such hauteur, I crack up.

"Was it really that bad?"

"Oh, worse. It was so atrocious, she'd lift a tile in my office and write her opinion on the back of it."

My shoulders shake. "That is pretty funny. What made you think of it just now?"

She jerks her chin at the screen. "Because I had all the carpet replaced after this contract. After this software launch, every square inch of Castor was recarpeted. Then I threw a massive party for our clients. Even Lee came up from the city for it because she didn't believe me."

Because I'm starting to understand the sentimentality of the woman just beyond my reach, I ask, "What did you do with her piece of the carpet?"

She looks away. "The last I know, it was hanging in a frame in my office. I'm certain Ivan's had it removed and shipped to my parents." She puts her food to the side and leans her head on her folded arms.

My ears prick up, even as my heart aches over her obvious pain. "Who is Ivan?"

After she collects herself, she mutters, "Ivan Forfa, Castor's chief data scientist. Sometimes friend, often a pain in the ass. Overall, a solid employee with creative ideas."

I jot down his name and make a note to have him run through Hudson's systems. "Where did you meet him?"

"MIT. He was in a few of my classes my senior year. Pissed him off he couldn't catch up to my GPA." Her voice holds a note of smugness.

"You know, I did look you up. I assume certain elements are true," I remind her. Once Leanne informed me of who she really was, I wanted to see how much of that was available through a Hudson background check. I had one pulled and dropped into the file, explaining it away as, "There might be something in here that could lead us to the answers we need."

I was wrong. As she expected it would, on paper, Leanne came off as the young, brilliant CEO of a successful software firm. There's nothing in her dossier that would trip anyone performing a deep background investigation of her extracurricular activities. So, either she's right about her sister's death being something to do with Kylie, or it's buried here in one of these contracts.

"Of course there are. I just do special things with these." She wiggles her fingers in my face.

Yeah, I know what I'd like her to do with those. To keep myself under control, I clasp my fingers behind my head. "So riddle me this. How did you not manage to graduate valedictorian of your class? Who in the hell is possibly smarter than you?"

One breath, two. Then Leanne topples sideways in stitches. "Oh, God, Kane. You just did the best imitation of my dad."

Disgruntled, I mutter, "That wasn't exactly what I was going for."

She rights herself and declares, "I'll tell you exactly what I told him. I didn't need to be valedictorian. I already knew what I was going to be doing with my life. In fact, I was thrilled to remind him I was graduating college with quite the hefty nest egg between the collection of bug bounties and the software I'd already designed. Plus, well, there was the other thing," she concludes.

Right, the government work. I flip open the file next to me, and my eyes bug out. "You were a millionaire at twenty-one?"

"It's not uncommon. People do remarkable things to earn money. Some are athletes and earn sponsorships. It wasn't too much longer before Kylie was singing and garnering the attention of the media. Success requires hard work and luck."

And her image fades away as I recall a dull metal barrel pointed at my chest. My head drops before I mutter, "And sometimes it's helped along by cheating, lies, and outright deception."

"Hey!" she exclaims indignantly.

My eyes flick up to meet hers. She's leaning up on her knees, and her hands are on her hips—a modern-day Valkyrie ready to go to battle. "It wasn't meant as an insult to you. But the real world, Crash, isn't ones and zeros. It isn't a computer program to be manipulated for gain. It's warfare. And in the sociopolitical mess soldiers like me were left to clean up, sometimes saying you made a mistake doesn't make everything all right."

My breath rasps out as she stares through her screen into my soul. For long moments, she doesn't say anything, and I think, *Fuck it.* I'm about to call it a night when her soft voice asks, "What caused you to join the Marines, Kane?"

Not what caused me to leave.

"I went to school on a NROTC scholarship. Up until the time I got there, I was certain I was going to go Navy."

"What school?"

"NC State. And let me tell you, for a boy from a flyover state, living somewhere I could go to Myrtle Beach for spring break was the shit."

She smiles but doesn't interrupt me further. "*Semper Fidelis.* Always faithful. It was my eternal commitment to protect not only this nation but the people I fought alongside."

"What feels different?"

"If you'd asked me this a month ago, I'd have said my honor."

"What changed that?"

I pause to think about the necessity of the work I do, the bond the team I work with has now, and admit, "Me. I suppose the only thing that's changed over the last few years is I let go of the pain and resentment."

I thump myself against my heart. "Something happened on my last mission, which made me question who I was here. It took me this long to realize I wasn't the one that changed, even if I'm no longer in uniform. But you know what's helping?"

"What?"

"I get to stand behind the curtain watching a woman sing who has every right to lie down and give up. She's about to bleed in front of the whole world. That takes a hell of a lot more courage than finding your best friend turned out to be a traitor."

She rubs her hands up and down her sweater before biting her trembling lower lip. "Kane."

I lean forward. The little box shows my camera fills her screen. "Trust me, Leanne."

She slides off her sofa until her face is all I see. She whispers, "How can you look at me and not see what's been lost? Everyone else is."

"Because when I look at you, the only thing I can do is feel."

Her breath shudders out. Then she quickly leans forward and presses her lips to the camera. I tip my face back a bit so I can see her eyes as she pulls away. Wet, wild, she wonders, "God help me, Lee. He's who you wanted me to meet—isn't he?"

Then her camera turns off.

I fall back in my chair, stunned. "I've never had a single date that intense, let alone an online date."

A message pops up on my screen. That wasn't a date. That was a working session that got a bit out of hand.

My fingers fly. Semantics, Crash. Two people eating together...

Work dinner, she fires back.

Sharing intimate details about each other's lives? I counter.

Could still be a work dinner.

I'm not convinced, I type.

Knowing details about your co-workers is important to building strong business relationships.

She's right, of course. Which is exactly why I won't let her off the hook. Then why don't you come down here to work? It would be much easier for us to do this together, partner.

No answer.

I'm certain we could get through these files better together.

Still nothing.

Put in a little extra effort to clear the desk, as it were. Then we'll know for sure where to focus our attention.

I press Send, and within seconds, her face pops up on the screen, flushed.

"All right, already. I can't come down there."

"Why?" I demand.

"First, because your boss banned me from the office. He said my showing up as 'Kylie Miles' would be suspect. And he's right. I have to focus on what I'm doing, Kane." Leanne's voice breaks.

"That wasn't going to be an issue..." I begin, but her next words stop me from going on.

"Because we have a problem. Or maybe it's just me. I have a problem."

I swallow. "And what's that?"

Her voice becomes husky. "You. You're in my thoughts, where I should have nothing but retribution. You're following me into my dreams, when there should be nothing but nightmares."

Lord deliver us. I slap my hand up to the computer. Hers is immediately there. "Then stay away, until we can't any longer, Leanne. That's the Grammys," I manage to rasp.

"After all, I'm going to need someone to hold me after I lose it onstage anyway. Didn't you read all about me singing 'Landslide'?" Her words are bittersweet.

"Fuck the world. You just lost your sister," I growl in response to the damn paparazzi.

She half laughs, half sobs. "God, Kane. Don't make me fall in love with you. I just lost my sister. I can't lose anyone else."

At that, she slowly pulls back and closes the computer for the night.

KANE

Everyone is speculating what Erzulie is going to wear on the red carpet. Will she be as outlandish as she has been at past events or more toned down due to mourning her twin sister, Leanne?

— **Eva Henn, Fashion Blogger**

Tonight we're focusing on data she passed to my superior just before the off-shoot assignment in Azerbaijan that rocked my whole world. Strangely, since I exposed my past to Lee, what losing Gene, Brit, and Maddie meant to me, I'm less fearful about what's coming.

Or maybe that's because of the woman who won't let me handle it alone, despite the overwhelming pain she's still working through herself. Leanne's making me roar with laughter as she engages me with her own war stories as her fingers fly.

"It's nice to see you got a new system there to work on," I remark drolly.

"Listen, my laptop is good in a pinch, but I need more than one screen."

"What does your setup look like now?"

"I have a quad of monitors, two drives with six terabytes of storage on each, and enough RAM to power... Oh, this is interesting." The next thing I know, there's a file on my machine. I begin scanning it. I'm no longer surprised at the markings at the top. I just pray Leanne was right and both of our clearances are still active or that they have conjugal cells at Leavenworth.

Her fair imitation of my base commander drags my eyes away from what I'm reading. "God, I hated dealing with that misogynistic prick. What a complete turd. 'Triple-check it, *Qaza*.' What was his problem anyway? Did he somehow figure out I was a female, even though our interaction was limited to online, or was it because a platoon of Marines couldn't get the stick out of his ass?"

"I seem to remember someone saying he was encouraged to retire early last year."

"Please tell me a woman took over. That would make my night." She twists up her long hair with a pair of pens, stabbing them in like the chopsticks she used to eat with the night before. My gut clenches as she inadvertently flashes me a glimpse of her flat abdomen.

"You know it utterly fascinates me how you do that?"

"It's pathetic, Kane. All I use is a combination of a Python script, plus..." she begins.

"I meant your hair," I murmur, causing her to pinken. "Do you play with your hair every time you need to concentrate?"

She blows a strand off her face that didn't quite make it into her haphazard bun. "I need it out of my face."

"And the pens?"

"I use whatever I have handy." Her eyes flick downward, a straight line to where my hands rest on my own keyboard.

Immediately, my mind wonders what it would be like to stand behind her before sliding my hands through her thick tresses. I'd lift it off her neck, let my lips linger where the fine hair curls just beneath. It would ensure Leanne was completely distracted from diving deeper into the murky territory she navigates with such ease.

I feel a warmth surge through my body. Standing, I shuck my jacket and tie before undoing my collar and cuffs. At her sharply indrawn breath, my head snaps around. "What is it? Did you find something?"

She stammers, "I...um...no. It's nothing."

I lean forward, planting my fists against the desk. "What did I miss?"

"Nothing," she denies.

"Leanne," I warn.

"I'm not a damn saint, okay? It's a little more than I can handle when I'm front row to a live striptease. Next time, cover your camera." I gape at her. She groans, "Oh, God. I miss Lee. This is the kind of thing we would be saying to each other on a Friday night. I sure as hell shouldn't be saying them to you." She draws her knees up to her chest to hide her face.

What she doesn't realize is by doing so, she's providing me with a spectacular view of the curve of her ass in the cutoffs she's sporting. I don't bother to hide my hard-on. Instead, I growl, "Explain to me— again—why it's a bad idea for us to do this in person?"

Her deep blue eyes capture mine. "You almost had me agreeing to it until our last call. I'm almost positive we're close to melting circuit boards. You stay right where you are, Kane McCullough. We need to work."

"We're going to be in the same location in just a few days," I point out logically.

Her breath rushes out. "Yes."

My voice drops to a growl. "Aren't you even slightly curious?"

She edges closer. I capture a glimpse of the side of her breast in its flimsy covering beneath her oversized shirt. Our eyes clash before she whispers, "About what? You? Us?"

"Yes."

"No."

"Liar." I mouth the word.

Her lips curve in a purely feminine smile before she reaches up and slowly pulls the pens from her hair. Long strands of blonde cascade over her shoulders. "Am I?"

The screen goes black, causing me to howl my frustration out loud. I storm over to the window, hoping the cooler air from the overhead vent might calm me down. I inhale and exhale, trying to regain some control, when my phone buzzes in my pocket. Hoping for a distraction—I can hope Beckett robbed a bank or something equally inane—I slide it from my pants. I frown when I find a text from an unknown number with an image. I open it cautiously.

And promptly drop my phone on the plush carpet. Bending down, I hope I don't snap off any critical body parts because they're as hard as granite.

The shot shows Leanne's shed her shorts and propped her legs on either side of her keyboard. The shirt she's wearing is mostly open, displaying her perfectly flat stomach. And, more importantly, the hand shifting beneath the scrap of nothing protecting her from my vision. "Sweet Christ," I moan, my hand reaching down to grip my dick through my pants.

That's when I hear her voice come at me from the computer. "Not fair. I want to see."

I clench the phone in my hand, not turning around to see what my body's craving. "Are we really doing this?"

"I'm not a liar, Kane, so I'll give you this. I've wanted you since the first moment we touched all those years ago."

My head bows under the sweet honesty of her words. I curse my acute hearing as the material of her clothing slides against her skin. Skin I can't touch, but I can demand she touch. Get dizzy by the way she looks when she falls over the edge.

Because of me.

"Be certain, Leanne. Because there's no stopping once we start," I say with my back still to her.

Her response is to lock the door and begin lowering the security shields. I bark out a laugh. "That's one way to respond."

"So's this." I look over my shoulder just in time to find her standing and slowly beginning to unbutton her shirt.

"Stop!" I command as I stalk over to the computer. I'm breathing heavily, and I've walked four feet instead of running the usual five miles I put in each day. Christ, this woman has me twisted in knots and I've barely spoken a word, I muse ruefully.

An uncertain look crosses her face. Her hand slides to the right, and I reprimand her, "Stop moving, Crash. I just want you to slow down. I want to savor this. You."

"Us," she whispers.

"What we can have of us," I agree. "Sit down."

She immediately plops back down in her chair. I gently question, "Have you ever done this before?"

And it's like a dam bursts. "No! At first I thought it would be easy. I mean, I think about you enough when I...I mean..." And that's when the most delicious blush begins at her open collar and spreads upward.

A small smile plays about my mouth. "You're not the only one."

Her eyebrows skyrocket. "Really?"

"Oh yeah." I kick my long legs back up on the desk and begin palming my cock through my slacks, keeping my eyes on her the entire time. Her breasts move up and down with the force of her breath. "Stand up, Crash."

Like she's in a trance, she does. "Unbutton your shirt. Do it slowly. Pretend it's my hands on you."

"I want my hands on you, Kane," she throws back.

God help me, I want them there too.

I surge to my feet and quickly make fast work of the buttons. That's when I hear her, "Tsk...slower, baby. My hands, remember."

I croak, "Whose idea was this?"

"Mine."

"When I finally get my hands on you, remember that." Still, I slow down as I yank my shirt from my slacks. For good measure, I unbuckle my belt while I still have complex motor function.

Her throaty laugh causes my cock to weep a little. But I'm soon rewarded by a full view of her barely there panties. And the fact the shirt's the only thing hiding her breasts from my view. "Lose the shirt, Crash. Drop it to the floor."

"Same goes."

I nod, high on the illicitness of what we're doing combined with the fact I'm now staring at the most beautiful woman I've ever seen. "God, you're exquisite."

She turns, and that's when I see it. A long scar running up her side. I recognize what it is, having seen it on too many soldiers in combat. It just shouldn't be marring the satiny skin of the woman I'm falling for. Stepping closer to the screen, I ask, "Leanne?"

She dives for her shirt. Quickly, I plead, "Let me see it. Let me know *you*."

This time when she stands there, she shakes in her vulnerability because it's not just her naked. She's baring her whole self before me. I'm paralyzed by the expression on her face as I study her—all of her. I may not be the first, but I feel like I am. That no one has gotten in as deep as I am, yet I haven't physically touched her. Not yet, at any rate. "Lift your left hand," I whisper.

She does so, confusion marking her face. "Now kiss the tips of your fingers." She again follows my instructions. "And place your hand on your scar, Leanne." Even as she follows my instructions, her right hand comes up and slaps against her mouth. Am I the first to see the woman who hurts and not the operative?

"Kane," she chokes out.

Casually, I flick open my pants and reach inside to hold my cock back while I unzip them. "You might want to sit down for the next part, sweetheart."

Her entire demeanor changes, knowing I'm not about to reject her because of who she is. I watch as her fingertips brush over her turgid nipples, and my fingers ache— actually ache— because I'm not the one making them elongate as she twirls and twists them. "Keep doing that," I groan.

Then I pull myself out and begin stroking myself. I use the moisture leaking from the head to coat my hand as I pull firmly on the downstroke.

"Touch your nipples," her husky voice whispers. "I would if I was there."

"Christ," I bite out. But when I go to demand how quickly she wants this over, I find she's scooted down in her chair, one leg thrown over the arm. Her fingers have snuck down back inside her panties, and her fingers are obviously dancing back and forth. "Let me see," I snarl.

She slides her hand out, and there's a web glistening between her fingers. I'm panting as she shifts her fingers to the front of the gusset and slips them back in.

We both moan simultaneously. My eyes are locked to her; hers are on me. I stroke, and she dips until it becomes too much. My thighs are quivering with the need to come, and come hard. "Crash, I'm close," I moan.

"Me too," she breathes as she swirls her wetness around her tight nub before dipping her fingers back inside.

I aim my cock for my chest, too far gone to reach for my shirt or anything else. With a slight roar, I climax, her name on my lips. I snap my head up, just in time to see her hips roll and her hips jerk as her orgasm takes her over the edge.

Holy fucking hell. My mind wants to blank out, but I can't. "Did that really just happen, or did I fall asleep and live out one of my fantasies?"

Her soft laugh makes me feel better when I reach in my back pocket for my handkerchief to wipe the mess off my chest. "Well, something came out."

I grin, loving this sense of humor I haven't been privy to before. It's another sign Leanne's healing.

Boldly, she admits, "I have to say, it was a lot hotter than taking care of myself thinking about you on my own."

I feel my cock stir back to life, and I glare at her as I tuck myself away and zip up. "You're killing me here."

She shoots me an angelic look. "Me?"

I slip on my shirt and begin buttoning it back up, ignoring her boo-hiss. "Yes. You're all I think about. I can't quite pinpoint how I got talked into having phone sex in one of my bosses' offices with the woman I'm counting down the hours until I meet again for the first time."

Her face morphs into one of simple happiness. "The answer is ninety-six hours. That includes the time zone change, in case you were wondering."

"Now, see, that's helpful." But I still wag my finger at her. "Still, no more of this. I'm just hoping I didn't hit anything of importance in Keene's office. You have magic fingers, but somehow, I don't think that extends to cleaning the carpet."

Leanne falls out of her chair laughing, giving me a magnificent view of her ass. "Damn, woman. Not helping. Put on some clothes."

"I'll remind you you said that," she gasps.

"No, you won't," I inform her smugly.

Her smile is everything I can imagine waking up to for the rest of my life. Now we just need to eliminate the threat against her so that can become a possibility.

Leanne

Washington, D.C. President Signs Executive Order Charting New Course to Improve the Nation's Cybersecurity and Protect Federal Government Networks. — **Whitehouse.gov**

It feels like an emotional wall has come down between us since we broke the seal on *us*, a burden removed inside of me that someone knows *me*. Even though we haven't directly spoken of my fears since that night, Kane said he'd find some way to ensure someone was keeping tabs on my parents. The suffocating welling up inside me from the moment Carys told me Caleb hasn't located anything in my twin's life that needed further investigating is beginning to ease yet sets my stomach churning.

Everything points to me. Me. I'm the one who got Lee killed.

The one thing I was adamant about was my rehearsals for the Grammys. If I'm going to walk out onto that stage and pretend to be my sister, I need to shove out all outside pressure. I couldn't walk into practice anticipating seeing Kane. So, I arranged with Carys to finish my studio time on my own. That doesn't stop her from dropping by to check on my well-being.

"Beckett thinks you're still angry with him for the comments he made the last time he saw you," Carys mentions as she leans against a wall while I lift the cover off the keyboard.

"Lee said once he was very intense. She was right," I remark without giving much away.

Carys chuckles. "That's one way of putting it. He can be a very good friend."

Sitting down, I stare thoughtfully out the window. "He's waiting for something. Is it really that he needs me to be all right?"

Startled, Carys jumps. "How can you tell?"

I press middle C, the sound echoing beautifully in the room. "He's pushing, over and over. He's trying to take the weight of the world off my shoulders, but of course, he can't. I'm just not certain if I'm overreacting and that's his personality or if it's something more."

Carys moves forward and leans on the baby grand. "You're very astute, Lee."

My lips curve in a faint smile, the first one I've shared with someone other than with Kane. "So I've been told."

"And you don't push. I'm not used to that in this business."

I don't mention I likely could figure out what's wrong with Beckett Miller in a matter of minutes if I cared enough to try. Instead, I shrug before I begin playing a catchy tune Lee and I learned very early on.

Carys laughs when she recognizes "Heart and Soul." "But much like your sister, you have a wicked sense of humor. Beckett is antsy about something personal, but much like you, he won't say much about it. I hope you'll let him make amends."

"Of course." Her eyebrows wing upward. I switch to Chopin before confiding the obvious. "I only hold grudges when my family is harmed."

She offers me a sad smile and turns to go. I stop my playing and call out, "Carys?" It's time to ask her for something critical.

"Yes?"

"Our trust was originally written so we left everything to each other. I need to update it. Would you help me?" Before she can say anything, I rush out, "You're the only one I can ask."

She steps forward. "I'm an entertainment lawyer, Lee."

My head drops. "Right." I let my fingers resume playing.

She stays them. "But I know someone who can help. If I remove the names, he'll look it over without questions. He'll just assume it's one of my premier clients. So, yes, I can help, but you're not going to need it for a long while. Take your time thinking about who you want to leave everything to. There's a lot at stake between the company and your sister's assets." Carys is careful not to disclose which sister's company and whose assets as we're out in public.

My thank-you is heartfelt. But something is prodding me to get this done. I've kept my promise to Kane and haven't hacked into anything, but I've brushed by my past haunts hunting for information. I'm on edge. Maybe it's due to the number of messages for *Qɑza* popping up, but I'm worried about the amount of time I have before something happens.

Then again, perhaps now that I'm "gone," it could be something as simple as someone assumed my former moniker.

Right. And I believe in Santa Claus again.

"What are you thinking so hard about?" Carys worries.

Deciding to lighten the mood, I begin to play a familiar tune and start singing a song Lee called "deplorable at best. If anyone with any taste ever hears it, they would never believe we're related."

"Well, let's see if she's right," I murmur before I start to sing.

On your mark, ready, set, let's go
Secure it now, I know you know
I go psycho when we flip that bit
Just can't sit
Gotta get stiggy wit it, ooh, that's it
Now SRG done lie
POAM all up in my eye
You gotta VM, swag with a lotta mods in it
Done gave it to your friend, let's spin
A new account for you and me, eye that bid
Wishin' they was lockin' the rig
Here it's been auto-mated
Ultra-laxed right to fuba-fubar
I just write it
It's in a nook, we don't like it
Locked away all day in the secure bay no Ray

Give it up stiggy, this is the way
Yo, grab the source from git
Ha ha
Automation's all in it
What? You wanna call with the pid?
Watch your grep, you might stall
Trying to do what it said
I'ma, uh, I'ma, uh I'ma, much closer
In the middle of the rules with the big ass club, uh
No love for the haters, the haters
Mad 'cause I got more locks on the visors
See us on the fifty-page mark in the papers
This prolly gonna need all the waivers
I got favor for the laser of a disc maker
You say, do another from the pages of this
My goodness, rollin' low wits through the fips
A to the s to the d to the f ——
Fought those bits and watch em roll off, roll off
Yes, yes y'all, you don't stop
In the center for the running time
I makes it nought
Cat-6a if you need the link
Macbook Pro on the drop
Who else? You in?
Walkin' that line some consider a rift
Mock from mouth, tweet, to shade a grift
Windows used to tease me
Gives it up now nice and easy
Since I moved on I feel less greasy
Seem to be rackin' 'em, fillin' it to maximum
Would you like to bounce with another that's trackin' 'em?
Never be chill when frackin' 'em
I rather change all when hackin' 'em, flatten 'em
Bike, kiddin'
Thought I modded wheel, but I didn't

Trust the way of my knife we cuttin'
Hit it with a "drop all" from the kitchen
Container mod with the promise of security
Wha? Check your specs, don't be silly

I'm really getting into it as Carys screeches, "What the ever-loving hell was that?"

"Sometimes you get inspired when you're staring at government requirements late at night," I inform her haughtily, but I can't quite keep the laughter out of my voice, recalling the way Lee literally fell out of her chair when I sang it to her during one of our late Friday calls.

"Never become inspired that way again."

"But I have at least three others I was hoping to pitch," I force my voice so it quivers deliberately.

"Oh, God, no. Yes, yes. I take it back. Sing it again. It's addicting as hell. I swear that was the funniest thing I've ever heard. Is there a recording of it somewhere? If so, I need it for personal use on those days I want to strangle people."

"Do I look like I've lost my mind?" I play a few notes and then shake my shoulders back and forth before plucking out the melody and singing, "Seem to be rackin' 'em, fillin' it to maximum."

Carys wraps her arms around her middle and stumbles back a few steps. "Please tell me you'll sing that for Kris at the Grammys."

I sober quickly. My hands stop moving on the keys. "Even if you gave me all the money of Fort Knox, Jeff Bezos, and the equivalent of the national debt, you couldn't get me to play that outside of this room." I stand and move away from the keyboard. "I've only sang that to Lee. I never should have..."

"What? Shared her with someone else who cared about her?" Sympathy laces Carys's voice.

I reel when it hits me that's exactly what I did. The heels of my hands come up and press against my eyes as I begin nodding frantically.

"Lee, in some ways, Beckett's right. You have to let go of some of this guilt you feel about her death. What happens if we find out it was nothing more than a true mugging and she was just in the wrong place at the wrong time?" Carys implores me.

"Then I pay the price for my decisions, but at least I—we'll—know," I rasp.

Her hand comes to rest upon my arm. "The price won't be that high. I promise, we'll find whoever did this to you, to your family, to your sister. We'll help you find peace."

If there's peace to be found.

My hands fall to my side, and I find myself staring down into the aqua eyes of this woman—dare I say, friend?—who has helped me with this charade. How much have I endangered her? Her family? Immediately, I begin putting a contingency plan in place in the event this goes to hell in a handbasket.

Because there's a feeling inside of me I'm going to get my answers, but what that means for everyone else around me? I have no idea.

KANE

I refuse to be jealous that @DaniMadison is wearing an #amaryllis-designs original on the #redcarpet while walking with hubby @brendanblake.

If I keep saying it enough, I'll really mean it.

— **Moore You Want**

"Are you ready for the Grammys?" I fling Leanne a lazy smile the night before she's supposed to fly out to Los Angeles. My feet are kicked up on Keene's desk, something for which I'm sure he'd kick my ass if he knew about it.

Her mouth curves, but the smile doesn't reach her eyes. "Oh, sure. I mean, just because they're expecting Erzulie and they're getting me, what's the point of worrying?"

My legs come down, and I straighten, concerned. "Lee, why wouldn't you let Beckett work with you?" My protectee's been squawking at his own rehearsals, wondering how his protégée is. In the precarious position I've been placed in, I can hardly say, "Fine, full of sass, and out for vengeance." So, I've been listening to him worry and rant for days.

"Because I have to stop leaning on people, Kane! I have to figure out how to survive on my own. I can't endanger anyone else any more than I have!" The pain of her words drowns out the actual words themselves.

"What's happened?" I ask her.

She stubbornly refuses to answer.

"Leanne, tell me."

"Maybe I should go."

"Maybe you should talk to me," I counter.

"I've already involved you enough."

"Not nearly."

"Damnit, Kane, I'm trying to protect you. Trying to give you that second chance at life you're hoping for," she bites out.

"No, you're closing me out. Why?" And the hurt that causes surprises me.

Instead of answering me, she reaches off camera for something. Much to my surprise, it's a guitar. Strumming, Leanne morphs into Erzulie in the span of seconds. It's disconcerting, to say the least, when her mouth opens and "A Hard Rain's A-Gonna Fall" comes pouring out.

In Erzulie's iconic voice, Dylan's infamous lyrics of black days, evil, and foreboding fill the air. Even down to the head shake her sister gives, the far-off stare during a particularly emotional stanza, Leanne has Kylie's mannerisms down pat. There's no one who sees her on television who would ever suspect the woman singing isn't her twin sister.

But as she wraps up, my stomach begins to churn when I get a good look at the desperation in her eyes. "Tell me what's wrong," I push.

That's when fear truly sets in. "I left something with Carys. Promise me you'll go get it."

"Lee..." I begin.

"She doesn't know to give it to you, specifically. She'll only release it with a..."

"Damnit, Leanne."

Her lips curve crookedly. "I can't give you the information you need if you don't let me speak."

"Crash, I swear to God, if you don't tell me what the hell's going on right now, I'm reading everyone in. To hell with oaths."

"I met with Carys to redo my estate earlier. It left me feeling gutted, all right?" She drops her head.

I release a sigh of relief before confiding, "The hardest feeling was taking Gene off of every life insurance policy, every property I own, every benefit."

Her navy eyes fly up to mine. "It was?"

"He was my brother in every way but blood, and he betrayed everything we stood for. And by 'we' I mean team, company, and country. I had to swallow the fact he was a traitor as well as the fact his blood was on my hands. I may never recover from that betrayal."

"And what would you do if you found out tomorrow it was all a waste? That Gene's death was for nothing?" she whispers.

I stiffen. "What do you mean?"

"Whoever it is wasn't after Kylie, but me. Which means when they catch up to me, I'll become expendable. Obviously."

My mind can't process what she's saying. "How could you be expendable?"

She throws up her hands. "I don't *know*! But they must have killed Lee thinking she was me. Obviously, someone thinks I am. And once I go onstage in front of all those people..."

Sudden fear grips me by the throat. "No. You can't go."

"I have to. We both know it. I can't stay here and hide."

"Don't." The plea is torn from my throat.

Her eyes shimmer like deep sapphires. Her smile is tragic when she modifies the song's lyrics to sing to me, "Where have you been for these last two years?"

Then she hangs up.

And since she's the fucking hacker who instigates all these calls, I can't contact her back. "God damnit," I shout. For half a second, I'm tempted to haul Sam Akin's ass out of bed before I use my training.

Once I start writing out the pertinent parts of what Leanne said, I underline Carys Burke's name.

I know who I will be visiting tomorrow.

"This is most unusual, Mr. McCullough." Carys Burke leans back in her chair. "The instructions I received from Erzulie..."

"Lee," I correct her, just to gauge her reaction. I'm unsurprised when her eyes widen.

"Very well, Lee. The instructions I received from Lee involved a word. I've yet to hear it."

"A single word?" I question. Damn, now I wish I'd listened to Leanne instead of losing it last night.

"Yes."

"Leanne," I throw out.

Carys's expression doesn't change when she says, "No."

I give it a moment's thought before, "Crash."

There's a tiny flicker in her eyes, but again she says, "No. We could do this all day. If you don't mind..."

But there's something important in that information. Something she's not telling me. Leaning forward, I breathe, "*Qəza*," and wait for Carys's reaction.

She inhales sharply. Without a word, she moves over to a cabinet that conceals a safe. After spinning a dial back and forth, she reaches inside for an envelope. Removing it, she closes and locks the safe before standing. Holding it out, she murmurs, "Please be careful on your flight. Tell Beckett to break a leg. We'll be watching on TV, of course."

I nod, slipping the contents inside my jacket. "It's going to be perfect."

She follows me to her door. "I certainly hope so."

After I depart the law office of LLF LLC with a quick wave to their administrative assistant, Angie, I slip the envelope from my pocket. After I open it, I read a quick note scrawled in feminine handwriting. The words send a chill down my spine.

Kane,

If I don't find out what is going on, no one I care for will ever be safe. That includes you.

If I've left, it's because it's no longer safe. You're going to have to trust me. No, I take that back. This goes beyond trust. No matter what may happen, I'm trusting you beyond trust with everything: my heart, my mind, my very soul.

Never doubt my feelings for you. They're real.

Love,

Crash

It's the last two words that galvanize me into action. Pulling my phone from my pocket, I tell Caleb, "I'm coming in."

"After I'm done pulling her fat out of the fryer, I'm going to enjoy slaughtering the both of you. Then I'm roasting you both on the grill I got last Father's Day. I'll enjoy every morsel of you I consume—you realize that, don't you, McCullough?" Keene roars.

Caleb, much calmer, is working on his tablet to get Sam Akin an update about a potential threat to Erzulie. "Really, Kane, you should have simply come to us."

"I was ordered—" I begin.

"Not to be dumb. I believe that's part of our contract, since I wrote it," Keene thunders.

My own temper begins to fire. "She wasn't mine to protect, Keene."

Shrewdly, Caleb notes, "Until she was. That's when you should have come to us."

I open my mouth to refute his observation, but I can't. Leanne Miles is mine in every way, and I'm not stupid enough to refute it. "Do I remove myself from Beckett's detail?" I offer as a solution.

Both of them eye me like I've just grown two heads. "Are you insane?" Caleb asks mildly before returning to his tablet.

"Well, there might be a conflict of interest," I retort.

"For one night." Keene yanks at his hair. "Okay, a few nights. See, this is why Carys should have convinced her to get her own detail when she was on tour last summer. But then..." He abruptly stops talking.

I know where his mind was going. *But then she died.* And who would have thought the death of her twin would have stirred up this hornets' nest. "Then things quieted down. Likely because she wasn't in the spotlight as much after her sister's death."

Keene jumps on the bone I throw him. "That. Exactly that. But if she suspects someone's targeting her again, why not come to us?"

"I can't say I blame her, Keene. She went to someone she can trust." Caleb nods in my direction. "We just can't sacrifice Beckett's protection for Erzulie's."

It takes everything in me not to correct him and call her by her proper name, but I manage to refrain. "So, what do we do?"

Caleb and Keene stare at each other, lost in thought. That's when we're interrupted by a knock on the door. "Enter!" Keene barks.

Tony pops his head in. "Kristoffer Wilde on line two. He wants to go over some last-minute security questions for LA." He ducks back out.

The two men don't move. In fact, their stillness is starting to alarm me. "Um, hello? Do you need me to take the call?" I start to press the flashing button.

Caleb brushes my hand aside and addresses Keene. "She could stay with Kris."

"She could. He's already made the offer," Keene concurs.

"That place is like a fortress."

"It is."

"Plus, she couldn't bitch about security—it's a part of his entourage."

"That's so."

"Would either of you mind letting me know what the hell is going on?" I demand.

"Go ahead." Keene jerks his chin at Caleb, who presses the flashing button.

Within minutes, my heart settles down to a normal arhythmic rhythm as the shorthand between the two men segues into a brilliant plan—Erzulie will stay at the estate of Kristoffer Wilde during her stay in Los Angeles.

"Except when she elects not to—with the proper bodyguard," Caleb adds smoothly, raising a brow in my direction. I catch his meaning immediately and nod. He ducks his head but not before I catch the smile on his face.

Her body will be guarded from all angles, except when she's with someone who will give up his life for her. Me.

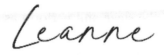

Leanne

Celebrity stylist Dee, whose credentials include stints at Gucci and Stella McCartney, was spotted leaving Beckett Miller's estate in Beverly Hills. The exclusive women's designer was mum when contacted about what she delivered. But it leaves us all to ask, who could he be escorting to this year's Grammys?

— **Eva Henn, Fashion Blogger**

Right now I'm so grateful Kris knows who I am because I'm fairly certain the jig would be up about fifteen minutes into the Grammy rehearsal at the Staples Center.

We've just stepped into the middle of a well-executed project plan that has me frozen in awe. I mutter to him quietly, "If I still have a company when this is over, I'm stealing their project manager. I don't care how much they cost."

He coughs to hide his laugh around the milling people before pulling me aside to allow a forklift to pass. We step over miles of carefully laid cable that is bundled together before it enters into a receiver that will broadcast this week's performance all over the world. I hide my fear as we step into the wings just as lights are being flicked on and off, and that's when I catch sight of the cameras.

Today is one of the final dress rehearsals for the performance. No one has been surprised Kris has been glued to my side as I've been in off-site rehearsals, but this is the first full run-through—the moment every act will get on the stage and perform as if every seat is filled with bodies.

I've been practicing the song I'm going to sing for weeks. There's been speculation in the media whether or not "Erzulie" is going to perform something old or new? Will she be able to make it through the performance? And, as I shared with Kris in the limo on the way over from the villa we're sharing with his family and enough armed guards to make a president feel comfortable, "I refuse to let anyone else down."

Now, as I stand center stage, I close my eyes and pretend the noise around me is the thousands of people who will be in the seats. I tip my head back and begin to sing my sister's number one song, "Inner Peace," without thinking.

I was never afraid
Our souls grew as we lay
In our thicket of grass
Holding hands.
I charge through life
With you right by my side.
As the days go by.
You never let go of
Holding my hand.
I want the stars, but I know
I'll be all right
So long as I have the earth
And your hand
One, two. Years pass.
Your heart still beats with mine
Together we fly towards the sky
And there's peace as you hold my hand.
Always our inner peace.

I stop singing to find a small entourage gathered around the side of the stage. It's no longer just Kris but Beckett Miller, Mick Ceron,

Carly Stolliday, and a security team spread out around them. One man stands apart slightly from the others, his hands typing on a phone.

I don't find it surprising there's a buzzing at my hip when he raises his head and my eyes meet his intense ocean-blue eyes I've never forgotten despite the many years since I've seen them in person.

Finally, after all this time, he's standing in front of me. The arc of electricity that happened that first moment we met each other starts sparking. And from the intensity on his face, he's feeling it too.

Soon, my mind whispers. Just a few moments more and...

Before I can make a move in his direction, Beckett steps out onto the stage with an unusually demure outfit on. I joke, "Going for a new look?"

He rolls his eyes before demanding, "Is that what you're singing tomorrow night?"

I rapidly shake my head. "I can't. I wrote it for my sister. It's just the first time I've been able..." I look past him and catch Kane's eye. His lips curve in understanding. One night during our many conversations, I told him I hadn't yet been able to successfully perform Kylie's music. *The paparazzi is going to have a field day*, I remember saying.

Then let them. This isn't your life, Leanne.

A landslide of emotions cascades over me as I stare at him. "I can't let them dictate what I do." Even though I'm saying the words to Beckett, they're for Kane, and he knows it, judging by the smile that breaks out across his face.

But it's Beckett who responds. "I agree. You handle what you can, Ky. And know we're all here for you." He waves Mick and Carly over. Soon, I'm engulfed in the caring concern of people my sister hobnobbed with regularly, and I understand why she kept them as close as she did.

"So what are you singing?" Beckett pushes.

"What are you singing?" I counter with Lee's sass.

"You'll just have to see at rehearsal." He thrusts his chin up in the air. I narrow my eyes as I glimpse something poking out under his collar. Just as quickly, it's hidden when he looks down his nose at me. "Now, spill it."

"I know it's not a word you're used to, Becks, but no." He looks so crestfallen, I can't help but genuinely laugh.

Kris chooses then to step in. "Come on, Erzulie. You're due in Costume. Then Sound needs you."

Beckett is still pouting. I back away, wiggling my fingers, and back into a warm body. "Umph." Strong arms slip arms around me to stabilize me. My head snaps up, and there he is. His arms tighten slightly.

Kane.

He whispers, "Check your phone when you have a moment, my Leanne," before setting me away from his warm body. His eyes spear through me, suspending my heartbeat as his hands side up my side enough to stabilize me.

I nod before hurrying toward Kris. I have to escape now, or I know I never will. I feel stunned over eight words and my name whispered in his husky voice. Why? We've talked so many times over the last few weeks. What is happening to me?

And for the first time since she died, I hear my sister laughing hysterically in my head. I begin cursing.

"Well, that was interesting," Kris muses.

"I told you, I'll be fine singing," I throw off airily.

"I didn't mean the singing."

I growl just as we hit the door for costumes. "Later, Kris."

He leans forward and whispers, "I've never known you to back down from something you want."

I glance about and hiss, "You don't know *me*."

His smile softens his hawkish features. "Don't I? It's amazing what you find out about people when they honor those they love." Before I can respond, he saunters away, leaving me stunned, which is probably a good thing as they're about to dress me in clothing my twin would wear onstage.

I close my eyes in mild fear. *What happened to the matching outfits Mom used to dress us in?* Bravely, I shove open the door to Costume.

I feel the heat of the spotlights as they clean burn through the simple white dress I'm wearing. I feel more exposed than when I overheard this is supposed to be the most-watched Grammys in years. Strumming Kylie's guitar, I center myself. Out just beyond the lights are people who believe in me, us.

And it's with the strength of those short-lived but strong friendships I'm able to read the teleprompter with the words I prepared and speak into the microphone as my sister. "A year ago, I was presented with the Best New Artist award." When I was flying out, I remembered the words Kylie said to me, her excitement, what she believed. And those words echo from my mouth. "I knew this was it. This was the beginning of the rest of my life. And that night—" I swallow hard. "—I thanked my twin for always being there for me. So, tonight, I'd like to honor one of Recording Academy's past Best New Artist winners, as well as my sister, by singing a song that eclipsed so many of the dreams we shared."

As I begin strumming the notes to Norah Jones's "Come Away With Me," the people hustling around the dress rehearsal hush. Then my voice, Kylie's voice, rips through the arena, lending passion and power to the words we whispered about in our bedroom so long ago. Words about taking the hand of love and disrupting life, no matter where we were, so long as we could grab hold to it.

My eyes drift to the wings where Kane stood just a few short hours ago. I feel his presence even if I can't make him out. And the words of his text fill me up with the courage I need.

Sing with your voice. You have it inside you to do this, Crash. I believe in you.

Knowing he's been a touchstone, that he understands the emotions I'm experiencing, the irony strikes me hard. In a roomful of strangers, I feel safe because a man of honor has been silently standing behind me offering me his strength, and no one but me is aware of it. My head falls forward as I pick out each note and sing.

When it's over, I touch the fingers still holding Kylie's pic to my heart, then my lips, before I raise it skyward. *I love you, Lee. Always.*

I stand, and the moment I do, I almost collapse under the force of the applause that is flung at me—and this is just a dress rehearsal. I absorb it so wherever Kylie is, she knows this is for her. Everything I'm doing is for her.

And without another word, I glide from the stage.

I can do this. In a few days, I can be my sister, prolonging the masquerade so we can find out who killed her. When I do, I hope like hell they suffer as much as I am, my family is, the people who loved her will.

Even then, it won't be enough.

KANE

Conversation starter: When are you most vulnerable: morning, noon, or night? What causes it? Reminder, keep it PG rated! I do *not* want to hear about your sex lives. Give me your emotions. You know what those are, right?

For those of you who need a refresher, Oxford's definition is: e·mo·tion

- a natural instinctive state of mind deriving from one's circumstances, mood, or relationships with others.

- instinctive or intuitive feeling as distinguished from reasoning or knowledge.

— **Viego Martinez, Celebrity Blogger**

I'm waiting for Leanne when she floats offstage barefoot. She's dressed in a white maxi dress with shimmering sheer accents that were made opaque by the lights shining down on her. Her hair is in loose waves down her shoulders, artfully tangled.

She appears feminine, earthy, and strong. Yet, I know if Kylie were alive and standing right next to her, even dressed the same, I'd immediately be able to tell the difference between the two of them. She's a protector, brave, and willing to do anything for those she loves. It calls to me on some elemental level. There's something in the direct way she meets a challenge head-on. There's a confidence that exudes from her when she sees something she wants.

And right now, her eyes aren't hiding what that is.

Gliding past Beckett, he reaches out to get her attention, but she disentangles herself as she makes her way to stand directly in front of me. Her free hand reaches out for mine, and I clasp hers like a lifeline. Maybe it is for both of us. "How was it?" Leanne asks me anxiously.

"If you sing half as well tomorrow, they're going to be clamoring for a new record the day after," I tell her honestly.

Her pert nose wrinkles. And I laugh aloud. I'm about to pull her in my arms when a shadow descends over us both.

He's muscular, tattooed, and anxious. Crap. A pissed Beckett Miller I can handle, no sweat. An emotional one is an entirely different story. "Ky? Kane? Everything all right here?"

I open my mouth to explain, but Leanne beats me to it. She reaches over and touches his arm briefly. "When you were in Texas, I reached Kane instead of you one night. He's...helped." She turns her face upward at me and smiles.

Beckett blinks. "He did?"

"We have some shared experiences, Beckett. It's not a club others should be in." She moves away and lays her head on his chest briefly. "But I'll never be able to thank you for literally carrying me during the worst of it."

He swallows convulsively. "Okay, Ky—"

"Lee," she reminds him. "Remember, that's what she used to call me. Lee. I can't be someone I'm not without her."

Beckett's head tips to the side as he tries to reconcile *this* Erzulie with the one he's known the last several years—hell, even the last several months. I recall everything Leanne charged through until her laser focus cut through the possibilities of what happened to Kylie. But to an outsider, it must have appeared as if Erzulie spiraled out of control. I can't help but appreciate the fact that despite our talk last night, he struggles a bit before accepting. "Okay...Lee. Just remember, we're all here if you need us."

"I wouldn't be here without knowing that," she reassures him.

Beckett looks like he's about to say more, but he's called onstage. "Kane, we'll talk more later."

He's a few feet away when I mutter, "Must we?"

Leanne begins to laugh softly.

Beckett hears her and whirls around, shock evident on his face. Then the shock morphs into a look of resigned acceptance, a brother passing along the responsibilities of watching over his sister to another. I feel Leanne's hand on my arm as Beckett is tossed his mic and begins to sing on the upbeat. "He is pretty special, isn't he?"

"Not as special as you," I tell her honestly, drowning in the dark blue eyes staring up at me.

Her lips curve. "How about I get out of this get up and we figure out when we're going on that first date you promised me?"

I wrap an arm around her waist and nod at Kristoffer Wilde. He frowns for a moment before slipping out his phone. I figure by the time I'm done escorting Leanne to Costume, he'll be looped in on the fact I know everything. At least, I hope. We reach the doors she needs to enter. I hate to let her out of my sight for a second. "What were you thinking?"

"Anywhere with you, Kane. I just sang you a whole bunch of ideas. Pick one." Her smile is filled with challenge. Then she slips inside.

As the words to "Come Away With Me" float through my mind, I'm glad I have an idea to start our tomorrow, which—God willing—will lead to a forever with this complex woman.

After forever, I'll leave the rest of eternity up to her.

KANE

It's my parents' wedding anniversary—fifty-two years today. Happy anniversary, Mom and Dad! They'll kill me for telling the world, but their first date could have been a catastrophe if my dad wasn't smart. Apparently, my dad was supposed to go out with my mom's sister, but he brought a buddy along to make up the slack. Good planning, Dad. Even better Aunt Shirley fell for him.

Now, for a chance at a Zoom call with yours truly, tell me about your best or worst first date.

— **Moore You Want**

Leaning across the hall from Costume, I wait for Leanne to emerge. Expecting her to be tricked out in something flamboyant to match the Hollywood vibe suffocating the already smoggy air, I'm pleasantly surprised to see her emerge in a pair of worn jean shorts, a black tank, and an unbuttoned flannel, which floats behind her as she dodges around people to make her way to me. Her trademark blonde hair is tucked beneath a baseball cap, dangerously proclaiming her a Sox fan amid Dodgers territory. My lips curve at the sight. Proclaiming her allegiance to her favorite baseball team is likely the least dangerous thing Qɑza's ever done.

The only thing I want to change is when she whips out enormous sunglasses that take up over half of her face, hiding her eyes from me. I understand why she's slipped them on. It's not to hide from me; it's to protect us both once we leave the shelter of the arena. But she has no idea of the pains I've gone to in order to protect her identity—including exposing my own feelings to the one person who could have made today impossible by sending my ass on a plane back to New York.

Despite how uncomfortable last night was, I hold more respect than ever for Beckett, and I know once he finds out the truth about Kylie, he's going to be completely gutted. It's obvious he truly does consider her a kid sister and—with that understanding—appropriately grilled me after I explained how Erzulie and I were discovering feelings for one another. To say he has an overprotective streak is putting it mildly, I recall with some amusement.

"She's vulnerable, Kane!" he shouts. I merely recline on his couch while the wild man paces back and forth, fuming. "She could just be looking for comfort. Have you thought of that?"

"It's not like that, Becks. If it were, I would have kept my distance. I didn't think I had the heart to fall in love with her, yet it wasn't that. She threw me a lifeline when I didn't realize I needed one. Somehow, she wrapped herself inside me when I wasn't looking." Starting with the first time we crashed into one another years ago.

He freezes. "Love?"

I arch a brow at him. "If it was something less, do you think I'd be risking something as important as your respect by having this conversation?"

He storms over to the windows overlooking the Pacific. For a long while, nothing is said between us as he absorbs the information I've given him. I start to push off the couch to leave him to his thoughts when his words float over me. "I never would have imagined the two of you together, but there's something about her that's changed."

I don't reply because it's unnecessary. We both know the trauma of losing her sister caused a catastrophic shift inside her. But he believes it's Kylie he's worrying over, whereas I know it's my Leanne. I offer, "If anything, you're likely noticing qualities in her that are more like her sister."

"Maybe that's it," he muses. He keeps his back to me. "If she's giving you a shot at her heart amid all of this, don't let it go. No matter what."

Something untwists inside me. "I won't."

"You're a good man, Kane. From the first moment we met, I always thought you were too good to be around the likes of me."

Startled, my head jerks up to find Beckett's turned to face me. His foot is braced against the window. "What the hell makes you say that?"

"You were a damn hero, man. And I grew up a worthless piece of garbage." Beckett's eyes drop to his booted foot.

"Neither of those things are accurate," I inform him forcefully. "Yeah, you grew up in shit, but that never stuck to you. And I'm not a hero."

"Could have fooled me." I go to interrupt, but his face morphs into a slow grin. "Captain fucking America and the Indie Princess. The press is going to have a field day with this."

"Must you remind me?"

"Well, it's better than the rumors going around about me," he remarks cheerfully. He pushes off the window and slaps me on the shoulder as he passes me. But instead of letting my shoulder go, his hand clamps down until I meet his eyes. "I'm glad it's you. Not just because she'll be looked after, but because you're one of the best men I know."

And after completely astounding me with that remark, Beckett strides from the room to find the others occupying his enormous beachfront mansion.

As she finally lightly jumps over the final bundle of wires taped to the floor to land in front of me, I know there's no way to fully protect her. She wouldn't be the woman I fell for if there was. But today, I can do my best on our first date. I hold out my hand, palm up. She slips hers into it. And we both feel the surge of power. Tugging her closer, I whisper against her ear, "Let's get out of here."

Dropping my hand, Leanne wraps her arm around my waist, as comfortable as if we've been doing this together for years. Her words ring in my head. *God, Kane, don't make me fall in love with you.* And after the hottest sex I've ever had, regardless of whether I actually touched her skin, I know we're both already reached the same place.

We're together, mind and soul. The last thing to join is our bodies.

I guide her down a hall that darkens almost to pitch-black midway through. Her breathing accelerates next to me, but I'm certain it's not fear but the same anticipation coursing through me.

When we reach the darkest part of the hallway, where I'm certain the cameras will only be able to register two bodies, I whirl her around and push her until her back presses against the concrete. I knock off her hat and rip off her sunglasses. A breathless "What..." escapes her lips before I press my body against hers. There's just enough light for me to capture the smile in her moonlit eyes as I lean my head forward.

As I get closer, I can feel the hot burst of air escaping her parted lips as she manages to whisper, "Kane."

I rub my thumb over her jaw, back and forth. The setting sucks. I want to be able to absorb her into every one of my senses when I take her lips for the first time, but I won't let this moment become fodder for some tabloid.

Instead of relying upon sight, I give her the pressure of my body, wrap her in my scent, and whisper her name as I brush my lips against her ear. "Leanne." Then, I feel the satin of her skin against my lips as I drag them across her cheek before I fasten them to hers, capturing the moan she lets out as it slides down my throat.

My tongue slides past her lips, and I get my first taste of her. Mint and dark, like she'd just munched on a piece of chocolate before meeting me. I pull her tighter against me, even as her hand slides up my chest. Leanne grips me by the back of the neck, holding me in place as her lips devour mine. A nip, a soothing swipe of her tongue.

I eat at her lips, leaving no part of the plump flesh unbranded. We've been building toward this moment, this kiss, for longer than anyone has suspected. Even us. My hands trace the length of her body, finally settling on cupping the back of her head, the other arm banded around her waist as I fuse us together. Fucking hell. I need more.

Long moments together, I realize this was the biggest tactical mistake I've ever made. I never should have kissed her here when all I want to do is pull her beneath me and join our bodies together the way we're both craving. Tearing my mouth from hers, I bury my lips against her shoulder and murmur her name.

"Why are you stopping?" Her voice sounds like she's just run a marathon. And in some respects, we have. We are. We're running to catch up with the emotions that are miles ahead of us.

Slowly, my hands drop down. Instead of running them over her body the way I'm almost desperate to, I find her hands, now desperately clenching my hips. I pull them away so I can lace our fingers together. I can't help but open my mouth on the skin I've bared by nuzzling away her overshirt. My breath rasps against her skin when I declare, "Because we need to get out of here before I take you right now. That isn't what I have planned for our first date."

"It isn't?" I'm thrilled her voice comes out a bit wild.

"Not for the date," I inform her as I step back. Flicking on my flashlight through my pants, I spot her glasses and cap. Bending over to pick them up, I hand them to her. She quickly stuffs her hair beneath the hat and slides her shades back on.

I grab her hand and begin dragging her toward the light. She's silent until we reach the street and I'm edging her to the SUV Mitch is guarding. He nods before quickly disappearing. Once we're settled, she asks, "Then what's our plan, Kane?"

"How does a picnic sound?" I start the car and check traffic before I pull a U-turn.

"In LA? We'll have the paps surrounding us in no time," she scoffs.

"We're leaving LA," I announce.

Her jaw drops in surprise. "For real?"

"Yes. Now, no more hints." I give her what I hope is a reassuring smile and follow the directions Beckett gave me this morning. "We have twenty hours."

"For a first date?" she yelps.

"I'm out to make a hell of a first impression," I inform her haughtily.

That's when I hear her whisper, "You did that years ago."

Leanne

The pre-Grammy events are all abuzz, but Erzulie hasn't been spotted at any of them. We wonder where she's at or who she's with.

— **Sexy&Social, All the Scandal You Can Handle**

"Where are we?" I gasp as I step down the stairs into the cold. I'm grateful Kane handed me a pair of his workout pants and told me to slip them over my shorts while we were on board the jet. Beckett Miller's jet. I feel Kane's arms wrap around me before I joke, "I know I've been living in an alternate reality. I just didn't know it included a stop in crazy town."

Kane laughs and guides me toward a familiar-model black SUV, as it's the same model Beckett's driven around in. A man nods at him before pitching the keys in his direction. Kane catches them one-handed. "Thanks," he calls out.

The man jerks up his chin before disappearing inside the ante building.

"Do I want to know?" I ask because we both know that with a few minutes with my computer, I could find out everything.

Kane gets me settled into the front seat before jogging around the front. Although they're a security nightmare, right now I'm saying a million thanks for keyless starters as the car is as toasty warm as the jet was. Kane slides in and immediately puts the car in gear. Once we're on the main road, he answers, "One of Hudson's guys is here on assignment. I called in a few favors."

"For me?" I ask breathlessly, unable to tear my eyes away from his handsome face.

"No." He reaches over and lifts my hand to his lips. He darts his eyes to the side. "For us. Is it too much too soon?"

I contemplate his words as he places my hand on his thigh. I immediately begin tracing the seam of his jeans with my fingers. "If it was any other man, yes."

"Why not me?" he asks. And I know it isn't because he wants an ego boost—he needs to know this is right for me, for us.

"Because I've been searching for you everywhere. Kane. Somehow, someway, you're everything I ever needed and never knew I couldn't live without. Even Kylie knew that."

His muscles jerk beneath my fingers. "What makes you say that?"

"A few weeks before she died, she told me she wanted to introduce me to someone on Beckett's security team," I muse.

"That's what you meant that night," he recalls.

I nod. We drive for a while in silence before we pull off to a classic cabin that has enormous frontage to Lake Tahoe. "Wow," I breathe as I slide from the car. "You do realize we have to be back in like twelve hours?"

"Sixteen. And I figured this was better than some hotel where you'd be recognized." His arm circles my shoulder as he guides me toward the back deck, which boasts postcard views of Tahoe. While I gawk, Kane unearths a key from beneath a welcome mat and unlocks the sliding glass door. He joins me for a few moments before resting his chin on my head. "There's no expectation for us inside. No pressure. I just want to give you the freedom to be you for a little while."

I rotate so my head falls forward against his chest. "I've wanted you from day one, Kane."

I feel his lips curve against my hair. "Since you realized who I was?"

"No, since the day we crashed outside of Free People." I feel his hard body jolt. "I'm tired of pretending. I need you. Now."

I tip my head back and find his ocean-colored eyes are hot on mine. He begins plucking at my borrowed sweatpants. "And I want these pants back."

My head tilts coquettishly, and I peer at him through lowered lids. "You do? Then how am I supposed to stay warm?"

He slides his hand in the front and yanks me to him. A wicked smile crosses his face, one I recognize from our play the other night on the phone. I wheeze out a breath that doesn't go unnoticed. His fingers wedge between the band of my jean shorts and my skin. "Oh, God. Kane."

I begin to pant and have to clench my thighs together to prevent a rush of wetness from just the slightest touch of his fingers against my bare skin.

Hot? Forget hot. His eyes are flaming blue, and I'm ready to be burned. Judging by the way he backs me toward the open door, he is too. "Let's find out."

As soon as we cross the threshold, Kane sweeps me over his shoulder and heads for the first bedroom he can find.

By the time my back hits the bed, my sister's killer could present his or herself gift wrapped in handcuffs and I might not remember why they were there. Maybe, maybe if Lee herself was laughing at me from the doorway, I might recall something beyond moaning Kane's name.

Other than that, I'm not certain.

I've had sex, even good sex. Kane's hands and mouth on me are beyond that. His heat and hunger are diving into the core of my heart and amplifying my emotions back at me a hundred times. It's need spiraling out of control at its most basic level.

His lips caress my jaw, down the line of my throat to the sensitive juncture where my shoulder and neck meet. It elicits divine shivers. His hands begin slowly divesting me of the clothing I hastily threw on in LA in my hurry to get to him.

But I forgot what else was beneath.

His hands and lips pause as he reaches the stiletto strapped to my kidney. He draws in a deep breath before it shudders out. Pushing the eject button, he tests the quick release before sliding it back home. Without a word, he removes the harness.

"Kane," I start to explain.

He shakes his head. "You do whatever you have to do to remain safe, Crash. I don't care what that takes." Moving over me slightly, he drops the rig onto the side table before capturing my lips in a fierce kiss. "You being alive is all that matters."

And just that easily, I slide the rest of the way into love. I whimper as I slide my fingers into the hair at the nape of his neck. While I engage him in a bruising kiss, Kane busies himself tugging down my shorts, leaving me mostly naked before him. When we come up for air, I breathlessly inform him, "You need to catch up."

A fingertip scrapes over the lace bralette and thong I'm left in. "I wish we had days to explore." His voice is filled with regret.

"We will," I promise him.

He gives me a crooked smile before he stands and quickly yanks his shirt over his head, revealing powerful muscles that clothes mask. Toeing off his shoes and socks, Kane quickly shoves down his slacks, revealing, like the night we were on the phone, he's commando. My eyes immediately latch onto that part of him that seems to throb on its own. He croons, "Ah, Leanne. I feel like I've waited forever for this."

His hand drops down as he strokes himself, reenacting our phone call from the other night. "Oh, is that what you want?" I taunt. I stretch back across the bed and slide one hand to my breast and start slowly sliding the other hand lower when I hear a low growl.

And feel a large object in my way.

Kane's head has already beat my hand there.

His lips cover my bareness, first sucking me entirely into his whole mouth. Then he parts my folds and begins flicking at my distended nub. I arch my back, both hands plucking at my nipples. "Uhh." And then my hands slap the side of the bed when he slides one of his thick fingers inside of me.

Preparing me.

For him.

For us.

Another finger joins the first as he surges up, his lips still wet with the taste of me as he consumes me with a fierce kiss. Words are unnecessary as I wrap myself around him. Mine. Yours. The necessary commitment doesn't need to be reiterated just because we're physically touching. I've already given this man my body.

This time it just happens to be in person.

His head drops, and he captures the tip of one of my aching nipples. I cry out as he feasts on it, his fingers still moving diabolically inside of me. The deep pulls combined with his fingers drive me closer to orgasm, but I'm fighting it. Just like the first time, "I want it to be with you, Kane."

He slides his fingers out slowly. My greedy body doesn't understand what my heart does—that I need more than just a release. I need completion. Spreading my thighs, he nudges his hefty cock against my folds. "Do I need protection, Crash?"

At first, I don't hear him. I'm too busy staring at his swollen lower lip. I lean up and lay my lips against it before I fall back, panting, "It's so close, I just want to bite it."

"Bite it when I'm inside you," he says raggedly. "Do I need protection?"

"No, I'm on the..."

I don't get to finish the sentence before Kane drives his hips forward and pushes his heavy flesh inside me. My hands fly to his ass, digging my nails deep as I adjust to the size of him inside of me. His hips don't move until I start to writhe restlessly beneath him. Even then he merely adjusts, keeping a close eye on me.

Finally, I snap, "What are you waiting for?"

He leans down, driving himself a little deeper when he does. I moan, my head snapping back before I whip my eyes to his. There's a fierce light of something glowing in his eyes, way beyond lust. It warms my heart as much as his words. "You said you wanted to bite it, Crash. I was just waiting for you to get on with it."

I surge up and take a sharp nip of his lip. "Happy now?"

His eyes glow down into mine as his cock drags back. "With you? I'll always be happy."

I pull his hips back into mine as his head drops. His lips become busy as he sucks first one nipple, then the other. Streaking pleasure has me tightening my legs around his hips.

Kane grunts as his thrusts become harder, faster. Finally, just as I'm about to go over, he fuses his mouth to mine. He presses his hand down onto my hip, pinning me into the mattress. And as I ripple and clench around him, I tremble when I feel him release inside.

Kane holds himself off me for as long as he can, but finally, his arms give out. Shifting his body weight to the side, we both lie there panting—perspiration dripping off our bodies. A while later, he catches my chin in his hands, and he whispers the only thing I need to hear.

"Leanne..."

Then his lips curve a sated smile at me before he drifts off. And before I do the same, I realize that whether I have a weapon or not, I'm defenseless to holding him out now.

Kane McCullough is firmly embedded inside my heart.

KANE

Who are you most excited to see perform at the Grammys tomorrow night? Brendan Blake? Beckett Miller? Erzulie? Hell, why choose! Make sure to tune in early as they walk the red carpet. We will be!

— Sexy&Social, All the Scandal You Can Handle

Leanne's tucked up against me, our bodies locked together like she's the missing piece I've needed to complete me. "In that moment, I felt like I'd rather have been dead right alongside of him than have dealt with his betrayal." My voice is hushed as I share with her what I've shared with no one else about Gene.

She remains quiet while I gather my thoughts, but her hand is stroking my chest, continuously coming back to rest over my heart. Occasionally, she'll shift to drop a kiss over it before relaxing back in my arms.

"We grew up together. Hell, we even shared the same birthday."

"When is it?" Her throaty voice asks.

"January 16."

"Right after mine. Is it too late to wish you a belated happy birthday?"

"No, considering I've refused to celebrate it for years."

"Even with your family?"

I nod, my head brushing against hers. She doesn't criticize my choice, merely says, "You know about my private celebration with Kylie this year. I'm not certain I could have handled much more."

"Ma understands. So does my sister. I just...can't."

"Like you said, the firsts are tough."

My lips curve against the top of her head. "What are you—a genius—doing listening to a guy like me?"

I feel hers curve against my shoulder. "Must we discuss that?"

"What, you being a genius?" A teasing note enters my voice.

I can practically feel her roll her eyes. "Yes. How about we leave it at I have a fondness for computers?"

"That's like saying Mozart had a fondness for pianos. Or Beckett has a few tattoos."

She laughs, and the openness of the sound does more to heal the wounds we've each sustained than any amount of time. Tucking her close, I confess, "I locked everything that had to do with Gene out of my life—celebrations, laughter. Well, everything except my family, Brit, and Maddie."

"Who are they?" Her fingers have resumed their comforting glide over my skin.

"Gene's wife and daughter. Even at the end, as he was trying to hand off the drive, he claimed..." My voice catches.

She nods. And I realize I don't need to tell her the specifics. As Qaza, she would have had access to the mission files. But her next words shock me. "That mission almost broke me."

"What do you mean?" I clip out.

Her hand stops moving. "I was twenty-two, Kane. It was next to impossible for me to absorb what I had just unearthed. I had no idea until after that it was my actions that caused the lives of our soldiers, caused another to lose his career. I couldn't function. What the hell was I doing? My mission was to stop the bad guys, not ruin the good ones. There was no order to this. I began to unravel and..."

"Hold on. None of what happened in Azerbaijan was your fault, Leanne. The fault belongs to Gene. The man who was a traitor to our country—for what? Money. Someone got to him." And as I'm saying the words to convince her, they unlock something that's been burning inside of me for years.

The truth.

"Christ. They got to him. What the hell did they have on him? Do you know?" I surge up to inspect her face.

She opens her mouth and swiftly shuts it. "Does it matter now?"

I drop back and drape my arm back over my eyes, tucking her back against my body. "No. The only thing that I regret is there was no recording of what transpired in that field."

I feel her frown against my skin. "There wasn't? Don't you wear a recording device when you're on an op in the event your live transmission doesn't go through?"

God, there are times when I love her brain. "Which was pointed out during a subcommittee hearing. Apparently Gene's was turned off, and mine was damaged—though I have no idea how. That plus my friendship with Gene played a huge part in the manner with which I was initially questioned by the subcommittee."

Leanne growls. "That's bullshit. You were a decorated soldier with no history of—"

"Yeah. That's probably why I was offered a desk job instead of a court-martial."

Her harrumph tells me exactly what she feels about that. Then her wicked eyes raise to mine. "I could always..."

"No."

"Come on. You've never played on the edge. You never know what files will turn up suddenly, Kane."

"Or manufactured," I laugh. "I know how you agency types work."

"Well, that too. But sometimes, it's for the greater good."

"This isn't the greater good, Leanne. Things worked out the way they were supposed to."

Her chin lifts, but she doesn't argue the point. Instead, she asks me, "Will you tell me about Brit and Maddie?"

I tuck her back into place where I want her before I explain about Gene's high school sweetheart and the baby they had. Reaching over to the bedside, I pull up the photo she sent the night Kylie died. I'm absorbed as Leanne enlarges it and smiles at the innocence of the little girl. "She's worth fighting the world for." Just as I'm about to agree, she hands the phone back to me. "Not betraying it."

I roll away to slide the phone to the end table. When I roll back, the fierceness in her eyes snags the last piece of my heart. Everything these last few weeks I've been feeling about this woman—the intense attraction, the protectiveness, the admiration—all coalesce.

And I can't not reach for her.

She moves into my arms easily. When she does, I tighten them around her before murmuring into her hair, "I never could have imagined this."

"What?" Her head tips back so I can fall into the never-ending depths of her midnight eyes. She's holding nothing back: neither secrets nor her feelings. It's all there lying as open on her face as her body was before.

Tenderly, I twist a lock of her fair hair around my fingers and give it a tug before teasing, "Falling for a woman I've been dating online. I mean, we all know the hazards of that, Crash. She could have been a complete psycho when I met her in person. I'm so glad you turned out not to be completely batshit crazy."

Leanne tosses her head back against my arm as she screeches with laughter.

My lips curve indulgently as she enjoys this carefree moment, something she hasn't had since Kylie was murdered. Wanting to be a part of it, to feel the laughter as it vibrates through her, I roll her to her back. Pressing my lips against hers lightly, I whisper, "I've think I started to fall the night you trusted me with your blood, Leanne."

I absorb her gasp as I go on. "You're everything I always dreamed a woman could be—strong, stubborn, loyal, and so fucking smart it makes my head spin trying to keep up. I don't know what the hell you could possibly see in a guy like me, but as long as you do, I'm here. Just know that..."

I have to pause because her fingers come up and lay across my lips. "Hush." Her lashes are spiky with wetness as she stares up at me. "Now, it's your turn to listen."

I don't protest when she rolls me to my back and straddles me. "This, you, me, it's once in a lifetime for me, Kane. I've lived so long in the shadows, I felt like I was destined to be there. Yet, you understand. You don't try to make me step away. You bring the light to me. And all you have to do is simply be there. No one's ever just been there. Someone I can trust beyond trust. It's everything I've been looking for and..."

"And what?" I squeeze my arms.

"I found it in you."

"Not Kylie?" I probe, not because I'm doubting her words but because I want her to let go of some of her grief.

Her head shakes just before she lies down on top of me. "No. She's a part of me, Kane. There's no real way to explain this. I'm always going to feel like I've lost a part of myself because she's gone."

I rub my hand up and down her back. "You don't have to."

"I do for me." With that, I quiet and let her explain herself. She pours out her story from the beginning, concluding it with the order to subdue her grief. The emotions she lets out tumble clean through her in a way she hasn't had a chance to let go of. My chest is damp with her tears by the time she's finished. In the end, I'm inclined to find Leanne's handler and kick his ass, but she hasn't given me his name. "God knows what I'd do if I had it," I mutter.

"Hmm?" Her breath flutters across my neck, causing a chill to race through me.

"Nothing." I run my hand through her hair, lifting it from her neck. "Now what?"

"Now, I finish what I started. Then..." Her shoulders move up and down. "I guess it's back to life. I don't know."

"What about your parents?"

Her laugh is full of bitterness. "What more would you like to know about them? Name? Address? The fact that since Lee died they can't bear the sight of me? My mother blames me for my sister dying because I should have 'done something,' though what more I have no idea."

It doesn't take a genius to identify the underlying devastation her parents' actions have caused. "You love them." I pull back so I can judge her true feelings.

"Yes. I love them the way I love Kylie, the way I love you. Always. Forever. But it hurts because with them I know I'll never have those emotions returned again." Her chin wobbles briefly before she firms it up.

I groan before I push her onto her back. I cover her body with mine, kissing her lips, which are so soft from the tears she's shed. I have to have her again, touch her, brand her to me. To show her how much I love her.

How I always will.

So I set about reminding her there's more to life than the shadows of despair we've both been living in. There's the light that spins from two people loving each other.

KANE

March

Is rock god Beckett Miller carrying indie goddess Erzulie away from the scene of the crime so his newest lover won't know? Shh, we won't tell. #tryst #lifewithbeckett #grammys #tsk #wewouldtoo
   — @LFrederickShadowOfficial

All hell is breaking loose. And to keep myself from taking it out on people who don't deserve it, I'm running on the treadmill. Hard.

We've been back from the Grammys for half a minute and a shit-storm has evolved, and I'm caught right in the eye of it with my lover on one side and a man I respect on the other. And because I'm sworn not to reveal who Leanne is since that's tantamount to revealing a national security secret, Beckett can't fix his love life. So the rest of us are paying for it. It took weeks to pry out of him what happened, but when I pieced the dates together, an overwhelming guilt crashed over me.

His relationship is on the rocks because I distracted Leanne.

One afternoon when I had a break and was over at her place engaging in some midday shower sex, a post with a picture of Beckett carrying Leanne the night she was drugged from Snowy-T's party emerged, only it insinuated it was from the Grammys. The problem is that not only has he tried to deny it, no one can find any semblance of the photo because—I amp the speed just a little more—Leanne has a miracle script that scrubs photos of her sister from the web. It's like she's some sort of benevolent demigod who decided what information the public could absorb to formulate an opinion about her sister. In my less infuriated moments, I must admit it's fucking brilliant. Just not right now.

"What the hell. Just put it back," I shout.

"Don't you take that tone with me, Kane. It's not that fucking simple," she yells back.

I remind her of our earlier conversation. "I thought you didn't deal with photos."

"I don't." I'm about to shout something snarky when she grits out, "But a member of my team wrote this for me."

"What kind of bonus did you have to give them to do it?" I snark.

"A Porsche. Fucking customized. So, yeah, that's how I know the damn picture isn't retrievable. It's that damn good."

"Christ." I scrub my hands over my face. "Why not give him some Bitcoin?"

"Because he wanted the new car. He had enough of the other."

"Of course. So, what the hell am I supposed to do to help fix this?"

Leanne stares at me openmouthed before stomping off, muttering under her breath. "Let yourself out when you leave," she calls over her shoulder as she slams the door to her bedroom.

That was three days ago, and I still haven't heard a peep out of her. I know I owe her a huge apology. None of this is a part of our relationship, but I owe Beckett so much. After Gene, working for him gave me a sense of purpose. Then, somewhere along the way, concluding with our conversation in LA, our relationship has shifted. He's still the person I'm responsible for protecting, but he's edged his way into a place I thought I sealed off when Gene died.

Beckett Miller's somehow become a friend.

I test the thought out as I slow down before I can't walk tomorrow. "I suppose it was inevitable."

"What? That Carys would yank my head out of my ass? Ward

would work a miracle? I'd hope so considering what I pay them." The man in question leans against the doorjamb.

I stop the treadmill and lean against the top as he approaches. "Did they? Does this mean there's not going to be any more '80s ballads being played at all hours?"

He sniffs. "That wasn't because I was devastated."

"Then what on earth would make a man as talented as you listen to that?"

"Inspiration. You should try it. It might help you get back into Lee's good graces."

I open my mouth and shut it before offering, "For a man who's up shit's creek with his own relationship, how about keeping out of mine?"

He slaps me across the shoulder. "No can do, Kane. Because I suspect you did the same thing I did back when it first happened—chewed her ass out over that photo. Only this wasn't her fault."

I chew on my lip before asking, "Ward found it? How?"

"He found the picture on a deleted page on the blogger's website. And here's the best part." He tips his chin. "Notice anything different?"

My eyes zero in on the new ink I drove him to get while we were in LA. "That won't be on the picture unless someone got a load of it in LA."

"Exactly. It's not there. So, I'm planning on ambushing Paige to get her to listen."

"Do you think that's a good idea?" I towel off my face.

A flash of uncertainty crosses his normally overconfident face. "It's the best one I've got. What are you going with? How are you going to get Kylie to forgive you?"

My lips open to automatically correct him, to call her Leanne, when I freeze. Leanne. She did this. She fixed this because she knew it was important to me. "God damnit," I swear.

Beckett's lips curve. "You're off for the next few days. Go make things right." He turns and makes his way out of the gym.

"Who's covering your ass?" I shout.

"If I'm very, very lucky, the woman I owe a few dozen apologies to," Beckett says seriously. Before I retort that isn't what I mean, he disappears, leaving me to yank out my phone and coordinate his coverage with Mitch before I figure out how to deal with my own screwup.

I knock on her door about three hours later. I have a bag in my hand that contains what my mother assures me will make the perfect apology dinner.

"Homemade lasagne shows you care, Kane. It takes time and effort to make."

"I get that, Ma. I got to go if I'm going to swing this by dinnertime," I tell her for the millionth time.

"But I want to hear all about this woman," she protests.

"You'll hopefully get to meet her." I ignore her gasps as I search my phone for what I'm looking for.

"When?" she demands.

"I'm not sure. It might be a bit."

"Kane," she warns.

"Later, Ma. Love you. Bye." I disconnect before she can interrogate me any further. *"Christ, the Marines should have mothers come in to teach courses."*

Now, I'm praying I don't drop the scalding bag before she opens the door. If she opens it, I amend glumly.

I hear the tumblers turn before she's standing there in front of me. Her arms cross over her chest. "Can I help you?"

Judging by the way her eyes are narrowed on my face, her anger hasn't abated much. Not that it should. I basically blamed her for something that was in no way her fault.

"That's a good start." That's when I realize I've been vomiting my thoughts aloud. "Keep going."

"I'm so sorry, Crash. There was no blame to place; it was an accident."

She nods but still doesn't move to let me pass. I try again. "I brought an apology dinner."

Her head tilts in curiosity. "What constitutes an apology dinner?"

"Homemade lasagne. Ma swears it works every time."

Her face softens a bit. "You made me lasagne?"

"Hell no. I want you to live, for Christ's sake. I went to Daniela Trattoria and bought a pan of the shit. The only thing I can cook decently is an MRE. I want to apologize, not give you salmonella," I grumble as I lift the bag to tantalize her with the incredible scents wafting from it.

Leanne bursts into laughter as she backs up. "Well, I appreciate not having to go to the hospital. I'm not a fan."

I put the heavy bag on the counter and hold out a hand. I'm grateful when she doesn't hesitate to lay hers in mine. "I'm sorry. I hate to see him hurting, but I had no right to take that out on you."

With a small sigh, she moves into my arms. "I could have handled that, Kane, but it was as if you believed I'd hurt him on purpose. I wouldn't do that."

I breathe in the sweet scent of her hair. "I know."

She pulls back a bit, searching my face. "Do you? Do you really? Because I spoke to Carys today. She said you picked up the letter."

In the hype of the Grammys and the hoopla after, the words she wrote on that piece of paper slipped my mind. It's like a body blow when I recall what she asked of me. I frame her face before leaning in and pressing my lips to her forehead. "Trust beyond trust, Leanne. You have it."

She leans forward and rests her head against my chest. I hear her murmur, "I hope so, Kane. I truly hope so because the kind of trust

I'm giving you goes beyond love. It's the kind you'll still have when I've been laid in the ground."

Fear pinpricks along my skin hearing her talk about death as easily as she speaks of love. I just tuck her tighter and grip on to our now until it's not enough to hear her heartbeat against my chest. I tip up her chin and brush her lips with mine. "Want to know how things with Beckett worked out? Ward found a photo."

That's when the woman I love gives me a smirk. "What makes you think I don't already know that?"

Stunned, I'm immobile as Leanne pushes out of my arms before making her way into the kitchen to put the oven on warm. Sliding the lasagne in, she faces me again. "I fixed it before you left the other night. The rest was up to Beckett and his team." At my narrow-eyed glare, she shrugs. "It's like time travel, Kane. I can only nudge things in a certain direction. I can't force people to make certain moves."

"You have before!"

Her frustration boils over. "Yes, as Qəza. But Qəza is dead. I can't do the things I used to. Do you get that? I don't have the same access I used to. I can't call Carys and say, 'I reloaded the picture to save Beckett from eternal depression because the man I'm in love with said it's a good idea.' Life doesn't work that way. I made amends for what I perceived as *my* error. That's all I could do. As it was, I took a risk to do even that!"

I was all set to engage when her last words freeze me. "What do you mean, you took a risk?"

"Nothing. Forget about it." She turns away.

"No. It's not nothing, Leanne. Tell me." I lay my hands gently on her shoulders. She whirls around, her eyes blazing.

"I had to hack a few systems to get the data I needed, okay? But without accessing my secure system to do it, there's a possibility I might have left a trail."

I count to ten. Then I do it again. I finally get a grip on my emotions before I ask, "Is there a reason you didn't use the secure system?"

And I'm knocked back six paces when she declares, "Because if I'm caught, the system I used is associated with Kylie Miles."

"Shit." I yank her forward as I realize just what she risked to put things right. "So while I was off pouting like..."

"A petulant child," she fills in.

"Right. You were standing in front of me, Beckett, and a woman you don't even know." I think about Paige Kensington and how much she would like Leanne, how different yet similar these two women are.

She squirms. "I'm used to it, Kane."

I dip down so our eyes meet. "Not for me. Not anymore. Okay? Don't stop any more bullets without talking with me first. I need you whole."

The luminescent smile that brightens her face could light the night sky. "I can work on that."

"I've missed you." I lean down and brush her nose with mine.

"It's been three days," she notes.

"Three days where we haven't talked. That's the longest we've gone since Christmas."

Her soft laugh grabs me by the throat. I kiss her neck and luxuriate in her long moan. "Think the lasagne will hold?"

"Do you care?" She asks as she runs her hands over my shoulders.

"Not really. You?"

"Nope."

I swing her up into my arms and head for the couch so this way I can tell if the place catches on fire. That's the only way I plan on moving from her side in the next three days that were a gift from Beckett.

KANE

April

The popularity of online ordering is on a mushrooming rise. Interesting fact: 60% of U.S. consumers order delivery or takeout once a week.
— **Fab and Delish**

"Do you want me to pick up anything special for dinner tonight?" I ask Leanne as I slip my arm through my suit jacket.

She's lying delightfully spent across her bed from where I left her after our early morning lovemaking. Shoving her hair out of her eyes, she accuses, "You're way too awake in the morning."

"And you're a slug," I inform her with good cheer.

"But you love me anyway."

I love the way the ghosts are disappearing from her eyes, slowly but surely. Maybe it's true. Time can heal, and I'll be there by her side to help her sidestep some of the pitfalls I landed in after Gene. "I do. That still doesn't answer my question of what you want to eat."

Her eyes drift downward, causing me to laugh even as I move back from the bed before I rejoin her in it. "You're insatiable."

She rolls to her back, holding my pillow to her chest. "It's you. My life was filled with so much structure and routine. Then I meet you and poof!"

Unable to resist her, I lean over to press one more kiss to her swollen lips. "It's only been a few months."

"I meant since the beginning, Kane."

Ah, hell. I glance at my watch and pray the gods of traffic are on my side because her earnest statement grabs me by the heart.

And once Leanne wraps her long legs around me, I'm grateful over time I've left more than one suit here as well.

Leanne

May

Although some people wear scars with pride, others may feel the need to hide those marks. It truly is in the eye of the beholder. If you're someone who wants to cover their scars, getting a tattoo is one way to possibly cover the area. However, the process isn't as simple as you think. According to celebrity tattoo artist, Kitty, prepare yourself for several consultations. And do your homework. "Meet with your tattoo artist face to face several times so they can touch and feel the canvas they'll be working with to come up with the best design. It's your body and their art. Both of you want it to be perfect."

— **Moore You Want**

"Are you ever going to share with me how you got the knife cut?" he asks me.

I pause, my water bottle paused halfway to my lips. "I can't tell you everything."

His lips curve wryly. "I figured that."

"Plus, it doesn't say much for me as..." Releasing a heavy sigh, I admit, "I still struggle to use the word 'operative' because that's not who I am in my heart. I gather data, I analyze it. Just sometimes it's under extreme circumstances."

"Understood."

I lean on the breakfast bar and twist the bottle between my hands.

"It was about two years ago. There was some information needed I couldn't access unless I was at the mainframe. We needed that data."

"What was at stake?"

I don't reply at first, too lost in the memories of the horror of the brutality being conducted to women the fuckers had sent halfway around the world. "Leanne?"

"People's lives." I finally answer.

"And it FUBARed." It's a statement.

"That's putting it mildly. One of our analysts was on the take—we found that out from the data I yanked off the drive. But because of that, they left guards behind."

"You could have been killed." His voice is devoid of emotion.

"I could have. I'm grateful I wasn't. I was trained well enough to escape."

"And the guards?"

My eyes lift to his. He needs to know he's not the only one who's taken lives when necessary.

"I see." He walks around the counter and smooths his hand up my side. "A badge of honor."

"I hate it," I blurt out. "Lee and I were going to get tattoos to cover it. I was so pissed she got hers before she died. It was going to replace the agony of that memory with something good."

"And now?" His fingers press against my skin, leaving warmth in their wake. "Now, what do you feel?"

I stare into his eyes while his fingers make their way under my shirt to the scar beneath. There's no judgment, just acceptance of me. Of who I am. "Maybe there's no reason to hide it."

"Get the ink if you want to, but never hide the woman you are, Crash. That's who I love."

When he lowers his head to kiss me, I know if his kiss had the power to heal, my skin would be smooth by the time his lips lifted from mine.

After all, look what he's done to my heart.

Leanne

June

Regardless of the tragedy, moving on doesn't mean you have lessened your grief. It simply means you're being gifted with another chance to keep living.

— **Beautiful Today**

"There's been nothing," I spit out.

"Sometimes operations take time."

Frustrated, I pace back and forth. "I can't live her life forever, damnit."

"I know. And to be honest, there are things that need your attention here."

"Then end it. Announce there was a mistake."

"Not yet."

"Why?" I cry out.

"Call it a gut feeling."

"You and your feelings."

"They've saved my ass more than once, *Qəza*," he retorts hotly.

True. Too true. I recall some of the missions this man went on first as a SEAL, then as an operative himself before he stepped into his current administrative role. "When, then?"

"By the anniversary of your death. If we don't hear anything, we'll come forward. I'll start working on a strategy to extract you from this mess."

With that, he disconnects without giving me the chance to ask more. Like, does extracting me include leaving me the opportunity to continue to be with Kane because that's nonnegotiable.

He's a part of my life.

Always.

Forever.

Leanne

August

Speculation is high on when indie goddess Erzulie is going to drop her next album. Some wonder if she's writing a tribute to her late sister. Now that her relationship with rock god Beckett Miller has been explicitly clarified, maybe the two will turn up the heat another way by putting out a duet? We can only hope. — **Moore You Want**

Even though months have passed with nothing, something's coming. I can feel it. Hell, I see it in the slight movement of the traps that were set. I've been warned to be on the lookout because they took out Lee publicly; whoever it is isn't going to hesitate with me. *I wish I knew more, but I don't. Be on the lookout everywhere, Qɔza.*

Right, I responded.

In the meanwhile, I'm living half a dream and half a lie. Maybe I always have been, just like Lee. It makes me appreciate the words my twin scribed in her journal more than ever before.

The more time I spend as her, the more I understand her frustration of who she was. Music fed her soul, but to have it at the level she did, she had to play a part. That included someone directing her life —well, as much as they could. A burst of anger at myself unleashes when I think about the handbag the police found in the suite at the Plaza the day Lee was killed. "If I'd have known the constant turmoil your soul was under, I'd have done more," I whisper fiercely at my reflection in the window.

Kane's arms slip around me. We're together every night he's not with Beckett. Some of his clothes have made their way into my closet, which both comforts and terrifies me at the same time. Leaning back into him, I feel my breath catch when our eyes meet in the reflection. Normally, I take comfort in the way he looks at me and sees me— Leanne. But this is different.

My pulse quickens, and my cheeks flush.

He's a weakness I shouldn't have.

I never thought I would fall in love, have someone who loved all of me—the woman and the operative. Somehow, he was created just to appreciate the real me. And even standing on a stage pretending to be my sister in hopes of luring her killer out of hiding doesn't hold the same fear of this man turning from me.

A tidal wave of emotion crashes over me. What will I do when I have to leave if he's not here to lean on like he swore he would be?

As he leans down to brush his lips against my shoulder, I shove the thoughts aside. *Trust beyond trust.* It's what I demanded, and he swore he'd give it to me. It may be the only thing to keep me alive if things heat up any more.

Either that or I'll have to take drastic measures to ensure they cool down.

And if I can't trust Kane, the man I've let so far into my heart I'll never be able to get him out, I know I'll never be able to trust anyone else. Not even if my life depended on it.

Leanne

A fast trajectory from an interesting source. Prepare yourself for the crash once you fall to the ground! There's no way to brace yourself from the impact once it hits you.

Texas-born Beckett Miller, always so reticent about his early years, has reason to be. The handsome rock god was abused as a child. Good for him for escaping that mess.

But tsk, tsk, Erzulie. All we have to say is snooping should really be left to the experts. But it's not your fault someone hacked your cell phone. Guess you're not as good as your sister.

Don't worry, we'll clean up any blood sure to be spilled over this. Maybe you'll actually attain true goddess status you enjoy in life.

But we've been waiting forever. Is it too much to ask for an album to go live in the hours before you ascend?

— StellaNova

I knew it was coming, but still, my hands shake as certain words from StellaNova's post leap out at me.

Fast trajectory.

Fall to the ground.

Snooping.

Hacked cell.

Not as good as your sister.

Hours.

Blood.

Crash.

I toss the personal cell to the side and reach for my secure cell. Frowning, I notice it's off. I immediately try to power it up, but there's nothing. Damnit, I let the battery die. "Fuck! How could I be so stupid!" I scream. I leap for the curtains, throwing them shut. It will only buy me a few minutes, but that's all I need.

Quickly, I try to dial Kane, but it goes straight to voicemail. "Shit. I need you to answer. Why aren't you?"

Then I realize he's working. He told me he'd be primary on Beckett for the next few days. "I love you and I'll miss you," he murmured into my neck.

"I love you too. Always. Forever," I replied before reaching up to try to tempt him back into bed.

God, I wish more than ever it worked.

I need to get to Kane. I need to call this in.

I need to... God, I can't think about it yet.

First things first. Get to Kane. Tell him the truth. Remind him how much I love him.

Then I can prepare for whatever is coming.

Even if it's the end.

KANE

So Beckett Miller—rock god of the ages—grew up with less than nothing. Who the fuck cares? Does that make me love his music less? Hell no. If anything, it makes me respect him more.
— **@PRyanPOfficial**
Preach it, @PRyanPOfficial
— **Viego Martinez, Celebrity Blogger**
"Kane."

Beckett's voice is despondent as I cross the floor of his expansive living room. His fiancée is curled to his side. It's obvious she's been crying, if only by the sheer number of tissues at her side. "What's wrong?" I ask.

"You need to sit down." When I remain standing, he drops the tablet in his hand and gestures to a chair near his side. "Please."

"What did I do?" are the first words out of my mouth.

"I have a question for you," Beckett begins.

"Yes?"

"Did you ever share any of what you knew of my childhood with anyone?" Beckett swallows hard. Paige reaches over and takes his hand. "If you did, I understand. You likely were trusting someone you care about."

I frown. "Of course not. I'm not permitted to discuss any information with anyone, even Paige. Sorry."

Beckett's lips curve, even if the smile doesn't reach his eyes. "Consider this my unofficial authorization there's nothing you can't share with Paige. That being said, do you want to revise your answer?"

I can't understand why there's such shock in his eyes. Or why Paige has a hold of his fingers so hard, her own are turning white. "Becks, man, I swear. I'll even volunteer for a lie detector if it would make you feel more comfortable. The only people who have an idea of what I know are those I normally report to."

"And that's Keene, Caleb, and Colby," he validates.

"Yes, sir," I say formally, because the situation appears to call for it.

His head drops. His hand with the ankh rises up and scrubs over his face. "I've already spoke with Hudson. Back when Kylie was acting out after her sister's death, you asked Sam a question about Kylie's computer skills. Why?"

My heart begins to thud heavily in my chest. "I was getting to know her."

"And she'd sent you an email. Caleb's already told me the story; you don't need to protect her."

"I hope you won't. You wouldn't be the same man I respect if you do," Paige hisses fiercely. She leans over, kisses Beckett on the cheek, and murmurs in his ear. He rests his head against hers a moment before she stands and leaves the room.

When she leaves, Beckett opens his tablet and hands it to me. "That's what we woke to this morning."

I begin reading the article on StellaNova. And then I click to the next.

And the next.

Beckett's childhood laid bare for anyone to read.

Fuck, Leanne. What the hell did you do this for? I curse her silently. "What's on the agenda for today?"

"We're going to see Carys," Beckett says simply.

Caleb's words from long ago come back to haunt me. Protect the principal. Keep Lee away from Beckett. She's a powder keg ready to explode.

In my mind, all I hear is the sound of a gun being shot. And I can't help but flinch.

She bursts from the stairwell, completely out of breath, and I let out a string of curses. I didn't post a man at the stairway entrances. I should have. I should have known an operative of Qaza's caliber wouldn't let anything stop her.

Certainly not something as nominal as avowals of love.

"Get out of here, Lee," I growl as I approach her.

She comes to a dead stop. Her beautiful, deceptive eyes are haunted as she pants out, "Kane. I have to...tell you..."

I lift my wrist and mutter, "Mitch. Cover the door. I have to handle something." After hearing his acknowledgment, I grab her by the elbow and drag her back into the stairwell. After a quick dash up and down to ensure we're alone, I charge her. "What the hell is wrong with you?"

Confusion clouds her face for just a moment before her jaw goes slack. "You think I did it. You think I gave that story to StellaNova."

"What the hell were you thinking? Did you find out that information about him and were saving it up?"

Her lower lip trembles, but she firms it up. "That's not what's happening!"

"That's the only thing that's happening. Right now, they're in Carys's office discussing what kind of legal action they can take. Against you." Instead of jabbing my hand into her chest, I turn and grip the railing.

"You're not listening to me. Beyond trust, Kane. Do you remember that?"

"I remember the look on his face this morning, Leanne. You gutted him. Her. Who the hell are you trying to save—your sister or yourself?" I lash out. My words echo over and over again until they fill all the available space in the stairwell between us.

Leanne staggers back. I automatically move toward her, but she cowers as if I'd raised my hand to her instead of speaking a truth that I should have made her face long before now. "She's gone, Leanne. I wish there was something I could do, something I could say to make it easier on you." My voice falters when her spine snaps straight, but it's the broken expression in her eyes that I need to steel my heart against.

"You won't even give me a chance to explain. You promised me you'd trust me—beyond trust means just that, Kane. Trust even when you're faced with something you can't handle. I've given that to you—my body, my heart, my soul. It's too bad you can't remember that when I need them the most. Can you?"

"Leanne, you don't understand how bad..."

Leanne doesn't give me the opportunity to explain how badly Beckett's wrecked at the idea the woman he thinks of as a kid sister has betrayed secrets he wasn't aware she knew about—for a price. And betrayal isn't something I can let stand. There was nothing I could have done to have changed the circumstances surrounding Gene's death. The only thing I can change is my reaction to it. Just as I open my mouth to defend my actions to Leanne, she races down the stairs.

"Where do you think you're going?" I call out furiously.

Her face is ashen, eyes enormous. "I have to go."

"Now?" My mind whirls with what she's throwing at me. "Are you telling me it's not safe for you?"

Her laugh is brittle. "Focus on your now, Kane. You have other things to worry about. Despite having told me you loved me, I know where I stand—and it's after your loyalty to Beckett Miller. Meanwhile, it's time for me to do what I do best."

"And what's that?" I'm infuriated, but now I'm questioning at what. The more she talks, the less I believe it's Leanne who harmed Beckett. God damnit, if it wasn't for *Qəza's* mask dropping down over Leanne's face, I might get some answers. I jog down the stairs until I halt just in front of her. "Listen, Crash, it hurts seeing him— them—in this much pain." I reach out a hand to touch her golden hair.

"I understand." My sigh is audible. Just as my fingers are about to make contact, she scratches out, "I'll fix this as soon as I'm safe. This, at least, I can get right."

Then before I can ask her what she means, Leanne whirls away from me and flees. Before I can stop her, she ducks inside another floor. Damn the timing, she ducks into an elevator just as it opens, and the heavy stairwell door swings shut before I can determine which direction it goes in.

And just like that, she's gone. I fall to my ass, wondering what the hell to do. "I just completely fucked up everything," I say aloud. Sitting for long moments, I replay the entire conversation. Did I even give Leanne a chance to explain? No. Oh, holy hell. My elbows hit my knees and brace there. I begin rocking back and forth.

I treated her like she was a bogey—a threat. I didn't believe in her, in our love.

And instead, I treated her like a damn traitor. Like Gene.

"Kane, he's getting ready to leave. Do you want to meet us downstairs?" Mitch's voice is in my earpiece.

For the first time, I hesitate. Should I stay, or should I go follow Leanne and try to work this out? I know if it was me, I'd tell me to go to hell. Deciding to give her a little time before I apologize for my harsh words and lack of understanding, I answer Mitch. "No, I'll meet you outside the office. Give me five."

"Right."

Briefly, I close my eyes in agony before I jog up the few steps. I jump when the elevator pings, hoping against hope. My heart sinks when Austyn Kensington flies out. She throws a glare in my direction. "Get out of my way."

My attempt to stop her is half-hearted at best. She plows past me into the office of LLF LLC, bellowing Beckett's and Carys's names.

Knowing this is just going to delay Beckett's departure, and possibly make things worse for Leanne, I hold my post and enumerate my sins. I should have known better.

I should have believed when I distrusted.

Then why was I so quick to believe Beckett when Leanne was the one who yanked me from the dark spiral of despair? Because betrayal can suffocate the light of love out in an instance.

And I've been schooled in it before.

Unfortunately, I let the training I endured take over instead of the new lessons I've been taught.

Leanne

Wildcard Records has stated they will not be releasing a statement about Beckett Miller. "Beckett's private life is just that—private. What he chooses to share is up to him. We fully back him on that decision," said Kristoffer Wilde, CEO. He also refused to take questions about Erzulie with a simple "I have no comment at this time."

— StellaNova

I run as fast as I can to a pay phone near Lee's condo—God knows there's a reason they're still around—and dial a number I've had memorized for the last six years. I wait for the series of clicks before a banal voice asks me what I'd like to order.

"I'd like item 57, the snodgrass. Put some extra bang into it."

"One moment, please."

Seconds later, his deep voice whispers, "What the hell happened?"

Without preamble, I tell my handler, "I'm gone."

"How do I know it's..." I press a button on my tablet, causing a small shriek to radiate out of his speakers. "Damnit, Qaza. You're a pain in my ass."

"Listen to me—a blogger had a coded message published today." At his sharply indrawn breath, I quickly tell him about what was in StellaNova's article. "I counted it down to the last possible second before I took off. I don't know if they're still tracking me."

"You honestly think they're going to try to assassinate you?"

"We've seen it happen," I remind him.

"Not to one of my people! We're the ones who stop it!" he thunders.

My eyes stare blindly at the throng of people scurrying by. "Well, now it has. I'm out."

"It's not that easy."

"Why not?"

"Because your mission's not over," he reminds me.

My head drops forward until it touches the sticky glass of the phone booth. "I'll finish the job. The answers aren't here. They're behind the screen. I know that now."

"I've been where you are, *Qəza*. You won't heal without finishing the job," he informs me, not without sympathy.

Heal. Will there ever be enough time to recover from Lee's death, from the slice of Kane's words, to trust the nebulous emotion called love again? Maybe I'll live long enough to find out. "I'll do the job, but I'll do it my way."

"What does that mean?"

"It means I'll be there unless you hear otherwise. That's the best I can offer you."

He's clearly unhappy when he snaps, "Fine."

"Will you do me a favor?"

"So long as I don't end up burying you, you can have it. What do you need."

"Give me thirty minutes? Then sweep Lee's place? Put everything but the bare essentials in storage. Leave his stuff by the front door. He'll come by, I'm sure." Maybe. "If I don't end up buried next to her, I'll deal with it later. But I can't bear for my parents to have to go through her place if that's what happens." And I know if I do end up taking a bullet, the man on the other end of the line will explain everything. He'll have no choice.

There's silence for a long moment before I get my reassurance. "Done. How can I reach you?"

I laugh bitterly, knowing that since I just asked for a favor, nothing comes free. "I'll contact you if I need you. You'll know it's me."

He grunts his response. I hang up the phone and walk away. Immediately, the cell I've been carrying for months rings. "Be safe, Leanne. You know I'm saying that as more than your boss."

I stop to stare up at the cluttered skyline. I hang up without another word, not that I could manage to get one out. After all, why bother lying to him? There's no one at my back anymore: not my job, not my family, and sure as hell not Kane. I immediately pitch the cell into the nearest trash can, knowing that within a few hours, the battery signal will die and I won't be able to be traced from it.

Knowing I have mere minutes before someone spots "Erzulie," I dash upstairs and grab my go bag, and with it the ability to temporarily disappear. After we flew back from LA, I augmented it with the most important things: copies of pictures of me and Lee, my secure computer, and a wad of cash. I slip my fingers in the front pocket and finger the photos of me and Kane I slid in just a few days ago. Bunching up my hair beneath a beret, I jam on an enormous gender-neutralizing coat that visually gives the impression of a shit-brown marshmallow.

Five minutes later, I'm strolling down the street with tears falling. *I failed, Lee. I let you down. Someday, I hope you can forgive me since I'll never be able to forgive myself.* I wipe the snot against my sleeve and debate where I should go.

Though, it's not like I have anyone left in my life who gives a damn about anything other than what I can do for them. Then again, did they ever care about more than that to begin with? With that thought, I jump on the nearest bus and silently disappear into the throng of people going anywhere.

Four hours later, I've added more black marks to my name. Yet, I hope the thousands of dollars I've dropped into their Uber accounts to compensate them for borrowing their IDs to get me where I am makes up for the inconvenience.

A few hundred yards ahead of me lies a pinnacle of wood and glass, my house and all the creature comforts inside of it. It's lit up like a beacon in the dark, beckoning to me. I ignore it and walk down the road until I come face-to-face with an enormous boulder. Shrugging off my backpack, I lean against it for a few minutes. It was a risk to come back here, but everything I need is just behind this rock: shelter, equipment. Most importantly, safety.

During the hours in the car, I began berating myself for not coming here first. Instead of trying to lure Lee's killer out into the open, I should have just done what I'm about to do—set a trap with myself as bait.

Cleaner.

Swifter.

Over.

I shove off the rock and slide my weapon out of my bag. Leaving the bag where it is, I circle the rock to check nothing has been disturbed since I was last here. I slide a pair of night goggles from my pocket, slipping them on before scanning the surrounding area. Nothing but a couple of deer. I deliberately rustle my feet in the leaves to determine if they're plants or real. They bound off, fearful of becoming prey themselves.

As certain as I can be I'm alone, I reach down and lift the storm drain situated just behind the boulder. Slowly, it creaks as it's pried open. Once it's propped enough, I grab my pack and toss it down into the fathomless darkness, certain the cushioning will protect the contents inside. I start lowering myself into the dark, keeping my weapon level until I have to slide it behind me to lower the grate. I do so quickly before I reach for it again until the darkness shrouds me and I'm alone.

It's how I should have been and how I will be for however long it takes to find out the answers I started searching for before I was distracted by myself and my heart.

Unknown

"Qɔza is going under. Give her any and all assistance."
   "Should we keep trying to flush out the perp?"
   "We don't have much of a choice." A chair slams into a desk in fury.

Leanne

Who would have ever thought Erzulie was that cold beneath her sweet and light act? I promise, Beckett, if you need some comfort, you come right on over here and I'll comfort you.

If I actually owned one of her albums, I'd return them as fast as I could.

— Sexy&Social, All the Scandal You Can Handle

Follow the money.

And when the money doesn't make sense, figure out why.

Why disparage Beckett Miller? Because he's media gold. Anything with his name will generate hits, shares, videos. But the person had to have known about Beckett's past. On the surface, that would initially lead someone to believe it was someone within Beckett's inner circle.

His fiancée.

His daughter.

Carys and David.

Angie and Ward.

His security team. Kane. And as a byproduct...me.

My training automatically kicks in as I strip apart every person on that list, cross-checking them against the employees of StellaNova, starting with their editor in chief, Aerk Ronan.

I'm flabbergasted when I find a connection of sorts, though not the kind I was expecting, between Carys's assistant and the social media's ridiculously wealthy owner. "Shit. Poor Angie." But I shove my softer emotions aside and keep digging.

Then the data slams to a halt when I bump up against something I never expected to encounter—Dioscuri. My own fucking software? I probe around it without tripping the tentacles I know are lying in wait to alert my people in Saratoga Springs. "Why is Dioscuri attached to a bunch of fucking social media servers?" I wonder.

Backing out, I attack this from a different perspective. When I do so, I get an overview of StellaNova's network map. Only three of their servers are encrypted by Dioscuri.

I study the systems connected to it before sneering at the commercial off-the-shelf software that has so many security holes I can get to the data I want simply by pulling the data down. And because the access control on the tables is completely out of the box, plain as day is the data I'm looking for—the identity of who provided the data to StellaNova. "People really are that stupid," I declare before my fingers start to fly.

When the data appears on my screen, I have to bite my fist to hold back the wail of pain even as the denial escapes. "No."

He wouldn't. For what? Money? Power? He already has it all. I'm supposedly already dead. What more could he want?

And that's when I start to dig and lay my own traps.

Leanne

September

Beckett Miller, who rose to an enviable rock stardom, is more than just a musician. He's a human, something we forgot in our recent disclosure about his horrifying childhood.

The notorious tattooed rock god, who recently debuted *The Golden Lady* on Broadway, is a music virtuoso, teaching himself how to play the piano, guitar, drums, and several other instruments by ear. Overheard recently to say, "Music was what saved me from disappearing in my soul before I had a chance to spread my wings and live," he's been making inroads to endow a portion of his fortune to underprivileged school systems in his home state of Texas.

But if you think it's his sexy voice, his moves on stage, or those hot as hell song lyrics that got him as far as he has, think again. Someone with half a brain at this trash rag unearthed Beckett Miller made his first million long before he ever took the stage. Writing jingles for everything from dog food to computers, he's a savvy businessman.

Not only do we owe a huge apology to Beckett Miller, his fiancée, and his loved ones, it makes us think twice about what you can do with a degree in art and music.

Edited to add: StellaNova will match every employee's contribution to art and music in our schools donated through https://www.networkforgood.org/topics/education/creative/ up to $50,000.

— StellaNova

When I installed the combination computer/safe room beneath my house years ago, I never imagined it would be used for more than middle-of-the-night phone calls from the office that couldn't wait for me to drive to Castor. It takes up a large portion of the footprint of my basement, but unless you know exactly how to access it from either the detached garage or beneath the boulder through the sewer system, you'd never know it was here.

Only Lee knew. And I put up with so much noise from her about, "Did we watch the movie *Blast from the Past* with Brendan Fraser too many times, babe? I mean, for real? I know you thought he was hot and all, but this is a bit much."

Little did I know the hyperawareness instilled in me during my training would be worthwhile, and the bunk room and kitchenette would come in handy, Brendan Fraser be damned.

Completely soundproof with copper wire running through the walls to shield transmissions, my only access to the outside world is through a hard line directly into the cable company. Not that I'm ready for more than a quick transmission—not by a long shot.

It's just time to wipe the first mistake off my list.

Accessing StellaNova from the safe room computer, I upload the article retracting what they wrote about Beckett for their blog tomorrow, completely erasing any evidence of what they had planned. Then I tag it through a cloud bucket so it will overwrite the top news story on any search engine when someone looks up Beckett Miller's name. It's a nasty trick used in search engine optimization marketing to block out competitors, but one which will suit my purposes nicely. I hate screwing with people's right to choose, but this tidy piece of work will allow Beckett Miller to regain his credibility instead of being painted as a hillbilly yokel. Mentally, I send him the apology I'll never be able to make in person. *I'm so sorry, Beckett. They used you and your past to get to me. It's my fault. I made the fatal mistake of falling in love.*

I slam the door on those thoughts because they'll lead me to think about Kane. And I can't. I can't allow his words to penetrate into my thoughts. I simply absorb the pain and log off before turning my attention to the other screen. The only thing I can do to prepare myself to stare into Death's eyes with no recrimination is to get answers. After all, by becoming *Qəza*, I lost the right to love, to live a life of free will. They were the rights I was supposed to give to Lee, and someone killed her instead of me.

My eyes scan a secondary monitor with the flat blue line a final time before I switch it off. I'm fairly certain with the program I'm writing, the moment I connect my secure laptop to the internet, they'll have me—if they want me. It wasn't hard to narrow it down once I knew where to look—Dioscuri. The question is, how long will it take him to find it? I'm not trying to hide the fact I've got him. I want him to come and get me.

It's time we end it.

I just need time. I have a few final things to do—a self-imposed order. My lips curve with no humor as I contemplate about how many messes I can clean up in the amount of time I have left. I'll protect them all if I do. Then I can finally rest.

The first part of my penance complete, I push to my feet and head toward the bunk in the back—my new "master suite." There are no more questions, no more answers. Nothing. "Soon, I'll be able to go home and rest. A few more months. That should do it," I whisper aloud. The sound of my voice startles me. I'm surprised by the sound of it. After all, there's no one here.

Then, I dig down deep for my resolution. I still need to be strong and fix as much as I can when it comes to those I love. Then once it's done, I can tell Lee all about it.

After all, no one has ever understood me better than the other half of myself.

Unknown

"He's back," I'm informed. I hear the quiet comfort of the keys clicking from his desk in New York.

"What's he doing?"

"Looking to see if she's returned."

My hand slashes through the air. "If the threat's credible, she won't endanger anyone by returning."

His chair creaks. "You've lived this life for too many years."

"So have you, my friend," I remind him.

"Do you think it is?" he asks me bluntly.

I think back to when I recruited Qaza at MIT, long after Sam and I settled down from our adventures. I recall the way she stood up to me—intimidation not even in her vocabulary. "Yes. I do."

"Then, should I tell him?" Sam asks.

"No."

"Why the hell not?" he demands.

"Because if she loves him the way I think she does, he's her vulnerability. She'll do anything to protect him. It may be our only way to protect her."

Sam's silent for a long while before declaring, "You're an asshole," before he slams down the phone.

After I know the line's disconnected, I say aloud, "I know. But I'm an ass who's trying to keep everyone alive."

KANE

October

Washington, D.C. Messenia challenges recent cloud computing contract issued to Argo Industries for $2 billion. Messenia has filed a protest with the Government Accountability Office against the Department of Defense, challenging the recent award of a cloud computing contract to a competitor.

— **InfoSec Gov News**

It's been three months.

She ran away from me in tears.

Now, mine are threatening to overflow.

There's no way around it. She's gone.

The first night I came here, my duffle was outside. I pounded on her door, and there was no answer. Nothing.

I've tried to call, no answer. I stop by every day, knocking, pleading. It's eerily quiet inside.

I snapped when she was trying to explain what happened. She explained how things worked, and yet I cast blame. Her fault? I wish someone loved me the way she loves Kylie. But there's been no chance to explain. I've been trying to reach her to remind her I love her, to beg, to get on my knees. To let Leanne know everything's been fixed. To tell her I'm so damn sorry.

Beckett and Paige are okay. But I can't reach her. When I try on the phone, it goes directly to voicemail. And as of today, that voicemail is full. I'm certain her doorman is sick of seeing me day in and day out. And when I check, Carys hasn't heard from her. Neither, she said worriedly, has Kris.

Today, the something that had a lockdown on my emotions shook loose inside me. I'd slid my hand inside my suit pants and found the letter Leanne had written before we went to Los Angeles. When I read it again, her words jumped off the pages and slapped at me— like she should have done that day when I was spouting off nonsense in her face.

My determination to shield someone who's become more than just a protectee caused me to break the single promise I made to Leanne—trust beyond trust. I didn't even give her a chance to speak; I just went on the offensive—selectively choosing not to protect someone as a pawn in her own game. I should have known better. I knew her mind long before she came into my life as Leanne Miles. And throughout the gamut of emotions, I fell in love with her.

What did I show her except I'm a complete ass?

Now, I'm standing beneath her balcony. I see there's nothing out there. It's as if neither she nor her sister ever lived there. There's no Adirondack chair, no colorful curtains fluttering in the breeze. All the plants that lined the balustrade are missing. It's as if she never existed —just like those years in between when we first crashed and we reunited. "Damn you!" I shout it at the wind but targeted at the one person who deserves it most. Myself.

A hand grips my arm. I whirl around to snarl at the offending touch. Mitch drops his hand. "Come on, man. We have a meeting."

I shake my head as I stare upward toward where Kylie Miles's condo is located. Leanne's supposed to be there, but she's hightailed it. How could things have gone so wrong? Days before everything went to hell, I laid in bed with her, "I told her I loved her." My voice cracks. And then I refused to listen as she stood before me pleading with me to listen. My mind just associated the scene like a fucked up flashback. I wasn't myself. I stood in front of Leanne trying to negotiate like I tried to get Gene to listen before I ended his life before he had the chance to end mine.

Crash.

I feel my heart tumble and shatter at my feet. But really, how many people let her heart break and she had to piece it back together alone? It takes several swallows, but I choke out, "I'll be able to fix things. Right?"

Mitch winces but doesn't say anything. He just tugs my arm to pull me out of the crowd to the vehicle waiting to take us back to the penthouse.

Blindly, I follow him, uncertain of what to do next or what other nightmares may be waiting just out of reach until I close my eyes.

Unknown

Unknown: Take care of the duplicate.
   Unknown: We have no idea where she is.
   Unknown: Then find her.
   Unknown: You're asking the impossible.
   Unknown: It's the only way.

Leanne

November

Beckett Miller states emphatically he will not discuss Erzulie's location or what she's working on. "What she's doing is healing." But the way he clutched his fiancée's hand belied those words.

With Wildcard Music refusing to comment as well, we're all left wondering, has something happened to the sexy Kylie Miles? Has she walked away from music entirely after her stunt this past summer?

— **Viego Martinez, Celebrity Blogger**

I plot and wait on the edge as two lives stand ready to crash together, not giving a damn about either. If they want me bad enough to have killed Lee, to have threatened Kane, they can have me.

But I won't bleed alone.

I'll take everyone involved in doing so out with me.

So help me God.

My fingers fly as my lips curl into a cruel smile. "You wanted it all, you motherfucker? Come and try to get it."

I pluck a picture of Kane and me that I tucked in the corner of one of my monitors. "It's not just for Lee anymore." Pressing my lips on top of his beloved face, I drop the photo next to my keyboard before my fingers begin dancing.

KANE

December

It's been over a year since singer Erzulie lost her sister. It's also been about that amount of time since she's put out any new music. Fans appreciate her grief but are getting restless for her songs that have been described as "sending quivering tingles down my spine." When can we expect to see the artist on stage again as well as a new record? @wildcardmusic

— **StellaNova**

"You'll never guess who came by today," my mother tells me.

I've just returned from a session with my trauma therapist, and I was hoping a call home might lift my spirits. All it's doing is reminding me is the world goes on, even if my heart is stuck in neutral. Waiting for direction. *Something. Anything, Crash. Give me some sort of sign*, I plead silently.

"Who?" It's a tight squeeze for my heart and lungs to fit inside my throat, but somehow, they all fit.

"Well, she has short dark hair," Mom teases.

It's possible Leanne cut hers, though the thought of her long blonde tresses that were spread across my pillow being hacked away pains me. "Mom," I push sharply.

"Son, you are seriously lacking in a sense of humor as of late. Brit. And she brought Maddie with her." My mother waits for my reaction.

Any other time, any other universe, the news would release the tight squeeze around my heart. But it's four months to the day since I've heard Leanne's voice. I've just stepped out of a meeting where Caleb declared her missing. *"Unless we go to the government and start snooping, we have absolutely no leads."*

My breath comes out roughly. "Great, Ma. Can we talk later? I'm at the office."

"Kane, you've waited years for Brit to heal enough to come see this family again," my mother spits out. "What is wrong with you?"

What the hell am I supposed to say? I fell in love, Ma. And within months, I drove her away because I'm a fucking ass? Oh, and now she's missing? Plus, she's an operative for an agency I don't even know the name of? So, I don't know if she's been pulled into some basement onto a computer or is dead. I rub my hand over my forehead. *"It's just been a rough couple of months."*

She clucks. "I saw the news about Beckett and that Erzulie. You should keep him away from her."

Her words cause me to snap. "Don't say a damn word about her. Nothing. None of this was her fault and...never mind."

There's a long silence. "So, that's the way of it."

I laugh, but the sound is hollow. "It was. Everything was beautiful. When I was with her, I was just caught up in her. I forgot who I am, who she is. There was no one else in the world. "

"What happened, sweetheart?"

I think back to the day I snapped. "I let other people, memories, in. I fell back on training instead of instinct."

My mother draws in a deep breath. "Gene."

"In a nutshell. Lee...something happened. I can't get into it. And it took me back. Right back to the moment when I held that gun. Only instead of a bullet, I used words."

My head falls back against the headboard in my room—a place that feels more lonely ever since the hours I spent with Leanne, even though she never spent a minute here. It doesn't matter. I've dreamed of her in this bed even before I first kissed her. Outside of the bed where we made love, or hell, Keene's office, it might be where I feel closest to her. I'm just grateful that despite the fact I've been temporarily removed from Beckett's detail, he's insisted I remain here. "Fix what's wrong and get back to riding my ass," he insisted.

"I've been trying to figure out the trigger. Every day, I have a session with the trauma therapist recommended by Keene and Caleb." As my mother tries to find the right words, I distract her by asking, "What did Brit want?"

That does the job temporarily. "Well, apparently, she received a letter. Do you remember how she just wanted closure—to know what Gene said in those last minutes?"

"Yes," I reply caustically. Despite the number of times I wished for someone, anyone, to have overheard my conversation with Gene, it wasn't to be.

"Someone found a recording. She's being asked to drive to Tulsa to listen to it."

My whole body locks. I leap from my bed and tug on some pants. My voice is raspy when I say, "Can you repeat that?"

"Kane." Her voice is exasperated.

"Mom, hold on a moment." I fling open the door and dash over to the neatly stacked mail. Like a beacon, it sticks out.

I tear the envelope open, but even as I'm reading the words with a sense of disbelief—an invitation to listen to a recently unearthed recording that could have a substantial impact on my retirement—the only thought coursing through my mind is how serious her blue eyes were when she said, "You never know what files will turn up suddenly, Kane."

"Or manufactured," I'd laughed.

"Well, that too. But sometimes, it's for the greater good."

A tear falls from my eye and lands smack-dab in the middle of the paper. Roughly, I manage, "I've got to go, Ma. I have to call the office."

"About Gene?" she says knowingly.

"It ties into something else." Boy, is that the understatement of the year.

"Take care, son. I love you. See you soon."

"I love you too." After hanging up, I immediately call Sam. Before he can get a word out, I inform him, "She's putting her affairs in order."

There's silence on the other end of the line before he asks, "How do you know?"

After I tell him what the letter says and absorb his reaction, I let the letter flutter to the table. "She's altering history. Leanne's trying to erase the worst of the past by making lives better for other people. This way, Brit will get some closure about Gene to be able to fully move on."

"Brit's always known you pulled the trigger," Sam reminds me carefully.

"True. But there was that kernel of doubt about her husband being a traitor." We're both quiet a moment, lost in our own memories at the awfulness of humanity.

Slowly, I recount to Sam everything Leanne did to fix the situation with Beckett and Paige. Her words haunt me. *Life doesn't work that way. I made amends for what I perceived as my error. That's all I could do.* "Lee has some faulty logic though."

"What's that?"

"She's not the one with anything to fix. She wasn't the first time either." And with that, I hang up on him and prepare to let my emotions out.

KANE

I'm spinning up Jose Feliciano and the Waitresses. Hell, who am I kidding. I'm spinning up the booze.

Happy Christmas to everyone!

— **Viego Martinez, Celebrity Blogger**

There might be a star on the tree, but it's not as bright as the lights in her hair.

The moon shines, highlighting the midnight sky, but it just reminds me of her eyes twinkling up at me.

Every tinkle of glass reminds me of those first moment she laughed. "I'd give anything to hear that again," I whisper in the cold Oklahoma night.

The fierceness in her eyes as she defended her choice to become the shadow operative, *Qəza*.

The hope she tried disguise when we talked about a future—a future I blew up with brutal words and distrust. *Beyond trust.* The words in her letter haunt me. The one thing she asked of me, and I didn't give it to her.

Now, on a night where a single star is supposed to represent blessings, the nightmares of Gene's face have been replaced by the hurt brutally accepted by Leanne. And I've quickly learned waking up—both physically and psychologically—hasn't dragged me from this nightmare.

Where is she?

"I don't want anything more than for her to be safe. Please, God, let her be safe." I stand on the porch for a few more moments before giving up on waiting for an answer and heading inside into the bedlam of my sister's family.

January

Have you ever watched something so real you felt like you were transported in time? That was me tonight at *The Golden Lady*. Evangeline Brogan made me feel like I was Adele Bloch-Bauer. I still have chills and a wad of used tissues in my bag.

It's a must-see.

— Moore You Want

I wake with the whisper of his name on my lips. "Kane."

I curl my knees up to my chest. Remembering.

The first moment we crashed into each other on the street. Being unable to forget his ocean-colored eyes. Passively searching for them. Him.

Lee's death. Awash in darkness. Broken. My body starts to shudder under the force of emotion I know I'll never recover from.

Fear. Agony. Blame. My fault. Knowing it, hearing it. And then, like a lifeline, Kane typed my name in that crucial moment of emotional exhaustion when I needed to know someone was there.

My realization Kane was part of the Marine unit that almost caused me to walk away all those years ago. That bond of trust snapping into place, regret flooding through me when I recall the words I lashed out at him when he's managed to stay standing.

Like a movie reel, the moments ping and flicker: nosing around the Hudson network to find he had joined the ranks of people searching for answers. Our banter. The first time I weakened enough to turn on my microphone.

I should have known then. I was falling.

Then there was the night he ordered me to turn on the camera. And I was rewarded with his first smile at me. "There you are." As if he'd been waiting for me.

Just me.

The shock. Then the acceptance.

The meant to be.

Kane.

I lay on my cot, running every moment together over and over.

The way he laughed.

The broadness in his smile.

The glint in his eyes as he raked them over me head to toe like a caress.

I accepted we were meant to be just as easily as I accepted his outstretched hand. Touching my absolution.

Instead, I handed over the weakest chink in my armor—my heart.

The feeling causes a sickening rush of nausea, causing me to lurch for the bathroom. I leap from the bunk, knocking everything to the side in my process. Barely making it there, I dry heave over and over, terrified of what might happen if I get this wrong.

I love him.

Even if it means my own life, I'll do anything to make certain he stays safe once I make up for my mistakes.

And that will take a little more time, but judging by the interest I'm generating, it's almost time for the reckoning.

Unknown

"I feel like I'm violating her privacy. This is personal stuff they're..."

The muscled man with the trident tattoo leans over the computer terminal. "Do I look like I give a flying fuck about privacy right now? Hers or his?"

"Uh, no, sir."

"If we don't find her and they crack that code, more than just evidence is at stake." The man storms into the other room and quickly dons a suit and tie, completely incongruous with his muscled appearance. When he returns to the anteroom, he barks, "Well?"

"I have a lock."

"Good. Let's go."

KANE

"These Dreams" is a song by Heart from their 1985 self-titled studio album, Heart. It was released on January 18, 1986. I don't know why that's important to know except I woke up this morning singing it. I guess that kind of ages me, huh?
    — @PRyanPOfficial
    A lot ages you, Ryan. That's the least of it.
    — @CuTEandRich3
    The holidays have come and gone with nothing. No message from her.

    The only time I feel anything is in my dreams. I don't want to live a life without moonlight because that's the only place I can reach her —my dreams.

    And every day I wake up, I hate myself just a bit more.

    I couldn't give a shit today's my birthday, but at least I'm back to work protecting Beckett. When I head in to the office, there's the routine of paperwork and investigations. But to my surprise, there's a large cake with a single candle burning and a vase of white roses. But it's not the gifts that make me stumble in shock; it's the card.

Life's too short not to celebrate your birthday, Kane, just because you shared it with someone who is gone.
After all, weren't you the one who told me the firsts suck?

Well, let me assure you, so do the seconds, especially when you're alone.
Have a bite of cake for me after you make a wish.

After recovering, I called down to Security to have the messenger stopped. I interrogated the poor kid for over an hour before realizing he knew nothing more than it was an internet order. There was a gleam to Sam's eyes when Caleb told him, "Have fun and don't get caught." For just a moment, I had a small measure of hope this was it —my birthday, a new year. Maybe Leanne was finally coming out of hiding. But those hopes were soon dashed, though in a momentarily amusing way. Later, I'll let the agony of her brushing up against my life get hold of me. Right now, I'm too busy enjoying the way Caleb's hysterically laughing at Sam's disgruntlement.

Dutifully, I say, "Thank you for my birthday flowers and cake, Sam," as he lets loose a string of curses when he realizes it was his own card that paid for my gifts.

"I sure as hell overpaid. Christ, she dropped a thousand dollars toward my credit card bill to cover it."

"Can't you trace that?" Caleb asks, his own amusement depleting at the way Sam was being bested by Leanne—again.

Sam shakes his head. "Offshore account. It would take me a while. And her computer needs to be on for the final trace. Damn, I love and hate and love how frustrating this girl is."

"I just love her," I admit out loud to both men for the first time. Scooping up the card, I make my way for the office door. "Anyone mind if I take off for the rest of the day?"

"Not at all." Caleb grants permission somberly.

I nod, before walking through the good tidings toward the elevator without acknowledging a single one. I need to be close to Leanne, and there's only one place I can think of to do that—where I know she loved me.

Nodding at her doorman, I head upstairs and knock. There's no answer. There never is. I turn my back and sit down with my back to the door. My phone pings with an incoming text. I reach for it with a sigh. "Probably Mom."

Unknown: Happy birthday.

Unknown: No, it's not your mother.

Unknown: God, Kane, this really would have been easier if you stayed at the office.

Afraid to hope, I type a single letter. *L?*

That's when I get a screen filled with *"I'm sorry,"* scrolling over and over. I yell, certain my microphone is on. "Stop! I don't care. Do you hear me? None of this is your fault. I realize you would never have done something like that to Beckett and Paige. I've been working with someone; I swear it. I got lost in my head and muddled what happened with you with what happened with Gene. It was never you; it was me. You asked for trust, and I'm the one who screwed up. Me. Please, if I have to type it a thousand times, let me. If I have to say it a million times, give me a chance to."

I clutch the phone like it's my lifeline. My fingertips have to be embedding into the surface. Then the blood rushes to my chest. It's all my fault, Kane. Every moment of pain. There will never be a minute I will stop loving you, but it's too late. I have to finish this.

"Finish? What the hell have you been doing? Damn you, get on this phone and call me right now!" I roar.

"Hey, buddy, keep it down." A man who has arms that are easily twice the size of mine flings open the door across from where I'm sitting. "Don't make me get physical."

Despite the gray edging at his temples, I catch a glimpse of a trident on his forearm. Yeah, I'm not a fool. Even with as much adrenaline as I have coursing through me, I know better than to fuck with a former SEAL. I lift my hands in the air. "Sorry, man. Won't happen again."

His eyes rake over me, giving me the once-over before he slams the door in my face. I scrub my hands through my hair, and when I pull my hands away, I almost miss her face filling up my screen. Tears pour down her cheeks. She doesn't say anything, just absorbs me. When she finally speaks, her voice is everything that's been living in my heart. "I have to do this, Kane. It's too late for me to stop it now."

"Please, baby. Let me help," I beg.

Her lips curve sadly. "You can't. I haven't stayed away because I don't love you, but because I love you enough to keep you alive."

My lips part. "You know who..."

"Shh..." She holds a finger to my lips through the video. Her eyes dart around as if someone is listening in.

"Christ, hang up if this is putting you in more danger."

An almost ethereal expression crosses her face. "It doesn't matter anymore. Go back to the office. They'll be waiting for you."

"I love you. Please, God, tell me you know that."

"And I love you, Kane. Always. Forever."

I start to make my way to the elevator. "Do you forgive me?"

Her eyes dart away. "There's nothing to forgive. I tried to make amends. I hope it worked."

"Lee," I say firmly. Her eyes bounce back. "There's only one thing I won't forgive."

"What's that?"

"If you leave me. Everything else, we can spend our lives working out." My voice breaks.

My knees almost buckle when her video suddenly cuts off. Her voice whispers, "I hope to God it won't cost that."

Then her voice disappears as well.

"*No!*" I pound the door of the elevator. Fortunately for me, when the doors choose then to open, there's no one inside. I bound in and jab the button for the first floor as hard as I can.

When I reach the first level, I'm greeted by a cadre of men. I note one of them happens to be my enormous friend from across the hall. He's shrugging into a suit jacket. "Mr. McCullough, can I give you a ride back to your office? I believe we both have something to discuss with your colleagues."

I back up a step. "Who the hell are you, and how the hell did you get down before me?"

He shrugs. "Fire escape. Much quicker than the elevator. Besides, I didn't want to interrupt your conversation."

"Great. That answers my second question; now how about the first?"

He reaches into his pocket and flips open his wallet before handing it to me. I almost swallow my tongue after realizing exactly who this man is.

His facial expression doesn't change when he openly declares, "*Qəza* is mine."

"The hell she is," I snarl.

A look of what might be respect crosses his face. "Fair. Now, let's go find her before she does something stupid to get herself killed." He holds out his hand for his wallet.

I slap it back into his palm as I move forward. He's already in stride next to me.

We hit the door at the same time for the darkened SUV that wasn't there when I arrived.

As we exit the elevator a short time later on the executive floor at Hudson, I feel like every mile we drove from where I last spoke to Leanne is wrong. "I should be with her," I argue fruitlessly with the large man next to me.

"Your wants, Mr. McCullough, don't mean much to me. Getting *Qəza* back alive does," he booms.

His voice carries so far, Tony doesn't have to notify Caleb or Keene of his presence. They both come out of Caleb's office with Sam, who immediately declares, "Shit."

Keene demands, "Who the hell are you?"

Sam groans, "Now? Right now?"

The behemoth's arms cross, straining his suit jacket. "Sam, really?

Like you didn't expect me to show up when I'm tracking one of my people."

"Thorn, she lost herself. You're the one who taught her that shit. Not me," he fires back.

Caleb wades in—bravely in my estimation. "I'll ask again. You are?"

I answer for him. "His name is Parker Thornton."

Sam tacks on, "I've worked with him for years—as early as when he was a SEAL."

"And we care about that why?" Keene interjects coolly.

Thorn uncrosses his arms, his stance shifting to one of cocky arrogance. "What neither Sam nor Kane are sharing is I'm also Leanne Miles's boss." His lips twist slightly, as he uncaringly unleashes information about Leanne being alive in a roomful of people who may or may not be aware of the situation.

Even on the car ride over, I got the impression quickly Parker Thornton gave up coloring within the lines a while back.

"Do you know where she is?" Caleb demands.

"I have a better idea now, thanks to Mr. McCullough's persistence." Thorn's eyes cut to me. "And now that I have that last piece of my puzzle, it's time to extract her safely."

"I agree with that," I agree grimly.

Thorn gives me a once-over. "Suit up. Weapons, body armor—whatever you think you'll need. We're wheels up in an hours."

"Hold on. No one move. On whose authorization?" Keene demands.

Thorn reaches into his back pocket and pulls out his wallet again. He flips it carelessly toward Keene, who snags it out of midair to open it. After scanning the contents thoroughly, he tosses it back. "Do you think the picture of your kids with the director adds something?" Keene asks scathingly.

Thorn shrugs. "The wife added it. I know better than to touch it."

Keene's snort causes a grin to cross Thorn's face.

"Who do you need?" Caleb asks, cutting through the bullshit.

"McCullough for Leanne, Sam for the tech. Too bad Cal's in DC, Sam; it would be just like old times."

Sam rolls his eyes. "Go to hell, Thorn. The only time you and Cal get along is when the wives are around to mediate. Now, let's go get our *Qəza*."

"My *Qəza*," I clarify. "And leaving is an excellent idea."

Thorn turns his cobra-like stare on me. "Because it's your birthday, McCullough, I'll let you get away with calling the shots once."

"Because it's my birthday, I'll let you live for letting her go into this with no backup. Are you out of your ever-loving mind?" I get up into his face, comfortable now that I'm on my own turf and I know he can't dump my body. Well, maybe he could still manage it but not without a hell of a lot of cleanup.

A hand clamps down on my shoulder. I spin and meet Sam's aggrieved face. "Frequently. But it makes him exceptional at what he does. If he's here, it means he knows he fucked up. Let's get on the plane and get comms established."

I step back and stomp toward the elevator without a word when I hear my name called. "Yeah?"

Thorn's head is downcast. "She's always been strong, fierce. She would have hated for me to coddle her, but it's instinctive to want to. You have to remember, she's been trained by the best."

"You?"

"Myself and others. Plus, she has incredible intuition. If she's hidden herself away, there's a reason. The threat against her is very real."

"So we could be placing her in more danger?" I take a step forward to throttle Thorn after all. Sam grips my arm to hold me back.

"It's too late now. We're going to have her back if she needs help. Everything else is up to her. It always has been."

Chest heaving at the picture his words paint, I yank my arm away from Sam before storming away from the group.

I need to lay eyes on Leanne. Then, my heart can rest, even if my mind won't until she's out of danger.

Unknown

Unknown: What do you want?
  Unknown: The access key to Dioscuri.
  Unknown: Acceptable.
  Unknown: What do you want for it?
  Unknown: More than you'll ever be able to give me.
  Unknown: We'll see about that.
  Unknown: Message unable to send.

KANE

She's alive! Erzulie was spotted at her sister's grave sporting some of this winter's brightest winter gear. From a distance, it was difficult which twin she was. For just a moment, Erzulie held herself with Leanne's mannerisms. With her hair twisted up, much like the older Miles sister was notorious for wearing, it was as if the other sister had risen from the snowy grave Erzulie was singing over.

Who knows how long she'll be in Silverthorn, so if you're out to get your hands on her, this may be as close as you get unless you're super fast.

— StellaNova

In the few hours since we've landed in New Hampshire, everyone has been called in. Sam, Thorn, his agents, and I are on a teleconference with an assortment of Hudson agents, including Caleb and Keene. Much to my surprise, Thorn ordered Leanne's parents to be brought in. "It's time they know everything."

If there's one place I'm glad I'm not, it's at Hudson. Keene is seething as his finger taps to advance through whatever is on his screen. Caleb's face is grim. "Now that you've read everything you're able to, do you have enough of an understanding?"

Keene's eyes glitter malevolently as they lift to the camera. "I do. And right now I feel like there's going to be some people who are seriously shocked when they find out what's been going on." He nods to the screen to indicate the people on our side of the lens.

"Let's find out." Thorn slams his hands on the table. I bob my head almost automatically as he begins to drone on but quickly tune back in when he summarizes, "Basically, what I'm about to tell you about Leanne Miles is to be considered protected until declassified by the US federal government or your death—and I suspect the latter will happen first. Do you all comprehend me?"

The Mileses look at one another, confused, but still speak in unison. "Yes."

"Sam. First, the most critical piece of information. What is Leanne Miles's present location?" Thorn demands.

Just hearing him ask the question so bluntly after the heartbreak of my conversation with her a few hours ago causes me to shake. But my body seizes when Sam declares, "Unknown but alive and in the area."

Chaos erupts from her parents. "Say that again, young man? And what makes any information about our daughter so important to our government?" her father demands.

Sam turns to face him. "Sir, Thorn is her handler. He and I worked together for many years before I left that part of my life behind. However, I was fully read in the moment Leanne disappeared from her sister's apartment months ago. She's running, because she feels she'll endanger anyone she comes into contact with. He never had the chance to disclose to her I'm his inside contact here at Hudson."

"What?" is shouted from multiple directions, including me. Her mother manages a weak "Handler?"

"Yes, ma'am." Thorn completely ignores the small explosion Sam's words cause—from everyone including myself to the Hudson employees on teleconference—to address Leanne's mother. "There are others higher ranked than myself who would have preferred to have been here to explain, but they asked me to stand in their stead. Your daughter is one of our finest patriots. She's rose to serve a call of duty when asked with pride and honor. She's spent years unearthing intelligence that's saved American lives. From a young age, she's done so without accolades."

Renee Miles is visibly shaken. "Leanne? My Leanne?"

Sam nods his head sharply.

"Is that why her sister was...killed?"

Keene intercepts the question. "According to the report I just reviewed, Leanne wasn't certain. She's been investigating the possibility of this night and day while trying to also determine if there was something about Kylie's own life that might have caused this. She was completely transparent with one of my agents, who she determined had an active and proper clearance level to be read in about this part of her life." Keene cuts his eyes in my direction before returning his attention to the Mileses. "She's selflessly set aside her own grief to find Kylie's killer. But in the course of the investigation, several attempts have been made on her own life."

Renee gasps before turning on her husband. "Did you know any of this?"

Frank's lips thin before he shakes his head. She whirls back to Keene for more information. He continues. "Not counting Kylie's own death, the first attempt was in Silverthorn, just days after Kylie's funeral."

Renee cries out and collapses unto herself. It's her husband's arms that keep her standing.

I cross my arms behind my back while Keene explains about the drug she was slipped at the party. But even I'm stunned when I hear the details about StellaNova's post. I clutch the back of the chair in front of me to keep my footing. Leanne ran to me for help, and I pushed her away. She told me to trust her. She tried to remind me to "Trust beyond trust, Kane. Please." The words echo through my head.

"Christ. Oh Christ." The words escape my mouth before I can stop them. I can hear my sanctimonious voice lecturing her about Beckett. And all the while, she was trying to let me know an attempt was going to be made on her life.

Again.

Caleb leans in and bares his teeth. "Be very grateful she's as smart as she is, Kane. She's managed to keep herself alive thus far. And with luck, there's still a chance we can help her do that now."

"Where is Leanne now?" The question comes from her father.

"Sam?" Caleb nods.

Sam presses a few keys, and Leanne's voice fills the room. "I promised to avenge her. And I will. I need to tie up a few loose ends. Then, I'll find my way to say my final goodbye."

Her voice, as cool as the first time when she asked me about *Qǝza*, fades away.

"When was that sent?" I demand.

"Hours ago, it was received by Thorn, right before he introduced himself to you, Kane." I turn my heated glare on the larger man, who merely shrugs.

"What does she mean?" Renee cries frantically.

Her husband's trying to soothe her when there's a knock on the door at Hudson. Tony slips in. He bends over and whispers to Caleb, whose head snaps in my direction. "Kane, there's something else. Beckett Miller."

Cursing, I step forward. "What about him?"

Carys saunters into the conference room. "I came to let you all know he's on his way to New Hampshire. He took Paige to pay his respects to Leanne without his security team."

I curse roundly. "Why now?"

"Why does he do anything?" Carys counters.

I groan, "Because he's trying to escape the media, and he had free time on his hands."

"Exactly. And with what was printed today by StellaNova..." Carys's voice trails off.

A hand lands on my shoulder. I whirl around and find Sam there. "What was printed?"

I open my mouth to ask why it matters, but Carys acknowledges. "Hey, Sam."

"Carys. What happened?"

She explains what StellaNova posted a few moments ago, and

several people's teeth snap together. Sam's jaw locks. "Do you have the URL?"

Carys drops her hand to her folio and draws out her phone. "Why, I have that very thing right here," she drawls.

He drops back down to his chair and starts typing in the URL she calls out. I crowd in behind him as his fingers pull up a terminal window next to StellaNova's website. He bellows, "Thorn, over here. Stat!"

I lean over his shoulder to see if I can understand anything amid the garbage of characters on the screen. There are only two things I can read. The first is the Dioscuri copyright. And the second, a few lines down, is a small cracked heart.

Her flat voice echoes in my head. I need to tie up a few loose ends. Then, I'll find my way to say my final goodbye.

And the feeling of dread that began in the conference room coalesces into something much stronger—abject fear—when Sam snaps, "She accessed Dioscuri. No, she's not even trying to cover her tracks. Her equipment is hot. She's luring them to her." His fingers begin flying at a familiar pace I've become accustomed to.

My voice is broken when I step forward. "Stop."

Thorn's voice is like a whip. "What do you mean, 'Stop?'"

"You heard what she said. There's only one place she's going to say goodbye." You could hear a pin drop, everyone has gone so quiet. I swallow and push the words out. "Kylie. No matter how long it takes, she'll go to Kylie."

"Did you hear that?" Sam demands of the people on the other end of the conference call. Without waiting for confirmation, he pushes a button to disconnect New York before turning his attention back to his laptop. We wait until he mutters a curse. "Holy hell. She laid a trap inside of Dioscuri."

"What kind of trap?" Thorn presses.

"The kind that will require a special passcode to access all of the data inside. If she's wrong about the identity of who's after her, Leanne just painted a multinational target on her back because there isn't an enemy nation who won't want the data she just laid out as bait—access to Dioscuri's mainframe."

I swallow the lump and ask, "How do you get the password?"

His fingers still for a whole five seconds before they resume their furious typing, in an effort to do what, I'm not entirely certain. "She's using a biometric blockchain cryptography."

"And?" He doesn't respond. I shake his shoulder to get his attention. "Come on, Sam. And? What do you need? That's some sort of special code, right?"

He whirls around to face me, whereupon I note the blood has drained from his face. "You could say that. Leanne's done something I've rarely seen before. She's using physical attributes as part of the passkey. And she chose not one, but two items to decode it—her retina print and a fingerprint."

Thorn yells, "That's impossible."

"It's not," Sam argues, pointing at the screen.

"It has to be. She doesn't have any fingerprints, Sam."

His eyes widen before he whirls around, and he looks at the coded bomb Leanne may have set off. "Then whose is she using?"

Thorn pounds the table next to him. "Faster, Sam!"

Sam brushes him off with a "Not now, Thorn!"

"There's a note. We need to know who she left her note to? If we get it, we'll know whose prints we need."

My back snaps up straight. I hiss, "How in the hell did you know she left a note?"

"It was part of her code when she asked us to clean out her—their —life in New York. She let us know one person had the instructions on what to do next. Whomever she trusted has the key to shut this down."

Beyond trust. I scrub my hands over my face. "Sam, stop."

"Kane, I have to figure out who Leanne left the message to."

"Beyond trust." The words come out choked.

That's when his fingers still. He jumps up from the chair and types a few commands. The screen goes blank from the lines of scrolling code. Once it does, he drags me back into the fray, where an astounded Renee Miles is demanding someone finds her daughter and brings her in safely.

"We're trying, Mrs. Miles. We have the where. We have the who." Sam jerks his thumb at me. "We just don't know when. We need to get Kane to Leanne as quickly as possible."

Renee turns and grips my arm. "Save her. Whatever you have to do, save my daughter."

Thorn jerks my other arm. "We don't have time for this. Let's go."

Without a word, I shake her off and go after him. I don't pay notice to the number of people who follow me. I'm only focused on one thing—finding Leanne and making amends for letting her crash after all those times she prevented me from doing the same, even when I didn't know it was her who was keeping me from falling.

The most important thing is on the line—and it has absolutely nothing to do with whatever secrets are contained within the confines of her brainchild. The only secrets I care about are the ones inside her heart.

The woman I love is in danger. And so am I because if Leanne doesn't survive, there's no way I will either.

Leanne

Don't blend in! Show your personal style when you're hitting the slopes this season. There are so many choices, you can swoosh down the slopes without sacrificing your personal style. There's nothing you can't stash that Mother Nature doesn't want you to have. Make certain your gear is water-repellent and has ample ventilation and pockets for all those last-minute-item must-haves.

— **Eva Henn, Fashion Blogger**

I drop to my knees and trail my fingers over the stone. "Hey, Lee. I've missed you."

The wind is whipping all around me, but I don't care. I lie down in the snow and wrap my arms around my sister and just hold on for dear life. "God, Lee, it hurts just as much now as when I found out you were murdered. Probably more so because I know the truth. The only thing I still can't figure out after all this time is why you had my ID on you."

I inhale the chilled air, unafraid of what's going to happen at this point. "I cleaned up as much as I could, Lee. Mom and Dad will be taken care of—I promise. I redid the trust. Mom and Dad will inherit all the money. There should be enough to take care of them and anyone they care for well into their hundreds. I promise you, they'll never want for anything."

I go on telling her about small gifts I've left here and there when my voice finally starts to crack. "I was up half the night trying to figure out what to leave to Kane. It was his birthday yesterday. Oh, don't think I didn't see your hand in that, Kylie. How did you know he would be absolutely perfect for me?"

"How did she know that indeed?" a husky baritone murmurs behind me.

I roll to my back, automatically reaching for the gun I have nestled in the small of my back, when I hear a delicate female question, "Beckett?"

Quickly scrambling to my feet, I take an automatic step away from the couple. Her dark hair and creamy skin are a perfect match for his tattooed hotness. But nothing prepares me for the sorrow in his voice as his eyes scan my features. A myriad of emotions chase one another across his face: devastation, fury, acceptance. Slowly, he nods. "You must be Leanne."

My breath releases so forcefully, steam rises from my lips. "Yes."

"Can I ask..."

I immediately begin to shake my head. "No. Not yet." Soon, everyone will know.

His arm immediately wraps around Paige protectively. "Is it safe for us to be here?"

My eyes scan the area. "For now." Still, I check my holster to ensure my weapon is in easy reach.

Beckett's eyes bulge before a small laugh escapes. "Christ. Now, it all makes sense."

I frown. "What does?"

"There was one night when Ky told Kane the two of you would be perfect for each other..." I adamantly begin shaking my head. Beckett merely cocks his. "Why are you denying something so obvious to the rest of us? Right, sweetheart?"

Paige hums in agreement. I gape at them both. "What is wrong with you two?"

"What's wrong with you?" he counters. While I'm sputtering in an effort to string words together, Beckett calmly explains, "We weren't the ones who had an issue with the past coming to light, Lee, just with the way it did. We always suspected it would someday. Truth be told, there's something a little more sensitive we're trying to keep a lid on for a while."

My eyes immediately drop to Paige's waistline, and Beckett roars. "Leanne? You've got a lot of your sister's sass in you."

At his words, I turn away to face her gravestone before he can see the hurt his words cause. "People have accused me of abandoning her."

"That's a damn lie." This beautiful man I inadvertently hurt in my search comes immediately to my defense.

"Maybe I did. Maybe I lost sight of finding the answers," I whisper harshly.

"Because you fell in love? Cut yourself some slack. That's honoring her by *living*. She would be devastated if you didn't. Remember? I knew her," Beckett states calmly.

His words cause a wrecking ball to slam into my heart. I can barely manage to nod before a shadow drifts in front of me. My head whips up, and the compassion in Paige's green eyes causes my composure to wither.

But it's the way she opens her arms to me that causes the last of my defenses to completely shatter. I manage to choke out, "I'm so sorry. I never thought they would target me through people I cared about. It turned into such a huge disaster. I swear, I never meant for you both to be hurt, despite what others might think."

I dive forward as her arms wrap around me—the first embrace I've felt of its kind since before Kylie died. And my body shakes under the force of my tears. Over and over, I keep whispering, "I'm so sorry."

Paige doesn't say a word. She just smooths her hand up and down over my back, murmuring encouraging sounds against the top of my hair. Beckett approaches, declaring, "There's nothing to apologize for, Leanne. You loved your sister."

Which only causes me to choke out, "I did. I do. I love her so much."

I feel myself being passed from Paige's soothing arms to Beckett's strong ones. He slowly rocks me back and forth. "I should have known something was up. Kylie would never have gone to that party.

She called Snowy-T a royal piece of shit who deserved to be run over by a New York City bus."

A watery giggle escapes. "That's what she wrote in her journal as well."

"Then why did you go? I mean really, kid, pajamas are not my best look."

Paige snorts out her disagreement. "My love, I get caught by Sexy&Social wearing pj's to pick up coffee and it's a scandal. You wear them and everyone races to look it up online."

My hand slaps over my mouth to hold back the laugh that wants to escape at the disgruntled look Beckett delivers to his fiancée. He ignores her before addressing me, "Forget about what I was wearing. Why go?"

I give an uncomfortable shrug. "I knew it wasn't one of her friends who had hurt her, so it had to be one of her enemies." *Or one of mine.* I shake away the chill that courses through me and explain, "For me to find whomever killed Kylie, I had to submerge myself in her world— even the awful parts of it." I shudder when I recall the nauseated feeling the next day.

Beckett tips my chin up before he demands, "No more, then?"

My body sags in defeat as I reach out and graze the top of Lee's headstone. "No. There's nothing left of Kylie's life to dig up."

His eyes narrow. "The StellaNova recant? That was you?"

My shoulders square, and I lift my chin. "They deserved to pay." His lips curve into a smile that I'm sure reflects my own—sinfully evil.

Paige draws me away from Beckett. "True. But..."

"Just say what you're thinking, Paige," I declare bluntly, bracing myself for her ire.

"You need to speak with someone, release your anger." Her hand lifts before coasting over my hair. I don't rear back in resentment of her assessment because I'm absorbing her touch like a sponge.

I open my mouth to deny her claims, but what comes out is "I know. I'd have given Lee the exact same advice."

"I was concerned you'd feel I was overstepping, even if I am a doctor," Paige explains.

"Paige, after everything the press has printed about you both to get to me, I think if you want the right to meddle, you pretty much have it."

She flashes me a quick smile, which fades as her eyes lock on something over my shoulder. I whirl around and find Beckett staring down at Lee's grave. Paige squeezes my hand. We're both silent for long moments until his rough voice manages, "She was like a kid sister to me. It's unbelievable to know she's gone."

"She deserved everything, but above all things, she deserved to know who did this to her and why." I wipe my fingers beneath my eyes. "It's just been so hard to deal with."

"Today," Paige states calmly.

"Excuse me?"

"Today, it's impossible to deal with. And tomorrow, it likely will as well. It doesn't mean time won't dull the wounds." Just as she finishes, Beckett turns away from Lee's grave and wraps his arms around her. "Healing happens when it's supposed to, Leanne. It always does."

I open my mouth, but no sound comes out. Paige leans forward and presses her lips against my cool cheek. "Take care. Call someone, please?"

Then she shifts, and Beckett wraps me in his arms tightly. "When you come back to the city, have Carrie get us all together." I squint at him in confusion. He clarifies, "Carys. We'll introduce you to our daughter. You'll like her."

"Umm, I'm not too good with small children," I waffle.

"Then it's a plus she's only a few years younger than you." Beckett beams proudly.

My jaw falls to the floor at this unexpected acceptance, not that I didn't know it. I'm so astounded by it, I forget I have no plans to head back into New York because I'll likely be lying right next to my Lee soon. "Well...sure."

Beckett whispers, "I was devastated thinking it was you—so was Paige. Kane knew it."

My eyes drop to the grass in shame.

"They have no idea what true love can overcome. He's waiting for his chance to show you." And with that, Beckett Miller leans down and presses a kiss on my forehead before he and Paige move away.

I scrunch my eyes closed for just a second. Taking a deep breath, I call out, "Beckett!"

He stops and looks over his shoulder. His clear blue eyes are clouded with the news about Lee, but unlike what Lee described to me, there's nothing else shadowing them. The words flow out of me. "She was worried about you. She knew something was wrong in your heart." I lay my hand on my sister's stone, and my lips curve. "She'd be thrilled to know it's fixed."

Even from a distance, I see moisture brighten his eyes even further. He swallows visibly before ordering, "Call Carrie," as he turns away.

"I'll get right on that. Was he always this autocratic?" I murmur to the cold marble.

I don't get an answer from Lee, but a male voice I'd recognize anywhere responds, "You'll be able to ask her yourself soon enough."

Right before darkness envelops me, his arm reaches over my shoulder and a cloth is smothered up against my nose and mouth.

KANE

According to the Federal Highway Administration, close to 2000 people die each year due to car accidents on icy and snowy roads. Use common sense when leaving your home to drive in adverse conditions, especially when the only reason you're doing so is to run to the store for some last-minute groceries.

Your favorite snack can wait; your life can't.

— **Fab and Delish**

"Get your ass out of there. They've already grabbed her," Thorn's now familiar voice barks in my ear.

I immediately wheel away from the cemetery. "Tell me where I'm headed."

"To the airport."

"Who has her?"

When he tells me the answer, I almost run off the road. Fortunately, I correct my out-of-control driving to avoid both a ditch and an oncoming vehicle. But there's only one thing I care about. "Is she alive?"

"As long as she doesn't give them what they want."

"Which is?"

"Access to Dioscuri."

Leanne

Decorating is not all about function; it is about ensuring the place you spend a large portion of your time nourishes your soul. That's difficult especially when bulk office furniture is often ordered in drab, easy-to-scrub gray.

— **Beautiful Today**

I immediately recognize where I am the moment my eyes wake up. "I see you haven't bothered redecorating since I died, Ivan. You liked the decor in my office that much?"

I pay for my snark with the crack of his hand to my face. My head whips to the side. He snarls, "What the hell did you do to my software, you bitch?"

I outright laugh. "*Your* software? I'm sorry. Are you talking about Dioscuri? That would be *my* invention. You just worked on some of the coding."

He looms over me and declares, "If I didn't need you alive to reverse what you did, I swear, I'd already have the bullet in you."

I shrug, knowing that nothing short of a complete shutdown of Dioscuri using the biometric keys will stop its destruction at this point. Still, "I'd like to know why. I deserve that."

"You deserve nothing," he spits at me.

"Oh, I don't know about that," a third voice says from a dark corner.

I immediately tense. "A partner? I'm surprised, Ivan. I would have thought *you* believed you had the balls to take me out on your own. I, of course, know otherwise."

He yanks his hand to club me across the face again, when the man in the corner calls out, "Enough. We need her alive."

I hold my breath until his face comes into view. "Linus Messenia? What the hell are you doing here?" My gaze darts between the two men.

Then Linus's lips twist in a familiar way—one I've never seen during our forced negotiation meetings set up by none other than Ivan. I direct my question at Linus, since he's obviously the one in charge. "Brothers or cousins?"

He jerks his chin back. "Does it really matter?"

"Well, when we're all dead, I'd like to be able to tell Lee who I killed on her behalf."

He laughs at me. "Oh, Leanne. I'd offer condolences for your loss, but it was such a pleasure to wrap my hands around your fucking throat and squeeze the life out of you—even if it wasn't you."

So, it was this monster who killed my Lee. Out of the corner of my eye, Ivan's howling with laughter, and the piece of Lee's journal finally connects with her cryptic messages the weeks before she died. As the memory of what Lee said clicks together with Ivan coming to our meeting late, everything begins to snaps into place. I hiss, "Don't get too cocky, Ivan. She saw you. Said you loved her outfit at the party. Your reaction must have been a doozy. After all, she left me a clue about wanting to run over you with a bus in her journal." That goddamn "I." Mentally, I'm kicking myself in the ass for not remembering it sooner.

"I searched her place. I didn't find a journal," he scoffs.

God, I'm so sorry, my Lee. You left me a clue, and I missed it. Berating myself, I sneer, "Obviously, you didn't check that closely. I'll admit it took me some time, but I, at least, have the excuse of grief. Once I was back in the game..." I let my voice trail off.

Linus turns to face him slowly. Ivan stammers, "I...uh...that is..."

"Did you see a journal?" Linus demands.

"Well, sure. But I didn't see what she's talking about."

"It was toward the back. Maybe if you went past the pages where the diary ended to make certain your name wasn't mentioned, you might have found it," I drawl at Ivan.

Linus cuts his eyes toward me. Within seconds, he pulls a gun—shit, my gun—from his slacks and shoots Ivan through his pant leg. "You motherfucking bitch!" Ivan shrieks.

"I'm not the one who shot you!" I yell.

"He wouldn't have hurt me if it wasn't for you. He never hurts me unless it's because of you." Ivan's rolling around on the floor, clutching his leg.

I coldly watch the blood ooze and mercilessly tell him, "I would have shot to the left."

Linus pins me with a snakelike smile. "And this, my dear Leanne, is why I wanted to merge our empires. Your heart is just as relentless as my own."

I wheel the desk chair back just a bit as Linus approaches. I'm mentally counting tiles as I scoot away. Five over.

"Now, let's forget Ivan."

Four.

"Tell me what you did to the software."

Three.

"What do you mean, 'did'?" I hedge.

Two.

"I mean, how the fuck do you stop Dioscuri from self-destruct-ing," Linus roars. He surges forward and holds the gun right above my shoulder. Without hesitation, he pulls the trigger.

Boom!

The force of the bullet hitting the high back throws the office chair against the wall. My heart stops when I realize I haven't been hit, just the chair. But I decide to stall. If I can get to my feet, maybe some of the training Thorn gave me will give me enough time to lock myself away.

"Speak!" Linus commands.

Taking a deep breath, I let out two parts of it before hedging, "I need access to the server room."

Immediately, Linus comes over and cuts through the bindings on my wrists and ankles. Gripping me by the arm, he drags me from the chair. Ivan starts to protest, and Linus yells, "I can't take this noise!"

Then he shuts him up. Permanently.

Even though I'm not sorry to see Ivan dead since he was privy to the plot of having my Lee murdered, I still shudder in Linus's grasp as I'm calculating what my options are. "For being your...?" I pause delicately.

"Cousin. Now, where is the illustrious server room of yours?"

"Even in the boardroom, you were never one for the small talk," I bite out as he drags me away from my office and down the hall. I catch a glimmer of headlights on the street. Praying to every god I can think of, I turn Linus in a circle when he asks me, "Left or right?"

"Left." We walk down another hall a few steps and come to a door. I lean forward and use my eye to open the retina lock. He jerks open the door and shoves me through it.

Immediately, alarms start going off.

"Shut it off! Shut it off!"

"I can't! You're not authorized. The technology doesn't recognize your biometrics," I shout over the alarms.

"That's the first fucking thing you're doing when we get into your server room."

I don't bother to argue with him despite the gun at my back because I know there's no way we're getting into my server room.

Finally, despite the screeches and sirens, we approach the door that protects Dioscuri. And not only is there another retina lock, there's a keypad, as well as a handprint lock. He taps me on the back of the head with the gun. "Open it up."

I step back and wait. "I can't."

"What do you mean you can't?" His face takes on a panicked expression. "Did we need fucking Ivan after all?"

"We need multiple biometrics, yes. But not Ivan's." With that, I cross my arms.

Linus grabs my wrist and slaps it onto the lock. A buzzer sounds. He grabs my other hand—same reaction.

Just as he's about to try it again, I hiss, "Do it one more time and it will set off a code to destroy all of Dioscuri from the inside out. I have a clause in my contract with the DoD for such an eventuality. I'll destroy it before I'll ever let a terrorist get their hands on it, you piece of shit."

"You lie, you bitch." He lifts his gun and aims it right at my heart.

A perfect shot.

I take a step back and lift my hand, letting it hover over the sensor. Throwing my shoulders back, I whisper, "For Lee."

Just then, there's a commotion outside the door. Both of our heads jerk to see what it is. Through the glass panel, I see Kane's face right before I make eye contact with Thorn. He nods.

For a brief moment, peace flows through me. *I did it, Lee.*

I let my hand drop.

After that, the world goes black after Linus pulls the trigger and it hits me exactly where he intended.

KANE

Erzulie—always believed to be folk-award-winning singing sensation Kylie Miles—was proven this evening to be her identical twin sister, Leanne, when she was rushed to the emergency room.

Leanne isn't available for comment.

— **StellaNova**

If I thought the scene at Castor was bad enough with the police, protocol, and statements preventing me from getting to her, the riot of reporters waiting for me at Saratoga Hospital almost sends me over the edge of insanity. I easily shove my way past them with the ease born of practice with Beckett, ignoring their questions.

Can you tell us what happened at the crime scene?

Is Beckett coming to visit Ms. Miles?

Are you here to protect Ms. Miles?

Finally, a male voice shouting next to my ear resonates above all the others. "Are you aware Leanne was an imposter?"

My head whips to the side, and I pause midstride. "What trash rag are you with?"

A flicker crosses his face. "StellaNova."

Figures. "All I'll say is this—neither Miles sister is an imposter." Certainly nothing Leanne has made me feel is close to a forgery of love. It's the real thing. Now, if I can just get her to forgive me for not believing in her when it could have cost her her life.

And with that, I push my way through the rest of the garbage barring my way to the hospital doors, and I hurry to the room I was told Leanne would be in once she gets out of her brain scan for her head slamming so hard against the wall.

Because once she wakes up, I may murder her for not letting anyone know she was wearing body armor beneath her ski wear. She took a hell of a gamble the lunatics she was dealing with would be so anxious to get to Dioscuri they would only check her for weapons, not protection. I'm certain my life expectancy shortened by several years until Thorn blew the lock and I was able to reach her while Thorn took care of the threat.

When I asked him what he wanted as a thank-you, he actually cracked a smile as he stared down at Leanne's rising and falling chest. "I think you're going to give it to me."

Then he disappeared, leaving me to clean up the mess.

I can't force myself to move away from her side. "You've lost weight, baby. You look like you've barely eaten, Crash." I run my fingers through the webbing of hers that doesn't have the IV through it.

She doesn't stir, even though it's been days. The doctors have come by twice a day to see if she's awake, making noises about sending her down for a new head CT if she doesn't begin to stir soon. The swelling on her brain isn't impacting her motor functions, but as they said, "It could be sheer exhaustion." Then they drew more blood and attached more bags to her overflowing IV.

Judging from that, I lend more credence to that theory than any long-term impact to her brain. She's just drained from the mental exhaustion of the last sixteen months. "Especially the last six." I lower the bed rail to get as close to her as I can. I just wish I could erase all the time and space between us as easily, but I need her awake to hear what I have to say. Instead, I focus on reminding her, "You got them, Crash. You kept your promise to Kylie. You figured out who killed her."

Her lips part, and a puff of air releases, encouraging me to keep talking.

A tremulous woman's voice comes from behind me. "I can't believe she did that." My head whips around, and I stare into Renee Miles's tearstained face. "No, I take it back. I *can* believe she would do that for her sister. What I can't believe is the life she was leading." Her eyes flick over to mine. "Can you?"

I nod. "But that might be because she saved mine a time or two before I ever knew who she was." I reach up and brush her loose hair off Leanne's face. She just sighs, head lolling to the side, instinctively trying to get closer.

I hope.

Renee sucks in a deep breath. "I've been so careless with her this past year...Kane? May I call you Kane?"

"Certainly, Mrs. Miles," I address her formally. When I think about the way Leanne cried in my arms about the loss of her family a year ago, it's difficult not to be reticent with this woman, yet what grounds do I have to stand on? I pushed her away in much the same manner. Right now, we're in the same lifeboat, hoping the only person who can rescue us from this river of hell will.

She rounds the bed and picks up her daughter's other hand expertly, inspecting the IV. "Make it Renee," she says absentmindedly. "Does Leanne know you're in love with her?"

"She does. And then I completely screwed up. I didn't listen, and it almost cost her everything." I lift her hand to my cheek and press a kiss to the palm. "I'll never be able to apologize enough."

Renee frowns down at me. So, I fill in a little more detail than what she learned in the conference room a few days ago before Leanne was kidnapped at her sister's gravesite. "I'm not certain I can forgive myself. Look at what happened," I croak out.

"Kane, people in love fight. And yes—some of them cause permanent damage. The true measure of a relationship is how you handle what happens next. Speaking as a bystander..."

I snort.

Her lips curve briefly. "I didn't say I was an objective one. But nevertheless, both of you ran—you, emotionally, Leanne, physically. Why?"

I open my mouth to respond, but I don't owe this woman the answers. It's the still body on the bed who deserves them. When I say as much to Renee, she tosses me Leanne's smile. I can't say it isn't disconcerting and heart-wrenching because the woman I want it from is motionless except for her chest rising up and down.

Renee drops into the seat across from me and runs her hand over Leanne's hair. "Did she ever tell you about the time she wiped out our mortgage and rearranged her father's stock portfolio?"

Amusement laces my voice when I lift Leanne's fingers to kiss them. "When was this?"

"It was her high school graduation present to us. She said her father needed the help with both of his daughters going off to pricey universities."

I bark out a laugh. "That sounds just like her."

"I thought Frank was going to strangle her," Renee reminisces fondly. "I have to say it's such a relief to know she's finally met a man willing to take care of her, even if she doesn't need it. No one else ever has, you see."

And reflected back at me, I find a woman who has been tested by the best and the absolute worst and still is willing to open her heart to love. It's humbling. "I have a lot to make up for."

"There's a lot of tomorrows. And even if there's not, then make today count. God knows she and her sister are the ones who taught me that." She opens her mouth to continue, but there's a groan from the bed. Leanne twists her head from side to side, moaning as she gets her bearings. Her eyelashes flicker as delicate as angel's wings. And in that instant when her pain-filled eyes lock on mine, I realize there's a secret no one shares about love. From second to second, it can change. It can flutter between hope or despair, laughter or tears, but until you're caught in its wings, experience the flight of your heart soaring, you'll never understand the undiluted emotions with it are never to be found anywhere else.

We both hold our breath as Leanne licks her lips before she rasps out, "How did I teach you that, Mom?" Dark blue eyes flick over and find her mother's as she tries to pull her hands away. I just tighten my fingers. Judging by the frustration that crosses her face, I'm certain Renee does the same.

"Oh, Leanne." Renee lifts her daughter's hand before lowering the bed rail. She perches on the edge of the bed and presses both of their hands against her heart. "There aren't enough apologies..."

"Mom, right now, I need a phone. Give me just a few minutes, please?" Leanne's voice is cool. Even with her chest likely on fire from where Messenia's bullet pounded against the Kevlar, she hasn't hit the magic pump ready to dispense the painkiller. She's *Qəza*, needing to ensure everyone and everything around her is safe.

I can't help but jump in. "Crash, it's okay." Renee slips from the room to give us privacy.

Her eyes jerk to mine. "A phone, Kane. I just need two minutes." Her anxiety causes her blood pressure to rise.

"Shit, fine. Any minute they're going to boot us out of here if you don't calm down." I whip mine out of my pocket and hand it to her.

She immediately begins dialing. I hear her spew out a code before demanding an odd combination of items. Once she hears whatever she does from the responses on the other end, her body sinks into the bed relaxing. Her eyes mist over even as she tosses the phone back in my direction. "It's done. It's truly done."

"What did you just ask Thorn to confirm?"

She sputters, "How did you know...?"

"It's a long story. He was staking out your place. He came to Hudson. By the way, did you know Sam was your contact inside of

Hudson? You should have seen Thorn barking out orders that sent a stick up Keene's ass." I smile crookedly at her.

She gapes at me. "For real?"

I nod, pressing her fingers between both of my hands. Then I break down. "God, when I saw that gun, I thought I'd never have the chance to hold you again."

"Kane," she starts, but I stop her.

I begin. "I was wrong, and it could have cost you your life. You ran."

"I ran because—"

"Crash, just listen, please?" She acquiesces. "You ran because you didn't believe you had anyone to trust in despite my promise to you—beyond trust. Right?"

"That's how it was supposed to be. Absolute trust." She winces when she shifts in her bed, turning her head away.

"Over the last six months, I've been working with a trauma therapist. He's helped me put into perspective the events of what happened—with Gene, with my career ending, and what caused the trigger to ignite that day when you came to me."

"What was it?" Instead of pushing me away like I deserve, her eyes focus on me for the first time. I can feel emotions I haven't allowed myself to feel boil up inside.

"I was blindsided." Immediately, Leanne starts nodding in understanding. "It's so stupid—working for Beckett, I constantly never know what's going to happen from one day to the next, but..."

"There's still a measure of control in those situations. You train how to react to them," she murmurs.

"Then in less than a few hours, it felt like everything changed: my heart, my job, my pride. And I chose the wrong things to hold on to."

"And you chose what you'd trained for," she concludes.

She gets it. A gush of air rushes out, and the words just flow out. "And I was wrong, Crash. So wrong."

For long moments, we sit in silence. My gut churns, terrified that at any moment, she's going to throw me out when I hear her whisper, "So, what happens next?"

My phone pings loudly with an incoming text. I frown since it's set to Silent. Flipping it over, I gape when I read the text.

Tell Qəza Dioscuri is secured. I personally enjoyed destroying her laptop which Sam deduced was the actual timer. Sorry, not sorry. Listen, on the begging front—let her know she can have anything she wants. Women seem to like that shit. At least, my wife does.

I don't reply. I simply turn the phone around and let her read Thorn's message. And when she lets out a primal scream that causes her mother and the nursing staff to come rushing in, I simply hand her the button for her pain medicine. "She rolled the wrong way," I explain blandly. They all back out of the room, still eyeing us both warily.

After everyone exits, she keeps her eyes pinned on the door before murmuring, "I can't stop what's going to happen next, Kane. The press, the media—there's only so much that even Thorn can do."

I bend over her and press my lips to her forehead, then her heart before I lay them against her lips and murmur, "I don't care. You're alive. I'll wait as long as it takes to straighten out this clusterfuck. I'll be right by your side. When I can't be, I'll be where it matters more—next to your heart. I love you, Leanne—not because of what you are, but because of who you are to me."

Her lips begin to tremble. "I love you. Always. Forever. I can't stop."

The words I feared I'd never hear her say again wash over me like a benediction. I slide my hand gently behind her neck and kiss her. "And I know that's a vow you take seriously."

"To death."

When I think about how close she came to that tonight, I pull back and lay my head on her stomach. I'm not certain how long it's going to be before I'll no longer witness the gun being held to her heart.

"Kane?"

"What is it?"

"I have to tell you something."

Oh boy. "Let's hear it."

"I think it's time to hit the pain medicine button for real now." I lift my head and catch the flash of pain cross her face. "Despite the fact I was wearing a vest, this hurts like a bitch."

Scooting as close as possible without putting any pressure on her bruise, I lay my lips on hers. "Just remember, the only thing preventing you from bleeding instead of just being bruised is the fact you had that vest on." My face crumbles. "Crash, I can't imagine what I would do without you again."

Her dark blue eyes begin dripping tears. "We'll work it out. We won't have to find out. Okay?"

"Swear it," I demand harshly.

"I swear."

And for long minutes until the doctor comes in to check on her now awake patient, I try to make up for the long months apart. Though in my heart, I know Thorn's probably right. I'm going to end up begging.

It's okay. It's the right order of things.

EPILOGUE
TWO YEARS LATER

"Did you see the garbage StellaNova wrote today?" I toss my tablet into Kane's lap as we sit on our couch after dinner at our home in Manhattan.

He reads the article aloud. "Is Kylie Miles spinning in her grave as she watches her sister take the spotlight 'in the name of love'? While we completely support the charity, is it necessary for the other 'Erzulie' to perform? But who are we to judge. The computer hacker is backed up on stage by Beckett Miller and Brendan Blake, so we're not going to miss a minute of the show." *His aqua eyes are lit with fury over the magazine's attempt to get a rise out of me since they damn well know I played fast and loose with their website to redeem Beckett a few years ago.* "I know what she'd say, Lee. She'd be damn proud of you. Look at what you've established in her honor."

I lean over to accept his kiss, even as my mind briefly touches on the memories of what happened when I got released from the hospital. Then I can focus on nothing but the heat of his lips.

And I damn well know my sister would approve of that and the three-carat ring sparkling on my left hand he slid on there for my birthday—almost two years to the day I found my sister's murderers.

After I was released from the hospital, it was a media circus with the press insinuating I was living my sister's life for glory—nothing more. There was a resurgence of the story about Beckett's past, that I truly did hack in for that information. And despite the very vocal protests that wasn't the case, we all stood together to fight that battle once again.

Thorn was out of his mind that what should have been him strolling in to declare the matter open-and-shut, wasn't. He argued with the New York State attorney general about the fact that yes, while I did technically live my sister's life, I did so with the knowledge of the key people who were instrumental in that life—as well as key people in the US federal government. Mentally, I gave him a high five for reminding the AG of his most salient point. "She didn't accept any monies that weren't hers to begin with."

But the AG wouldn't let me off scot-free. "It's a horrible circumstance, and I appreciate the justification. But all of you should have had encouraged Ms. Miles to go directly to the police. At the very least, come straight to me."

"And wind up dead?" I argued myself in his office, peeling away my shirt barely two weeks after I was shot with a wince—deliberately exposing where the bullet from the gun Linus shot me with left a plate-size bruise. "The police closed my sister's death with a nominal investigation."

"I've reviewed their files, Ms. Miles. They believed they had the correct information."

"And they were wrong. Even if it had been me lying on that ground, there's no way this would have been open-and-shut. If it wasn't for the fact the company I own has extensive classified contracts with the federal government, setting off the need for certain agencies to investigate my own 'death' and choosing to keep that information I was alive quiet, my sister's killers would still be on the loose. Your nose is just out of joint because you weren't one of the ones in the know."

His face turned a lovely shade of puce, but I plowed on. "No one in local law enforcement was acting as though Kylie's death was more than a simple mugging. And by not realizing they had the wrong sister, it was almost too late to stop them a second time. A third time. A fourth time."

He winced at my harsh words that were no less than the truth. Still, he tried again. "I am obligated to defend the law I too was sworn to uphold as it's written." Thorn began spouting words to defend my choices. He held up a hand. "But there are mitigating circumstances I can and will take into account."

And he did.

Our two years has evolved with love, healing, with spurts of uncomfortable reality thrown in. Wildfire Records spent the first few months publicly supporting my actions and mourning the loss of one of music's greatest voices—earning my eternal gratitude and devotion to Kristoffer Wilde. The attorney general was of course stressing the fact I should never have taken justice into my own hands, leaving the agency out of it. But in the end, we all accomplished what we could to seamlessly transition Kylie from front-page news to allow those of us who loved her most time to grieve. It's given us time to restore emotional order to our lives when we've barely had any in almost eighteen months.

I was more pissed off because the agency didn't have my back—all due to the fact Thorn never cleared our mission since I was dead.

"What the hell do you mean we weren't sanctioned?" I shouted at him in his office in an undisclosed location in the Metro DC area.

"You were dead. You said it yourself the first day. You'd signed your own death certificate. What the hell was I supposed to do, Qəza?" Thorn growled. "Besides, you're not the only one who has to pay."

"Aw, you poor baby. Did the director take a bite out of you too?"

"The hell with you, Leanne. Next time, I'll leave you dead."

I walked around his massive desk and gripped one of his massive biceps. Knowing his wife as well as I do since she helped me design the specs for my office in Saratoga Springs, I felt no qualms about leaning up and pressing my lips against his cheek. "No. You'd do exactly the same thing. Thank you, Parker—for everything."

He grumbled under his breath before he flung out an arm. "Get out of my office and let me get back to the donkey work I've been assigned."

As soon as I reached an open terminal just outside his office, I logged in and wrote a detailed report to the director informing him that if it wasn't for the dedication of my boss, not only would I have been assassinated but Dioscuri would be compromised. After sending it off, I left.

Parker called me two days later to thank me, but he informed me that for the good of public relations, "Your public punishment has to remain, Qəza."

"Absolutely." I'm still not certain how I kept my tone serious.

"I'm not kidding! The director is dead set on using one of us to make an example."

"Oh, I believe you, Thorn." The minute I hung up, I laughed my ass off.

"What's so funny?" Kane asked from the doorway as he made his way over to the couch in my home office.

I loftily told him that since the director knocked my personal clearance down a peg that, "It will only last until Thorn needs me to install an update on Dioscuri. Just watch. Then everything will be restored back to the way it was."

"You're too full of cock and sass," he declared, wrapping his arms around me.

I snuggled my hips against his. His shaft stirred to life, causing me to purr. "Not nearly full enough."

Those were the last words I spoke for a while that night.

And a few weeks later, I was proven right when Thorn texted me with a critical software update. My work life went back to normal with the exception of my informing Thorn I was permanently done with being a field operative. "From that standpoint, consider me still dead."

Even years later, I can still hear his laughter ringing in my ear—such a rare, sweet sound.

A ping from the tablet pulls me from the temptation of yanking Kane down on top of me. Groaning, I hope it's not Thorn interrupting us as he's prone to do. I tear my lips from Kane's before I reach for the offending device. Then my heart softens. "It's Becks."

"What does he have to say?" Kane sits up and pulls me into his lap.

I read the message aloud. "We're here for whatever you need, kid —and that's from Mick, Carly, Paigey, Austin, and me. Screw the press —are you ready to kick ass on stage again?" Meeting my fiancé's eyes when I lift them from the screen, I say huskily, "You know that day everything went to shit? The day I ran when you refused to listen with me? When everything came out with Becks?"

Kane winces. "Yes?" Despite his continuing his sessions with the trauma therapist, that day sent him spiraling—reminding him all too clearly of the events with Gene. My getting shot didn't lighten his guilt.

I press my lips against his before admitting, "He's a royal pain in the ass, but he deserves your loyalty. Just next time, choose your target better before you ready, fire, aim, baby."

Kane throws his head back and laughs, tugging my hips against his. "I promise to practice my target practice at your earliest convenience."

"Better yet, why don't you just show me?" I deliberately fall backward so we both go tumbling. And for a long while, we forget about everyone and everything. And I'm grateful that everything in our lives remains in perfect order for just a little while so we don't have any interruptions, electronic or otherwise.

"Those boots are pure Kylie," Carys declares.

I stretch out my leg and admire the sparkly Betsey Johnson ankle boots gracing my feet. "I know. They're totally something she would have worn." They look completely atrocious with the black, silver-studded, cape-sleeve sheath dress I have on. And I completely don't give a shit. "They're going to be perfect for the show."

"I completely agree," Paige concurs.

"Glitter!" Ben yells as he races by.

As we lounge around Beckett and Paige's penthouse, I recall all the moments that led me to right now. And I say a prayer of thanks for being loved the way I know I always will be—by both Kylie and Kane. Paige immediately picks up on my mood change. "What are you thinking about so hard over there?"

"The capriciousness of fate. A sequence of unstoppable events that led me to right now."

"I'd say your motivation had a hand in guiding a lot of them."

"I was determined not to let her be forgotten."

Carys holds out a hand over her pregnant stomach, which I immediately take. She squeezes my fingers. "And because of you, she won't be. Not by her fans, not by her family, and certainly never by you."

I think back to the relationships that have been repaired over the last two years. I listened to Paige and went to see my own specialist to deal with the trauma of losing half of myself—my identical twin. And I've dragged my parents along with me. "It's still so difficult for my parents. Dad is still shaken by the lengths by which I went to keep my promise to Lee. But Mom? Even though she's the one who couldn't bear the sight of me for so long, I think it's her abject grief that I understand the most. There's a fierceness in her eyes when they fall upon me now, an understanding.

Everything I did was worth it to help us heal.

"You'll understand why, one day," Paige assures me.

I shoot her a lazy grin. "Oh, I hope so." I catch Carys's son, Ben, as he races around the table and dive-bombs onto his mother. Lifting him up in the air, I blow kisses onto his exposed tummy.

All three of us burst out laughing along with him. "Eager to get started?" Carys drawls.

"I certainly wouldn't be upset by it."

"Kane will make a good father," Paige agrees.

My smile is wicked. "And I'm going to be an awful influence as a mother."

Carys frowns. "Why do you say that?"

I reach into my bag and pull out a sealed folder before handing it to her. "You're going to want this later."

She frowns at it. "Am I going to get spanked by my husband for having it?"

I shrug. "Unlikely. Unless that's your thing. Then maybe you'll enjoy it."

The three of us are still howling when we hear a faint ping and footsteps on the marble floors. I hear Kane's beleaguered sigh. "You gave it to her?"

I beam as I tip my head back over the sofa in Beckett and Paige's condo to await Kane's kiss. "Of course I did. Back so soon?" I ask curiously.

"Yes. Beckett couldn't stay away. I can't imagine why." His eyes track to where Paige is resting on the couch, her stomach out so far,

I've asked on more than one occasion if she's not certain if there's more than one baby in there.

Paige rolls her eyes before lumbering to her feet and glaring at her husband. "If you're lucky, I'll have this child in the middle of the charity...uh-oh."

"What do you mean, uh-oh? What the fuck is uh-oh?" Beckett bellows.

I didn't think it was possible, but for the first time since Kylie died, I can feel her. See her. And right now, she's rolling on the floor of Beckett's penthouse, laughing her ass off at her friend's meltdown. *Something's coming, Daddy. Better get ready!*

I wait for her eyes to meet mine, and I mouth, *I love you. Always.*

Her face softens in the way it always has when I say that to her. *I love you too, Lee. Forever. Thank you.*

And I blink away my tears just as Beckett swings Paige up in his arms and storms for the elevator. Kane leans down and offers me his hand. "Want to change your shoes before we head to the hospital? It's going to be a long night."

I shake my head. "No. I feel like Lee's with us. And for this, she should be."

Understanding me, he tugs me at a fast clip after Beckett, who we both know is going to ignore any and all security protocols to get his wife to the hospital. Carys hurries as fast as she can behind us, on the phone with David to meet us there.

Of course, every trash rag covers the event. But it isn't until just before the charity event a week later that Beckett announces his new son's name. And it's the next day when Carys rips open the envelope I gave her. Because there were only a few people in the room when he did—all of whom Beckett considers his closest friends.

So how on earth did StellaNova announce his son's name mere hours after the rest of us finding out?

Welcome to the world, York Miles Miller. The world is happy to meet you.

— StellaNova

PERFECT SATISFACTION

Are you dying to know what Leanne put into the envelope?
Be sure to sign up for my **newsletter** so you know the release date of
Perfect Satisfaction.
The answer is coming in 2022!

ACKNOWLEDGMENTS

First, to my husband who just shook his head when I told him the storyline. Your support gets me through the rough spots. I love you.

To our son. You are the best at helping Mama de-stress. Love you, baby.

To my mother, thank you for keeping my spirits up when I was so sick, for bringing me coffee, and being an amazing Mom. Love you!

To my Jen. This is what happens when worlds collide. And stop laughing. I love you. Always. Forever!

To my Meows, you made me better just by knowing you. I owe you everything.

To Sandra Depukat, from One Love Editing, my thanks. I know the timing of this one was a challenge.

To Holly Malgieri, from Comma Sutra Editorial, you are an eternal superhero. It's kind of like Captain Marvel calmly swooping in to whoop some bootty at the end. XOXO.

To Deborah Bradseth, Tugboat Designs. Talk about cover love! This one is going to be tough to beat.

To photographer Wander Aguiar, Andrey Bahia, and model Philippe Bélanger, you three are a dream team! Thank you!

Dan Fitzpatrick, I'm grateful our friendship has lasted over the years and blessed you said "Yes," when I asked if I could include your incredible lyrics in this story. You are one-of-a-kind. Have "M" give you a whopping big kiss for me!

To Gel, at Tempting Illustrations, you're images are a work of art. Thank you!

To the fantastic team at Foreword PR, there's not enough ways to offer my thanks for what you do behind the scenes!

Linda Russell, losing you would be like losing a twin. Never going to happen. Love you more!

To my Musketeers. Nothing can stop us but our own limitations.

To Susan Henn, October 20, 2021. You will be forever missed.

Amy Rhodes, from the beginning, Kane was promised to you. See? Now it's in print. XOXO.

Dawn Hurst, I don't know what I would do without you!

For my amazing individuals who are a part of Tracey's Tribe, thank you for being a part of my world!

And to the for all the readers and bloggers who take the time to enjoy my books, you are the heroes. Thank you.

ABOUT THE AUTHOR

Tracey Jerald knew she was meant to be a writer when she would rewrite the ending of books in her head when she was a young girl growing up in southern Connecticut. It wasn't long before she was typing alternate endings and extended epilogues "just for fun".
After college in Florida, where she obtained a degree in Criminal Justice, Tracey traded the world of law and order for IT. Her work for a world-wide internet startup transferred her to Northern Virginia where she met her husband in what many call their own happily ever after. They have one son.
When she's not busy with her family or writing, Tracey can be found in her home in north Florida drinking coffee, reading, training for a runDisney event, or feeding her addiction to HGTV.
Connect with her on her website (**https://www.traceyjerald.com**) for all social media links, bonus scenes, and upcoming news.

Made in the USA
Las Vegas, NV
03 March 2024

86636284R00233